Vertigo Alley
A DCI Finnegan Yorkshire Crime Thriller
Ely North

Red Handed Print

To contact ely@elynorthcrimefiction.com

Author's website at https://www.subscribepage.com/ely_north_home

https://www.facebook.com/elynorthcrimefictionUK

Cover design by Cherie Chapman/Chapman & Wilder

Cover image © Adobe Stock/Rambling Tog

Published by Red Handed Print

First Edition

Kindle e-book ISBN-13: 978-0-6455982-2-3

Paperback ISBN-13: 978-0-6455982-3-0

Also By Ely North

DCI Finnegan Yorkshire Crime Thrillers
   Book 1: **Black Nab** – Text M For Murder
Book 2: **Jawbone Walk** – Text V For Vengeance
Book 3: **Vertigo Alley** – Text K For Killer
Book 4: **Whitby Toll** – The Bell Rings... But For Whom?
Book 5: **House Arrest** – Escape Can Be A Deadly Road
Book 6: **Gothic Fog** – The Strawman Cometh
Book 7: **Happy Camp** – Discipline, Godliness, Fun!
DCI Finnegan Series Boxset: **Books 1 – 3**
DCI Finnegan Series Boxset: **Books 4 – 6**
   Prequel – **Aquaphobia** – The Body in the River (Free ebook for newsletter subscribers)

*Note: All books are available from Amazon in ebook, paperback, and in **Kindle Unlimited** (excluding Aquaphobia). Paperbacks are distributed widely via online retailers (Apple, B&N, Kobo, Amazon etc). **Boxset print editions are one book compiled from three books. They do not come in a box. ***** Pre-orders only apply to ebooks.

1

Friday 13th November

Late afternoon and it's been a long week at Whitby Police Station.
Frank glances out of his office window as the daylight rapidly
fades. He has a bird's-eye view of the harbour and the promenade
festooned in twinkling illuminations. His expression is glum. It's
an hour until knock-off. His typical routine at the end of the week
is to head to the pub near Collier's Hope accompanied by a few
willing comrades and wind down with a couple of pints before
heading home, where he typically cooks the Friday night meal for
his wife and himself, before settling down in front of the telly.
It's a pleasant way to end a stressful week. Tonight, it's different.
He's on a strict deadline and must be home by six as Meera has
invited friends around for a meal—her friends—Stan and Glenys
Corbett. Frank ruminates. He'd rather stick a red-hot poker
through his kneecap than spend the night with the Corbetts.

He winces at the thought of it and glances at the clock on the
wall as he awaits the arrival of Detective Superintendent Banks. It
is unusual for the super to be still hanging around in Whitby this
late on a Friday. On the rare occasions she even visits on a Friday,
she's usually flown the coop by midday. Standing up, he stretches,

the bones in his arms and back emit a satisfying crack. Opening his office door, he pops his head out into the CID room.

'Okay, gang, in here!' he shouts at his small team of officers.

The trio troop into his office with little enthusiasm. It seems everyone is waiting for the clock to tick over to knocking-off time.

'What's all this about, Frank?' Prisha asks.

Frank holds his hands in the air, palms splayed outwards at the side of his head. 'You know as much as me. The super pinged me an hour ago and asked me to get the gang together for a briefing at four o'clock.'

DS Cartwright and DS Stoker slump into chairs opposite Frank's desk, less than enthused. Prisha sees her chance and delicately grabs Frank's elbow and leads him towards the window.

'Frank, did you mention to the super about my acting inspector role becoming permanent?' she whispers, glancing furtively over her shoulder.

Frank fixes her with a warm smile. 'Yes, Prisha. I have mentioned it twice.'

'And?'

'She's mulling it over.'

Prisha grimaces. 'What does that mean?'

Frank's chest heaves. 'It means—she's mulling it over.' He spots movement in the CID room as the diminutive figure of Anne Banks enters the room accompanied by two men—one of whom appears distinctly familiar.

'Bugger me! Is that who I think it is?' he murmurs.

'Who?' Prisha queries.

Before he has time to answer, Anne Banks and the two men enter Frank's office.

'Ladies and gents, sorry to have kept you waiting!' the super declares.

Frank shoots another glance at the clock. She hasn't kept them waiting. She's early. Anne takes up position behind Frank's desk, much to his annoyance.

He smiles and chuckles as he stares at an old acquaintance. 'I thought it was you! Hedley Keegan how the...'

Anne cuts him off sharply. 'We'll get to the introductions in a minute, Frank.' She glances at the other man in their midst and nods. DS Beale is of medium height, thickset, and in his mid-forties, with a bulbous nose and flaky skin. He has the face of a hardened criminal, or possibly a cynical police officer who has spent too long in the job.

Beale runs his eye dismissively over Prisha and Cartwright. He sidles over to Zac. 'Stand up please,' he says in a deep Glaswegian baritone steeped long in nicotine, and possibly alcohol. Zac throws Frank a puzzled look but rises to his full impressive height. 'Aye. He'll do,' Beale says.

'DS Cartwright and DI Kumar, you're dismissed,' Anne declares officiously. 'You may return to your duties.'

Jason Cartwright gives a nonchalant shrug, glad to have escaped something which may have impinged on his propensity for feeding his face or malingering. Prisha is less than enamoured at being asked to leave the room in such a curt manner, but she does so with a certain amount of grace, tinged with an adolescent dirty look to everyone, including Frank, who once again holds his hands out, apparently as bamboozled at the proceedings as Prisha.

As the door shuts, Frank erupts into a good-natured guffaw as he moves towards his old friend. They shake hands and slap each other on the back. 'How long has it been, Hedley?'

Hedley Keegan grins. 'A long time Frank! Over twenty years.'

'What was the case we were working on together?'

'The A1 Panther—as the media dubbed him.'

'That's right,' he confirms as he turns to Zac and Anne. 'Roger Bartholomew, a truck driver from Kent. He picked up young women hitchhikers heading north on the A1 late at night. You got the bastard in the end, though,' he says, returning his smile to Keegan.

'It was a team effort, Frank.'

'Is he still inside?'

'No. He served eighteen years. Got out on parole a few years back. Reformed character, apparently. Studied acting while he was inside... of all things.'

'Reformed character, my blue arse. And what are they doing letting him study acting? It's not supposed to be a bloody weekend retreat.' Frank scoffs. 'Anyway, what about you, Hedley? You'd be what—Superintendent, Chief Superintendent by now? You were always aiming high.'

Keegan shuffles, embarrassed. 'Ahem, no. Still a DCI.'

Frank laughs. 'Nowt wrong with that, Hedley. I'm in the same boat and happy to stay here. Although I have twenty years on you, so there's still plenty of time for you to climb that greasy pole. Now we must...'

'Gentlemen!' Anne shouts. 'As interesting as this old boys' club reunion is, you can continue the mutual tittle-tattle after we've finished our meeting. It's late. It's the end of the week, and I'd really like to head home. I have a dentist appointment at five-thirty, which is a good hour's drive away. Now, please be seated and let DCI Keegan explain why he and DS Beale are here.'

Keegan holds his arm out. 'Let me introduce you to DS Beale from Police Scotland.'

As names and handshakes are exchanged, DS Beale nods and says, 'Hallo. Gled tae meet ye.'

Keegan takes his jacket off and glances at the small whiteboard opposite Frank's desk. 'Can I?' he asks Frank, pointing at the scrawled shopping list in the centre of the board.

'Wait, hang on,' Frank replies as he quickly scribbles down the words—teabags, milk, porridge, dishwashing liquid—onto a notepad on his desk. 'Aye, Hedley. She's all yours.'

DCI Keegan wipes the board clean and picks up a marker pen. 'What I'm about to say is strictly confidential. No one outside of this room must be privy to the information I'm about to impart.' An uneasy silence descends as everyone's interest is piqued. Keegan quickly draws three boxes on the board with arrows leading back to a large circle above them with the words "Operation Dragnet," written neatly below it. 'I'm sure you've all heard of Operation Dragnet, the task force put together to stop or at least curtail the importation of Class A drugs via sea.

The operation was launched six months ago. Beneath Operation Dragnet, there are three other operations running concurrently, which all report back to the umbrella operation.'

'What are the other three?' Frank asks, leaning forward in his chair.

Keegan swiftly fills in the boxes on the board. 'Operation East Net, West Net, and South Net. East Net's jurisdiction is from Lincolnshire up to the Scottish border. West Net's coverage is from the Bristol Channel, again, up to the Scottish border, and South Net...'

'Covers the south of England,' Frank murmurs absentmindedly.

'Correct. There's also Operation North Net, under the jurisdiction of Police Scotland. It's not about catching dealers, or the crime gangs, it's about catching the importers.'

'The big fish,' Zac says.

'Precisely. Cut off supply at the top and it impinges on everyone down the line. We're working with the coastguard, the National Crime Agency, Interpol, and our own specialist boat services to wreak havoc on the illegal importation.'

'And what are your results like so far?' Superintendent Banks queries.

Keegan rubs at the stubble on his chin. 'We've had a great amount of success, especially on the east coast. As you will be aware, the street price for class A drugs has skyrocketed by two hundred per cent over the last six months. Last year, a gram of cocaine would have cost you thirty to forty pounds. Today it's selling for up to a hundred pounds and rising. Likewise with heroin, crack, ecstasy, and methamphetamine.'

'Sweet merciful crap!' Frank exclaims, receiving a glare from the super.

'In response, we've seen a huge drop off in drug use by so-called casual users.'

'What about the long-term addicts?' Zac asks.

'Our data shows they're switching away from illegal drugs to prescription drugs. Diazepam, Zopiclone, Codeine, Ritalin, Fentanyl and the like.'

'That doesn't really solve the problem, does it?' Zac says.

DCI Keegan nods thoughtfully. 'No, it doesn't. Not for long-term addicts. Although we have seen a sharp spike in people checking in for methadone treatment.'

'And how many people have been charged so far?' Frank quizzes.

'I'm sorry. That information is confidential, Frank.'

'This is all very interesting DCI Keegan, but where do we fit in?' the super says, eyeing the clock.

Keegan smiles. 'Yes. I'll get to the point. I'm senior operations manager for East Net, and although we've been having great success in disrupting the supply from the sea, about a six weeks ago a blip appeared on our radar. Namely—Hull.'

Frank chuckles. 'Hull has always been a blip on the radar, amongst other things.'

'Frank!' the super snaps at him.

'Sorry, ma'am.'

'We suspect someone has circumnavigated our operation, and it appears a certain nightclub in Hull is a hub for organising the distribution of high grade cocaine.'

'Where are they getting their supplies from if you've disrupted the usual avenues?' Frank asks.

'That's the problem... we don't know. But what we do know is the cocaine is cut with a lot of filler, mainly creatine. And what's different is they're all in tablet or capsule form.'

'No little white bags of powder?' Zac says.

'No. They look like any other over-the-counter drug you'd buy from a chemist, except they have a distinctive marking or logo stamped into them.' He fumbles in his pocket and pulls out a snap lock bag and drops it onto the desk as the other officers inspect the contents.

'A pig's head?' Zac mutters, rolling a tablet around in his fingers.

'Yes. They're known on the street as Boars.'

Superintendent Banks is becoming distinctly impatient. 'DCI Keegan, you still haven't explained how we can assist you?'

He stares her down. 'I always think a little backstory is best before getting to the crux of the matter, ma'am. The name of the nightclub in Hull is called Mr Bojangles. It's owned and run by Brian Cassidy, although he prefers the nickname "Butch". He's completely clean; no police history and the local uniform indicate it's one of the better run clubs in the city. Strict door policy, responsible serving of alcohol, very little after-hours violence. Cassidy has been in the business for fifteen years with an unblemished record.'

'You think Cassidy has either gone over to the dark side or someone else is organising the drugs without his knowledge?' Zac asks.

'Yes. Over the last four weeks, from all over North England, and the Midlands, the heads of regional crime gangs, or their deputies, have paid a visit to the club.'

'Are they picking the drugs up from the nightclub?' Frank asks.

'We don't think so. We think it's simply a meeting point to organise the deals and for potential clients to be vetted by this new outfit.'

'What about phone taps?'

'Completely dark. Again, this is supposition, but we think after the initial meeting they communicate via an encrypted messaging app.'

Superintendent Banks taps her fingernails against the desk. 'Can you not set up electronic surveillance in the club?'

'We've thought of that, but nightclubs are extremely noisy, and dark, ma'am. What we need is for someone to pose as the head of a crime gang and set up a deal. That's where DS Beale comes in. Over to you Danny.'

DS Beale stands up. 'I've been given a false identity—I'm now Talbot McGovern.'

'I've heard of him,' Frank says as his memory bank struggles to put a picture to the name.

Beale laughs. 'I'm not surprised. Talbot McGovern is a real person. He's second in command of the Scottish crime gang—The Caledonian Boys. And the reason I was asked to join this sting operation is because my ugly mug is the spitting image of McGovern's.'

He pulls a photo out of his jacket and hands it around.

'Christ!' Frank exclaims. 'You could be twins.'

'Uncanny,' Zac gasps, looking between the photo and DS Beale.

'Aye, it is uncanny. We look the same, similar age, height, and size and we both come from Glasgow.'

'You ever nicked him?' Frank asks.

'No. Believe it or not, I've never even laid eyes on him. You'd have thought our paths would have crossed over the years. But the Caledonian Boys are canny operators these days. A cut above your usual crime gangs. They're smart.'

'What will be your modus operandi?' the super questions.

'I'll go to the club next Friday and introduce myself. We have intel that the head bouncer, a guy called Tiny, is the man to talk to. Although we don't even have a photo of him. We don't believe he's anything more than a go between, a starting point, but it's all we have to go on at the moment. He and whoever's in charge will naturally be suspicious until they've checked out my credentials. I'll return on Saturday and place an order. Twenty kilos of cocaine to begin with. I'll tell them if the product is as good as I've heard, there'll be bigger orders to come.'

'And what do you hope to achieve by this?' Superintendent Banks asks, patently unconvinced.

'Firstly, gain their trust. Secondly, gather intel on where and how they're getting the drugs into the country, and who the main players are. My personal theory is that these are new kids on the block, chancing their arm while the street price for coke is at an all-time high.'

'And for the third and final time, I still don't see where we come in? DCI Keegan, you appear to have unlimited resources at your disposal as part of Operation Dragnet. Why do you need us?'

He winces, momentarily closing his eyes. 'We cannot be one hundred per cent certain that there hasn't been a breach.'

'A mole?' Frank asks.

'Yes. A mole, an insider, someone who has been paid off to turn a blind eye. It could be someone in the coastguard, the specialist police boat units, the port authorities... we don't know. We are investigating. That's why we need someone unconnected with Operation Dragnet to get closer to the source.'

'You're not going rogue on this are you, DCI Keegan?' the super demands. 'You have authority from your superiors?'

'Yes, of course. We want to keep this as low-level and hush-hush as possible. That's why there will be only two officers involved. DS Beale and one of your officers,' he replies, eyeballing Zac.

DS Beale cuts in. 'That's my request, ma'am. If I'm going undercover, then I want someone to cover my back. When I'm in that nightclub, and heading back to my hotel on a night, I need another set of eyes and ears—that's where Zac comes in.'

'DS Beale also needs a point of contact to relay the intel back to me. There can be no direct communication between Beale and me,' Keegan adds. 'His false identity must not be compromised.'

Superintendent Banks huffs as she rises from her seat. 'There are forty-three police forces in England and Wales. North Yorkshire has the fifth largest geographical area to cover, and yet we have the fifteenth smallest force in terms of manpower. We are always understaffed. In the grand scheme of things, Whitby is a small fish in a big pond, yet you want to me assign one of my very few officers from this station to your fishing trip?'

'It's not indefinitely, ma'am,' Keegan replies. 'Maybe a couple of weekends night time work, and a few hours relaying information back to me.'

Superintendent Banks pouts and stares at Frank. 'Your thoughts, Frank. Can we spare him?'

'I think so, ma'am. Things are pretty quiet at the moment—touch wood.'

The super adjusts her jacket. 'Zac?'

'Aye. I'm up for it, ma'am. A bit of overtime never hurt,' he adds with a grin.

'Yes, overtime paid by my department. Very well. I'll authorise it. But you are there as an extra set of eyes and ears—only. If you feel threatened or in danger, then you call uniform immediately—do I make myself clear?'

'Crystal, ma'am.'

'Good.' She heads towards the door. 'And Frank, I want a daily update on this. I don't want it going pear-shaped.'

'Understood, ma'am.'

'DCI Keegan, you could have requested an officer from any force in the country. Why did you pick our little station?'

'Two reasons. Whitby's not too far from Hull. And having worked with Frank before, I know he's a man of integrity and discipline. I figured the officers under him would be of similar calibre.'

Superintendent Banks eyes Frank and Keegan suspiciously. 'Hmm... I see. Have a pleasant weekend, gentlemen.'

DS Beale sticks his fingers in the blinds, parts them slightly and stares out. 'Christ, where the fuck did you dig her up from? I bet it's a brutal laugh riot around this place.'

2

Prisha reaches into her backpack and pulls out a bottle of water, swiftly glugging down the remaining contents. She paces up and down the room, occasionally throwing a glance at the window to Frank's office, the interior hidden by the closed Venetian blinds.

'What do you think they're talking about in there?' she queries.

Jason Cartwright lifts his head from the sports section of the newspaper and yawns. 'Not sure, and to be honest, I don't care,' he replies as he relaxes back in his chair and lifts his feet onto the desk at the side of Prisha's monitor.

'Who were the two new faces? Did you recognise them?'

'The smart looking, well-spoken guy looked familiar, but I couldn't place him.'

'And the other?'

'Don't have a clue,' he says, returning his attention to the latest footy transfer news.

Prisha eyes him disdainfully before walking over and slapping his legs away. 'Get your feet off my bloody desk!' she snaps.

Cartwright's feet fall heavily to the floor. 'Christ! What's up with you? You've been like a bear with a sore head since you returned from sick leave.' She ignores his barb and takes up her seat behind her laptop.

'Bit bloody rude if you ask me,' she mumbles to herself.

'Hey, I was relaxing. My shoes are clean,' Cartwright explains with a hint of regret.

'Not you. The super. First, she gets us all together, then dismisses us two like a couple of naughty children.'

'Do you ever let up?' Cartwright folds his paper and puts it on the desk. 'So, anything interesting lined up for the weekend?' he asks, trying to navigate the conversation into smoother waters.

'What? Oh, yeah, I'm going rock climbing tomorrow at Malham Cove.'

'Rather you than me. Who are you going with?'

'A guy I met online.'

'Tinder, e.Harmony, or Match.com?' he says with a cackle and a leer.

'Hilarious. It's a rock climbing forum, and the guy is one of Europe's most famous sports climbers.'

'Handsome, is he?'

'As it happens—yes. Not that it's got anything to do with you.'

'You could do with a fella. Maybe then you wouldn't be so grumpy.'

Prisha shakes her head and purses her lips. 'You really are a good old-fashioned male chauvinist pig, aren't you? You think if a woman is in a foul mood, it's because she's not getting enough sex?'

'Or any sex,' Cartwright chuckles. 'Do you want to know what I'm doing for the weekend?'

'No.'

'My mate's got a spare ticket for the Toon game against city.'

'Toon?'

'Newcastle.'

'Oh, football. What a bore.'

'Then on Sunday...'

Prisha spots the door to Frank's office open and Superintendent Banks stride out. She bolts from her seat and makes a beeline towards her.

'Goodnight Prisha, Jason. Enjoy your weekend,' the super declares.

Prisha falls in at the side of her. 'Ma'am, can I have a word, please?'

'Not now Prisha. I'm already running late for an appointment.'

'It is important, ma'am.'

'Can it not wait until Monday?'

'Not really.'

'Very well. But you'll have to walk and talk,' the super says, clearly annoyed as she pulls at the door and heads out into the corridor. 'Go on then, what's it about, although I think I can guess?'

'It's about my role as acting inspector. I know Frank mentioned it to you. I was wondering if you've given any further consideration to the position becoming permanent?'

They descend the stairwell, side by side, in double-quick time. 'Yes. I've given it careful consideration, and I intended to catch up with you next week to discuss it, but I may as well tell you now.'

Prisha's heart skips a beat with cautious optimism. 'Very good, ma'am.'

They round a bend on the landing and clatter down the last flight of stairs. 'As of the end of this month, you will be returning to your normal duties as detective sergeant.'

The dagger is embedded firmly in Prisha's heart. For a moment, she's lost for words as they both swipe their security passes and head out into the car park.

'But, I thought, I…'

The super doesn't let up as she marches briskly towards her Volvo. 'Don't take it personally, Prisha.'

'How else am I supposed to take it? Do you not think I'm up to the job? Have I shown a lack of leadership? What is it?'

The car emits a double beep as the lights flash on and off. 'I've set aside an hour next week to discuss it with you in more detail. But in brief I have several reasons. As superintendent, I always have one eye on the budget.'

'The budget? I'm sorry, ma'am, but the difference between a sergeant and inspector's annual salary is hardly going to break the bank.'

'No, it's not. But if I gave carte blanche to every request I receive, then that would break the bank. I must be judicious in my fiscal responsibilities. It's the taxpayer's money, after all.' She yanks at the door handle of the Volvo as a bitter wind picks up strength.

'You said a number of reasons, ma'am. What else?'

'You transferred from the midlands in what... mid-August? It's now mid-November. You've barely been with us three months, during which time you were also on sick leave for three weeks.'

'Enforced sick leave! I never wanted it,' Prisha bristles.

'You witnessed a horrific murder, were hunted by a pair of assassins for twenty-four hours and taken captive. You needed time to recuperate. My officers' welfare is paramount. Anyway, that's by the by. I think you need more time to acquaint yourself with the area, build up contacts, informants, a network. And lastly,' she says as she drops into the driver's seat and fumbles for her seatbelt, causing her to become distracted.

'And lastly?' Prisha prompts.

'I was surprised when Frank put your name forward as acting DI for the major incident involving the missing teenagers.'

'Why?'

'Because DS Stoker has been under Frank's tutelage for a number of years and he's a damn fine officer—in the making. During that time, he's built up extensive local knowledge and contacts. He's also disciplined and is respected by his colleagues.'

'Meaning I'm not?'

'Don't put words in my mouth, Prisha,' she states indignantly as the seat belt finally clicks into place. 'If I made you inspector after such a short period of time, people would see it as blatant tokenism. They'd think you'd got the job because—one, you're a woman, and—two, because of your colour and ethnicity.'

Prisha false guffaws at the irony of the words. 'I see! So, for you to avoid accusations of tokenism, you don't give me the job because I *am* a woman. My skin's brown and my last name's Kumar! It's the perfect catch-22.'

Superintendent Banks eyes her with a mixture of understanding and pragmatism. 'Prisha, in case you've missed it, I'm a woman, and I've been around a lot longer than you. We've come a long way, but we're not there yet when it comes to equality. Prove yourself and you'll earn respect, then when you are promoted to inspector it will be because of your ability and that alone.' The car engine reluctantly growls into life as the super slams the door shut and the window slides down. 'I know it must feel like a kick in the guts, but don't take it like that. Give it another twelve months and we'll revisit the subject. Although, you must remember DS Stoker will also be in the frame, should he put his name forward. Goodnight, and try to relax this weekend.'

Prisha stares in disbelief as the car turns a corner and disappears. She tries desperately to quell a range of emotions, but no matter how hard she tries, at this moment she could literally kill someone!

3

Saturday 14th November

Albert and Maxine scurry down the steps of the guest house, backpacks on, wet weather gear protecting them from the elements. They turn and wave goodbye to the landlady. Smiles, anticipation, and enthusiasm radiate from their weathered faces. Both pensioners but their countenance contradicts their age. Nimble, fit, and in love, they have a spring in their step. They could be love-struck teenagers—in spirit.

The market town of Settle, nestled like a jewel in the bracelet of North Yorkshire, is mostly still asleep, or at least engaging in morning ablutions. The couple fumble for each other's hand, exchange a peck on the lips and set off with gusto towards the trail which will lead them to Malham Cove.

Wrathful clouds hang low over Malham Tarn. Occasionally, in an outburst of pique, they discharge their contents onto the dejected moorland below. On clear days, the sweeping vistas are magnificent and attract a steady stream of walkers. Today, only two seem to have ventured out into the cold, brooding conditions.

Menace is carried on the wind that buffets the couple, as they trudge over grit, sidestep muddy puddles, and occasionally wipe drips from their faces. The light is fading fast, and although not outwardly expressed, Albert and Maxine are feeling the occasional prickle of anxiety.

'Albert, are you sure we're heading the right way? I think we should have veered left at the last crossroads.'

He pulls the ordnance survey map from his backpack, fumbles spectacles onto his head and stares at the chart. Large droplets of rain create a lonesome pit-a-pat noise on the protective plastic cover.

'I don't think so, Maxine. The last signpost we passed indicated Malham Tarn was only three miles away. Anyway, according to the map, even if we did take the wrong route, this path still leads to the cove and joins up with the Pennine Way again at Watersinks car park.' His voice appears authoritative, but Maxine picks up a shard of doubt in his words.

'Maybe we should turn back. The weather is getting worse, and the visibility is fading fast.'

'By my calculations, we are well past the halfway mark. It would make more sense to carry on.' He puts an arm around her and gives her a kiss on the cheek. 'Another hour or so and we'll be sitting in a warm, cosy tearoom eating scones with clotted cream and strawberry jam.'

She offers up a reassuring smile. 'I hope so. I'm cold, wet, and hungry despite the large breakfast. Hiking is fun in summer, but late autumn can be so changeable.'

Albert pulls away, puzzled. 'What's that noise?'

'Sounds like a truck. Are we nearing a road?'

'A few miles away, but that engine is really close. I think it's an aeroplane.'

'If it is, it's very low.'

They gaze up into the swirling mist and pick out the aircraft.

Albert wipes a drip from his nose. 'Hell! What are they playing at? That would be like flying through pea soup. The damn fools are way too low.'

'Oh, my god! What's that falling from it?'

'I think it's...'

They're his last words.

There's a dull, squishy thud and something splats onto Maxine's raincoat. Still fascinated with the falling object, she half turns to look at Albert... but doesn't quite make it.

4

Prisha readjusts her backpack as she climbs over the stile, drops to the other side and gazes in awe at the distant cliffs of Malham Cove.

'I think this is the most beautiful spot I've ever visited,' she murmurs as Lewis Visser takes a glug of water. 'Mind you, I've lost count of the number of times I've said that when I find myself in a new part of the countryside.' She pulls her eyes away from the enchanting view and smiles at Lewis. 'I'm really grateful. You must get loads of people pestering you to do this sort of thing.'

Lewis grins. 'Not as many as you'd think. I may be famous in the sports rock climbing fraternity, but to the rest of the world, I'm just some skinny old guy who's stupid enough to climb up vertical rock faces.'

'You're not old, and you're not skinny. I'd call you lithe, sinewy.'

'You mean skinny?'

'I've never seen an overweight rock climber.'

They amble along at the side of the stream as Lewis throws out interesting snippets of information.

'Malham Beck merges with Gordale Beck outside the village and forms the source of the River Aire.'

'The river that runs through Leeds?' Prisha asks.

Lewis chuckles. 'Yes, and many other places.'

'So where does Malham Beck come from?'

'Malham Tarn. It lays above the cove a few miles to the north. On top of the cove is a limestone pavement famous around the world. It's where some scenes of a Harry Potter film were shot.'

They walk briskly on as Lewis plays the local tourist guide and Prisha listens in silence.

'I'm sorry... I must be boring you,' Lewis says as he stops for another drink of water.

'Not at all! It's fascinating. Harry Potter, the River Aire, the Water Babies, limestone pavements.'

'You're winding me up—right?'

'No! Absolutely not. I mean it. I love things like this. It takes my mind off my job.'

They walk on. 'And what is your job?'

'I'm a police officer. Detective with the CID. Based in Whitby at the moment, but I can end up anywhere in North Yorkshire depending on staffing levels and the seriousness of the crimes.'

'A police officer. Well, well...'

'What?'

'You don't look like a police officer.'

'And what does a police officer typically look like?'

'Well... CID... I always imagine an overweight, pot-bellied, middle-aged white man, who's a chain-smoking alcoholic, estranged from his children and has a toxic relationship with his ex-wife and his superiors.'

Prisha laughs hard. 'Yeah, there's plenty of them about. Sometimes stereotypes do contain a grain of truth. And what do you do for a living?'

'I own and manage a handful of high street shops along the east coast.'

'Oh, very flash. What are they called?'

'Price Slashers.'

'You mean they're discount stores?' Prisha says with a cheeky grin.

'No, no! We're a bit more upmarket than that.'

'Really. What sort of things do you sell?' she questions with an element of doubt.

'Make-up, toiletries, perfumes, aftershave. A mountain of stuff. Sometimes I think we carry too much stock.'

'I'll have to pay a visit. Can't say I've noticed one around Whitby.'

'Nearest one to you is Scarborough, or Middleborough.' Lewis gazes up at the white blanket of clouds above. 'Come on, let's lift the pace. I don't like the look of the weather. We may not get much climbing in today. It's true it's a beautiful place, but the weather can be a harsh mistress!'

———◦———

Pain floods through Prisha's body. Her fingers are numb, forearms on fire as the lactic acid in her bloated muscles renders her immobile. The rain intensifies. She wedges a knee under an overhang, allowing her to rest her arms for a moment. Sucking in air, she looks down, then up, searching for the next handhold in the limestone crag. She dips a hand into the chalk bag, sitting below her left hip, then reaches up for the next hold point. Her potential saviour, the belayer taking the slack out of the safety rope, is forty feet below. He calls out, his voice bouncing off the limestone cove.

'Prisha! I think it's time to come down. The conditions are worsening.'

'I'm fine, honest!' she yells.

'You're forgetting the first rule of climbing—respect the rock!'

'Damn it!' she whispers under her breath as she clips the rope into the carabiner. 'Okay, a few more feet and I'll come down!' Reaching up, her fingers find a pocket. She pulls herself upwards while simultaneously searching fruitlessly for a foothold. Gentle rivulets streak down the rockface, eradicating the chalk from her fingers. Panic swoops as she loses traction. Her scream reverberates across the countryside as she falls backwards from the cliff. She knows the routine—the belayer will pull the rope and engage the brake mechanism, their weight negating the fall. Still, when in freefall, such logic evaporates. She plummets towards the harsh rocks below, dropping ten feet in a split-second before the safety routine kicks in, arresting her fall.

———◇———

She swigs thirstily from the bottle of water and stares at Lewis as he packs the ropes away.

He's probably a good fifteen years older than me, but he's handsome, rakish, the picture of health and vitality. Stop it, Prisha! Stop what? You know what. You always do it. Anyway, a catch like him would definitely be married. Only one way to find out, girl.

'That's the hardest climb I've ever attempted,' she pants, screwing the lid back on the bottle.

'It's supposed to be hard. It's graded 9b. One of the toughest in England. You did well.'

'How far did you think I got up Rainman?'

'You climbed Raindogs, part of Rainshadow, Batman, and Batroute.'

'That wasn't the question?'

'Oh, maybe ten feet into Rainman,' he says with an apologetic wince.

'Ten bloody feet!'

'About that.'

'Does it get harder from where I fell?'

Lewis chuckles. 'Ahem, yes, a little.'

Prisha is disappointed. 'Damn! I thought I was at the hardest point with the overhang.'

'Hey, c'mon! Your first attempt and you managed two-thirds of the climb? You should be celebrating. I didn't complete the climb until my fifteenth attempt. I've been coming here for the last eight years. I'm an old man now. You've plenty of time left. In fact, you could try it again next week—weather permitting,' he adds.

27

Prisha doesn't miss the opportunity. 'Wouldn't your wife or girlfriend be suspicious if you accompanied me two weeks in a row?'

'I don't have a wife or girlfriend,' he says, kneeling and zipping up his backpack.

Damn it! I bet he's gay. Just my luck. Why didn't I pick up on that?

'Oh,' is her confused response.

'And before you jump to any conclusions—no, I'm not gay. I was married, but we divorced five years ago. Nothing tawdry—we just didn't share the same interests. And as for girlfriends, well, with managing the business and indulging in my passion of climbing, I never seem to find the time to meet anyone. What about you?'

She tries to remain cool. 'Me? No, I'm single. Came out of a long-term relationship last year. Nothing since.'

He smiles benevolently at her, like a caring older brother... much to her annoyance. 'I'm sure you'll meet a nice young man of a similar age soon. If I was ten years younger, I'd definitely be asking you out. Come on, I suspect it's going to bucket it down any moment. We'll jog back to the village and grab lunch at the pub. They do good counter meals—my treat.'

Nestling in lush rolling countryside is the eighteenth-century stone pub. It stands tall and proud, like a sentinel surveying its domain. The outside walls are swathed in a thick blanket of emerald and blood-red ivy. A jingling stream only adds to the serene and peaceful setting. As Prisha and Lewis near, the heavens open up and they make a mad dash for the entrance, laughing like children.

'What's your poison?' Lewis asks as they make their way to the restaurant area and discard their packs and jackets next to an empty table.

'Oh, I'm driving so I best stick to a lager shandy,' she replies. As Lewis orders the drinks, she studies the menu. 'What do you recommend?'

'The cheese and caramelised onion pies are especially yummy.'

'Okay. I'll go for that. What are you having?'

'Think I'll go for the ale battered fish and chips.' Lewis places the order, and they head back to the table.

'Not many in for food,' Prisha notes.

'No, not at the moment. You should see it on a warm summer's day. Packed to the rafters. Right, excuse me, I'm heading to the bathroom to freshen up.'

She takes a gulp of her shandy and inwardly smiles as he disappears through a door. A tiny flame is growing inside, dispelling the disappointment and frustration of her last few weeks on the job. Her gentle reverie is rudely dispatched as a loud, angry voice travels through from the main bar. She lifts her head and peeks across the counter. A tall, ruddy faced, middle-aged man is holding court chaperoned by two older men.

'I've had it up to the bloody gills with ramblers tramping all over my land! They leave gates open, they shit everywhere, and they scare the livestock.'

'Tourism is good for the area, George. They bring a lot of money with them,' one of the friends explains in a conciliatory tone.

'I don't give a damn about tourism! This is farming land, has been since time began. Last week, one bugger walked through the farmyard, bold as brass, asking if I had any eggs to sell. I told him straight he had ten seconds to get off my property, otherwise he'd be getting a backside full of buckshot. You should've seen the bugger run!' He bursts out laughing, gesticulating wildly as he slams his empty pint glass down on the bar. 'Stick another one in there, sonny,' he shouts.

The young barman shakes his head. 'Sorry, George. But you've had enough. Why don't you get yourself home and have an afternoon kip?'

George doesn't take kindly to the words of wisdom. 'Don't you tell me what to do, you jumped up little prick! Now pour me another pint before you cop a hiding!'

His friends remonstrate with him, but it only infuriates the situation. His head has now taken on the shape of a giant, angry beetroot accompanied with flying spittle and hands clenched into fists the size of Christmas hams. Prisha considers intervening, but quickly discards the idea. It would be hot oil to water. As the fracas escalates, Lewis returns.

'What's the commotion?' he says, heading towards the table.

'Angry farmer alert. I don't think he likes tourists or ramblers.'

Lewis stares across to the scene, does a quick shake of the head, then leaves the restaurant area. A few seconds later, Prisha spots him in the main bar. The angry farmer seems surprised at the sudden appearance of Lewis, who gently guides him into a corner. There are no raised voices, merely gentle gesticulations from Lewis as he stares at the man, who steadfastly gazes at the floor, apologetic, maybe ashamed. Lewis pats the man on the back. The farmer apologises, grabs his coat and leaves the pub as Lewis returns to the restaurant.

'Well, well,' Prisha chuckles. 'You're a dark horse. He was twice the size of you. What did you say to placate him?'

'I told him a senior detective from North Yorkshire CID was sitting in the restaurant and if he didn't button his big mouth and go home, I'd have no other choice but to tell her about his illegal activities.'

Prisha cackles and takes a sip of her drink. 'Ha, ha! Very funny. No, honestly, what did you say to him?'

'I told him he was making an arse of himself and it was in his best interests to go home and sleep it off. He agreed. He's a loudmouth and looks intimidating, but he's a gentle giant. A nice man... when he's sober.'

'How do you know him?'

'George Baxter is the guy's name. I have a holiday home on the outskirts of Malham, and when I'm staying here, this is my local. George and I share an interest in the local history of the place.'

'Your accent; it's a mixture of Yorkshire and something else?'

He laughs. 'Ah, yes. My father was born and bred around these parts, but my mother is half Dutch, half German. In my early childhood, I grew up around North Yorkshire. When I was ten, my parents relocated to Holland where they still live, happily retired. I always missed the stunning countryside around here, so when I saw a business opportunity a few years ago, I moved back.'

'A business opportunity? You mean the discount stores?'

'Yes. Ah, here comes the food now! I'm ravenous.'

5

Sunday 15th November

Frank gazes at his reflection in the full-length bedroom mirror for longer than he should. It's inevitable, and it happens to everyone, at least everyone who lives long enough. Thirty years ago, even twenty, he would have seen a young, strong, handsome man, full of vim and vigour. A head full of ideas, and hair, and a heart full of hope and optimism. He closes his eyes and imagines what he used to be.

'Frank!' Meera calls out again as she hustles into the bedroom dressed in her Sunday best. She stops in her tracks and glares at her husband. 'Whatever are you doing? If we don't set off now, we're going to miss the beginning of the service. I hate walking into church late. It's disrespectful.'

Frank remains mute to the spot, eyes still tightly closed. 'Yes, Meera,' he reluctantly replies.

Meera's face flashes concern. 'Frank, are you feeling all right? It's not the chest pains again, is it?'

'No.'

'Then what's the matter? Why are you standing in front of the mirror with your eyes closed?'

'I'm reflecting.'

'Oh no... not about...'

'No.'

'About what then?'

'About life, time, and what happened to it.'

'You're making no sense, man.'

His eyes flicker open and fixate on his wife. 'Do you remember when we first began dating and I'd race you up the 199 Steps? I'd give you thirty steps start and I'd still fly past you—not that you were a slouch by any means. We'd go for long drives around the moors or into the dales and find a secluded spot by a river. Picnics, flasks of tea, egg, and cress sandwiches. I can almost hear the skylarks now.'

Meera's concerned expression takes a turn for the worse. 'Frank, should I call for a doctor?'

'No, I'm bloody fine!' he snaps.

'Sorry.'

'What happened, Meera?'

She drops onto the bed and clasps her hands together, and stares at the carpet. 'We got old, Frank. Same as everyone else does.'

'But I'm not old. My mind is still twenty-one. It's this bloody, creaky old body that lets me down. Aches and pains and...'

She rises, takes his hand, and stands at the side of him as they both gaze at their reflections. 'It's fine to remember the glory days of your youth, but you're not dead yet. We've both still got a lot of living to do,' she adds, gently rubbing his back. 'In a few years we can retire, then we'll really start living.'

'Will we?' he asks morosely.

'Yes, we will.'

'Do you know what I really miss, more than my youthful looks, more than my physical strength?'

Meera purses her lips disapprovingly. 'I can imagine what you're going to say.'

Frank smiles. 'I wasn't going to say sex.'

'Really?'

'No. What I miss is the energy. I used to fire on six cylinders. Up at five, run three miles, beat the crap out of a punch bag for twenty minutes. Eat whatever I wanted and never put on an ounce of weight. I'd tackle the day and whatever it threw at me with gusto, then drop into bed at midnight and sleep like a babe until the alarm clock rang, then I'd be up and ready to do it all again. I was a force of nature, Meera. These days it takes me an hour to have a shower, a shave, a shit, and a shoeshine.'

She slaps his arm and spins him around, kissing him gently on the cheek. 'It's not like you to be reflective?'

'Isn't it?'

'No. But what you say has some truth to it. We are getting older. Our looks fade, our skin sags. The lines and wrinkles accumulate. Our bones ache and we are slower than we wish to be.'

'Don't sugar coat it.'

'But you're missing something—something deeper. Our body may age, but it's merely a vessel for our mind, for our soul. Working in the hospice, I see it on a daily basis. Some people have but weeks left. Others, a few days, and some... hours. For many, their soul still shines through, as though they know this time is about to pass but another one is about to start.'

'Meera, don't get onto the religion and spirituality thing again. You know we agree to disagree about god, the afterlife and...'

She presses a finger against his lips. 'Shush. I'm not. Each to their own. All I'm saying is there's something within every human being. A light that can still shine bright no matter the pain, the heartache. It is the soul, Frank... it is the soul. And you shine brighter now than I've ever known you shine. Your mind is still alive. Your memories, experience, your wisdom mature like a fine wine. You may be slower on your feet, but in your head you are still razor sharp. Now stop maudlin, old man. Straighten your tie and let's head to church and give thanks to our Lord for what we have.'

'Your Lord, not mine.'

'Frank!'

He checks his watch. 'It's not even nine-thirty yet. What's the rush?'

'It's a good twenty-minute walk.'

'Walk?' he quizzes as though he's been asked to explain string theory.

'Yes. You heard—walk. Now come on.'

'Why can't we drive?'

Meera's frown is severe enough for Frank to drop that particular line of questioning.

6

Monday 16th November

'How was your weekend?' Frank asks, as Prisha enters his office.

'Had a ball Saturday. Went rock climbing at Malham Cove. Actually, managed to get about ten feet up Rainman.'

Frank is busily organising paperwork on his desk, slightly distracted. 'I take it Rainman is the name of a route up a rockface, and not a person?'

Prisha grins. 'You're on fire, Frank, and it's a Monday morning.'

'Ten bloody feet, you say? I reckon I could manage that and I'm nearly twice your age and weight.'

'Rainman actually starts about fifty feet up. It comes off another route below it.'

'Ah, I see. I've never understood why people voluntarily flirt with danger.'

'It's the adrenalin rush, boss. Best drug in the world. Anyway, you used to be a boxer, that's far more dangerous. All those bangs to the head.'

'At least with boxing, your welfare is in your own hands, literally. With rock climbing, you're hoping and praying one of those thingamabobs doesn't come away from the rock.'

'A piton. Even if one comes away, you're still attached to the others below, and you have a belayer.'

'A what?'

'A partner on the ground who's holding onto the rope. How was your weekend?' she enquires as she takes a seat and sips on her coffee.

'To be honest—not good! Friday night was ruined thanks to a visit from some of Meera's friends. Most boring couple on the planet. Saturday, Meera had a list of odd jobs for me to do around the house. And to cap it off, Sunday morning I was guilted into going to bloody church.' He leans back in his chair and eyes her a with a hint of sympathy. 'By the way, Superintendent Banks messaged me Friday night and told me she'd broken the bad news to you about the inspector's position. I'm sorry, Prisha. I did push your case.'

'I know you did, Frank. I don't blame you.'

'How do you feel about it?'

'Bloody pissed off! She said it would be seen as a token gesture if she made me inspector after such a short time here. Which begs the question—why did *you* promote me to acting inspector for the missing girls investigation? Why not Zac?'

Frank picks up a pen and twiddles it between his fingers and thumbs. 'It was a test. I knew Zac was up to the task, but I wanted to see how you handled it. You were an unknown quantity to me at that stage. I also wanted to see how Zac reacted. To see if he carried on in a professional manner despite the disappointment.

And I'm pleased to say you both passed the test with flying colours.'

Prisha stares directly into his eyes and slowly nods. 'Fair enough,' she says without emotion.

Frank exhales. 'You've just turned thirty, Prisha. Why the rush?'

'There was no rush until you appointed me acting DI. To go back down to sergeant feels like a demotion, as though I'm being punished for something, and no one's telling me what it is.'

'That's not the case. Next year at this time you may well be inspector.'

'Then I'll feel bad for Zac, and if I don't get it, I'll feel sorry for myself. This station isn't big enough for two DIs.'

'And how long do you think I'll be around for? Two, three years? Then they'll need an inspector to step up to DCI, plus there are always opportunities arising all over the force—York, Northallerton, Harrogate.'

'I like it here. Anyway, can we change the subject? I don't want to dwell on it. What have you got for me? Hopefully something nice and juicy I can get my teeth into.'

Frank pushes a sheaf of papers across the desk. Prisha excitedly picks them up and skims them. Her enthusiastic countenance soon morphs into a pained expression.

'Oh, come off it, Frank. A missing person risk assessed as absent! This is uniforms jurisdiction. Ever since I came back from sick leave, you've given me all the shitty jobs. I know what you're playing at; you're treating me with kid gloves. You think I'm traumatised and will fall out of my trolley if you give me anything taxing. I've done all the psychological tests, the medicals, and passed. I still have a weekly session with the psychologist—not that I need it. I've done everything that's been asked of me, and you still won't trust me.'

'Whoa! Calm the farm, lass! First up, none of that is true. We've had a quiet few months on the serious crime front. No one's had anything spicy to tickle their taste buds—and thank god for that. And if you care to read the mispers report more carefully, I'll explain why I want you on the case.'

There's an angry silence from Prisha as she rereads the report, before shaking her head.

'Nah, don't get it,' she states, clearly irritated. 'Albert Shaw, aged seventy, a keen walker set off early Friday morning from his home in Pickering for a three day walking trip. Was due back late Sunday afternoon. His wife reported him missing this morning. Has no pre-existing medical conditions; doesn't suffer from depression; there was no family altercation. Is an experienced walker; took adequate clothing and always carries snacks and water. No mobile contact as he turns his phone off to conserve the battery in case of an emergency. Has not contacted any other family member or close friends.'

She pushes the papers forcefully back across the desk to Frank, who instantly pushes them back, more forcefully, in her direction.

'Where's that detective brain of yours, Prisha? Why aren't your spider senses tingling?'

'Because there's nothing to tingle them. He hasn't even been missing a day. You know as well as I do the majority of missing people are found within forty-eight hours. There could be a dozen explanations why he's missing. He could be pulling up outside his home right now. His car might have broken down last night. He might have left his wife or stayed the night with his lover. He could be lying in a ditch after breaking a leg or suffering a heart attack. He may have undiagnosed Alzheimer's. Whatever the reason, there's nothing suspicious that warrants CID getting involved—yet.'

'Why did his wife not raise the alarm last night? It's mid-November and bloody freezing on a night. He may be as fit as a fiddle, but he's still in his seventies. How do we know if he left to go on a walk? All I want you to do is call around and see Mrs Shaw. Leave your preconceived notions at the door and get the full story. See what your gut instinct has to say? If you come back happy that everything is legit—then fine. We'll leave it to uniform. But something smells off to me and it's not just Cartwright's BO drifting in from the incident room. By the way, take Cartwright with you.'

She huffs. 'Really?'

'Yes, really. And don't throw me that look.'

'Fine!' she stands up and yanks at the door.

'Oh, Prisha,' he whispers, 'shut the door a moment.'

She obliges and glares at him 'What?'

'Whilst we're discussing Cartwright's body odour, do you think you could have a motherly word with him in his lughole?'

'Motherly?' she hisses.

'Yes. It would be better coming from a girl.'

'The hole you're digging for yourself, Frank, is getting bigger.'

'Sorry. What I mean is... it would be better coming from a woman. He's more likely to take notice. If I broach the subject, he could take offence. I tried dropping a big hint on his last birthday. I bought him an industrial sized box of Lynx deodorant, a dozen of the buggers. Cost me a small fortune. Alas, it's Cartwright we're talking about and he's not quick on the uptake,' he adds with an air of disappointment.

'Frank, do I have to?'

'Please, for me,' he adds with begging eyes. 'Or, if not for me—then take one for the team, and for the sake of everyone's nostrils—including your own. It can't be easy sitting in there with him.'

She closes her eyes and sighs. 'Very well. But I'll only bring it up if the opportunity should arise, so don't hold your breath.'

'I won't need to. But you might, sharing a car with him to Pickering.'

'Very funny,' she says, turning to leave.

'By the way, go softly, softly, with him. He may be an average copper, lackadaisical, and scatter-brained but he's still one of us. We look after our own.' He pauses deep in reflection for a moment. 'Actually, with those attributes, I'm surprised his career stalled at detective sergeant. He should be Deputy Chief Constable by now.'

Prisha masks a smile. 'Don't worry. If I bring the subject up, I'll do it with care, empathy, and understanding—in a motherly way.'

'Good lass.'

'I'll tiptoe across eggshells.'

'That's the spirit. Everyone has feelings—even Cartwright.'

'Anything else, boss?' she asks as pulling at the door again.

'No. Report back to me after you've interviewed Mrs Shaw.'

'Will do. By the way, where's Zac? I haven't seen him this morning. Is he sick or has he a rostered day off?'

Frank averts his gaze and hastily scribbles his signature on the first sheet of a mountain of official papers in front of him.

'What's that?' he replies, deliberately preoccupied.

'Zac. Where is he?' Prisha reiterates.

'Oh... Zac! He's on a... sort of thing...'

'Sort of thing? A training day?'

'Not exactly.'

'Then what?'

'Ahem... a sort of special, no, not special, but kind of special operation. It's all hush - hush, so I can't say too much.'

Her voice lowers an octave. 'A covert operation?'

'Covert is rather a strong term.'

'Undercover?'

'Erm... I suppose so—sort of. As I said... it's hush - hush.'

She crosses her arms and taps her foot aggressively on the floor. 'Hmm... I see. Been rather quiet on the crime front lately—hasn't it, Frank?'

'Now, Prisha, what you've got to under...'

The slamming of Frank's office door sets every pane of glass on the top floor rattling.

'DS Cartwright! Shift your arse, now! You're coming with me to Pickering!'

7

Prisha types the address into her GPS and clicks on her seatbelt. 'Haworth lane, Pickering. About thirty minutes,' she says as Cartwright jumps in and immediately cranks the heater to high. Prisha turns it back down.

'Eh, up! It's freezing!' he laments.

'The car's cold. Give it a chance to warm up, otherwise all you're doing is blowing cold air into the car.'

'If you pass a roadside food van on the way, pull over, will you? I'm famished.'

Glaring at him, she relents. 'Your stomach always comes first with you, doesn't it?'

'I'm a growing lad.'

'You can say that again,' she murmurs as she hands him the report and risk assessment on Albert Shaw. 'Here, read this and get up to speed,' she says wearily as they head towards town.

'Hell's bells! He was only reported missing this morning. Why are we involved?'

'Frank insisted.'

'I sometimes wonder if Frank's losing the plot.'

Prisha spots the sign for Pickering as they hit the outskirts of the pretty market town. She edges her window down another notch as the heater blasts out hot air.

'What's the point of having the heater on if you insist on winding your window down,' Cartwright complains as he devours his second hot dog, smothered in ketchup and mustard.

'I get car sick unless I'm driving,' Prisha replies, praying for the journey to end.

'You are driving,' he says, wiping his mouth on the sleeve of his jacket.

'Have you collated a set of pertinent, probing, yet sensitive questions?' she asks.

'No. I'm telling you, this is a wild goose chase. But it's been a pleasant drive out.'

Prisha doesn't share his sentiments as she sucks fresh air in through the window. The car turns onto a narrow lane hemmed in by well-to-do houses on either side.

'Here it is, on the left,' Prisha says.

'Hmm... impressive,' Cartwright says taking in the detached brick house with a large, classy conservatory addition, and substantial gardens.

'You're a local—what would it be worth—ballpark?'

'Oh, nudging five hundred grand, I'd say.'

She steers the car up the driveway and parks at the side of a battered green Land Rover Defender.

'At last,' she mumbles, quickly releasing the seatbelt.

'Told you. Looks like the old fella's back already,' he says nodding at the Land Rover.

Prisha sighs. 'If you had actually read the report, Albert Shaw set off in a 2014 Land Rover Discovery Sport—not a knackered old defender.'

'Oh, aye,' he says as he hands the risk assessment back to Prisha. She takes it and stares at the blob of tomato sauce on the top sheet. Pulling a tissue from her pocket, she carefully wipes the stain as best she can. Cartwright exits the car and brushes food detritus from his one-size too small suit. The shortish journey from Whitby to Pickering has been hell on wheels for Prisha. Apart from his body odour, Cartwright has as much personality as a pickled egg. She gazes at the food and drink wrappers in the passenger side footwell. In less than forty minutes he's munched his way through two hot dogs, two Mars bars, and a packet of biscuits washed down with a carton of chocolate flavoured milk. She quickly exits the car and takes three deep breaths to refresh her lungs.

'I suggest you get rid of all your rubbish when we get back to the station,' she advises. 'If Frank sees the state of the car, he'll blow a gasket.'

'Don't you worry about Frank. His bark is worse than his bite,' he says with a chuckle.

'Don't say I didn't warn you. Right, let me do the talking unless you have anything which tickles your curiosity.'

'Suits me.'

'And remember, Mrs Shaw is not a suspect. She'll be undergoing a lot of stress at the moment. Our job is to offer hope and reassurance whilst piecing together a more complete picture. Oh, take down the numberplate of the defender,' she adds, walking towards the front door, still performing deep breathing exercises.

'What for?' Cartwright quizzes with a pained expression.

Prisha's patience is waning fast. 'Forget it!' she hisses as she pulls her phone out and fires off two quick snaps of the vehicle. As she's about to knock on the door, it's flung open, and she stands face to face with a medium-sized, well-built man, probably in his late thirties. He has jet black hair swept back and a well-manicured beard. His eyes are deep brown pools as he stares directly at her. For a moment she's lost for words, caught off guard by the man's attractiveness and something else... a natural magnetism.

'I'm Detective Inspector Kumar from North Yorkshire Police and this is my colleague DS Cartwright.'

'Pleased to meet you,' he says narrowing his focus onto Prisha's face before his eyes quickly wander down her body. She can feel herself blush. Without turning away, he calls inside. 'Mam! The police are here again to see you.' Concern suddenly spreads across his face. 'It's not bad news, is it?'

'What? Oh, no. We don't have any news at the moment. We want to go over some details with your mother.'

The man's demeanour changes again. 'The plods only saw her this morning... what details?' he adds with a hint of concern.

'Let them in then, Craig, let them in,' a frail woman's voice from inside the hallway calls out.

Craig stands aside and holds his arm out as Mrs Shaw comes into view. He turns and pecks her on the cheek.

'I'll call around later, mam, with a takeaway for your tea. If you hear anything, give me a bell, yeah?'

'Yes dear.'

'I'll have a drive around, see if I can spot his car anywhere. A job the police should be doing,' he adds as he eyeballs Prisha and Cartwright with barely concealed disdain.

He heads towards the defender as Mrs Shaw ushers the officers inside.

———————

Prisha quickly evaluates the situation. If Frank had any suspicions about Mary Shaw, then he's wrong. She's frail and uses a Zimmer frame for support. Late sixties, possibly early seventies, she's skin and bone.

'Here we go,' Cartwright says enthusiastically as he bustles through the kitchen door carrying a tray containing three cups of tea and a small plate of chocolate digestives. While he was making the tea, Prisha was explaining how the police treat missing person cases, trying to put Mary's mind at ease.

'So, you see Mrs Shaw...'

'Please, call me Mary.'

'Mary. In the majority of cases, most people are found within the first forty-eight hours. Now with Albert, because of his age

49

and the circumstances, we'll be considering changing the initial risk assessment from absent, to high risk if he hasn't returned home or been found by tomorrow morning.'

'I see.'

'I've studied the report that was submitted by uniform this morning, but I want to ask you a few more questions,' she continues as Cartwright hands out the refreshments, then takes a seat at the side of her on the sofa—much to her dismay. 'You may find some questions unnecessary or even intrusive, but that's not their intent. The more information we collect, the better chance we have of finding Albert. Are you okay with that?' she says in her softest, most soothing voice.

'Yes, dear. I understand.'

'According to the report, you last saw Albert last Friday morning. Is that correct?'

'Erm... no it's not.'

Prisha tries to read the words through the smudge of tomato ketchup. 'The report says...'

Mary cuts her off. 'I think that's what I may have told the officers who turned up this morning. But I was confused. I blame the medication. The last time I saw Albert would have been on Thursday night. We watched All Creatures Great and Small on the TV and I think that finished about eight o'clock. Then I said goodnight and went to bed. I heard Albert come to bed about an hour later. We sleep in different rooms, you see... so he can get a good night's sleep.'

Prisha jots down notes in bullet form. 'And what time on Friday did he leave for his three day walking trip?'

'I'm not sure. I didn't hear him leave. During the summer, he likes to be off at first light. But this time of year, he usually leaves about seven, or later.'

'I see. And he gave absolutely no indication where he was going on his walk?'

'He's always been the same. We were both keen walkers for most of our married life, but I had an accident about ten years ago. My own fault. I wasn't paying attention and walked out into the road without looking and got side swiped by a car. It shattered my leg. I've still got pins in it. Anyway, that was the end of my walking days.'

Prisha blinks. It's going to be one of these, she thinks. A situation where you ask a question and the respondent goes off at a tangent without actually answering the question. Patience.

'So, no indication where he was heading?' she probes gently.

'No. He gets in the car and drives, then on the spur of the moment he'll pick somewhere to head to.'

'You said you were expecting him back on late Sunday afternoon or early evening?'

'Yes. That's what time he usually gets back.'

'But you didn't report him missing until 7 am this morning?'

'I was exhausted yesterday and went to bed about six. I thought I'd wake up this morning, and he'd be home. Then when I saw his bed hadn't been slept in, I knew he hadn't returned.'

'Has he ever not returned home on the day he said he would?'

'No, never. Oh, hang on, yes, he has.'

There's an audible huff from Cartwright as he snaffles another biscuit.

'How long ago was that?' Prisha asks.

'A couple of years ago. But he rang me to let me know on that occasion. The walk had taken him longer than he anticipated. He was in the Lake District somewhere and didn't fancy a two hour drive back home when feeling tired.'

'I see. If he'd intended to extend his trip, he'd have definitely let you know?'

'Yes, definitely.'

'Mary, I know you gave us a recent photo of Albert earlier, so we know what he physically looks like. Can you describe his personality for me; his traits and mannerisms. What sort of husband is he?'

'He's a good man, caring, loving, considerate. He's always on the go. I wish I had one tenth of his energy. Always positive in his outlook. Methodical, neat, fit and active. Does all the cooking, cleaning, shopping. Takes care of all the finances—you name it, and he does it. Well, he has to you see. I can't manage it these days. The walking weekends are his time to recharge the batteries. Once a month without fail, he'll spend two to three days away. He'll stay in a bed and breakfast or a pub for the night. It was my idea... after my accident. Just because I couldn't walk anymore didn't mean he had to give up his passion.'

'You said he's methodical; what sort of provisions does he take with him?'

'He has a proper walking backpack—you know, the big ones. He takes wet weather gear, first aid kit, maps, and compass, emergency rations, water sterilising tablets and one of those silver thermal blankets that retain your body heat.'

'Well prepared,' Prisha mumbles as she adds to her notes. 'Mary, you're doing well. I now need to ask some questions which may seem invasive—are you okay with that?'

'Yes.'

'Does Albert suffer from any depression, panic attacks, social anxiety?'

'No.'

'Does he have a short fuse? Prone to physical violence, or coercive behaviour?'

'No.'

'Is it a stable marriage? Any domestics, arguments, fallings out?'

'No. None. We may have the odd quibble, but that's all. It's soon forgotten.'

'You stated he has no known medical conditions. How often does he see a doctor?'

'He has regular check-up twice a year.'

'Could he be suffering from an undiagnosed medical condition? Has he complained recently of chest pains, tingling in the arms, headaches... that sort of thing?'

'No. Nothing.'

Prisha clears her throat and adjusts her position on the sofa. 'And what about extra-marital affairs?'

Mary pulls back, shocked. 'Albert? Good lord no! One of his other personality traits is honesty and loyalty.'

'I see. Sorry, but I had to ask.'

'That's right,' Cartwright jumps in. 'A lot of missing people have done a bunk with their bit-on-the-side. It's not uncommon.'

Mary appears appalled as Prisha glares at her colleague, who is busily picking crumbs from his shirt and dropping them onto the carpet.

Cartwright for once takes the hint. 'Albert sounds like he was the perfect husband, Mrs Shaw.'

'*Is* the perfect husband,' Prisha quickly rephrases, hoping to obliterate Cartwright's past-tense faux pas.

'He's one in a million.'

Prisha takes a deep breath, silently cursing Frank for insisting Cartwright accompany her.

Why didn't I leave the twat in the car?

She gathers herself. 'Moving on. What about finances, Mary? Any unpaid debts or money worries?'

'No. We've been financially stable for many years. The house is paid off. We have no loans. We receive the state pension and have plenty of savings, and we get dividends once a year from some investments Albert made many years ago. We're not extravagant.'

'So, you'd describe yourself as comfortably off?'

'Yes. We're very lucky.'

'I met your son, Craig, as we arrived. Do you have any other children?'

'No. Just Craig. Albert has a daughter from his first marriage. She lives in Australia.'

'What about close relatives?'

'My sister, Karen, lives up the road in Kirkbymoorside. I have some cousins who live in Scotland, and Albert has a brother in Cornwall. I called him before I rang the police this morning. He hasn't spoken to Albert in over a month.'

'Okay. We're about done, Mary. You've been very patient and helpful. I mentioned before that if Albert hasn't returned by tomorrow morning, the risk assessment will be re-evaluated, and from past experience, Albert will be reclassified as high risk. That elevates the case and brings in more officers, search teams, and public notifications. We'll need to obtain warrants to access Albert's phone and bank records, and other documents, and conduct a thorough search of the house.'

'Oh, dear. I'll give my permission for you to search whatever you want. I've nothing to hide,' Mary stammers, concerned at the mention of warrants.

'It doesn't work like that, Mary. You may give *your* permission, but Albert isn't here to give *his* permission. That's why we need warrants. Banks and telcos are very funny about the privacy of their clients' information.'

'Oh, I see.'

'You said you don't know where Albert went, but if you could pick three of his favourite walks, where would they be?'

Mary ponders the question before a brief flicker of a smile flits across her wrinkled features. Witnessing the smile sends a stab of sympathy through Prisha's heart.

'He loves Malham.'

'Malham Cove?' Prisha quizzes, briefly thinking of her rock climbing exploits on Saturday.

'Yes. And the tarn. He likes to do the loop from Settle. The Cleveland way is also one of his favourites, especially from Staithes to Robin Hoods Bay. Although, he prefers that walk during the summer. It can get very blowy up there this time of year. Another of his favourites is The Coledale Horseshoe in the Lake District.' She reflects, hands wringing together. 'That's not to say he walked any of them.'

'In general, how far would he typically travel? Would he ever go up to Scotland or down to the Midlands?'

'No. Mainly North Yorkshire, occasionally Cumbria and sometimes he'd venture into West Yorkshire—Haworth, you know—Bronte country.'

'Oh good. That narrows it down a bit,' Cartwright declares, his words dripping with sarcasm.

Prisha closes her eyes for a moment, then continues. 'Thanks for your time, Mary. You've been very helpful. The first thing we need to do is locate Albert's car, and with the information you've provided, at least we have a start. If you hear anything, then please let us know. You have a point of contact, don't you?'

'Yes. The young PC this morning gave me a number,' she replies as Prisha and Cartwright stand up.

'Good. And if we have any new information, we'll be in touch. Now remember what I said—most people turn up within forty-eight hours.'

'That's right,' Cartwright chirps in. 'After that, the chances of finding people alive quickly diminish.'

Prisha stabs him in the back with the car keys, then hands them to him. 'Why don't you go and start the car, sergeant?'

'Ow! That bloody hurt,' he says rubbing at his spine as he makes his way to the entrance.

'Don't get up, Mary. We can see ourselves out. Oh, two more questions. Before you retired, what did you and Albert do for a living?'

'I was a primary school teacher for over thirty years and Albert drove a taxi for the last twenty years. Before that, he was a mechanic. Why, has it any significance?'

'Probably not. Does he have any distinguishing features—a birthmark, piercings, tattoos—that sort of thing?'

'He has a tattoo on his right arm, up near the shoulder. It's of a boar's head with the letters BMC underneath it.'

'What does BMC stand for?'

'It was a motorcycle club he was in way back. Before I met him.'

'Can you remember the name of the club?'

'He mentioned it once or twice, but I can't recall the name now.'

'Thanks for your time, Mary. Take care and try not to worry.'

Prisha slams the car door shut and sticks the keys in the ignition. 'I've worked with some first-class pricks in my time, but you take the biscuit!' she yells.

Cartwright is taken aback. 'What have I done now?'

'A lot of missing people have done a bunk with their bit-on-the-side! Very eloquently put! Then as you left—after forty-eight hours, the chances of finding people alive quickly diminish. You're unreal!'

'It's true. No point giving her false hope.'

'She's a fragile and vulnerable old lady with health issues. She needs to be given hope, a lifeline, something to cling on to. All you've done is water the seeds of doubt. You have zero empathy or sympathy, and are completely lacking in social intelligence. There's only one word for you—bleeding dickhead!'

'That's two words,' he mumbles as Prisha starts the engine.

'Right, I'm calling HQ to get a squad car out here with two uniforms and you're going to organise a door-to-door of every house on this street.'

'What for?'

'To see if anyone saw Albert leaving, and if so, on which day and at what time?'

'I don't see what good that's going to do.'

'I know this may be foreign to you, Cartwright, but it's called police work, investigative police work.'

'And what are you going to do?'

58

'I'm heading back to Whitby.'

'And how am I supposed to get back?'

'Get the patrol car to drop you back once you've done your house-to-house,' she snaps, reaching for her radio. 'Oh, and by the way—you stink to the high heavens! You've been funking out the incident room for the last month. Try showering twice a day and use antiperspirant before you spray on your deodorant. And lose some weight!'

'That's fat shaming. I could have you up on a harassment charge.'

'Cry me a river, big boy.'

Superintendent Anne Banks doesn't knock as she enters Frank's office.

'Ah, Frank. I'm heading off early today as I have a late luncheon with the newly elected councillors and Lord Mayor. It's tiresome work, but one must keep the wheels oiled. You never know when we may need them on our side.'

'I was hoping to grab ten minutes with you to discuss your decision about Prisha.'

'Sorry, Frank. Not today. I'll set aside a half hour tomorrow after lunch. Say one-thirty?'

'Very good.'

She turns to leave. 'By the way, for the last few weeks, whenever I enter the incident room, my nostrils are assaulted by a rather unpleasant smell. Has something died in there?'

'It's sometimes hard to tell with Cartwright, ma'am.'

'Cartwright?'

'Yes. You may not have noticed him. He's only been with us ten years. He's the rotund, slovenly individual who nests in the corner reading the newspaper whilst stuffing hot dogs into his face, or burgers, or donuts, or...'

'Don't be facetious, Frank. I'm not in the mood. If Cartwright has an odour problem, then you need to tackle it.'

'Actually, Anne, as head of this department, I believe it falls under your remit.'

'Nonsense. He answers directly to you.'

'I think it would be better coming from a woman... don't you?'

'I'll ignore that sexist remark. Deal with it and deal with it quickly, otherwise he'll find himself back in uniform.'

'You can't put him back in uniform simply because he has a body odour problem. He'll have the union and HR onto you.'

'I may not be able to put him back in uniform because of his odour problem, but I can, based on his lacklustre performance, over the last few years.'

'Ma'am,' Frank replies dejectedly as she leaves the office. 'Don't choke on your canapes.'

8

Prisha takes a seat as Frank pours something from a plastic bottle into a glass. She stares at the cloudy brown liquid which settles with a small creamy head.

'Bit early to be hitting the bottle, Frank,' she says as she pulls out her notepad.

Frank sips from the glass and winces. 'Shit with sugar on,' he groans.

'What is it?'

'Sambuca or something. One of Meera's work colleagues makes it. It's supposed to reduce inflammation. Full of antioxidants... apparently. Tastes like pond water with a bit of fizz.'

Prisha chuckles. 'It's called kombucha. Sambuca is an aniseed flavoured liqueur.'

Frank pulls a face and pushes the glass away. 'Right, how'd you go with Mrs Shaw?'

'On face value, it appears to be a straightforward missing person case. A logical explanation would be that Albert Shaw got into difficulties whilst out walking. Maybe he got lost, broke a leg or ankle, and he's hunkered down somewhere. He's well prepared and has food, water, and a thermal blanket to keep warm.

However, you'd have thought another hiker would have stumbled upon him by now.'

'Which means he may have gone off the beaten path.'

'Possibly.'

'You don't think Mrs Shaw is hiding anything? Didn't bump Albert off and dig a hole in the back garden?'

'No. She's not in the best of health. Skin and bone. She can barely walk.'

'Why the delay in reporting him missing?'

'She went to bed early yesterday evening and assumed Albert would be there when she woke up this morning. He has once returned home a day late. But on that occasion, he telephoned to let her know.'

'So what's wrong, then?'

'Who said anything was wrong?'

'I can read you like an open book. You left here looking like someone who'd lost a shilling and found sixpence.'

Prisha's confused expression paints a picture. 'Boss?'

'You were down in the doldrums, despondent and bloody crotchety, to boot. Now you have a spring in your step and a twinkle in your eye. So come on—out with it.'

Prisha puts her notebook down and leans forward, tapping at her chin. 'Nothing tangible, Frank... just a feeling. Albert sounds like the perfect husband, and although he's got a lot on his plate, I don't think he'd do a runner.'

'But?' Frank says, slightly exasperated.

'It's not much, but... they live in a flash house. He drives a newish Land Rover Discovery. No money worries. She admitted herself they're comfortably off.'

'Get to the point.'

'She was a primary school teacher most of her working life and he drove a taxi before retirement. Plus, they get dividends from their investments. Which means they've got a bundle.'

'They may have been frugal all their lives, or won the lottery, or been left the money.'

'Yeah, I understand all that,' she says, wiggling her mouth from side to side. 'You asked me to speak with her and tell you what my gut feeling was. Well, I'm telling you—there's something a little off.'

'Children?'

'One son. We bumped into him as he was leaving, and Albert has a daughter in Australia from his first marriage.'

'What's he like, the son?'

Prisha grins. 'Drop dead gorgeous.'

'Keep your hormones in check, inspector. What was his demeanour?'

'Seemed caring enough towards his mum. Said he'd pop back later with a takeaway for her tea. He was on his way to search for Albert's car, then made a snotty remark about that's what the police should be doing.'

'Typical reaction.'

'Yeah, I know.'

Frank stands and hitches his pants up. 'Okay. If Albert hasn't turned up by eight-thirty tomorrow morning, then I'll raise the risk assessment to high and we'll swing into action. Uniform will be in charge of organising search teams and public information bulletins. You and Cartwright can work alongside them in case this is something more sinister. Talking of the Caped Crusader—where is he?' he asks as he stares into the empty incident room.

'Left him in Pickering with two uniforms to conduct a house-to-house with the neighbours.'

'Good thinking.'

'There was method in my madness. My nostrils couldn't take another thirty minutes in the car with him. Anyway, hopefully one of the neighbours will have seen or heard something. We're not sure what time Albert did leave, or even if he left on Friday. If we can establish a time, it will give us a starting point. The first thing we need to do is locate his car. At least that will narrow down our search area.'

Frank taps his desk and lowers his voice. 'Erm, did you have time to, you know, discuss Cartwright's odiferous predicament?'

'His smell?'

'Yes.'

Prisha throws a glance outside. 'Erm, yes. I dropped a subtle hint.'

'Softly, softly?'

'Yes, Frank. I tiptoed over eggshells.'

'Good lass. And?'

'I think he got the message.'

'How did he react?'

'Yep, yep, pretty good actually.'

Frank breathes a sigh of relief. 'Well done. Let's hope that's the end of the matter. I had the super in earlier, breathing down my neck about it. Back to Albert Shaw. Mrs Shaw initially said Albert didn't tell her where he was going. Any developments on that front?'

'Possibly. Albert likes to wing it, spur of the moment, but she specified three of his favourite haunts.' She opens her notebook as Frank picks up a marker pen, dons his spectacles and moves to the whiteboard.

'Go on?' he says.

'The Malham Cove loop, starting in Settle.'

'Aye, that's a grand walk unless it's blowing its arse off,' he says, jotting down the location on the board.

'Part of the Cleveland Way—specifically between Staithes and Robin Hoods Bay. She said he prefers to do that walk during summer, as it can be blustery this time of year.'

'Yep, another majestic hike. Me and Meera do that at least once a year.'

'And lastly, The Coledale Horseshoe in the Lake District.'

'That's near the village of Braithwaite.' He finishes jotting the place-names down and moves across to a large ordnance map of north England stuck to a cork board. Squinting, he studies the map, then sticks a red pin into the town of Pickering. 'Staithes, Settle, or Braithwaite,' he murmurs, pushing white pins into the place-names. 'Quickest route to all the destinations is via the main A-roads. Although, it is possible to reach any of them by B-roads if he likes to take the scenic route. Check the cameras.'

'I'll feed the details into the ANPR and see if it comes back with anything.'

'And expedite the warrant process to access the records for his telco and bank. We may as well be one step ahead of the game.'

'Already on to it, Frank.'

'Okay, good work inspector.'

'Soon to be demoted back to sergeant.'

'Don't start that again.'

9

Tuesday 17th November

The early morning fog, damp, unforgiving, and baring icy fangs, hovers low over Whitby. Chimney pots poke out above the shroud, gasping for breath. The impressive ruins of the abbey, high on the hill, are eerily visible. A heady cocktail of salt air, seaweed, and smoke from the old kipper house lingers in the thick blanket of mist.

As Prisha strolls along the harbour front, she experiences one of those unforgettable moments in life. A sense of place, well-being, and purpose. An elixir. She has misgivings about her transfer from the Midlands to North Yorkshire. Doubts and imposter syndrome torment her more often than she'd like. And yet... this place has an atmosphere, a long history, and ghosts which reach deep inside her. On special days like these, she feels reincarnated, as though in a past life she lived here. A fisherman's wife, shelling mussels, shucking oysters. Maybe a seamstress in a dusty old shop in one of the cobbled backstreets. A mother struggling to feed her brood while her husband is away at sea, hunting whales or seals.

Stopping off at her usual haunt, she orders a takeaway coffee. The town is deathly quiet apart from the distant noise of the rubbish wagons and their heavily muted beep-beeps. Happiness was never a frequent visitor, but recently it has dropped in to say hello to her on a more regular basis. This place has a pull, an allure, a charm she's content with—and the old, weathered town appears to be content with her.

———◦———

Entering the incident room, one lonely, flickering fluorescent light illuminates the bland, soulless interior. She sidles up to her workspace. Glancing at her neatly organised inbox, she doesn't spot anything from Cartwright. She was expecting a written report about the door-to-door of the Shaw's neighbours.

Hmm... maybe he's entered it into the database already? Although that would be out of character.

After a quick check on her laptop, she ascertains there is nothing in the database from Cartwright in relation to the Albert Shaw case. She wanders over to his desk and stares at the mess. Papers are strewn everywhere. The inbox is a puzzle never to be solved, accompanied by indistinguishable food stains, within a two-foot vicinity—varied, and repulsive.

'Slob,' she murmurs.

Returning to her seat, she glances at her wristwatch—seven-five. She pulls out two earbud headphones, taps her phone, and waits for the fifteen-minute meditation app to begin. It's her start to the day. Get in to work an hour early. Meditate for fifteen minutes. Calm the brain. Wipe it clean, then come out of the zone, and slowly let the thoughts jostle for position. It's a good start to the day. As she lifts the second bud to her ear, her routine is rudely interrupted.

'Slap my big red arse!' Frank's voice booms out.

Prisha pulls the bud from her ear, closes her meditation app, and sighs.

'Well, there goes that,' she mumbles as she heads towards his office. Knocking once, she enters.

'Frank?'

'Oh, morning Prisha. You're in early.'

'Yes. I sometimes like to...'

He interrupts. 'I'm the same. You and me must have been plucked from the same flower bed.'

'What does that...'

'Just read the overnight reports. Another missing person case came in a few hours after we knocked off last night.'

'Not unusual. North Yorkshire is a huge area. We can sometimes get two or three mispers a day.'

'Aye, true. Except this missing person is a sixty-eight-year-old female.'

'And?'

'Comes from Pickering. Not more than five minutes' drive from the Shaw's house.'

'You're shitting me?'

'I shit ye not!'

'Could it be a coinc...'

Frank holds his hand up aggressively. 'Stop! Don't even utter that word.' He tosses the report across the desk.

Prisha grabs at it and quickly scans the contents as Frank continues. 'Maxine Wood. A widow. Has one daughter, Julie, who lives in Scarborough, a midwife who's on call over the weekend. She visits her mother every Monday. Arrives about 5 pm, sleeps overnight, spends the day with her on Tuesday then leaves early evening. Arrived yesterday. House all neat and tidy and tickety-boo...'

'Tickety what?' Prisha quizzes, momentarily taking her eyes from the report.

'Everything as it should be,' Frank offers. 'The daughter calls her mother's mobile and guess what?'

'Switched off or out of range?'

'Exactly,' Frank confirms. 'The daughter said that once a month her mother goes away with a local walking club. They leave on a Friday morning, do a couple of medium graded walks, return home Sunday evening. Sound familiar?'

'Has Julie, the daughter, been in touch with the walking club?'

'Yes. They cancelled last weekend's hike because the weather was iffy, but the president of the club said Maxine hasn't been out with the walking club for over a year.'

'Hell! Are you thinking what I'm thinking?'

'Aye. It smells fishier than a trawlerman's underpants after a month at sea.'

Prisha winces. 'Thanks for the mental image.'

'My pleasure. Right, plan of attack. I've already escalated the risk assessment on Albert Shaw to high. Uniform will take care of that. But I want you to pay a visit to Julie and get some more details. She's still at her mother's place. Address is on the report. Oh, and drop in on Mrs Shaw. Explain about the escalation and that uniform will want to search the house. Reassure her it's simply standard procedure—we have to tick all the boxes.'

'Yes, Frank.'

'And ask her if she...'

'... knows Maxine Wood, yes, Frank. You don't have to spell everything out for me.'

Frank stops pacing and removes his spectacles. 'You're right. I can tend to micromanage. I apologise,' he adds softly.

'Apology accepted.'

'Good. Now, have you got the results back from the cameras? Have we got a positive ID on Albert's vehicle?'

'Haven't had time to check yet, boss.'

'Well, get on to it! And what about Cartwright? Did he get anywhere with the door-to-door yesterday?'

'I can't seem to find his report.'

Frank shakes his head and yells, 'Call the slack bugger right now and find out. And tell him to get his sorry arse in here—pronto!' He pauses and scratches at his cheek. 'It's looking like Albert, the perfect husband, and Maxine, the widow, may have been having shenanigans.'

'A relationship, you mean?'

'Didn't I just say that?'

'Sometimes, I'm not familiar with your expressions. Any chance you can speak in plain English?'

Frank is aghast. 'You can't get any plainer speaking than a Yorkshireman. We call a spade a spade.'

'No, I meant.... It doesn't matter. I'll ring Cartwright now, then check the ANPR results.' She heads to the door.

'And Prisha, while you're at Mrs Shaws, check that Albert...'

'... didn't take a suitcase full of clothes with him. And confirm he hasn't taken his passport. I'll also check the telco and bank have received the warrants for Albert's records. You see, Frank, I'm wearing big girls' knickers today.' She quietly closes the door behind her as she reaches for her mobile.

Frank sports a wry smile as he studies her through the window and chuckles. 'She wants to be careful. Any sharper and she'd cut herself.'

———⋄———

'Hello,' Cartwright says, answering his mobile, still half asleep.

'Jason, it's Prisha.'

'No shit.'

'Where's the report from the house-to-house?'

'Still in my notebook.'

'What! That was a two hour job at most. What did you do the rest of the afternoon?'

'Thanks to you, I spent most of it in the back of a bloody patrol car. We finished the door knock and were heading back to Whitby when the patrol was called to a traffic accident. By the time I got back, it was way past knock-off time, and I had a darts tournament last night.'

'Right. Well never mind that now. Did any of the neighbours see or hear anything?'

'Yeah. Mrs erm, Mrs… from across the road at number eighteen—or was it sixteen?'

'Get on with it!' Prisha snaps.

'Seven-thirty Friday morning. She'd set off from her front gate to walk the dog when she says Albert passed her in his car.'

'And she's one hundred per cent certain it was Albert?'

'Aye. Described the car. She only saw the back of his head, but she said it was definitely him.'

'And she was sure of the time and day?'

'Yes. She was adamant. She's one of those types who sees and hears everything. A real old busybody. Got their nose stuck into…'

'Yep, got it. Frank says to get your backside in here ASAP.'

'Easier said than done.'

'Why?'

'I need to take a shower. Apply my antiperspirant, followed by deodorant. Make sure I have fresh, clean clothes. All those things take time. I mean, I wouldn't want to funk out the office, now, would I?'

'Stop being a baby.'

'Your remarks were quite hurtful.'

Prisha reflects as a stab of regret gnaws at her. 'Look, Justin, I'm sorry. I admit I was a tad harsh.'

'A tad harsh! You were brutal.'

'I'm sorry, you're right. I wasn't very tactful. I was annoyed at the way you behaved with Mrs Shaw. I apologise. Friends?'

There's a pause. 'Yeah, friends. I'll be with you in thirty minutes.'

'On second thoughts. I'll pick you up from home in fifteen.'

'What's the bloody rush?'

'Another misper. A woman of similar age to Albert. Gone missing from Pickering.' She ends the call before he can offer any more protestations, then knocks on Frank's door and sticks her head inside. 'I'm heading to Pickering now, boss. I'll pick Cartwright up on the way out of town. We have a confirmation that Albert left Friday at around seven-thirty. Can you run through the ANPR records and call me if you find anything? Thanks.'

'Who's in bloody charge here?' he grumbles, watching her march across the incident room with a spring in her step.

10

By the time they reach Pickering, Prisha has laid out their plan of attack, but she knows Cartwright only too well and goes over it one more time.

'Mrs Rutherford is the president of the local walking club. We're nearing her place now. She's expecting you. Confirm the last time Maxine Wood walked with the club and find out if she knows Albert Shaw. I'll call in to get a statement from Maxine's daughter, Julie, then pop over to Mary Shaw's place and inform her about the search escalation for Albert.' She shoots Cartwright a glance. 'Did you get all that?'

'Yeah,' he replies, clearly distracted.

'What's the matter with you?'

'Nothing. Thanks for cleaning the car out, by the way.'

'No problem.'

'Am I in Frank's bad books again?'

'No more than usual. Why do you ask?'

'I'm thinking of throwing the towel in,' he states glumly.

'What!' Prisha exclaims as she pulls up outside the address of Mrs Rutherford.

'You heard.'

'But why?'

'Don't talk daft. You know why?' he says as he removes his seatbelt and pushes open the door.

'No, I don't. What's brought all this on? It's not because I had a go at you yesterday, is it?'

'No, not really, but it got me thinking. The fact is, I'm nearing forty. Been on the force nearly twenty years and been a DS for nine of those years.'

'So?'

'Let's face facts, Prisha, I'm a shit copper and everyone knows it. I'm not going any higher. I'm surprised I was ever promoted from DC to DS, to be honest. You know how it works in plain-clothes; if you haven't been promoted in over ten years, they kick you back into uniform.'

'That's a fallacy, an old-wives' tale.'

'Is it? Anyway, I can't go back to uniform. Can you imagine me organising a team and dealing with people's personal and work problems?'

The truth is, Prisha can't imagine it, but now is not the time for honesty. 'Jason, you have a lot to offer,' she says with as much conviction as she can muster.

'Have I. Like what?'

That's a curly one. 'Like... well, you're—you're easy going, affable.'

'Is that it? Jason, the easy going slob?' He steps from the car and takes a deep breath of the frigid air.

Prisha stares at a man standing at a crossroads. She leaps from the car and walks up to him.

'Take a look at you!' she declares, beaming.

'What?' he replies, non-plussed.

'A smart new suit. Crisp white shirt. Shiny shoes. Ironed trousers. Neat hair with a side-parting. And I've got to admit, you smell damn good.'

Cartwright visibly grows an inch as he pulls his shoulders back and attempts to suck in his protruding gut. 'You think?'

'I don't think; I know. Now you look the part—act the part. You're in CID, one of the team. If you look good, you feel good. And when you feel good, everything is much easier.'

A thin smile spreads across his lips. 'Now you mention it, I do feel sort of different. Sort of like a new man.'

'That's the spirit.' She moves in and grabs the knot of his tie and adjusts it slightly, then pats him on the shoulder. 'Okay detective sergeant, go and do your job. And remember the salient part of your title.'

His brow furrows. 'What?'

'Detectives—detect.'

The notion is a novel idea to him as he considers the simplicity of the words. 'Right,' he nods with a wide grin. 'Detectives—detect.' He strides to the garden gate with confidence and pushes at it—except it sticks, and he tries to force the situation without success. Prisha saunters over, lifts the gate up and it swings freely open.

'Ah,' he murmurs, slightly embarrassed.

'Did you get time for breakfast?' she asks.

'No.'

'Nor me. I tell you what; once you've finished here, have a stroll up onto the high street and find a caff. Text me the name and I'll meet you there in about thirty minutes and we'll swap notes—yeah?'

'Yeah. Now you're talking. And Prisha?'

'What?'

'Thanks.'

Prisha places a plate and a cup of fresh coffee on the table and takes a seat.

'What'd you get?' Cartwright asks, finishing his full English fry up, then washing it down with a hearty glug of hot sweet tea.

'Scrambled egg wrap with avocado. How'd you go with Mrs Rutherford?'

'Interesting. Maxine Wood had been a member of the walking club for about five years. There's about thirty in the club. They typically do a two day walk once a month, although not all the members take part all the time. They stay over at a B&B or local pub. Anyway, about a year ago, Mrs Rutherford said she had a falling out, or a misunderstanding with Maxine.'

'What about?'

'She said it was much ado about nothing, but she appeared evasive, reticent.'

'Go on,' Prisha says as she attacks her wrap.

'Then I drop in Albert Shaw's name. She said she knew him, as Maxine had introduced him to the club a few months before the falling out. I knew I wasn't getting the full story from her, so I kept prodding away, little by little.'

'Good.'

'Finally, she cracks wide open. At first, when Albert joined the club, everything was fine. Then Mrs Rutherford noticed that Maxine and Albert were getting a little too friendly for a so-called platonic relationship. She caught them holding hands a few times at the back of the group whilst walking. Anyway, one morning she catches Maxine coming out of Albert's room in a guest house they stayed in overnight. She confronted Maxine about it and said she should be ashamed of herself, as Albert's wife had only recently been diagnosed with cancer and she was using the walking club as an excuse for her disgraceful behaviour.'

'Cancer?'

'Yes.'

'What type?'

'Ah, well, here's where it gets really interesting. Mary Shaw had been having treatment for breast cancer for several years. She was in remission for a while until it was detected the disease had spread to her lymph nodes.'

'Shit! That means it can spread to any other organ.'

'About six months ago Mrs Rutherford heard on the grapevine that Mary had been diagnosed with pancreatic cancer, and she was refusing to have any more treatment.'

'Which means she hasn't long left.'

'Three to six months, according to Mrs Rutherford. Of course, that's her supposition—not fact. How did you go?'

'Maxine's daughter, Julie, confirmed what was in the overnight report. When I asked if she knew Albert Shaw, she seemed a bit surprised. But yes, she knew him. He came around occasionally to Maxine's house to do odd jobs.'

'I bet he did.'

'Julie was naturally suspicious when I brought his name up, but I said Albert had also gone missing and we wanted to join the dots to see if there was a connection. Still, she's not thick, so I know what will be going through her mind. Maxine had taken her walking backpack, but nothing else seemed to be missing, and her passport was still there.'

'So she hasn't done a runner with Albert?'

'No.'

'And Mrs Shaw?' Cartwright asks, swallowing the last of his brew.

'Worried to death—and rightly so. Again, Albert's passport was in his office and no suitcases were missing. I told her uniform would arrive to search the property, which made her even more anxious. A Family Liaison Officer is on their way now, and Mary's sister, Karen, is planning to come and stay.'

'And does Mary know Maxine Wood?'

Prisha stares at the table. 'I didn't ask.'

'Why not?'

'She's in enough pain—mental and physical. If I mention another woman's name who has gone missing at the same time as her husband, then she'll draw only one conclusion. I couldn't do it to her. Things are bad enough without her worrying about if her husband's cheating. Anyway, her knowing Maxine or not adds nothing to the enquiry. We know Albert and Maxine were probably having an affair, and that's all that matters.' Prisha finishes her breakfast in silence, then dabs at the corner of her mouth with a tissue. 'Oh, and one last thing I forgot to mention from yesterday—probably nothing, but I asked if Albert had any distinguishing marks; scars, birthmarks, piercings—that sort of thing.'

'And?'

'He has a tattoo on his upper right arm. It's of a boar's head with the letters BMC below it.'

'BMC?'

'Yes. I did a bit of research last night in bed. It's the Brigante Motorcycle Club.'

'The outlaw biker gang?'

'Yes. The Brigantes were an ancient Celtic tribe of Northern England, or modern-day Yorkshire. In fact, the Italian word Briganti translates as brigands, which is a thief living in the countryside who ambushes and robs outsiders passing through.'

'You're not telling me seventy-year-old Albert Shaw is part of a biker gang?'

Prisha chuckles. 'No. He used to be forty-odd years ago. Mary said he quit before she even met him.'

'Ha, quit... right,' Cartwright scoffs, swilling the last of his tea down.

'What do you mean by that?'

'About seven years ago, I was part of an operation to bring down a biker gang. They were into all the usual shit; drugs, money laundering, illegal weapons. It was fascinating the way they operate, but I learnt one thing—once you're a member—you're a member for life. The only way out is death or to distance yourself from them and hope you fade from memory. Even so, it's no guarantee they won't come knocking on your door one day calling in a favour.'

'Hmm... nothing to suggest Albert Shaw is still involved with them, though. Mary would have said.'

'If she knows.'

'Anyway, let's not get distracted by the biker info. We've swapped notes, now tell me what it all means—police detective,' she adds, sporting a mischievous grin.

Cartwright grimaces but takes the bull by the horns. 'It looks like Albert and Maxine were, are, having an affair. It appears they've gone off together for the weekend and something's happened to them.'

'Which probably rules out what?'

The cogs in Cartwright's head slowly grind around. 'It means... it means the likelihood of both having an accident and being incapacitated is slim. If *one* of them had been injured, the other would have raised the alarm.'

'Correct. And from that likelihood, what can we deduce?'

'Slim to no chance they've eloped. Slim to no chance they're both injured. Which leaves a very good possibility they're dead.'

'And what do we need to do, first, before we go off on a wild goose chase?'

There's a long pause until Cartwright has a lightbulb moment. 'We need some sort of proof that Maxine was in Albert's car on Friday. Otherwise, our assumptions are flawed.'

Prisha laughs. 'Excellent!'

'If they are dead, then how? And was some other person, or persons involved and if they were, why?' he says, surfing the wave into shore.

Prisha fixes him with a firm stare. 'Let's not get ahead of ourselves, Jason. Methodical police work—right? Step by step, building block by building block.'

'Yes. Sorry.'

'What's our next course of action?'

'Get a fix on the car from ANPR. Then any towns the car drove through, we locate CCTV footage from roadside shops, petrol stations, to ascertain that both Albert *and* Maxine were in the car together. Hopefully, we'll also get a fix on where their likely destination was. Once we have that, we get the local patrol to check the place out and locate the car. Then we need eyewitnesses or CCTV to tell us which direction they set off on their walk, which should point us to the trail they took.'

'If they did set off. There's always a possibility they didn't.'

'Very true.'

'Good work, sergeant. I'll give Frank a call and see if the cameras clocked Albert's car.'

11

Frank squints as he studies the images and corresponding data on his monitor.

'Come on, come on, keep going,' he urges. 'Bingo!' he yells. 'Got you.'

He swiftly moves to the corkboard and sticks another red pin into it as his mobile rings.

'Prisha, I was about to call you. Good news. We have a confirmed sighting of Albert's Land Rover. Have you a pen?'

'Yes, boss. Go on.'

'His vehicle was picked up in Pickering at the roundabout intersecting the A170 and the A169, at 7:37 am last Friday. I have a photo, but it's impossible to tell who was in the car. The vehicle was clocked at regular intervals along the A59 until he reaches the roundabout near Thorlby, where he hangs a right onto the A65. He's next clocked at the roundabout just past Cleatop, at 9:45 am where he takes another right onto the B6480—and there the trail goes cold.'

'Shit! And where does that road lead to?'

'Settle,' Frank says with a certain amount of satisfaction.

'The Malham loop from Settle, as Mary Shaw suggested.'

'Exactly. But let's not put the cart before the horse. There are plenty of places which splinter off from that B-road. The area is awash with walking tracks.'

'Understood. But Settle is a start.'

'Aye, it is. Now, before you go racing off, there's a few things you need to put in place...'

Prisha, as calmly as she can, interrupts him. 'Frank! You're doing it again!' she yells down the phone.

'What?' he asks in all innocence.

'You know what! Micro-managing.'

'Am I?'

'Yes, you are.'

'Sorry. I was going to say...'

'Call the Desk Sergeant at Settle Police Station and give him the details of Albert's vehicle and ask him to send a patrol car to search for it.'

'Aye, and...' Frank begins.

'Check CCTV along the route Albert took through Pickering and confirm who was in the car.'

'Yes, but always check the petrol stations and jeweller's shops first. They typically have very good CCTV cameras. And it's possible Albert pulled in close to home to fill his car up.'

A deep sigh comes down the line. 'Already on it, Frank. Me and Cartwright are parked up at the first petrol station on the way out of Pickering, right now. Cartwright's inside making enquiries.'

'Oh... I see. And don't forget...'

'To obtain some used clothing belonging to Maxine and Albert for the sniffer dogs.'

'That's right, and then...'

'Inform Inspector Pearson, at Northallerton of the developments, so he can put a search team on standby, and get a public bulletin out asking for eyewitnesses to come forward.'

Frank taps at his desk with his pen, feeling slightly surplus to requirements. 'Okay, well, you seem to have it all in hand. If the car is found in Settle, then I suggest...'

'I come back to Whitby, pack an overnight bag and my walking boots and get booked into a guest house for the night. Then head to Settle.'

'Right, righto. Ahem, have you anything else for me?'

'I'll give you an update when I finally hit the road. No point wasting time.'

'One last thing; is Cartwright a help or a hindrance? If the latter, then go to Settle alone and use some of their uniforms as resources.'

'He's been on the money today, Frank. I need him.'

'You need him?' Frank repeats, incredulous at her statement.

'That's what I said. Okay, I'll speak soon. Bye, Frank. Hang on... here comes Cartwright now, and he's running.'

'Cartwright's running. When did he pick up that skill? Prisha? Prisha?'

Frank waits nervously before opening the door to his bar fridge in the corner of his office. He stares at the chickpea salad in a Tupperware bowl, then at the wrapped Mowbray's pork pie sitting next to it.

'Why does life have to be so cruel?' he mutters.

'Boss! Are you still there?' Prisha's voice cries, telegraphing good news.

Frank slams the fridge door shut, clutching the pork pie. 'Aye, go on lass.'

'Cartwright's reviewed the CCTV. We have a positive. Not only do we have footage of Albert's car at the pumps, and a clear number plate, but also footage of him, *and* Maxine Wood entering the store to buy water and snacks. Cartwright says it's definitely them, boss.'

'Aye, well bloody double check it. Anyone else in the car?'

'No. Not unless they're hiding.'

'Excellent work! Now what you need to...'

'Bye, boss. I'm heading back to Whitby.'

The call goes dead as Frank gazes disconsolately at the pile of paperwork on his desk and an email inbox, which is nearing capacity.

'Bugger it,' he states sadly as he grabs a plate and knife from his drawer and pulls the wrapper from the pork pie.

12

Zac parks up in a pay and display car park adjacent to a nondescript carpet and flooring store. Exiting the vehicle, he makes his way to the ticket machine, jabs at a few buttons, then swipes his police issue credit card.

'Three pounds fifty for two bloody hours. Christ, I should arrest you for daylight robbery, you titanium twat.'

After displaying his ticket on the windscreen, he takes the short walk back towards the city centre, feeling mildly apprehensive about his clandestine rendezvous with DS Beale aka Talbot McGovern. He slips down a side street and stares at the hotel. It has a sleek, modular look, all boxes, rectangles, and glass. It was probably designed to create an enchanting visual effect when the sun shone down upon it at particular times of the day. Obviously, the architect had spent little time in Hull. The design is ugly now, give it another twenty years and it will look like a Soviet era tenement block.

Zac enters the reception and takes in his surroundings. It's minimalist and the three reception counters in front of him remind him of airport check-in desks. Spinning around, he does a three-sixty and spots DS Beale making his way from the bar.

There's barely a flicker of recognition as both men walk towards the lift. Zac pushes the button on the console and fumbles in his pocket.

'Now where did I put that card?' he murmurs as the lift doors open.

DS Beale pulls out his keyless entry card and flashes it in front of the scanner. 'Allow me,' he says. The doors close as Beale presses the button for the fourth floor.

Exiting the lift, they walk on in silence, Zac a good ten feet behind. Beale stops and swipes his card in the hotel door, which immediately clicks open. With a quick look up and down the deserted corridor he pushes open the door allowing Zac to walk swiftly into the room. The door slams shut.

'When I walked into reception, I thought I was at Manchester Airport for a moment. I even experienced a mild panic attack as I searched for my passport,' Zac says, admiring the clean interior.

'Aye. That's modern architecture for you. It's like living in fucking Legoland. I thought we'd got over building everything in boxes in the mid-seventies. Did they no learn their lesson?' Beale grumbles as he sticks his swipe card into a receptacle on the wall and the lights flash on.

Zac does a quick tour of the suite, before slumping into a Windsor dining chair which is about as comfortable as sitting on a pallet of engineering bricks.

'Pretty flash,' he comments, referring to the room.

'Aye, well, if I'm putting my neck on the line then I'm not going to slum it,' Beale says unscrewing the top off a whisky bottle.

'Anyway, I've got to look the part. If I'm some big shot gangster from Scotland, then I'm nay going to stay in a backpacker hostel, am I?'

'Suppose not.'

He holds the bottle up to Zac. 'Snifter?'

Zac checks his watch. 'I'm on duty, driving and it's barely past one o'clock,' he says shaking his head.

'So? I'm on duty too. Ah, well, suit yourself.' He dribbles scotch into a tumbler and sits on the edge of the bed. 'I asked for a room with a view,' he begins as Zac pulls back a net curtain and stares outside. 'I meant of the River Humber, instead I've got a bird's-eye view of the city. Some view. It's like fucking Stalingrad—after the siege.' He pulls a packet of cigarettes from his shirt pocket and sparks up a smoke before offering one to Zac, who declines.

'I'm sure I saw a no smoking sign in the corridor,' Zac says.

'I'm not in the fucking corridor,' Beale replies, drawing heavily on his ciggy. 'Oh, I have something for you,' he says making his way to a desk in the corner and picking up a white envelope. 'It was waiting for me in reception this morning. Hot off the press.' He tosses the envelope to Zac who pulls out the contents and stares at the pieces of plastic.

'A credit card and driver's licence?' he asks, bemused.

'Don't get excited. The credit card only has a grand on it, so don't get any funny ideas about absconding to the Bahamas with a pole dancer. It's to pay for your hotel room, meals, and a few drinks at the nightclub.'

Zac's eyes narrow. 'Hang on a minute. When I agreed to this, you said I was to be another pair of eyes and ears—I wouldn't be getting involved.'

'That's true.'

'Then why the fake ID?'

'Always prepare for the unexpected. The drug ring are an unknown quantity. Now I'm sure they're all a nice bunch of lads and send flowers to their mothers on their birthdays, but just in case they're not, you need a fake ID. If they were to find your warrant card on you, I'm not sure they'd be embracing you with open arms.'

Zac studies the cards more closely. 'Oh, come off it! You've got to be joking!'

'What's the matter?'

'My fake name—that's the matter! Nigel Crowther.'

'What's wrong with that?'

'Do I look like a Nigel Crowther?'

'Fuck knows.'

'That's the sort of name belonging to a software developer who stays up all night playing Grand Theft Auto and has a cup of cocoa before bed.'

'Dinna fash yersel. It's only a name.'

'Whose bright idea was this?'

'Your boss.'

'Frank or Superintendent Banks?'

'I said your boss.'

'Frank... the bastard. It's his idea of a joke.'

'It's fine. Nondescript, bland, forgettable. Oh, and if anyone asks—you're a tractor salesman.'

'It just gets better,' Zac groans.

'Can we move on... Nigel?'

'Very amusing. Aye, I suppose so,' he mutters, still staring at the name on the card.

Beale pulls open a drawer. 'Here's a burner phone. The only person to call you on it will be me. It will come up as a private number. Remember, I call you; you can't call me,' he explains handing Zac the phone. 'Have you had any further discussions with Frank about this operation?'

'No, apart from I told him I was meeting with you today to go over the plan in more detail.'

'I better fill you in then,' he says stubbing his cigarette into a saucer, then topping up his whisky glass. 'The meet and greet we had on Friday with Frank, DCI Keegan, and your super—was a bit of a ruse. DCI Keegan may be English, but we cannae hold that against him. Okay, maybe we can, but that's a different ball game for a different day. Keegan's a canny operator—one of the smartest. If it wasn't for his dickhead brother, he may have gone all the way to the top.' He lights another cigarette, then spits a stray strand of tobacco from the corner of his mouth.

'His brother?' Zac queries, intrigued.

'Aye. His brother—the boxer. Anyway, never mind about that now. I'll tell you later. Keegan, having worked with Frank many years ago—and being mightily impressed, got in touch with him to give him the heads up on this little fishing expedition. He knows he can trust Frank. Keegan explained the situation and told him we needed a good, true man, and one who could handle himself—just in case. Frank had no qualms in nominating you.'

'You're not filling me full of confidence here. Remember the eyes and ears bit? Last Friday you said if the shit hit the fan, then I was to call uniform.'

Beale shakes his head vigorously. 'No, that was your super who said that. You know what the pen-pushers are like—they shit their britches at the sight of a wee mouse.'

'So, if something goes down, do I call uniform or not?'

'Fuck me! You're nearly as green as you are cabbage looking. Calling uniform would be like calling Mary fucking Poppins to take down Mike Tyson. No, you don't call uniform. We don't want the keystone cops running around all over the place like a demented flock of headless geese. That's a sure-fire way to get someone killed. All I need is someone in my corner who can rumble if it kicks off. Frank said you were the man. Said you could handle yourself. Is that true, or no?'

Zac strokes his beard. 'Aye. I've had my moments.'

'Good. I need someone who can fight like a cut snake if needed. Someone who can grab whatever's at hand and batter a man, or woman, senseless regardless of the consequences. Someone who will fight to stay alive. I'm not walking into that abyss with no wire, no specialist unit on standby, no firearms unit at the ready unless I've got someone to back me up. Now, can you handle it, or no?'

'Aye. I can handle it. Frank has shown me a few moves over the years.'

'Oh aye, that's right. Keegan said Frank used to be a promising boxer when he was younger. Until he got disqualified. You can throw a good punch then?'

'I practice at the gym twice a week.'

Beale pushes air out through his lips in a frustrated manner. 'Christ... the thing with punchbags, sonny, is they don't fight back. Let me have a look at your mitts.' Zac holds his arms out and splays his fingers as Beale inspects them. 'Aye, big enough paws to do some damage. Of course, they're only good if you've got room to swing them. Do you know how to headbutt?'

'It's hardly rocket science, is it?'

Beale grins. 'There's an art to it, sunshine. Stand up.' Zac rises and towers over Beale by a good six inches. 'Right, forget about all that nonsense you see in the films when the whole head tilts back. It's a recipe for disaster.'

'Why?'

'Because it gives time for your opponent to jab you in the jaw. Now come at me in slow motion and watch what I do.' Zac raises his fists and moves towards Beale, who immediately reaches out and places his palms on top of Zac's hands. He bends at the knee, then shoots up and in towards Zac's head. 'Understand?' he asks. 'Trap the hands or wrists, bend at the knees, then launch up and use the crown of your head to connect with their nose. At the same time, ram your knee into the plums. If they're still standing, then smash your head into the side of their neck. Your opponent will automatically turn their head to the side, at which point you swing your elbow into his... pardon me for being politically incorrect—you swing your elbow into his—or *her* jaw. You can get an enormous amount of power into the elbow. It's a much under-utilised weapon, and it's a bony bugger, so you're not going to hurt yourself. Right, let's practice. Remember, you're using the hardest part of your head to hit the most vulnerable part of your opponent's head—the nose, the jaw, the mouth. Got it?'

'Yep, got it.'

For the next ten minutes they practice and refine the headbutt move until Beale is confident Zac has the technique down pat.

'Not bad,' Beale says. 'Although, I would nay be signing up for cage fighting anytime soon if I were you. Now, how to defend against the headbutt. You've got a long set of levers, so that automatically gives you a distinct advantage, unless you come up against a fucking escaped orangutan with arms as long as yours. Arms outstretched, fingers on your opponent's chest. If they try a headbutt from that distance, you'll feel their trigger movement, at which point you hit them with a double palm strike up and into the chin, or a finger jab to the throat. And if you want to take the initiative, hit them while they're talking. Let's do it.'

Another ten minutes pass by until Beale breaks off for another smoke, panting heavily at the exertion of slow motion headbutt evasion.

'It's all right giving me all these fighting moves, but by the sound of your chest, I'm not sure you'd last more than ten seconds before you'd need an EpiPen injection and half an hour in a hyperbaric chamber,' Zac states.

Beale pulls a snap lock bag from his pocket and drops it on the desk 'Don't you worry about me, sunshine. I'll be dropping one of these bad boys before I enter Mr Bojangles.' A worried expression takes up residence on his face. 'Hang on, that didn't sound right. Someone could get the wrong impression. Let me rephrase that. I'll be dropping one of these bad boys before I enter the nightclub,' he adds with a cackle. 'I'll be full of energy and false bravado.'

Zac picks the bag up and stares at the tablets with mild disbelief. 'Great! I'm putting my neck on the line to help bring down a drug cartel while you're popping the very pills they're selling. It's ironic, and illegal.'

'Calm down, Nigel Crowther, and have a sip of your cocoa. I'm not a regular user. Remember this; if I'm playing the part of Talbot McGovern, lieutenant of the Caledonian Boys, then I must think like him, act like him. I need to slip into his skin as a psychotic, deranged, Scottish fuck knuckle. It's the only way to be convincing. It's called method acting.'

'I'm not sure you need to act.'

A loud rap on the door has both men staring nervously at each other as Beale checks his watch.

'That's odd. I wasn't expecting my visitors so early. You best hide in the wardrobe,' Beale whispers.

'What?'

'You heard.'

'Why?'

'I can't be seen with you.'

Zac ungainly squeezes his tall frame into a wardrobe as Beale peeps through the spyhole and breathes a sigh of relief, as he opens the door.

'All right, sweetheart, what can I do for you?'

The young woman is smartly dressed in a blue skirt and blazer with the hotel logo imprinted below the lapel. She has a name tag—Ruby—pinned to her pristine white blouse.

'I'm sorry to trouble you, sir, but we've had a complaint.'

'I'd really like to help you out, lassie, but I've never worked for a complaints department before, so I'd be out of my depth. Maybe try one of the other guests. They may have some experience in that particular field.'

'No, you misunderstand. We've received a complaint about you.'

'Me!' he says with incredulity. 'I find that very hard to believe. I'm just keeping myself to myself, minding my own business.'

'It's about the cigarette smoke coming from your room.'

'I think you're under a misapprehension, Ruby. I dinnae smoke. Dirty, disgusting, filthy habit, and ridiculously expensive... ahem, so I've heard.'

'I can smell it all down the corridor, in the lift, and I can smell it drifting out from your room.'

'Ah! I know what that will be; it's my joss sticks.'

'Your what?'

'Joss sticks, you know—incense.'

'Then why does it smell of cigarette smoke?'

'It's essence of tobacco, although it is nicotine free.'

'May I come in and have a look?' she says, making a move forward.

Beale blocks the doorway with his arm and leg. 'I'd advise against that, Ruby,' he replies in a whisper.

'Why?'

He winces. 'I have an assortment of toys on my bed.'

'Toys—what sort of toys?'

Beale takes a quick glance up and down the corridor. 'Oh dear, this is a tad embarrassing. Let's just say there are certain toys that can help a man get off—if you catch my drift. They're not for a young girl's eyes like yours. It could scar you for life and I don't want that on my conscience.'

She pouts less than convinced by Beale's bullshit. 'Well, I'd appreciate it if you could refrain from burning anymore of your incense. It's upsetting one of our guests.'

He shoots her his most endearing smile, which could neuter a rabid rottweiler. 'I tell you what, sweetpea, give me their room number and I'll apologise in person. How does that sound?'

'I'm sorry. We're not allowed to give out that information.'

'Really? And when was that law passed in the Houses of Parliament, because I must have missed it.'

'It's hotel policy.'

There's a moment's impasse.

'Right, is there anything else I can help you with, darling? Only sometimes a man needs to do what a man needs to do. It's been well over twenty-four hours since the straining cyclops was let out of his cave and he's getting grumpy.' She throws him a disgusted look, turns, and marches away. He closes the door and goes back into the room, cackling as he sparks another cigarette. 'Nigel, come out, come out wherever you are. The coast is clear.'

Zac staggers from the wardrobe, slightly dishevelled and not in the best of moods.

'Who was it?'

'Hotel staff. Some snivelling, wee bawbag made a complaint about the cigarette smoke. I bet they dinnae think twice about jumping into their diesel powered SUV and polluting the planet. Two-faced, hypocritical bastard.' He sloshes another glug of whisky into his glass, gulps it down, then takes a giant gasp on his ciggy. 'I suspect the bald-headed fuck nut who was throwing me the stinky eye at breakfast. He was eating muesli and fruit—you know the type—sort of weirdo who likes to jerk off in front of the mirror in a pair of nylon pantyhose. Now, where were we?' he says, emitting a violent cough.

'We were about to discuss tactics and how it may play out at the nightclub.'

'Aye, so we were.' He glances at his watch. 'Right, let's get down to business. I have another appointment in forty minutes.'

———◆———

'Okay, we're about done for today,' Beale says checking his watch again. 'One last thing I forgot to mention. I'm bringing the operation forward by a couple of days.'

Zac does a lightning-fast calculation. 'A couple of days? That means tomorrow—Wednesday night?'

'Fuck me! Ever thought about putting your name forward for NASA?'

'What's the rush?'

'Wednesday night is ladies' night. The girls get in free and pay half-price for their drinks.'

'You mean you've changed the day, not for any tactical or strategic reason, but because you're hoping to get laid?'

Beale jumps to his feet sporting a wounded expression 'How dare you! Take that back! What type of man do you take me for?'

Zac winces, feeling a little ashamed and embarrassed. 'I'm sorry. I didn't mean it. I apologise,' he mutters contritely.

'Aye, well... we can all say foolish things sometimes. I accept your apology,' Beale says sitting back down. 'Anyway, it's not solely about getting a cheap shag. I have to be back in Glasgow by Friday. It's my ma's seventieth birthday and the whole family's having a big piss up. It had completely slipped my mind.'

'Oh, that's all right then. As long as it's nothing trivial.'

'And the truth is—I don't like it here.'

'Hull?'

Beale screws his nose up. 'England. The air doesnae smell good. The water doesnae taste right. It's all fucked up. And the sawn-off, missing links that wander around dragging their knuckles along the ground, like fucking rejected extras from the Hobbit give me the creeps. The place is in its final death throes. Get me back to the panoramic vistas of the highlands, the smell of heather wafting in the air and young fawns gambolling through the glens,' he says with eyes half closed, in a reverie.

'I thought you lived in Glasgow?'

Beale throws him a disdainful glare before resuming. 'I'll make initial contact with this Tiny guy tomorrow night. I'll give him and his crew twenty-four hours to trawl the internet looking for photos of Talbot McGovern, then return on Thursday night to set up a deal.'

Zac frowns, alarmed at Beale's erratic nature, and changes the subject. 'So, what's the go with Keegan? He doesn't seem like your typical copper,' Zac asks.

'In what way?'

'You know, posh accent, well groomed, educated. His accent alone tells me he went to a public school.'

'Don't let all that fool you. DCI Keegan was brought up in some inner-city shithole in Bradford. At eighteen, he was offered a scholarship to Oxford.'

'University?'

'No, the fucking football team!' Beale says shaking his head. 'I dare say that's maybe where he had the rough edges knocked off his accent. Like I said, he has the smarts.'

'What did he study?'

Beale gazes out of the window, increasingly bored with the topic. 'I dunno, some useless shite like philosophy or psychology, or proctology.'

Zac grins at the joke until he realises Beale was serious. 'How come he joined the police?'

'What is this—twenty-fucking questions?'

Zac has one major concern about a certain aspect of the Keegan Beale masterplan.

'There are several things that could go wrong with this op. You feeling good about it?' Zac queries.

Beale stubs his smoke and immediately lights another. 'Aye—like shelling peanuts.'

'You mean peas?'

'Same difference.'

Zac strokes his well-manicured beard a couple of times. 'Your intel says this new drug cartel is an unknown quantity?'

'Aye, that's right. They could be newcomers—chancing their arm, trying to make a quick buck while there's a shortage—or they could be a consolidation of old heads who have come together to form a cartel while things are tough. Let's hope it's the former.'

'And what if someone from this gang actually knows the real Talbot McGovern or anyone from the Caledonian Boys?'

'Then I'm fucked. That's why I want you there. But I've got out of worse situations. On the positive side, I've spent the last two weeks studying video footage of McGovern. I know him better than his own mother. We even employed an acting coach to train me in the way he walks, talks, his mannerisms, tics. For my sins I look like the weasel prick, and now I can act like him. Tomorrow I'm even paying a visit to a tattooist.'

'What for?'

'To buy a bag of fucking carrots! What do you think?'

'To get a tattoo?'

'Fuck me blue, North Yorkshire Police certainly have a rigorous selection process these days. Only the sharpest knives in the drawer—eh? McGovern has the words LOVE and HATE tattooed on the bottom part of his fingers. I'm getting false tatts to match.' Zac's apprehensive disposition doesn't go unnoticed. 'What's wrong with you? You look as nervous as a kitten. Cheer up. What's the worst that can happen?'

'It all goes tits up and we both get rumbled. Next stop the sausage factory.'

'It won't go tits up. Have faith, hairball. I'll put in the finest acting performance since Arnold Schwarzenegger played the lead role in Othello. It will run like clockwork.'

'Really,' Zac mutters, dejected and wishing Frank had never put his name forward for this dangerous pantomime.

Beale sighs. 'To be honest, and with no disrespect to you personally, I'd have preferred Frank in my corner. But a rotund sixty-year-old hanging around the bar of a popular nightclub for a few hours would have had Help the Aged descending upon the joint which may have raised suspicions. Righto, are we finished here? Because I need to take a dump and have a shower before my two escorts turn up for an afternoon of bizarre, bawdy, bedroom fun, and I don't want a pretty boy like you distracting their attention from my own magnificent body.'

Zac rises wearily. 'Aye, we're done.' He glances once more, disdainfully, at the driver's licence before dropping it into his coat pocket. 'Nigel Crowther,' he mutters, shaking his head. 'What was wrong with Luther Du Noir or Rufus Kane?'

'Or Twatty McTwatface the tractor sales rep,' Beale replies as he stubs his ciggy out and swills down the remaining whisky from his glass. 'Now fuck off and let me prepare for debauchery. I'll see you tomorrow at nine o'clock and we'll have a recap. And try to book a room on level four. Right, let yourself out. You don't need a swipe card for going down in the lift. I need to hit the cludgie, ASAP. The turtle's head has made an appearance and the little bugger's in a hurry.'

Zac heads towards the door then stops dead, as the penny finally drops. 'Oh, I get it. You nearly had me there. Well done, very clever.'

Beale is puzzled. 'What are you gibbering about?'

'You—you've been method acting, pretending to be Talbot McGovern, testing it out on me. You're not really an obnoxious, chain-smoking, delusional alcoholic, sexist nutjob. You're simply getting in character. I have to say—you've got it nailed.'

Beale stands and heads towards the bathroom. 'Afraid not. This is the real deal, sunshine. Now excuse me, but if I don't get to the cludgie right now, the hotel will hammer me with one hell of a steam cleaning bill.'

As Zac ambles back to his car, his initial apprehension has morphed into a mild panic attack.

'Christ, what have I got myself into? The guy's a loose cannon,' he murmurs.

13

Frank glances at his wristwatch then knocks on the office door of Superintendent Banks.

'Come in, Frank.'

He enters, sporting a grin. 'How'd you know it was me?'

Head down, pen in hand, she replies, 'Because it's precisely 1:30 pm, the designated time of our meeting and there's no one else in the CID room. Take a seat.'

He takes a chair and plonks himself down, pulling at his tie as he gives the tiny box room a derogatory glance. Anne scribbles away for another few seconds before she carefully replaces the top on her fountain pen and relaxes back in her chair.

She eyeballs him. 'I take it you wanted to see me about my decision on Acting Inspector Kumar?'

'Yes. But before we start, is this a formal or informal meeting—on the record or off the record?'

'What do you prefer?' she quizzes with her deadpan, poker-faced expression.

'Informal. Off the record.'

'Informal it is, then. But before we start, a few observations.'

'Go on.'

'When I entered the station a couple of hours ago, I experienced déjà vu. Whenever I'm downstairs, there's always a hive of activity. Uniformed police officers coming and going. Suspects being read their rights by the custody sergeant. Patrol cars in and out of the car park. There's an energy about the place. A feeling that things are being achieved.'

'Your point being?'

'When I enter the CID room, your domain, it's... how can I put it... moribund, depressing, usually absent of any form of life, apart from you in your back office—hidden away.'

'I apologise for that,' Frank states, already with his back up. 'But what exactly do you expect? I could hire a troupe of jugglers a few days a week. Perhaps a steel band playing calypso music with a few dancing dogs and a fountain of champagne.'

Her cold, grey eyes bore into him. 'Maybe some activity would suffice. And cut the jokes, I'm not...'

'... in the mood. Yes, I get it. You're never in the mood. It may have escaped your notice, but uniform has twelve regular officers, two Highway Patrol, four PCSO's and six special constables. In CID we number four. And as much as you'd like my team to spend their days tapping words into a computer, they do actually need to be out on the streets; interviewing, investigating, solving crime.'

She remains emotionless as she clasps her hands in front of her stomach and purses her lips. 'Why do we always butt heads, Frank?'

'Oil and water?'

'No. I think it's more than that.'

'Enlighten me.'

'It's a long time ago since I leap-frogged you into the position of superintendent. You really should be over it by now.'

'Get real, Anne. I never even applied for the position.'

'No, you didn't. Because you knew you wouldn't get it. If you don't apply, then you can't fail—can you? It's a protection mechanism to keep your self-esteem intact.'

'Thanks for the psychoanalysis. But you're wrong. I didn't apply for one simple reason; I want to solve crime and protect people. I don't want to manage budgets, chair forums on some hair-brained initiative, or ingratiate myself to jumped-up short-term officials from the council or chinless wonders from the government.'

She takes a deep sigh, unfolding her arms. 'Let's move on, shall we? In two hours, I'm due in York.'

'Another meeting?'

'Yes. It's a new focus group.'

'For?'

'Strategies to proactively involve community groups in the development of bi-lateral synergies which will engender a synchronicity between disparate ethnic groups in lower socio-economic areas.'

'I rest my case.'

'We're here to discuss Prisha. Although afterwards I would like a catch up with you about your future plans.'

'My plans?'

'Yes. May as kill two birds with one stone. Right—let's talk about Prisha. Get it off your chest, let's clear the air.'

'Okay. I'm bloody pissed off on several fronts.'

'Continue.'

'When I last discussed Prisha's position with you, I came away with the impression you were going to make her position permanent. Then on Friday afternoon you tell her of your decision, and let me know almost as an afterthought, by text. I find your actions disrespectful.'

Anne picks up her pen and spins it around. 'In retrospect, it was an error of judgement on my part. I'll admit that. She caught me on the hop. I'd left your office after the meeting with DCI Keegan about Operation Dragnet, and she collared me. She can be persistent. I didn't want the poor girl to spend the weekend worrying, so I told her of my decision. I realise now, I should have told... sorry, consulted with you first. Frank, I apologise. We can all make mistakes.'

Frank studies her scanning for artifice but can find none. 'Fair enough. I've been there and done that. Let's bury that one. Moving on—why?'

'I'm sure she told you.'

'Something about it being perceived as a tokenistic gesture because she's a woman of colour.'

'True. I did say that. And also, she's not been here long enough to warrant a permanent promotion. Next gripe.'

'I know our little station is a proverbial backwater, but I still need a chain of command. I'm DCI, and at the end of the month, once again I'll have three permanent detective sergeants. Prisha would have given me the opportunity to effortlessly pass things to her to handle, then delegate. Now I've got to juggle things between appeasing her and Zac and Cartwright.'

'Forget about Cartwright. His days are numbered.'

'What?'

'A discussion for another time, Frank.'

'A bit like the discussion we had about Prisha's position?'

'Let's keep it civil. Are you done or do you have you another kvetch?'

'No. Not a Grievance. But just this; Prisha is one of those rare breeds of officers you encounter once or twice in your working life. She has an intuition, a sixth sense, about cases. My god, I hate to blow my own trumpet, but when I was her age, I was damned good at my job. But Prisha would have run rings around me. For example, this missing person case we're working on—she's all over it like a rash. I asked her yesterday to nip down to Pickering and simply dig around. See what her senses told her. On a purely physical level, there was nothing of note; an older guy gone on a walking weekend, not returned, risk assessed as absent. The obvious summation is he's decided to stay out another day or possibly had an accident or medical episode and fallen in a ditch, out of sight.

'Not more than an hour ago, I get an update from Prisha. She's alive, buzzing with that feeling you get when know you're onto something. She's like a bloodhound that's been let off the leash with the smell of blood in the air. My point is this—if you stymie her too long, we'll lose her. She'll see an opportunity in York, or at HQ in Northallerton, or Middlesbrough or, god forbid, some other county. If you want to balance your budget and hit your conviction targets—then you need Prisha.'

Anne pulls her lips back without baring her teeth. 'I hear you, Frank. My decision on Prisha will not change, but nor does it mean I've discounted her. You seem to forget you have another highly intelligent sergeant in your midst—one who's been with you for a number of years.'

'Zac—yes, I know. And he's damned good—as a sergeant, but he's not at inspector stage yet. He needs a little longer in the oven.'

'And for all your fawning admiration of Prisha—the facts speak for themselves. One of the main suspects in the abduction of the teenage girls was Tiffany Butler—who Prisha managed to let escape. To this day, never been seen again. Then there were the two Russian operatives. Again, one of them escaped—one died. She may have a nose for weeding out the rats, but she's not very good at catching them and bringing them to trial—is she? You say Zac needs longer in the oven. I dare say Prisha does, too. As for your chain of command—I could understand it if you were overseeing ten, twelve officers. You have three, Frank—three—and one of them is useless. It's hardly taxing, is it? I won't revoke my decision on Prisha. However, give it twelve months and we'll revisit it—through the appropriate channels, of course. And I hope Zac will take the opportunity to throw his hat into the ring.'

Frank stands and pushes his chair back, aggressively. 'Okay, I think we're done here.'

'Not quite. Sit back down. We still have your position to discuss.'

He rests his hand on the back of the chair but doesn't sit. 'It's only three months ago since we had this discussion. I told you then, I'd give it another two years, then re-evaluate. Nothing's changed. You can't force me out.'

'No, and nor would I want to. But nothing remains the same, Frank. The only constant is change. You need to ask yourself if you're really still up for it.'

'We're nearly the same age, Anne. Maybe you should ask yourself the same question.'

14

Zac knocks once and enters. Frank is leaning back in his chair, staring out of the window, deep in thought. Zac wearily takes a seat opposite, exhaling loudly. Frank detects something is amiss and drags his eyes away from the view of the harbour.

'How'd you go with DS Beale? The meeting was in Hull, wasn't it?'

'Aye.'

'Spill the beans.'

'The guy's a raving lunatic. To be honest, Frank, he's about ten times scarier than the worst criminal I've ever come across. He's a certified fruit loop.'

'In what way?'

'In every way! Erratic, changing the plan on a whim, if you can call it a plan. He's physically unfit, a chain-smoking alcoholic, abusive, sarcastic and downright disgusting—and I'm no shrinking violet. The plan was to make contact on Friday night. Give them twenty-four hours to chew it over, then return Saturday night to set up a deal. Now he's brought it forward to tomorrow night because he wants to be home by Friday for his mother's birthday. He's supposed to be undercover, on a mission. James Bond—he is not!'

'Anything else?'

'Well, apart from the two escorts who were due at his hotel room after I left and the fact he's going to pop a pill before he hits the nightclub tomorrow—then no.' He leans forward. 'What's going on, Frank? I thought you rated this DCI Keegan?'

'I do.'

'Then why has he picked a raving lunatic for the job?'

Frank sucks air in through his teeth. 'Because he looks like Talbot McGovern.'

'There must be someone else in the force who resembles him. He's hardly unique. White, middle-aged, overweight, greasy-haired, and ugly. They're ten-a-penny in the police.'

'I dare say there is. But it's horses for courses, I guess.'

'What do you mean?'

'When you have to circulate with low-life scum, who would cut your throat as quick as look at you, then you need like for like. Obviously, Keegan sees that in Beale. Who's going to suspect he's a copper working undercover? If you didn't know him, would you think he was one of us?'

'No. I'd think he was a long-term inmate recently escaped from the local psychiatric hospital. And that's another thing—he said if the shit hits the fan, then I'm not to call on uniform for back up—which means it's me and him, alone.'

'Alone together. Do you want to pull out?'

Zac groans and shakes his head. 'No, I can't. Not now. I said I'd do it.'

'Trust me, Zac, you'll be fine. Nothing's going to go wrong.'

Zac stands up to leave. 'Do you mind if I knock-off early and go home? I need to do the shopping and get something for the boys' pack-ups for the rest of the week.'

'Kelly on night shift at the hospital?'

'Aye. And I'm going to have to organise a babysitter for the next two nights. The girl we usually use is on a skiing trip with school.'

'Hey, send your boys to stay with their Uncle Frank. Meera would be over the moon!'

Zac hesitates. 'No, I couldn't impose.'

'Nonsense. I'm telling you, the last time they stayed, Meera was as happy as a sandboy.'

'Well, it would get me out of a bit of a pickle.'

'It's sorted then.'

'Okay... well, if you're sure? I can throw some clothes in a bag for them and drop it off with you tomorrow.'

'What time do they finish school?'

'Three-thirty, but they both have football training tomorrow night. I normally pick them up around five.'

'Too easy. I'll collect them. They can walk to school from our house the next day. It's only a stone's throw away.'

'Cheers, Frank. It's appreciated.'

'Right, get yourself home, lad. Hey, before you go, I've a question for you.'

'What?'

'We've worked together for a number of years now. We get on well and we share an occasional beer after work—right?'

'Aye.'

'I'd like to think we were friends, mates.'

'Suppose. What about it?'

'When I ask you the question, I'd like a truthful answer, as a friend, not as a junior officer to myself.'

'Just ask the damned question Frank and stop beating about the bush.'

'Do you think I'm past it, over-the-hill?'

'No.'

'Do you think it's time for me to retire?'

'If I were you—then yes, I'd retire. But do I *want* you to retire—then the answer's still no.'

Frank offers him a thin smile. 'Good. Thanks for your honesty.'

'Not a problem. Superintendent Banks been poking the bear again?'

'Who else.'

'Aye, well, ignore her. You go when you're ready, Frank, you've earned it. It's your life. Right, I'll catch you tomorrow.' He pulls jadedly at the door then stops as a recent memory resurfaces. 'Actually, I take it all back. I've changed my mind.'

'Why?' Frank asks, concerned.

'Two words—Nigel Crowther!'

'You don't like the name? I think it suits you,' he replies with a chuckle.

15

Things are moving fast, a lot faster than the Ford Focus Prisha is driving, as it laboriously makes its way towards Settle. The winding roads and unusually heavy traffic are making the journey to the small market town tiresome.

Cartwright is on the phone to Sergeant Evans from Settle Police Station. 'Thanks Percy, we'll be arriving in the next twenty minutes. Yep, see you then,' he says, ending the call.

'What's the latest?' Prisha demands.

'They've located Albert's car an hour ago in the town centre, and it's all systems go. They've commandeered the local rugby ground as headquarters for the search. People are drifting in from Cave Rescue, Mountain Rescue and they're putting out a social media release to ask for volunteers to join the search at first light tomorrow.'

Prisha ducks her head and stares up at the ponderous, bleak skies above. It's just past three in the afternoon and the light is fading fast. Maybe two hours max before it's dark.

'What else?'

'Sniffer dogs will arrive later tonight, and an officer qualified as a drone pilot has turned up.'

'How many for the search team?'

'Percy reckons by tomorrow they should have a minimum of sixty.'

'You obviously know this guy?'

'Aye.'

'Is he coordinating the search?'

'From a command perspective—yes. He's done this thing a hundred times before. Probably gets thirty missing or injured people a year. Drives him nuts.'

'What's he like?'

'Percy? Oh, he's old school, methodical. Probably around Frank's age. He sums people up in a few minutes; he either likes them or doesn't until proved otherwise. But he knows his onions.'

'Hmm...'

'What does that mean?'

'It means he's coordinating a search and rescue. I think this has now turned into a search and recovery situation. And if that's the case, then it's suspicious.'

'Don't get on the wrong side of him, Prisha. Percy can be your best friend or a right pain in the arse. We're entering his domain. Let him handle things.'

'Bollocks to that. I'm not going to tiptoe around some old guy's ego if a crime has been committed. If there is a crime scene, then it needs to be preserved for forensics.'

Cartwright sighs. 'Okay, have it your way.' A nervy silence descends as Prisha attempts to overtake a slow-moving cattle truck. As she pulls out, the road ahead is clear, but a split-second later a car rounds a bend. She floors the accelerator, and the Ford Focus responds—a little, as the opposing car flashes its lights. There's a blare of horns as she tucks back in front of the cattle truck.

'Christ, that was close,' Cartwright mutters, releasing his grip from the door handle. 'Oh, one other thing, he said a small team of three were nearly ready to set off to do a speed search. That's when...'

'Yes. I know what a speed search is. How far to Settle now?'

He checks the GPS on his phone. 'Ten minutes, give or take.'

'Damn it!' Prisha says as she pushes the car way past the speed limit.

Cartwright takes a deep breath and tries to relax. 'I don't want this to sound wrong but...' he pauses.

Prisha focusses on the road ahead and any opportunity to overtake. 'What?'

'Well, today... it's been like...' He pauses.

'Get on with it!'

'Okay, it's been one of the best days of my policing career. I know that sounds wrong. Two people are missing. They could be dead. So that's not good, but I feel alive. For the first time in ages, I feel I might be making a difference—do you know what I mean?'

Prisha turns to him and smiles. 'It doesn't sound wrong—it sounds right. When you feel like that, it means you are making a difference.' Her eyes drift back to the road. 'One way or another, we're going to find out the truth. And that's important. Best-case scenario is that Albert and Maxine are injured but alive. And I pray to god that's true. Worst-case scenario is they're dead. Then we need to piece together the how's and why's. If they are dead, there's nothing we can do for them. But we can find answers for their loved ones. And that's what they need—answers. They want all the gory details, no matter how painful it may be, because then they won't have to wrestle with the unknowns for the rest of their lives. That's what destroys people—not knowing the truth. And by the way, for the record, I've seen a new side to you today. Hand on heart, I can say I'm proud of you.'

Cartwright beams. 'Really? Why?'

Prisha chuckles. 'Stop fishing for compliments.'

'Come on, tell me.'

'Okay. Because you turned up smart for work. Some might think, what's the big deal? But like I said, it puts you in a different frame of mind. Ever wonder why all the superheroes have costumes? Batman, Superman, Wonder Woman, Spiderman? They're ordinary dudes for most of the time, but once they step into their costume, they gain superpowers. Okay, I may be overdoing it a bit. But you got the info out of Mrs Rutherford, then the CCTV from the petrol station. Your star is on the rise, Jason. Don't hamper it.'

He stares at her for a moment. 'Thanks. You don't know what that means to me,' he says, choking up.

'Oh, harden up and don't go getting all emotional!' she shouts. 'How far now?'

His attention returns to the GPS. 'You're coming up to a roundabout. Hang right, and it's about five minutes up the road.'

Prisha navigates the car into the entrance of the rugby club. Numerous vehicles are parked up in orderly fashion; police cars, unmarked cars, a fire truck, Mountain Rescue, and Cave Rescue vehicles.

'If the sprint team hasn't set off yet, I'm going to go with them,' Prisha states. 'First thing I need *you* to do is get us lodgings for the night. Oh, and get us booked in at a restaurant or the local pub for a meal, say about seven-thirty. The place will be heaving tonight, and I want a decent meal and a comfy bed.'

'Already checking some places out,' Cartwright replies as he scrolls the screen on his phone.

They exit the car and quickly march into the clubhouse. A busy hum of activity greets them. At one end of the room, a whiteboard is set up and a large map of the local area is pinned to a back wall. Cartwright spots Sergeant Evans and moves towards him.

'Percy! How are you doing?'

The old sergeant spins around. 'Aha! Jason, good to see you,' he replies as they shake hands warmly. 'I see your team is through to the finals in the local darts tournament.'

'Yep. We've got this one in the bag,' Cartwright replies with a guffaw.

'Aye, well. You'll be into the regionals if you win then you'll come up against my boys. Then you'll know about darts.'

'Oh yeah. Last time we met, I seem to remember we gave your lot a good spanking.'

'True, but we've a new young gun on our team now. Only eighteen, but he's destined for great things.'

'Really.... I've heard that before. How's the missus?' Prisha clears her throat and coughs. Cartwright takes the hint. 'Oh, Sergeant Evans, let me introduce you to Inspector Prisha Kumar from CID.'

The old sergeant takes Prisha's outstretched hand and shakes it. 'I've heard of you, lass,' he says in his deep, gruff Yorkshire accent.

'All good, I hope,' she replies.

He stalls. 'Some good. Some not so good.' The smile drops from Prisha's face. 'But for a copper, you'd take that as a win every day of the week. Most buggers hate us—especially our colleagues,' he finishes with a crusty laugh.

'Has the speed team set off yet?' she enquires.

'No. They're heading out in about five minutes. Waste of time, if you ask me. This time of day the light is too...'

Prisha interrupts. 'I'll join them.'

Sergeant Evans leans back. 'Those lads are elite athletes. They don't just amble around—they carry heavy backpacks and jog. It's not for the faint-hearted,' he says staring at Prisha's diminutive frame.

'I do triathlons. I'm sure I'll be able to keep up.'

Sergeant Evans eyes her suspiciously. 'Okay. Have it your way.'

Prisha is about to leave to fetch her gear from the boot of the car when she has a thought.

'Sergeant Evans, I know you're treating this as a search and rescue, possibly search and recovery, but there's always the possibility of something more suspicious. I'd be grateful if I could inform your team before they set off tomorrow that if they come across anything, then it needs to be flagged and a barrier set up around the area. We must preserve the crime scene at all costs for forensics.'

Evans doesn't like this one little bit. He pulls his cap down further over his eyes as they narrow to slits. 'Crime scene?' he drawls slowly.

'Yes.'

'I was born and bred in these parts, inspector. If our missing couple are dead, the only suspect will be Mother Nature and man's lack of respect for it. This is a classic case of two people going unprepared and not checking the conditions.'

'I disagree. Albert and Maxine were both experienced hikers. Albert, at least, had all the gear with him; waterproofs, thermal blanket, map, compass, snacks. He wasn't... isn't a novice. The chance of both having an injury which incapacitated them seems highly unlikely to me.'

Evan's hates this even more. Cartwright shuffles nervously. 'Is that right? Know these parts well, do you, lass?'

'No. And don't call me lass—sergeant—it's inspector.'

'Let me educate you, inspector,' he says pointedly, his face reddening. 'I have upwards of forty missing or injured people a year that get into strife around these dales. It's a huge drain on resources and I can tell you right now, with thirty-five years' experience, ninety-nine per cent of the cases are down to under prepared fools. Last year a female walker coming down a very slight gradient tripped. Hit her head on a rock—stone cold dead. In another incident, a couple of so-called experienced walkers climbed Ingleborough. They didn't check the weather forecast or tell anyone where they were going. They died of hypothermia. I could go on and on.'

'I'm sure you could. Have you any local CCTV or eyewitnesses who saw Albert or Maxine set off on their walk?'

'What?'

'We need to find out what day and at what time they left to go on their walk—if they actually did. Was it Friday and if so, at what time? And if not Friday, then when?'

'Inspector, a search like this is a big operation. By tomorrow morning, we'll have sixty-plus bodies on the ground. They need food, drinks, and accommodation. I've been busy organising all that.'

'It wasn't a criticism sergeant, merely a question.' She fixes her attention on Cartwright. 'Grab two uniforms and have them door knock all premises that lead to the start of the walk and see if they can obtain CCTV footage. While they're doing that, I want you to ring around all the accommodation in town and find out where they were staying. That's B&B, AirB&B, hotels, pubs, cabins, campsites, you name it—check it out. For all we know, they could be holed up somewhere whispering sweet nothings to each other, oblivious to what's going on.'

Sergeant Evans emits a haughty laugh. 'Hardly likely.'

'You're right, it is hardly likely. But we must eliminate the possibility. Right, I need to change,' she says as she turns to leave.

Sergeant Evans shakes his head, half in anger, half in dismay as he confronts Cartwright. 'Who the bloody hell does she think she is? Bloody cocky, arrogant upstart. Out-of-towners coming here thinking they know better than me!'

As Prisha heads towards the door, she spots an officer sitting at a table as he opens a heavy-duty case and removes a drone.

'I'm Inspector Kumar. What's your name, officer?'

'PC Jarvis, ma'am.'

'You're the drone pilot?' she queries.

'That's right, ma'am.'

'Are you preparing to send it up?'

'No. I'm preparing it for tomorrow.'

Prisha is puzzled. 'Why not get it in the air now?'

'Because there's not much daylight left.'

'I thought these things had spotlight attachments?'

'Yes, they do.'

'Then I'd appreciate it if you could get it airborne as soon as possible. We can search the first couple of miles, at least.'

The officer winces and glances over at Sergeant Evans who ambles over.

'Is there a problem, Jarvis?' Evans barks at his officer.

'I'd like to get the drone airborne immediately,' Prisha interjects.

'It's getting dark, inspector.'

'Getting dark—but it's not dark yet—is it? As long as we have daylight left, then I suggest we use it.'

'Those things are expensive, inspector, and we wouldn't want to lose or damage the damn thing before morning, would we?'

Prisha turns to the drone officer. 'Correct me if I'm wrong—but can't these drones return to base unaided, and they have safety features to detect objects, so they don't collide with them?'

'That's right ma'am.'

'Is it a line-of-sight drone?'

'No, ma'am. It comes with a smart controller,' he replies, removing a small black monitor with a built-in joystick from the case.

'Meaning you can control it from anywhere by looking at the screen?'

'That's correct,' he says awkwardly as he glances at Sergeant Evans.

'Then get it in the air now. What are you waiting for?'

The officer waits for his sergeant's approval. Prisha glares back and forth at both men until Sergeant Evans gives a slight nod accompanied by a deep nasally snort.

'It will be in the air within ten minutes, ma'am.'

'Good. Keep in touch with me via radio. What channel are we on, sergeant?' she says as she notices three men heading out of the rugby ground with backpacks on.

'Channel nine,' Evans replies with barely concealed contempt as Prisha bolts through the door and races to her car.

She yells to the men to stop, then quickly pulls out a pair of lightweight walking boots and a heavy-duty waterproof coat. She throws her shoes into the back of the car, slips into the boots and runs after the men as she hurriedly fastens her coat.

As she nears, she flashes her warrant card. 'DI Kumar, CID. Do you mind if I join you?'

'Prisha! We'd be delighted, wouldn't we, boys,' Lewis Visser says as he pulls his balaclava from his head and offers Prisha a winsome grin.

'Oh, Lewis,' she says with an element of surprise. 'I didn't know... I mean...'

'I'm one of the coordinators with the Cave Rescue Organisation. I was doing some renovations at the house in Malham when I heard the call go out.'

He introduces her to his two colleagues as they set off through the town, making their way to the start of the walking trail that leads to Malham Cove.

'We'll only get an hour in before we'll need to set off back,' Lewis says.

'Better than nothing,' Prisha remarks.

'My thoughts exactly. No point sitting on our backsides waiting for sunrise.'

Prisha experiences a little tingle as she gazes at his weathered but handsome features.

'The drone will be up in a few minutes so keep in touch with the pilot and guide him,' she suggests as she pulls her radio from her lapel and offers it to him.

He waggles his own radio at her. 'No need. How'd you get on with Dixon of Dock Green?'

'Sergeant Evans?'

'Yes.'

'I don't think we got off to the best of starts. But I'm not here to win friendship awards.'

'Quite right. To give the old lad his dues, he's good at organising all the backroom stuff; food, provisions, getting the teams together, finding accommodation. But he usually leaves the logistics to the experts.'

'Experts?'

'Yes. Mountain Rescue, Cave Rescue.'

'I see.'

'Ready for a jog?'

'Yes. Let's do it.'

'Come on boys, let's lift the pace.'

As the four of them set off at a steady pace up the gravel incline which leads to the open moor, Prisha hears the angry buzz before she spots the flashing lights of the drone. She stops and gazes skyward. It passes thirty feet above as her heart explodes and adrenalin surges through her veins. A panic attack renders her mute and incapable of movement. Her mind plays tricks as the ghastly images of the two Russians, Kira, and Maxim, appear in front of her, smiling, whispering, plotting some terrible, violent deed. Behind them is Tiffany Butler, forlorn, alone, arms outstretched, imploring. A stab of remorse sticks in her throat.

'Prisha, Prisha... what's wrong?' The voice of Lewis breaks the waking nightmare.

'What? Oh, nothing.'

Lewis follows the path of her eyes as the drone heads up the hill. 'It doesn't seem like nothing.'

'It's the drone. I had a bad experience with one a few months ago. I thought I was over it, but obviously not.'

Lewis offers her a quizzical smile. 'Want to talk about it?'

'No. Come on, let's catch up with the others.'

16

The November night air is sharp and crisp, its chill creeping through the heather. The heavy grey clouds are an ominous promise of what the coming night has in store. A desolate silence pervades. Everything has taken on a sinister air, as if the moor is preparing itself to unleash some hidden surprise. Even the birds have stopped their song, as if they too are aware of an impending danger. The dying light of the unseen sun serves only to further enhance the feeling of foreboding, as though someone or something is lurking in the shadows, ready to pounce at any moment.

'Okay, that's enough for today,' Lewis says to his small team. 'The light's fading fast. Best we head back.'

'But we've only been going forty minutes,' Prisha protests.

'I know, but we can't risk it. There's a front moving in and it will be pitch black in another half hour. At least we've covered a bit of ground.'

Prisha pulls at her radio. 'Yes. You're right. I'll let the drone officer know. Inspector Kumar to PC Jarvis. Over.'

'Go ahead, inspector.'

'We're heading back to HQ.'

'Roger that.'

She has an afterthought. 'Lewis, how far is the tarn from here?' she asks as she gazes up at the spotlights of the drone in the distance.

'About five miles.'

'Inspector Kumar to PC Jarvis.'

'Go ahead.'

'Have you enough juice left in the drone to do a quick flight over Malham Tarn?'

There's a moment's silence. 'Yes. But it will have to be quick pass over.'

'Okay, do it. Thanks.'

The group turn on their heels and head back towards the market town, its lights twinkling in the distance.

'Why do you want to check the tarn?' Lewis asks as he leads the pack down the hill.

'Just being thorough,' Prisha replies.

'You've never seen the tarn, have you?'

'No. Why?'

'It's a benign body of water. There's a good gravel walking path around it and it's shallow at the edges. There are no cliffs or drop offs where anybody could easily fall in.'

'Still, it needs checking.'

'Hang on, the missing couple—you don't suspect a suicide pact, do you?'

'There's nothing to suggest that. How deep is the tarn?'

'About five metres in parts, but most of it is shallow. It's more like a boating lake.'

'If for any reason they ended up in the tarn, the temperature of the water would slow down body decomposition.'

'Meaning?'

'Bodies initially sink in water. When decomposition begins, it creates a build up of gases in the abdomen and chest cavity, making the body rise. Decomposition typically starts after twenty-four hours, depending on temperature. With the water of the tarn being extremely cold, it would have slowed down that process by another twenty-four hours or more.'

'So if they are in the lake, then they should have risen to the surface by now?'

'Possibly. It would help if we knew what day and time they actually set off. Hopefully, DS Cartwright has the answer to that by the time we get back.' Her foot catches a rock jutting up from the path, causing her to stumble. Lewis sticks out his arm and catches her.

'Okay, team,' he shouts. 'Walking pace from now on.'

'You were right about the light.'

The group slows down to walking pace as the other two men take the lead. Prisha and Lewis drop back slightly, and she spots her opening.

'Lewis, my colleague was going to book a table at a local restaurant or pub for dinner. It's going to be a bugger finding anywhere to eat with the influx of people. You're more than welcome to join us if you'd like.'

He grins. 'I'd love to, but I can't.'

'Why's that?'

'I'm heading back to Malham. I have a date.'

'Oh.' She tries hard to hide her disappointment, but fails miserably.

He turns to her. 'Not that sort of date. I'm planning an extension on the holiday house and I have a builder turning up at seven to discuss my options.'

She conceals a smile. 'I see. You'll be back tomorrow for the search, though?'

'I'll try. I need to ring around and see if I can get cover for me at work.'

'I thought you owned the business. Can't you do whatever you want?'

He throws her a toothy grin. 'It doesn't work like that. I have responsibilities. But like I said—I'll try.'

<hr/>

Prisha checks her watch after a quick debrief with Sergeant Evans at the improvised search and rescue headquarters. It's nearly six-thirty and her stomach is reminding her it needs feeding. She takes her phone out and taps at Cartwright's chubby, smiling face on her screen. Whilst waiting for him to answer, she takes in the surrounding scenes. The club bar is already open and a small circle of rescue volunteers, all male, are quietly supping on pints of beer. At the end of the room is a door that leads to a kitchen. Occasionally, someone will walk in carrying boxes of bottled water, milk, loaves of sliced bread. As the door swings open, Prisha glimpses the activity inside. People peeling vegetables, bread being buttered and topped with cold meats. Vast soup pans being scrubbed, someone mopping the floor. This time she notes, they're all women.

'Prisha?' Cartwright's languid drawl echoes from the phone.

'Jason, did you get us a table? I'm starving.'

'Yes, but you better shake a leg. The only spot I could get was at seven at the Oak heading out of town.'

'A pub?'

'Yes. I'm here now, wetting my whistle.'

She shakes her head disapprovingly. 'Knocked off early, did you? I hope you got the intel we were chasing first,' she snaps.

'Calm the farm. We've got CCTV of Albert and Maxine and I've also interviewed the landlady of the B&B they stayed at. Hang on a moment, I can't hear myself talk. It's packed to the rafters in here. That's better. You want me to fill you in now?'

'No. You can tell me over dinner. And where's our accommodation? I need to get showered and changed first.'

'Same place—Royal Oak. A two-minute drive from the clubrooms. There's parking at the back. Do you want me to tell you what's on the menu so I can place an order for you?'

'No. I'll eat anything as long as there's plenty of it.' She ends the call and spots the drone officer entering the building.

'Ah, PC Jarvis. I see you got it back in one piece,' she says, nodding at his precious drone. 'Did you spot anything in the tarn?'

'No, ma'am. But it was a quick fly past. I only had ten minutes left before the drone would have automatically returned home. I'm about to upload the footage to the portal. I'll send you a link.'

'Thanks, appreciated. Anything else of note?'

'Nah, not really. There was a farmhouse and some outbuildings close to the tarn. I took a quick peek around but to be honest, even with the spotlights, it was too murky to pick anything up.'

'Okay. Better luck tomorrow.'

The sound of barking dogs distracts her as Sergeant Evans hurries past.

'That'll be the sniffer dogs and handlers arriving,' he says, more to himself than anyone else. 'Cartwright informed me you have some recently worn clothing from the missing persons, inspector?'

'Yes. They're in sealed plastic bags in my car.'

'Excellent. Leave them there for tonight. The fewer people handle them, the better,' he adds, disappearing into the gloam outside.

'I said they're in sealed plastic bags,' she murmurs as the drone officer shrugs and throws her an apologetic smile. 'I'll see you tomorrow,' she says as the officer removes the battery from the drone and places it in a recharger.

Stepping outside, she squints at the floodlights surrounding the rugby field as they highlight the sleet, which is increasing in intensity. She buttons her coat and walks briskly to her car, passing Sergeant Evans on the way.

'Night, sergeant,' she offers.

Evans, distracted by an elderly gentleman wearing an overcoat from a different era, and a flat cap offers her a distracted farewell.

'Aye, night inspector. Briefing in the club rooms tomorrow morning. Six, sharp.'

She nods and pulls her collar up.

Evans turns to the elderly man. 'What is it now, Edward?' he asks, not attempting to hide his impatience.

'It's about those red lights I told you about, Sergeant Evans.'

'Not now, Edward. We're in the middle of a major incident, can't you see that?'

'Aye, but...'

'I said not now! If you've anything further to add to your earlier statement, then call in at the station in a few days' time.'

The restaurant at the Royal Oak is busy but nothing like the main bar, which is shoulder to shoulder with many from the rescue teams. Prisha spots Cartwright in a corner, sitting at a table for two, studying his notebook. She walks over and pulls up a seat.

'Nice tidy rooms,' she says, referring to her accommodation.

'Aye, very nice. Did you bring my suitcase in from the car?'

'Yes. It's in my room. Have you ordered?'

'Yes. Fifteen minutes ago?'

'What did you order for me?'

'The locals recommended the Guinness pie with homemade chips and winter veg.'

Prisha's mouth waters. 'Great! I'm starving.'

'Looks like it's here now,' he says as a waiter heads to their table carrying two large plates overflowing with food. He pushes a half pint towards her. 'Got you a lager shandy.'

'Cheers, Jason. You're a star.'

There's a few minutes silence as both officers attack their food with zeal. Prisha takes a moment to relax and slow down as Cartwright carries on unabated. She takes a sip of shandy.

'Okay, lay it on me. What have you got?'

Cartwright flicks open his notebook and finishes chewing his food. 'We got CCTV footage from a jeweller's shop of Albert and Maxine walking up Duke Street.'

'When?'

'Saturday morning 7:35 am heading north. Then again at 7:40 am walking along Cheapside from the bank's CCTV. Good quality footage.'

'Saturday?' Prisha muses. 'What were they doing on Friday?'

'Can I finish?'

'Yes, sorry. Carry on.'

'On Friday night they stayed at the Prince William guest house, which is a two-minute walk from where we're sitting. Booked in Friday lunchtime under the name Mr and Mrs Smith and paid in cash for one night's accommodation. They had a full English breakfast the next day at 7 am. Then left with their walking backpacks, at 7:30 am. They told the owner—a Mrs Winterbottom, they were going to do the walk across Malham Moor, circumnavigate the tarn *if* the weather was good, then head to the tearooms at Malham for a bite to eat before catching a bus back to Settle. Then they intended to drive to the Lake District.'

'And she was absolutely certain it was them?'

'Aye. Positive.'

'Did she notice if anything was off about them? Their mood, their disposition?'

'No. She said they were a lovely couple and seemed extremely happy. They were out most of Friday afternoon, then returned at seven. They had a quick chat with Mrs Winterbottom and said they'd spent the afternoon mooching around arts and crafts shops, visited the local gallery, then caught an evening meal at a local pub—they didn't state which one. After that, they went to their room. That was the last she saw or heard from them until breakfast the next day.'

'For all intents and purposes, an elderly loving couple spending a weekend away.'

'That's right.'

'Did she not think it odd they paid in cash?'

'No. She says it's not unusual for older folk to pay in cash. How'd you go?'

'No, nothing. The light faded quickly. There's some drone footage on the portal which I'll look at before bed, but I'm not holding my breath,' she adds as she tucks into her food again.

'Tomorrow, it will be five days since they were last seen. Which doesn't bode well,' Cartwright states, then takes a large gulp of his amber ale.

'No, it doesn't. Why have they not turned up either dead or alive? Those trails are well travelled, maybe not as much at this time of year. But you're not telling me there's been no walkers over the last five days.'

'They could have fallen down a ravine, or an abandoned mining shaft that wasn't fenced off.'

'Both at the same time?'

'It's possible.'

'But not likely.'

'You heard what Evans said about the couple who died of hypothermia last year. Maybe the same fate befell Albert and Maxine. When you become hypothermic, your brain doesn't work as it should. They could have wandered well off track.'

'Then why not use their phones? Which reminds me, I'm heading out on the search tomorrow, so I'll need you to stay back at HQ. Apart from keeping me updated on any developments, badger the phone telcos and the banks, and see if either of them left a digital trail.'

'Will do.'

'Right, I better finish my dinner, then call Frank and update him.'

17

Wednesday 18th November

The alarm from Prisha's mobile steadily increases in volume, playing a gentle classical piece. She rouses and fumbles in the dark, the only illumination a blue hue coming from the phone screen. The room is deathly quiet and a little stuffy. As her mind stutteringly moves up through the gears, she remembers where she is and why she's there. Rolling onto her side, she flicks a bedside lamp on, which offers a pale-yellow blush. She pads across to the one window in the room and throws back the curtains, gazing upon the tranquil street scene below. Alleyways and nooks are haloed in a faint orange glow from a streetlight, as a ghostly mist blankets the pavement. The nearby trees are bare, their withered branches jutting into the darkness like bony fingers on a skeleton. She opens the window and breathes in a deep lungful of icy air. Earthy aromas intermingle with a faint hint of wood smoke. Despite the chill of the morning, she takes in the quaint beauty of the town. A calming hush prevails, broken only by the occasional chirp of a bird. A sense of peace radiates around her, as a wintry breeze tickles her face. She is happy, content, and ready for the day.

The improvised headquarters at the rugby ground is a hive of activity. Prisha and Cartwright alight from the car, the earth beneath their feet vibrates with the steady thrum of diesel engines. Rescue workers and volunteers busily strap on boots and don their coats and headgear, preparing for the day ahead. The air is heavy with the scent of smoke, coffee, and food, while the background chatter is equal parts urgency and excitement. Prisha and Cartwright look around, impressed by the sheer scale of the response. Despite the commotion, an indescribable feeling of purpose and resolve hangs in the air. A mobile food and coffee van is already in action, serving volunteers.

They both enter the clubrooms where Sergeant Evans is orchestrating a cohort of search team veterans—four in all. At the far end of the room is a row of tables, behind which a clutch of middle-aged women are laying out oven trays full of bacon, fried eggs, sausage, and giant urns full of tea and coffee.

'Oh yes,' Cartwright exclaims with glee. 'Is there any better smell in the world on a cold, frosty morning than freshly fried bacon? I'm going to get a butty and a pot of tea. Want anything?'

Prisha is distracted as she takes in a diagram on the whiteboard. 'What? Oh, yes. A black coffee and a sausage sandwich, please.'

'No worries.'

She strolls over to the small gathering that circles Sergeant Evans and spots Lewis Visser. He lifts his head and gives her a smile and a wink. She nods and stares at the whiteboard once more.

'Ah, Inspector Kumar,' Evans begins. 'I'm about to brief my core team. Care to join us?'

'Thanks,' she replies, standing slightly to the back of the close-knit semi-circle.

'As you can see from the map, we have a large area to cover. But some good news; I had a quick head count a moment ago and we're already up to eighty bodies on the ground. I think that number will swell to over a hundred in the next hour. I've also received the latest weather report. The morning is going to be bright and clear, but chilly. At midday, it all turns to shit with a heavy front moving in, bringing rain, sleet and possibly snow. Now, if you care to look at the whiteboard.' He picks up a ruler and taps at the board. 'I'm splitting the search into four teams—red, yellow, blue and green.' He hands coloured armbands out to the four men, then focuses on the map on the wall. 'Red Team, led by Lewis Visser, will set off from Settle and follow the main trail to Malham Cove. Blue Team will splinter off at this point,' he says, tapping the map with the ruler. 'They'll head north to Cartrigg Force before doubling back and returning to Settle via Warrendale Knots. Green team will be taken by coach to Malham and follow the trail to Gordale Scar, and Malham Tarn where they'll complete a circuit of the tarn before returning to Malham via Malham Cove. Another bus will take Yellow Team to Watersinks car park, where they will head north along the track to Fountain's Fell and return to Settle via Langcliffe. Any questions?'

All the men shake their heads as they slip into their allotted armbands.

'Ahem, yes, I have a question,' Prisha says.

'Yes, inspector?'

'I'm curious why you're dividing the resources when we're pretty certain Albert and Maxine were taking the direct route to Malham. Mrs Shaw indicated it was one of Albert's favourite walks and Mrs Winterbottom from the guest house had a conversation with them before they set off on Saturday. She confirmed they were heading directly to Malham.'

Evans' heavy jowls involuntarily wobble. 'Have you organised a search and rescue before, inspector?'

'I've participated in many searches before, mainly when I was in uniform.'

'But your experience of organising a search is?'

'Well, no, I don't have that experience,' she replies meekly, feeling two feet small as all eyes stare at her.

'Then I suggest you leave it to those who have. But to answer your question—what people say they are going to do and what they end up doing are often different. The caves to the north and the waterfalls at Cartrigg Force are a top attraction for tourists, and only an hour's detour from the main walk to Malham. And as you will see from the map, there are numerous paths that lead to the village of Malham. As far as I'm *aware,* the walkers didn't specify which route they'd be taking to Malham. Unless of course you know different, inspector?'

Ouch!

'No, I don't.' Prisha's humiliation is complete and thankfully she receives a nudge in the arm from Cartwright.

'Here's your butty and brew,' he whispers, raising his eyebrows in sympathy. Prisha gratefully accepts the offering as Evans continues his instructions to the four men.

'You're all experienced in this. We've worked together many times before, so I'll leave it to you to organise your teams.' He picks up a sheet of paper and studies it. 'We have thirty-two police officers, ten cave rescue, eight mountain rescue, and six from fire services. I'm guessing there'll be about another forty to fifty volunteers from the public. You know the score—ensure the volunteers are wearing adequate clothing and walking boots. Check they haven't any pressing medical conditions. Anyone who looks unfit, then thank them for their time and send them home. The last thing we need is someone breaking a leg, getting lost or having a medical episode up on the moor.' He pauses and stares out the window as muted dog yelps are heard. 'Sounds like the handlers and the sniffer dogs have arrived. There's four in all—one for each team. They'll set off twenty minutes ahead of the main parties, accompanied by a police officer and an experienced hand from either mountain or cave rescue. Inspector,' he says turning to Prisha, 'we'll require the clothing from our missing walkers now.'

'They do have names, sergeant. Albert and Maxine,' she says pointedly.

His mouth shrivels into a prune shape. 'Pass the clothes to one of the handlers. They'll cut them into swatches. Right, I suggest everyone indulge in a hearty breakfast and we'll wait for daylight to break. I'll address the volunteers before they set off. Any other questions?'

'Sergeant, do you mind if I head out with the dog handler of red team?' Prisha asks.

Evans shrugs. 'As you wish, inspector,' he replies with indifference.

18

Cartwright is tapping at his laptop whilst munching on his third bacon and egg roll. Prisha enters the clubroom and sits down opposite him.

'Christ, Jason! Where the hell do you put it? When Sergeant Evans suggested everyone get a hearty breakfast, I think he was referring to the people actually going on the search. The only walking you'll be doing is from your laptop to the food table.'

'Got to keep my strength up.'

'Hmm... any info from the telcos or banks?'

'Albert's bank card has only been used once since Friday, and that was at the petrol station in Pickering. As for his phone, it's pinged at being near to his home address for all of Thursday night and early Friday before it goes dead. I assume he switched it off not long after he got in the car. Likewise, with Maxine's mobile. It goes dead at 7:40 am Friday, and is briefly switched on at 9:08 pm Friday night for about three minutes before dropping off the radar again.'

'She probably booted it up to see if she had any missed calls or texts when she was getting ready for bed. What about her bank card?'

'Used a couple of times around Settle on Friday afternoon. Once in a gift shop, where she spent ten quid. Then twenty minutes later at a coffee shop. After that—zip.'

'Then it confirms what we already know. They both keep their phones switched off, and Albert uses cash instead of his card to pay for things, so it doesn't show up on the bank statements. Poor old Mary,' she adds wistfully.

'Mary?' Cartwright quizzes.

'Mary bloody Shaw—Albert's dying wife!' she snaps, clearly irritated with his lack of recall.

'Oh, aye... Mary.'

'Jason, you had a stellar day yesterday. Don't let it be a flash in the pan.' Her eyes drift from Cartwright to PC Jarvis, who enters the room carrying his beloved drone case. She casually rises and approaches him. 'Morning, Constable Jarvis,' she says with a toothy smile.

'Oh, morning, ma'am. Did you get a chance to look at the drone footage last night?'

'Indeed, I did. Actually, that's what I want to talk to you about.'

'Go on,' he replies as he opens the case and tentatively removes the drone.

'After you'd flown over the tarn, you did a quick reccy near a farmhouse a few miles north.'

'That's right. What about it?'

Prisha frowns. 'There were some distinctive markings in one of the nearby fields, sort of square shaped. Do you know what they were?'

146

'To be honest, I didn't really notice them. Why?'

'Any ideas what they could be?'

He shrugs. 'Could be anything. Hay bales, old farming machinery, fencing, stock yards.'

Prisha ponders. 'Yeah, I suppose they could be hay bales. They appeared similar in shape and size, except they were scattered in a haphazard fashion.'

'That's not unusual.'

'Hmm... anyway, can you take a closer inspection today?'

Jarvis stiffens, then nervously squints over his shoulder as Sergeant Evans heads out of the door carrying a megaphone.

'Well...' he begins, hesitantly.

'What?'

He lowers his voice. 'Sergeant Evans gave me strict instructions to only follow his direct orders today. I got a bit of a roasting yesterday for sending the drone up.'

'Why?'

'He doesn't understand them. Thinks we'll run the battery down. I've told him they're rechargeable and we have five back-ups, but it never seems to sink in.'

Prisha stares him down with an enigmatic smile. 'Please? It could be important,' she implores.

Jarvis relents. 'Very well. But keep it quiet.'

'Mum's the word,' she says with a grin, tapping the end of her nose. She decides it's in her interests to humour him for a moment. 'What's the specs on that thing,' she asks, nodding at the drone which Jarvis assembles in a matter of seconds.

Jarvis sticks his chest out. 'Top speed of 70 kph. Battery life of fifty-five minutes—that's dependent on head winds and outside temperature, of course.'

'Of course.'

'640 by 512 pixel thermal camera. 32x digital zoom. Pin drop recall. Built-in anti-collision and return to base intelligence. This little beauty is cutting edge technology,' he says with pride whilst stroking the drone in an unnerving fashion which Prisha finds slightly perverse.

'Have you ever found anyone with it?' she asks, refocusing on his face.

His cheeks flush red. 'Ahem, well, no—not as yet, but...'

There's a short blast of a police car siren followed by chair legs scraping against the floor as people hurry outside.

'Attention! Attention everybody! My name is Sergeant Evans, head of the search and rescue operation.'

'I'd love to carry on this conversation,' Prisha says, 'but duty calls.' She spins to head out of the door. 'You'll upload the footage to the portal, as before?'

'Yes, ma'am. Each time the drone returns, I'll switch out the SD card and upload.'

'Good man.'

Prisha and Cartwright stand behind Sergeant Evans, who holds the loudspeaker in front of him like a weapon. He addresses the search team, which now number over a hundred. Unfortunately, he waffles on for longer than he should, as noted by the murmurings and impatient shuffling from members in the team.

There's already enough daylight to set off safely, but still he prattles on.

Prisha whispers in Cartwright's ear. 'Wish the boring old fart would get on with it. We're wasting time.'

Cartwright unexpectedly snorts tea down his nose and is met with an icy glare from Evans. Eventually, his overly complex instructions come to an end as he thanks everyone for their time. The assembled throng falls away. Some head towards the main entrance of the ground, others amble towards the two coaches waiting to transport the green and yellow teams to their destinations.

'Wait! Sergeant Evans, it was agreed I was going to have a quick word with everyone,' she shouts.

Evans purses his lips. 'Is that really necessary, inspector?'

'Yes—it is—*sergeant!*' she retorts angrily, emphasising rank. He reluctantly hands her the megaphone.

'Don't take all day. We've already lost enough time.'

She shoots him her most disdainful look, reserved specifically for a special few. 'Attention, everyone. This won't take more than a few seconds,' her voice booms out across the field, followed by a quick screech of feedback. Moans and groans drift through the air.

'Get on with it. We're wasting time!' A distant voice yells.

'I'm Inspector Kumar from CID. I realise this is a search and rescue mission, but there is a possibility it could turn into a search and recovery operation. If that scenario occurs, then the area around the bodies must be preserved as if it were a crime scene—no contamination.' She's suddenly got everyone's full attention as a wave of mutterings and gasps wash through the crowd.

'Stone the bloody crows,' Evans harsh voice blasts from behind.

'Thank you. That's all.' She hands the speaker back to Evans.

'Well done, inspector. It will give them all something to gossip about as they trudge the hills. Crime scene indeed,' he scoffs as he heads back to the clubrooms.

She faces Cartwright. 'Hand on heart, I hope and pray we find Albert and Maxine alive and well. But if they're dead—I'm hoping it's foul play. Is that a terrible thing to say?'

'Erm... yes, it is.'

'Too bad,' she says, racing to catch up with the Red Team. 'Call me if anything crops up!'

'Wilko!' He watches with admiration as she races through the slow-moving crowd and pushes past a line of people waiting to board a coach. 'Frank's right; she has balls of steel, that one. Right, I wonder if there's any bacon or sausage left?'

19

Catching up with the advance team, she introduces herself.

'I'm Inspector Kumar, but let's keep things informal. Call me Prisha.'

'PC Matthew Anderson, ma'am,' says the dog handler.

Prisha nods as she studies him. Of medium build and slightly overweight, with brown, messy hair, and a round face with a tiny chin.

'Matthew,' she says, shaking his hand. 'And who's this fellow?' She drops to her haunches and vigorously rubs the dog on its back.

'This is Torpedo. A three-year-old, male Cocker Spaniel.'

'I noticed the other dogs were German Shepherds and a Labrador. I've seen Cocker Spaniels at work during drug busts, but never on a search and rescue.'

'They're becoming more common, ma'am.'

'Prisha,' she corrects.

'Sorry, Prisha. The cockers have an excellent nose and strong endurance. They're also small enough to fit into tight places where a larger dog would have difficulty manoeuvring. And if you were lying on your back in the middle of nowhere, what would you prefer to be standing over you—a Cocker Spaniel or a bloody great, big German Shepherd?'

Prisha laughs. 'Yeah, you have a point,' she says standing and focusing her attention on a young female police constable.

'PC Darby, Claire Darby, ma'am.'

Either I'm getting old, or they've started recruiting adolescents, Prisha thinks as she gazes at Claire's youthful face.

'How long have you been with the police?'

'I finished my classroom-based training two months ago. I'm still on my probation period, working out of Northallerton.'

'Enjoying it?'

PC Darby beams. 'Yeah, I love it. Every day is different.'

'Good. This your first search and rescue?'

'No. My second.'

She turns to the strapping young man from mountain rescue who's dressed in black combat trousers, sturdy boots, and a hi-viz orange jacket.

'And you're Cody,' Prisha says. 'We met last night. Part of the speed team.'

'That's right,' he says with a smile.

'Okay, let's crack on. I guess Torpedo will lead the way.'

The dog is eager as it strains at the leash. The small group almost race up the steep gravel path, away from the town to the start of the moor. Twenty minutes in and they've already passed the ground searched the previous evening by the Speed Team. Prisha takes a mental note—despite Sergeant Evans' protestations, it was worth going out yesterday.

Cody holds his hand up. 'Okay, this is as far as we got last night before we turned around,' he states, staring at his handheld GPS. 'From here on in, it's fresh ground. Spread out, about arms width apart and walk in unison. If you see anything, a tissue, a sweet wrapper, a footprint, then call out.'

The dog handler pulls out a small plastic bag with a swatch of cloth inside. Prisha recognises the colour. It's part of Albert Shaw's red underpants she took from a wash basket. She suddenly feels a connection with the missing pensioner. Mary Shaw elicited Prisha's sympathy because of her failing health and the fact her husband is maybe cheating on her. But now she feels a twinge of empathy for Albert. He's been a good husband and it can't be easy caring for someone with a death sentence hanging over them. He's fit and active. So what if he's found a new love in his life? It doesn't mean he no longer loves or cares for Mary. He clearly does. She'll be gone in three to five months. Hasn't he the right to start a new life? To have hope for the future and grab a glimmer of happiness in an otherwise dark existence?

A sliver of his red underpants—it's pathetic! A man's entire life may come down to this.

The dog takes only a second to stick his snout near to the bag before he wags his tail excitedly and pulls vigorously at the leash. PC Anderson lets out more of the long lead as the dog zigzags from side to side, nose to the ground.

As they continue, her mind drifts back to earlier in the day. Men in charge—organising, barking orders and instructions, wittering on so long they lose their audience. The women—cooking food, preparing food, serving food. Nothing's really changed. Even Superintendent Banks, a gay woman, seems to have slipped into the persona of a nineteenth century man. As she ruminates, she discovers a new respect for two of her colleagues—Frank and Zac. Neither undermine or judge her. To them, she's a competent CID officer. She has earned their respect... and dare she say, friendship. Her focus returns to the job at hand.

'How long can a human scent last on the ground?' she asks PC Anderson.

'We've found people after seven days with sniffer dogs, but obviously it depends on the weather. If it's been carting it down, then it can disperse the scent.'

'Raining, you mean?'

'Sorry, yes. The sooner we begin the search, the better chance we have of the dogs detecting the scent.'

They walk on in relative silence for another hour until Torpedo explodes in excitement. He circles a patch of grass and emits a yelp.

'What does that mean?' PC Darby asks.

'He's picked up the scent of Albert. Maybe he sat down here for a bite to eat or took a leak.' The dog takes off again, dragging PC Anderson along with him. 'Here we go. He's onto something now,' he shouts, beaming widely.

Thirty minutes elapse as they trudge on. Torpedo appears to have lost interest in the original scent and keeps veering off the main pathway, then back across to the other side. PC Anderson holds his hand up.

'I think it's time for a break, and a reset. Torpedo has forgotten what he's here for. The back and forth across the path indicates he's been side-tracked by the scent of a rabbit or fox.'

The group sling off their backpacks, flop onto the ground, and pull refreshments from their bags.

PC Darby unwraps the foil and inspects her sandwich. 'Nice. Cheese and ham. What have you got?' she asks Prisha.

Prisha pulls the foil away. 'Eugh!'

'Don't tell me—egg mayo?' PC Darby says.

'Yes. Smells disgusting but tastes divine,' she says biting into it, as PC Anderson splashes bottled water into a portable dog bowl for Torpedo, who thirstily licks at the contents.

'Even sniffer dogs need a rest,' he says taking out a dog chew.

'What you said earlier, back at the rugby ground,' PC Darby begins. 'About if we find bodies, then to treat it as a crime scene?'

'Yes,' Prisha says as she swigs from a water bottle.

'Do you suspect foul play?'

'I have an open mind. Have you not been taught that?'

'Taught what?'

'Treat every dead body as suspicious until proven otherwise.'

'No. I haven't come across that.'

Prisha chuckles. 'I don't think it's officially in the police handbook, but it was explained to me by my first sergeant and most of the officers I've worked with since, use it as their motto—especially in CID.'

'But why? I mean, if you find a climber at the bottom of a cliff, then it's obvious what happened?'

'Is it? Did they fall or were they pushed? Was the rope cut? Had some drug been dropped into their water bottle? Until the scene has been thoroughly examined and recorded and the pathologist has delivered their findings, then the death is suspicious.'

'Until proven otherwise,' PC Darby says with a giggle.

'Yes. You only get one chance to preserve and examine the scene. It's a reminder to not rush in and contaminate the area.'

'I'll put it in my memory bank.'

Prisha turns to Cody. 'How long before we reach Malham Cove?'

'About an hour,' he replies, languidly lying on his backpack, arms across his chest, eyes closed.

She packs her bag and stands. 'We better push on. Is Torpedo suitably refreshed?'

PC Anderson attaches the lead and pats the dog on the neck. 'Yes. He's got his second wind now.' He offers the plastic scent bag for Torpedo to take another quick sniff. The dog becomes energised.

'I wonder how the other teams are getting on?' PC Darby wonders aloud.

'If they'd found anything, we'd have known by now,' Cody says, zipping up his coat as he studies the sky, the pale blue now replaced by heavy and oppressive clouds. 'I reckon the weather front could be here sooner than predicted. The temperature has noticeably dropped.'

The troupe reach the top of a small hill and stare down at the blackish waters of the Malham Tarn in the distance.

'And there she is,' says Cody. 'England's highest lake.'

'Really?' quizzes Prisha.

Cody laughs. 'No, it's not *the* highest lake, but it is the highest marl lake in England.'

'Marl lake?'

'Yes. Rich in carbonate.'

'I'm none the wiser.'

Their admiration of the stunning view is rudely interrupted as Torpedo emits a series of yaps and strains at the leash.

'Here we go,' PC Anderson says. 'I know that bark. It's a positive ID.' The dog scurries along the path for fifty feet, then abruptly stops and circles a tuft of grass.

'Rabbit? Fox?' Prisha asks, questioning the dog's abilities.

PC Anderson frowns. 'No. He's found something.'

Prisha joins the dog and kneels, studying the grassy area. 'Okay, pull the dog away!' she commands.

'What is it?' PC Darby asks.

Prisha takes a rubber glove from her pocket and pulls it on, then tentatively dabs at the grass. 'It's some sort of gloop.' The others near to have a look. 'Stop! Cody, do you have anything to mark this site?'

'Sure,' he replies as he fumbles in his backpack and pulls out a tin of fluorescent white paint.

'Spray a large X two feet to the left and right of this area.'

'Is it blood?' PC Darby asks, sporting a worried frown.

Prisha rubs at her fingers. 'Not sure. It's a very dark reddish colour. Almost brown, but that could be oxidisation,' she says thoughtfully as she scans the vicinity around the find.

Torpedo takes off again, diagonally away from the grassy area as PC Anderson is dragged along. 'He's definitely onto something,' he cries.

The four of them race up a slight incline, then come to a halt at a scar in the landscape. Below is a deep ravine about three hundred feet wide and a hundred feet deep. The sides are composed of loose scree. Torpedo is champing at the bit to go down and PC Anderson has to rein him in.

'Easy boy, easy.'

Cody quickly removes a climbing rope from his bag as he scans the area for anchor points but sees none. 'Just to be on the safe side,' he says as he swiftly fashions a bowline loop around his waist.

'What's this place called?' asks Prisha.

'It isn't named on the map, but the locals call it Vertigo Alley—for obvious reasons. Who's going down?'

'Me,' Prisha says. 'I'll handline down.'

'Done this sort of thing before?'

She grins. 'Once or twice. I do sports climbing in my spare time.'

'You should know what you're doing, then.'

Prisha slips on another latex glove. 'Not ideal, but better than nothing. It will give me a better grip on the rope. Let Torpedo off the lead,' she commands PC Anderson.

Cody throws the end of the rope over the side. 'Take it slowly going down. It's not dangerously steep, but the rock is unstable. Keep your body weight low to the ground.'

'Will do.'

As Torpedo is released from his tether, he dashes over the edge and zigzags down the hill in that unique way dogs have of navigating steep slopes. Prisha grabs the rope, turns her back to the ravine, and carefully steps over the edge. Tentatively she crabs backwards, her feet occasionally losing purchase with the flaky rock. The first drops of rain splatter her face as she gazes heavenwards at a thunderous black cloud that has silently moved in overhead. Torpedo yelps excitedly. She glances over her shoulder. The dog is about three-quarters down the gully and is frantically scratching at a pile of rocks. As Prisha traverses the steepest part, she spots a less hazardous route a little further down. Letting go of the rope, she spins around and sits on her bottom and shuffles downwards, her legs dragging her forward. Not more than fifty feet from Torpedo, the smell hits her. She instinctively sticks her nose into the crease of her elbow. She's hoping it may be a dead cow or sheep, but hope can be a cruel mistress. She's encountered the distinctive tang before on too many occasions. A pungent odour intermingled with notes of sour milk and ammonia. Once experienced, never forgotten. As she nears the dog, she pulls her hat off and places it over her mouth and nose. Torpedo has moved a few small stones from the cairn, but he's struggling fruitlessly with the larger ones. Prisha stares back up the ravine.

'Call Torpedo!' she yells.

A distinctive shrill whistle echoes down the hillside. Torpedo stops his work, glances at Prisha, then scampers up the hillside faster than he went down it. Prisha removes her mobile phone, hits the video play button and takes a detailed shot of the area before moving anything. Putting the phone away, she takes a deep breath and carefully lifts some of the larger rocks away, stacking them neatly side by side. Beneath the larger rocks are smaller pebbles which come away easily. Her throat stings and her eyes water as the rain intensifies. As she drags away another stone, she jumps back as if zapped by electricity. Eyes widen. Mouth as dry as desert sand. Her breathing is fast, erratic. She tells herself it could be a discarded boot from a walker. Maybe the sole split or it was causing blisters? It's funny how the conscious mind will grasp at any straw, no matter how fanciful and improbable. The sub-conscious is not as gullible. It knows the truth. It knew the truth on the path when she spotted the reddish stain. Still holding her hat to her mouth, she bends forward and, with fingers trembling, scrabbles a few more rocks away. If it is a discarded rogue boot, then it's connected to a discarded rogue leg. She tries to swallow, but the motion becomes paralysed in her throat and erupts into a gasp. Her eyes wander across the mound of stones to where they no longer look like they've been purposefully stacked. She knows what she must do—see the face—establish the identity.

Her phone rings, making her jump. Pulling it from her coat, she stares at the image.

'Not now mother!' she curses as she taps at the screen to decline the call. Sidling around the mound, she nears the opposite end, sucking in air through her woollen ski mask. She whispers encouragement to herself. 'Come on, Prisha. Get it over with.'

Crouching, she pulls the rocks away until she sees the grey lifeless skin, then the eyes—still open, staring at her. Then the gaping hole at the top of the neck above the larynx. And finally, the forehead and the thinning grey hair of Albert Shaw. She falls onto her backside and blinks. Rain rolls down her nose and onto her lips. For the first time, she hears the gurgling of a stream coming from the bottom of the gully. Pushing herself to her feet, she does a three-sixty, almost in a daze.

A few short strides away—is another pile of rocks.

The black tea, kindly dispensed by Cody, tastes like nectar. Prisha stares at her three colleagues.

'Well?' asks PC Anderson.

'It's them.' She realises there's no time for reflection. Things need to swing into action fast and the tea has given her a temporary boost of energy. Leaping to her feet, she presses at her police radio.

'Inspector Kumar to Sergeant Evans, come in. Over.'

A few seconds elapse before Evans' rather grumpy tone responds. 'Evans here. Go ahead inspector, over.'

'We've found them. I have a positive ID on Albert Shaw and Maxine Wood.'

Another pause. 'Alive?'

'No. Both dead. You can call in the public volunteers and send them home. We'll still require the services of the cave and mountain rescue teams. I'll hand you over to Cody and he can give you the exact coordinates. Over.'

'Wait, inspector. Any indication of how they died? Hypothermia? A fall?'

'No. They were murdered. This is now a major crime scene investigation and CID will be taking charge. I'll be seconding a number of your officers over to the murder investigation team and I'll need an office for myself and Cartwright at your station. I'll also be taking over the incident room—if you have one. If not, you'll need to think of an alternative—and fast. Over.'

20

Prisha was expecting a sense of schadenfreude as she spoke with Evans—but she felt none. No gloating, no sense of validation, no dish of cold revenge. Merely an empty sick feeling in the pit of her stomach as her mind conjured up images of Mary Shaw's tear-stained face, twisted in grief, and the doting daughter of Maxine Wood, soon to be receiving a knock on the door. A knock she would remember for the rest of her life.

Fuck! The world is a cruel place.

She snaps into action and issues orders to the other three.

'PC Darby, get on the radio and organise a team of officers to get here ASAP and secure the area. We'll need the grassy area cordoned off where the suspected blood was found. PC Anderson, speak with the other dog handlers and when they arrive, have them search near to that area for any other blood splatters—if it is blood. Cody, we're going to need some sort of rope system setting up. I'm not sure how long before a forensic team arrives, but most of them will struggle to climb down the ravine. Maybe a pulley system, and a seat like a Boson's chair. And we'll need stretchers to recover the bodies. Oh, PC Darby, get a team of paramedics out here as well, and organise mobile catering and portable toilets. Cody, where's the nearest road?'

'About two kilometres south.'

'Shit! How are we going to get vehicles up here?'

'Not a problem. The Pennine Bridleway runs almost parallel with the walking track. It's a bit bumpy, but we can definitely get access vehicles on site.'

'Great! Can you send out instructions for the nearest entry point from the main road?'

'Will do. Another thing you need to bear in mind, inspector...'

'What?'

'If the heavens open up, then Vertigo Alley can flash flood within a few hours.'

'Shit!' She pulls her phone out and calls Cartwright.

'Prisha, I heard the news over the radio. Well, done.'

'I can't take any credit. If it hadn't been for Torpedo, it might have been another day or two before we found them—or never. Listen, call the Family Liaison Officer who's assigned to Mary Shaw and tell her the news. Then get onto the desk sergeant at Pickering and ask him to send someone over to Maxine Wood's house. The daughter, Julie, was staying there for a few days. I don't want Mary or Julie finding out the news on social media. Also, get the address of Mary and Albert's son, Craig Shaw, and pay him a visit. Apart from breaking the bad news to him, if Mary doesn't beat you to it, see if he knows anything about Albert that Mary wasn't aware of—you know enemies, or if he'd recently fallen out with anyone.'

'I might not have to go and see him. I spotted him leaving this morning with the main search party.'

'Good. Everyone is supposed to return to the ground to sign-off against their name, so keep an eye out for him. And one last thing, dig up all you can on the Brigante Motorcycle Club. I want names and addresses, any recent illegal activity, police records on the members.'

'Is this because of the tattoo on Albert's arm?' he asks with reservation in his voice.

'Yes.'

'You don't really think they had anything to do with it, do you?'

'You said yourself that once a member, always a member. We have to look at every connection if only to remove them from our enquiry.'

'Aye, okay.'

'Right, time for me to call Frank. I'll see you back at Search HQ.' Before she makes the call to Frank, she kneels and pats her thighs enthusiastically. 'Good boy, good boy!' she encourages. Torpedo runs up to her and licks her face as she rubs and tugs at his torso. 'Well done, Torpedo! I was having my doubts about you. Tomorrow I'm going to buy you the biggest, juiciest bone you've ever seen. It will be as big as a dinosaur bone.'

Frank rubs at the excess flesh under his chin and smiles inwardly. Not at the news—that's shocking enough. Despite his number of years on the force, it always gets to him. He's smiling because Prisha's intuition was on the money.

'Leave forensics to me,' he says. 'I'll get onto Charlene Marsden straight away and get her to pull a team together.'

'The terrain is challenging, Frank, even for fit people.'

'I'll let her know, but forensic specialists are hardly ten-a-penny around these parts, so we'll have to work around it.'

'Oh, another thing. The mountain rescue guy, Cody, says if we get a big enough downpour, the ravine can flash flood very quickly. The bodies are about thirty metres from the stream, but still...'

'Christ! If it doesn't rain it pours—pardon the pun.'

'I take it you'll be heading up here to take over the investigation?' Prisha asks, hesitantly.

Frank pauses and considers the question. 'I'll head up there a few hours after the forensic team to assess the situation, but I'm quite busy down here, so best if you run with this one.'

'Really? Do you mean that?'

'Aye, of course I do. This is your show now. You let me know what you need, and I'll make damn sure you get it. How are you getting on with Sergeant Evans?'

'Erm...'

'I see. He can be a miserable old bugger. Don't take it to heart. This is CID's op now, so don't let him bully you.'

'One other thing, Frank. We'll need a ballistics expert. The gunshot wounds are unusual. The wounds are at the top of the neck, just below the chin. Now I'm no expert, but to me, they looked like exit wounds. Hell of a mess. Taken half the throat away.'

'That's odd. Maybe a close shot from behind?'

'Who shoots someone through the back of the neck when you've got a much greater chance of success with a bullet to the brain? Like I said, unusual.'

'No point speculating yet. I suppose it's too early to ask about suspects?'

'My mind hasn't really been playing with those thoughts, but now we have the bodies. I'll let it off the leash, see if anything jumps out.'

'Okay, good work, Prisha. I'll call you back to give you an ETA on forensics. One last thing—Cartwright?'

She chuckles down the line. 'He's doing great, boss. I think he's been low on confidence, that's all. He had a couple of wins yesterday and it made all the difference. I know you think he's a lost cause, but he's not. Admittedly, he's never going to be a Sherlock, but he can be a good old-fashioned meat and two veg copper.'

'You mean a methodical plodder like me?'

'Don't put words in my mouth, Frank. No, not like you.'

'Okay. I'll be in touch.' He ends the call, grimaces, and fights with a few demons. 'Unfortunately, for poor old Cartwright, it's too little too late. Her Royal Highness has already marked his card,' he mumbles to himself.

21

Cartwright is standing on the steps of the clubhouse as Sergeant Evans bustles past him.

'If anyone wants me, Cartwright, I'm on my way to the crime scene. I'll be gone an hour or two.'

'Righto,' he replies as he notices a few of the public search team returning to the grounds. He wanders over to a middle-aged man with a noticeable limp. 'Excuse me sir, which colour search team were you with?'

'Red team.'

'They should all be back shortly, then?'

'Yes. Although I spotted a few people stop off in town to grab a bite to eat.' He strolls across the ground to a temporary marquee where a search coordinator is standing, clipboard in hand. Cartwright can't hear what's being said, but words are exchanged along with a few downbeat smiles as the coordinator moves a highlighter pen across a sheet on his clipboard. Cartwright heads back into the clubrooms where the women who prepared breakfast and packed-lunches are now busily cleaning up and putting everything away.

'Any leftovers, Kath?' he asks an elderly woman who has taken a shine to him.

'Sergeant Cartwright, you must have hollow legs. Let me have a look in the kitchen,' she says with a wry laugh.

He smiles and quickly grabs a fresh brew of tea from the urn before it's also taken away. The woman returns with a plate, and something wrapped in foil.

'Couple of chicken legs,' she says.

'Oh, you're a star, Kath. I wish I'd married you.'

Kath giggles and blushes slightly. 'Into old women, are you?'

'Old? You're not old, Kath. I'd say you were mid-thirties—at a push.'

'Daft bugger. Double that and you'd be nearer the mark. Now be off with you. We need to mop the floor.'

He wanders outside as he attacks a chicken leg. 'Christ, that's good,' he mutters. 'Damn it!' Craig Shaw is walking away from the coordinator at the marquee. He puts the plate down, jogs down the steps and breaks into a sprint—of sorts.

'Craig!' he calls out. The man stops and turns. 'A quick word.' He only covers thirty metres but is out of puff by the time he reaches him. 'Ah, Craig, can you spare me a few minutes?' he asks as he retrieves his notebook and pen.

'Sure,' Craig says slowly, without emotion.

'First of all, I'd like to say how sorry I am about your father.'

Craig gazes at him and huffs. 'Why? You didn't know him.'

It wasn't the response Cartwright was expecting. 'Erm, no, I didn't. But still...'

Craig stares at the ground. 'Sorry. I shouldn't have said that. It's been a bit of a shock.'

'I understand.'

'Were they murdered?'

'I honestly don't know the exact circumstances yet. All I know is their deaths are being treated as suspicious.'

'I heard some of the others talking. They said it was murder. Both been shot, they said.'

'You know what it's like in these situations, rumours, Chinese whispers, half-truths. Forensics are on their way. We'll know more once they've finished.'

'Who'd want to kill them?' he says, shaking his head, sorrowful.

'Actually, that's sort of why I wanted to speak to you. Do you know of anyone who would wish to harm Albert?'

'No.'

'Had he been in any arguments or disputes with anyone recently?'

'No. He wasn't the type. Pretty relaxed, easy going sort.'

'We asked your mother, but do you know of any financial worries he had? Had he lent money to anyone?'

'Not that I'm aware.'

'Gambling?'

'No. Said it was a mugs game.'

'Did you know of his friendship with Maxine Wood?'

Craig shakes his head. 'No. Never heard of her until the news bulletins started circulating. Her face looked sort of familiar, so I may have seen her around town. Pickering's a small place. It will kill mam when she finds out. I'll have to make something up and say they were walking friends, and that's all, but she's not stupid.'

'Can you give me your details Craig; in case we need to get in touch about anything.'

'Yeah, sure.' Craig reels off his address and phone number as Cartwright jots them down.

'One last question, then I'll let you get off. Sorry to ask you this, but can you tell me of your whereabouts last Saturday from 7:30 am onwards?'

He takes a deep breath and sighs. 'Woke around eight. I went around to mam's place about nine to make her breakfast, knowing she was alone for the weekend. Probably stayed there until ten, then back to my place. I'm in the middle of redecorating. I was there until one-thirty, then went for a couple of pints at my local.'

'Local?'

'Yeah, The Sun.'

'And after that?'

'Back home. Carried on painting until six, then went to the local chippy and took fish and chips around to mam's place. Stayed until seven, then back home and watched TV the rest of the night. Bed around eleven.'

Cartwright finishes scribbling and puts his notebook away. 'Oh, out of curiosity—what do you do for a living?'

He puffs out his cheeks. 'I'm a handyman. Odd jobs, that sort of thing. Nothing major. Mainly joinery, fixing shelves and cupboards, painting and decorating.'

'Much money in it?'

'Nah, but I have a modest pension. I get by. Anything else?'

'No, that's all,' Cartwright says apologetically.

'I understand... it's procedure.'

'Yes. Have you spoken with your mother yet?'

'No. I'll wait until I get back home. It's a two hour drive, so it will give me time to compose my thoughts.'

'I spoke with the Family Liaison Officer about an hour ago, so your mother will already be aware.'

'That's a relief, of sorts.'

'And once again, I truly am sorry.'

'Yeah, thanks,' he says as he turns and trudges wearily away. Cartwright watches him with a certain amount of sadness before he heads back to the clubrooms.

'Hey, where's my bloody chicken gone?'

22

Frank gazes out of the car window at the throng of officers, rescue personnel, and forensic specialists dressed in their white bunny suits. The patrol car parks up in between an ambulance and a mountain rescue truck.

'Thanks, constable. If you don't mind hanging around, I'll need a lift back to the car park. I should only be twenty minutes or so.'

'Very good, sir.' He alights from the vehicle, stretches, then ducks under the barrier tape and strides towards the group of people standing outside the cordon. Sergeant Evans spots him and makes a beeline in his direction.

'Frank bloody Finnegan as I live and breathe!' Evans exclaims, breaking into a throaty guffaw as both men shake hands warmly.

'Percy. It's been a while.'

'How have you been keeping Frank?'

'Oh, fair to middling. What about yourself?'

'Can't grumble. No one would listen if I did,' he adds with another burst of laughter.

Frank's face hardens as he nods towards the edge of the ravine. 'Bloody rum do.'

'Aye, it is that. And a hell of a spot to access, but we've got a good crew around us, so we're managing. I take it you're here to take over the investigation. Now, you may have trouble getting accommodation tonight. The town is packed out, what with the rescue workers and the like. You're more than welcome to come and stay with me and Joan. We have a couple of spare rooms to choose from. Nothing flash, mind, but it's warm and cosy. And Joan does a mean steak and kidney pudding.'

'That's very generous of you, Percy. And as much as a steak and kidney pudding sounds enticing, unfortunately I have to head back to Whitby tonight.'

'Nay, Frank! You can't run a major crime investigation from Whitby—you need to be in Settle, close to the action.'

'I'm not running it. DI Kumar is.'

His face drops. 'What?'

'You heard.'

He removes his cap and strokes back the few strands of grey hair on his otherwise bald head, then pops his cap back on. 'Now Frank, don't get me wrong, but I'm not sure she's up for the job.'

'And why's that?'

Evans takes Frank by the arm and leads him a few feet away from the nearest eavesdroppers, and lowers his voice.

'She's nowt but a slip of a lass, Frank. And she's got too much brass—you know, cocky, arrogant. This is a double murder in the middle of bloody nowhere. It's above her pay grade. Surely, you see that?'

'Inspector Kumar is one of the brightest detectives I've worked with.'

'I'm not doubting that, Frank. But a case like this... well, you need experience. Bloody hell, she's barely turned thirty! She needs more cooking time, about another ten years' cooking time.'

'I disagree. She's sharp, intelligent, energetic, thinks outside the box and she's as tenacious as a randy Bulldog during mating season.'

'Come on, Frank. Me and you go back nearly forty years. We started on the force at the same time. We've seen it all. I'm telling you, we need an old head on this one. I dare say the unfortunate couple died on Saturday. That's over five days ago. The so-called golden hour has well and truly passed. You need local knowledge and a gut instinct for this one.'

'I heard it was Prisha's gut instinct, which didn't rule out the possibility of foul play. I believe you thought it was solely a search and rescue, or recovery operation. Am I right?'

'Oh, she told you that, did she? Blowing her own trumpet.'

'No. I spoke with DS Cartwright earlier. Prisha never mentioned it.'

His disposition changes and his face hardens as he realises he's backing a loser. 'Have it your way, Frank. But don't say I didn't warn you. This case calls for experience and an old head, not a young lass who's a bloody outsider.'

'Outsider? Because she's from the midlands or are you referring to her skin colour, or possibly her gender?'

'Don't pull that bloody shit with me, Frank! You know damn well what I mean—she's not from around these parts.'

Frank sighs and eyes him wearily. 'You know, Percy, I've been reflecting lately. Meera wanted me to retire when I hit fifty-five, a few years back. And lately, Superintendent Banks has been dropping not-so-subtle hints that it's time for me to go. The thing is, I'm not quite ready. A year ago, I wanted to stay on for my own selfish reasons. I still get a buzz out of the job. And what would I do in retirement? But over the last three to four months, I've put those selfish reasons aside. My purpose for staying on now is simple. I have a small but good team of officers working for me. Most notably DI Kumar and DS Stoker. It's their time now. They need to be blooded while I'm still here. There's no point throwing them in at the deep end once I've retired. Who will they turn to for advice, guidance, and a shoulder to cry on? It's time for the young ones to step up, Percy. I reckon I'll give it another two years before pulling the pin. It's time for me to take more of a backseat. Maybe you should think about doing the same.' He pulls the collar up on his jacket and moves away as Evans glares at him. 'I'll take it for granted you'll give DI Kumar every assistance—should she need it? And think about what I've said, Percy. By the way, give my regards to Joan.' He heads away from Evans towards the small team standing near the edge of the ravine. An A-frame has been erected with assorted ropes and pulleys attached to it, manned by three guys from the rescue team. Inside the barrier tape are four members of the forensic team; two on their knees and another two crouching.

'Frank!' Prisha cries, waving him forward. She points down into the chasm. 'I found the bodies down there,' she states.

He peers over the edge and sees another five forensic officers busily plying their trade. 'You mean where forensics are, examining those two corpses?'

She giggles. 'Sorry. Come on, I'll show you where I think they were shot,' she adds full of nervous energy, tugging at his sleeve. She leads him back down the incline towards the main walking track and points towards the two white X marks on the ground. 'That's where I first spotted what I suspected was blood, which has now been confirmed. Spreading out from there is more blood splatter. To the left of the white X marks is another similar pattern.' She turns and directs her gaze back towards the gully. 'Then two distinct trails of blood until the edge. They continue down the side of the ravine right up to the burial site.'

Frank does a double take at the X marks and the edge of the ravine. 'They were shot about here, probably looking out towards the tarn. Then their bodies were dragged up the slope, to the edge, but not tossed over... they were dragged down the gulley, then hidden under rocks?'

'Yep, looks like it.'

'That's odd. Why the care on taking them down into the ravine? Why not throw the bodies over the side and save yourself a lot of time and trouble, then bury them?'

'That's what I thought.'

'Have ballistics given you anything yet?'

'Only speculation, but I think they're on the money. They'll know for certain once they receive the pathologist's report.'

'Go on then, entertain me.'

'Comparing entry and exit wounds, he says it's most likely a hunting rifle. He rattled off all the specs, but they meant nothing to me except some rifles can be fired from over a mile away. He gave me an example,' she adds, pulling out her notebook and flipping the pages. 'A shooter, one mile away, fires a bullet which travels at two and a half thousand feet per second. It takes two seconds to reach the target. The sound from the gunshot would take nearly five seconds to be heard—dependent on weather conditions.'

'Meaning you'd be dead before you even heard the gunshot?'

'Correct.'

'A really top-class shooter can reload, aim, and fire in about three seconds. But they're freaks. A good shooter, maybe five to six seconds.'

A kerfuffle behind them interrupts the conversation. As they spin around, they witness the diminutive figure of Forensics Team Leader Charlene Marsden being helped from the Boson's chair. She steadies herself on the ground and waves at Frank, who reciprocates. Cody takes her by the arm to guide her down the slope.

She slaps his hand away. 'Get off me! I'm not an invalid yet, you know,' she says with a scowl.

Cody laughs. 'Sorry, Grandma, I was only trying to help.'

'Oi, watch it sunshine! You're not too old for a clip around the ear,' she says with a wry smile as she walks unsteadily towards Frank and Prisha.

Frank chuckles. 'Still some fight in the old lass,' he whispers to Prisha. 'Charlene, funny meeting you here of all places,' he says with a guffaw as he greets her.

'Most amusing, Frank.'

'What's the state of play?' he asks.

'Just about finished. We're preparing the body bags and stretchers. If we can get them up that bloody ravine without too much drama, we should be packed up within the hour. We've got all we can.'

Prisha pulls her phone out. 'Excuse me, Frank, I need to ring the undertakers. I have them on standby. I'll let them know they can set off. Charlene can fill you in on the other details,' she says as she sidles away.

Frank steps forward and puts a large meaty arm around Charlene's gaunt shoulders. 'You never age a day.'

'Bugger off, Frank. You're not fooling anyone. Now, did Prisha tell you about our ballistic guy's theory?'

'About the weapon being a long-range rifle?'

'No. About the trajectory of the bullets.'

'No.'

'Come with me.' He follows her as she ducks under the barrier tape and heads to the X marks on the grass. She manoeuvres him into position so he's facing the tarn in the distance, then stands to the left of him and slightly forward. 'Right, imagine you're

Albert, and I'm Maxine.' She places a spindly finger on the back of his head halfway up, then two fingers under his chin. 'The bullet entered here,' she says tapping the back of his head, 'and exited here,' she adds gently pressing at his neck. 'For Maxine, slightly different.' She repositions her fingers. 'The entry wound was above the right ear. Exit wound—on the left side of the neck.'

Frank ponders for a moment as he slowly peers behind him at the gentle gradient leading to the gully.

'It makes no sense. You're indicating a downward trajectory, which means the shooter may have been standing at the edge of the ravine.'

'We've scoured that area thoroughly, and there's no gunshot residue on the ground.'

Frank scratches his head. 'And why use a hunting rifle from that distance when a handgun to the back of the head, close up, would have been far easier?'

'Exactly.'

Frank pulls his wise expression. 'Come on, Charlene. Stop playing games. Tell me what you're thinking?'

She pouts. 'I don't know what you mean, chief inspector. My work is about facts and science. I leave theories to other people.'

'Charlene...' he encourages.

She finally relents as a bitter wind picks up. 'Fine. I'll give you my hypothesis.' Taking Frank's head in her hands, she gently tilts it back until he's staring vertically up at the sky. Tapping at the back of his head again, she says, 'If Albert was looking directly up, the trajectory of the bullet would have exited at chin level. Over a long distance, gravity gradually pulls down on a bullet.'

'And Maxine?'

'She's standing a little in front, detects something is wrong, and either turns to her right to look at him, or she hears the first gunshot and turns to the right. Bang! Hit above the right ear. Exit wound through the left side of the neck. Instant death for both of them.'

'A few seconds apart.' Frank slides his fingers back and forth across his mouth, still puzzled. 'That's some bloody excellent shooting if your theory is correct.'

Charlene grins. 'My theory is a long shot.'

Frank chuckles. 'Now who's the comedian? There is another possibility.'

'Which is?'

'There were two shooters.'

Charlene's eyebrows arch as she shakes her head. 'Unbelievable! That's exactly what Prisha said. Peas in a pod, Frank... peas in a pod.'

Frank notices another taped off area about thirty feet from where they're standing. 'You've recovered the bullets?'

'Yes. It took a while.'

'Metal detector?'

She nods. 'Yes. But there was no point looking for the shoot site,' she says turning around, gesturing over the landscape. 'To search that vast expanse would take a thousand-man hours.'

'Whoever shot them is a professional, or a damned good amateur. They'd have taken the empty shells with them.'

'Exactly. Right, time for me to head. I'll expedite the DNA samples, but I can't guarantee when they'll be back. Forty-eight hours... twenty-four if you're lucky. I'll send my report to you as soon as I can.'

'Send it to Prisha. She's running the show. She'll forward it on to me.'

Charlene bobs under the barrier tape and turns, puzzled. 'Prisha is in charge of the investigation?'

'Aye.'

She smiles and nods. 'My god! Frank Finnegan finally letting go of the reins. I commend you, Frank. Well done.'

'It's about time,' he says reflectively.

'Yes, it is. How long are you giving it?'

'Another two years—maybe. I need to lead the horses out of the stable—that sort of thing.'

'You'll see me out, then.'

Frank is visibly upset. 'Don't say that.'

She buttons up her waterproof coat to protect against the rain. 'The thing is, Frank, I've not been well for some time.'

'Hell... not the big C?'

'Not as yet. They've poked, prodded, sucked my blood out, put me under scanners and X-Rays and yet they still don't know what's the matter. I'd have taken early retirement years ago, but they don't have anyone suitable to replace me. I can't let them down.'

'What about the young guns coming through?'

'We train them up, then they bugger off to the big cities as soon as they have the experience. I can't blame them. Who wants to be in a backwater like North Yorkshire when you can experience the nightlife of London, Leeds, Glasgow.'

Frank nods, having dealt with similar for over twenty years. 'We're singing from the same hymn book, Charlene. Although Prisha did the opposite. She came from a big city to the country.'

'I know. Strange move for a young, single woman.' Walking towards the improvised carpark, the heavens finally open, sending down a torrent of heavy droplets. She breaks into a slow jog. 'She's a keeper, Frank! You look after her. I'll see you around!'

'Aye, see you around, Charlene,' he whispers as he fastens his jacket and pulls the hood up. 'But not for too much longer, by the sounds of it. Bugger... it's all changing.'

23

Prisha is sitting cross-legged on her bed dressed in her fluffy pink pyjamas, laptop on her thighs skimming through the drone footage from earlier in the day when there's a gentle knock on the door.

'Who is it?'

'It's me, Jason.'

'Hang on.' She slips into her dressing gown and opens the door.

'Here, I brought you this,' he says as he hands her a large mug and a pizza box. 'I know you said you weren't hungry, but you need to eat. I got one of the kitchen staff to make you a cup of hot chocolate with warm milk. I know it's your favourite.'

She gratefully accepts the offerings. 'Jason, that's so thoughtful. Come in and shut the door.'

'You sure?' he asks, hesitant.

'Don't be silly. Come in.'

She places the drink on her bedside cabinet and opens the pizza box. 'Oh, yes! My favourite—mushroom margherita with olives.' Grabbing a triangle, she takes a giant bite and closes her eyes in ecstasy. 'That is so good. You were right. I am hungry. Here, take a piece. I'll never eat all this. It's bigger than me.'

'Are you sure?'

'Yes, of course. Go on.'

'Thanks.' Cartwright takes a slice and positions himself in a chair as Prisha jumps onto the bed. 'What have you been looking at?' he says, nodding towards the laptop.

'The drone footage from today. Hey, did Evans set us up with an office and incident room at the station?'

He raises his eyes. 'Of sorts. Incident room is no more than a large office and our office is more of a box room.'

She shakes her head. 'Typical. Well, we'll have to manage. How'd you go with Craig Shaw?'

'Got his details, and he gave me his movements for Saturday. He visited his mother in the morning. Called at the pub, lunchtime. During the afternoon, he was at home decorating. Then took his mam fish and chips for tea. Still to be corroborated, of course. Have you determined an exact time of death?'

'No. And I doubt we'll ever get one, but let's look at it logically. They set off from the guest house at 7:30 am. Vertigo Alley, where their bodies were found, is just shy of two hours from Settle. We know they never reached the village of Malham. Now, assuming they didn't make any deviations during the walk, that would put the time of death around 9:30 am, give or take fifteen minutes.'

'But it's possible they made a deviation.'

'Correct. Which means they could not have been killed much earlier than 9:30 am but they could have been killed up to two, three hours afterwards if, for example, they took a detour to the waterfall at Catrigg Force. If we allow a bit of extra time, then it gives us a working timeframe of between 9:30 am and 1 pm.'

'What's the plan for tomorrow?'

'A nice early start. Then you and me will visit all the farms around the vicinity. There's four near to where the bodies were found.' She grabs another slice of pizza and tucks in. 'God, this is good. How'd you go with the Brigante Motorcycle Club?'

'Yeah, got some intel. Nothing mind-blowing, though. The club is run by two brothers—Mike "Razor" Roberts and Steve "Wolf" Roberts—President and Vice President, respectively. It's hard to determine how many members are in the club, but it's assumed there're about thirty hardcore and another thirty casual members. Mike is clean, but Steve has a record for growing and dealing marijuana. Got eighteen months, but that's eight years ago now. He also received a caution for a brawl in a pub with a rival gang, but no one wanted to press charges and not surprisingly, no one saw anything, so no witnesses. A guy from the rival gang had twelve stitches put in his back. Said he fell on a broken glass outside.'

'What about CCTV from the pub?'

'It wasn't running on that day, according to the landlord.'

'Unreal, aren't they?'

'Yep. The police are always enemy number one. There was an investigation into the gang about three years ago. Must have been when I was on long-service leave. They were suspected of knocking-off farm machinery—tractors, baling machines, that sort of thing. Anyway, we never got anything concrete on them, although during the investigation a steel shed was discovered, a few miles from their clubhouse outside the village of Forest Beck. It was a marijuana farm using hydroponics and LED grow lights. Again, not enough evidence to link them. Then there was the suitcase.'

Prisha stops chewing for a moment. 'Suitcase?'

'Yeah, suitcase. About a mile from the marijuana shed, in thick forest, a suitcase was discovered. Inside was a hacked-up body. Well, most of it. The head, hands, and feet were never found.'

'And the brothers were suspects?'

'Initially. They'd been having an on-off battle with another gang.'

'And?'

'And nothing. A thick veil of silence from both sides.'

'Was the body identified? DNA, body markings, recently reported missing persons?'

'No, no, and no.'

'How old are the brothers?'

'Mike is thirty-five and Steve is thirty-seven.'

'So the younger brother is the president?'

'Yep. He's the brains, apparently. Steve is a bit more of a loose cannon, and a scary looking bugger. Tatts all over his face, shaven head, scars.'

'Sounds like a real charmer.'

'Mike looks normal, whatever normal is these days. Oh, I forgot to mention, the investigation was led by none other than NYPs finest, DS Zac Stoker. You may want to have a chat with him.'

'Yes, I will.'

'To me, they're low-level villains, who may resort to violence with rival gangs. But knocking off an old couple is not really their thing.'

'Even so, there is a connection to Albert. Tomorrow, after we've finished the farm visits, I'll head to the station, and you catch up with the Roberts brothers.'

'What about Craig Shaw's alibi?'

'Where does he live?'

'Pickering. Close to his mam.'

'If you get time, check it out, but there's nothing that jumps out at me as to a motive. How was his appearance?'

'Downbeat. Shell-shocked, if I'm honest.'

'Understandably.'

'We don't have a hell of a lot to go on, do we?'

Prisha laughs. 'No. But it's day one of the murder investigation, Jason. Maybe when we visit the farms tomorrow, someone may have spotted something odd.'

'What about Maxine?'

'What do you mean?'

'We've focussed on this being about Albert, as though Maxine was collateral damage. What if it was the other way around?'

She nods thoughtfully. 'Good point. You're right. I have been a bit blinkered. Thanks for pointing it out.'

Cartwright holds back a proud smile. 'Has Maxine an ex-husband or boyfriend?' he asks.

'Husband died five years ago, and according to the daughter, Julie, Maxine hasn't had any man friends since—as she put it.'

'Maybe she kept it a secret and a jealous ex-lover killed them.'

'Long shot, but it's worth checking out. Have a trawl around the internet dating sites designed for older people and see if you can dig anything up. If you end up back in Pickering tomorrow, call in at Maxine's place and have another chat with Julie.'

'Christ! It's going to be a long day.'

Prisha chuckles. 'I have given you rather a lot to do.'

'No. I'm enjoying the responsibility. I'm usually treated as a gofer for the food and drinks.'

'Whatever you don't achieve tomorrow, do it on Friday.'

He stands and edges towards the door. 'Ahem, I was meaning to speak to you about that?'

'About what?' she asks, taking another slice of pizza.

'I know with Frank, on murder investigations, he likes to push everyone hard—long days, and work the weekends. It's just that I have a darts tournament Saturday night in Whitby, and if we win, we'll be through to the regionals. It's quite a big deal. But obviously, the job comes first.'

'That's the way murder investigations have always been done. It's ingrained. But to me it's not about quantity, it's about quality and you get more out of people when they're fresh, and relaxed. Everyone needs downtime. Unless something absolutely major blows up, we'll head back together to Whitby on Friday afternoon. And as I'm running this murder inquiry, take Saturday and Sunday off. Unwind, chill out and get back here Monday morning. You'll be a better copper for it.'

Cartwright beams. 'Brilliant! Thanks Prisha. It means a lot. Right, I'm down to the bar for a relaxing pint of Guinness, then bed. What time tomorrow?'

'I'll see you in the restaurant for breakfast at six-thirty.'

'Sounds good. Sleep tight.'

'Night, Jason. Thanks for the pizza and cocoa.' She places the pizza box on the floor, picks up her cocoa and takes a heavenly sip. 'Everyone's been wrong about him all this time, including me. Poor old bugger,' she murmurs, regretfully. 'Okay, back to the drone footage, Prisha.'

24

Zac opens his door and peers up and down the hotel corridor.

'All clear,' he whispers to himself. He walks past three rooms, then gently raps on Beale's door.

'Sorry, but whatever it is you're selling, I'm not interested. Fuck off!'

'Stop pissing about and open the door,' Zac replies in a forced whisper.

The door clicks open. 'Oh, Grizzly Adams, it's you. I do beg your pardon,' Beale guffaws, a butt of a cigarette dangling from the corner of his mouth. 'Come in and shut the door. You're late, by the way—by an hour.'

'You said nine o'clock.'

'I *said* eight,' Beale insists, stubbing his ciggy into an overflowing saucer of tab ends.

'Nine.'

'No... I said eight. Nine is my self-abuse in the shower time and I'm a creature of habit.'

Zac wanders into the room and notices sheets of paper and photographs strewn around haphazardly.

'What's all this?' he asks.

'What?'

'The mess.'

'No mess here, sunshine,' Beale replies as he pours a small shot of whisky into a glass. 'That, my Edinburgh born, lowland, turncoat, English loving bastard, is what we in the highlands call research.'

Zac sniffs. 'If you knew your Scottish history, Edinburgh isn't the lowlands, and neither is Glasgow the highlands.'

Beale slugs the whisky down in one hit and lights a fresh smoke. 'Ah, the old arguments never die, do they? That's the only problem with us Scots; we spend so much time fighting with each other, we overlook the real enemy—the Sassenach bastards. Friday morning cannot come around fast enough for me. This place is getting me down—which is not like me—I'm usually fun, frivolous, carefree.'

'Can we get down to business?' Zac snaps, impatient.

'Don't get your knickers all bunched up.' He waggles the bottle of whisky in front of him. 'A wee dram?'

'No, thanks.'

Beale frowns. 'I'm beginning to question your heritage. Are you sure your mother and father weren't Welsh?'

Zac ignores him and slumps into the armchair. 'Right, let's go through this step by step and take in every possible scenario.'

Beale puffs smoke into the air. 'No need for all that upper management, risk mitigation shite. It's quite simple. At ten-thirty you leave here and head towards Mr Bojangles. It's a ten minute walk—I've timed it. Go into the club and make yourself at home.

Try to appear relaxed—the opposite of what you look like now. And don't get hammered,' he says as he pours himself another generous shot of whisky. 'I need you to be on your game. This has to run like a digital clock. At exactly ten-fifty, give or take ten, possibly fifteen minutes, I'll enter and sit at the opposite end of the bar to you. You'll be playing the character of the good-looking, randy young git on the pull—after all, it is ladies' night, and it attracts sex pests; I'll be playing the sad old loser drunk whose wife has left him and taken the kids, and is massively in debt to the bank and is now living in a hovel of a bedsit in student land where they play that god awful fucking duff-duff music, or worse, Abba, until the wee hours of the morning. Bastards!' He drifts off into a reverie for a moment.

'Go on,' Zac eventually prompts.

'Oh, aye. Where was I?'

'Sad old loser?'

'That's right. I'll be using my highly tuned covert skills to surreptitiously check the place out. Once I've identified this Tiny guy, I'll make contact. It will be brief. I'll hand over my business card and ask if we can have a chat in private. He'll take me somewhere with cameras so they can get a good look at my gorgeous features, and I'll tell him who I am and who I represent.'

'Talbot McGovern from The Caledonian Boys?'

'Correct. I'll say I'm looking to purchase some of their product and if it's good gear, then we may be able to strike up a business partnership conducive to both parties. Then I tell him I'll be back tomorrow to shoot turkey.'

'Talk turkey?'

'Same difference. After the meet and greet, I exit Mr Bojangles and turn left. Five minutes later, you leave and turn right—but follow my path back to the hotel.'

Zac is confused. 'What?'

Beale throws him a map marked with red and yellow highlighter pen. 'Study the tourist map. My route is red, yours is yellow. Although, why in fuck's name the council went to the trouble of printing a tourist map for Hull is beyond me! Obviously, the so-called councillors don't fucking live here. Anyway, I digress. Out of Bojangles, you cross the road, turn left up the first street, hang another left, and it will bring you out on my route. I'll walk slow. You walk fast. That way, you should only be about two hundred yards behind me.'

'You think someone may follow you?'

'Don't know. Just being cautious.'

'Then what?'

'I'll call your room fifteen minutes after I get back to the hotel. Your phone will ring thrice...'

'Thrice?'

'Aye, fucking thrice!' Beale says angrily. 'That's the signal for you to pay me a visit and we'll exchange notes. You'll return to your room, contact DS Keegan on his personal number, and fill him in. It will be as easy as taking money out of the church collection box!'

Zac stands up and points at the mess of photographs and notes strewn on the floor. 'And what's all this?'

'As I said, research. To you, I may appear as a drunken, twat-faced, tit-juggler, but...' Beale pauses for a good five seconds. 'I *was* waiting for an automatic repudiation, but as it's not forthcoming, I'll continue. I may appear as a drunken, twat-faced, tit-juggler, but I'm actually a good copper who likes to get a back story.' He picks up a photo of a middled-aged man, not unattractive, with slicked back grey hair and hands it to Zac.

'Who's this guy?'

'Mr Brian "Butch" Cassidy. The former owner of Mr Bojangles. Sold the club six months ago for two hundred grand, about a quarter of its real value. The nightclub was never on the market. After fifteen years of running the club, it appears Butch Cassidy was eager to sell.'

'Meaning?'

'Someone put the squeeze on him. You know—made him an offer he couldn't refuse. He's now living in an isolated cottage on the coast of Cornwall.'

'Have you been in touch with the local CID to question him?' Zac asks.

Beale throws him the shitty eye. 'No. Too risky. If he still has contact with the new owners, the last thing we want is for him to mention to them he's had a visit from the plods asking about the club. It would raise suspicions.'

'Who are the new owners?'

'Good question,' Beale says as he slides a sheet of paper across the desk.

Zac picks it up and scans the official-looking document. 'Red Kite Solutions. Registered in the Cayman Islands. Is that all you have?'

'Aye, at the moment. You need to pass this intel onto Keegan, who can handball it to Interpol.'

'This new mob is quite sophisticated. Not your usual bums trying to make a quick buck.'

'There's certainly someone at the top who has the smarts, that's for sure.'

'They buy a nightclub at a discount, from which to run their business. Everything looks legit, but it's merely a front to organise their drug operation, and the nightclub would come in handy for laundering money.'

'Well done, Stephen fucking Hawking. Now, fuck off. I need my shower, if you know what I mean.' He takes a pill from the plastic bag on the table, sticks it on the end of his tongue and washes it down with whisky. 'Fifteen minutes from now, I'll be Superman... or at least I think I will. Sure you don't want one?'

Zac heads towards the door. 'No! One of us needs to remain compos mentis.'

Beale scratches his head. 'Didn't realise you spoke French, but anyway, suit yourself. By the way, I have your burner phone number set up as an SOS call on my mobile. All I need to do is click the start button twice in quick succession and it will ping you. I'll only use it if I'm in mortal danger.'

'Then what?'

He groans. 'Do I have to spell everything out for you? No doubt I'll be shown to a backroom to discuss things. Make sure you know where that room is. If you get an SOS, then bust the fucking door down and punch, kick, eye-gauge and stab any fucker you can see—excluding me, of course.'

Zac pulls at the door, agitated. 'This op is a dog's dinner.'

'Hey! Chillax brother. It will be a breeze,' Beale replies confidently.

Zac turns to him. 'You really think so?' he asks hopefully.

'Aye, of course.' He stops as his brow morphs into something resembling a wave pattern on a beach. 'Having said that, you gave your wife and bairns a farewell kiss before you left, didn't you?'

Concern spreads across Zac's face. 'What?'

'Ha! Ha! Look at that fucking mush! I was joshing with you, sunshine. Merely a bit of levity on my part. Right, shower time.'

25

Zac orders a bottle of beer and surveys the inside of the nightclub. It's quiet, with only twenty or so patrons, mostly women who got in for free. The music is loud, but not deafening. He leaves his drink on the bar and heads to the toilets and checks them out. They're clean and tidy, but there's only one tiny window, and it has bars over it. Rinsing his hands under a tap, he gazes at his reflection in the mirror, feeling more at ease than when he first entered the club. A quick glance at his watch tells him Beale should arrive at any moment. As he leaves the bathroom, he spots the emergency exit down a long corridor to the left. Apart from that, the only way out is via the main entrance. There were two bouncers on the door—a tall Afro-Caribbean guy and a short, stocky bulldog of a man with a neck the size of a tree trunk. He resumes his seat as a small group of women saunters up to the bar, laughing and joking with one another. There's five of them, all roughly aged in their early twenties, but who knows. They could be older women trying to look younger or they could be all underage trying to look older. These things are so hard to judge. One of them orders five glasses of prosecco. From the excited chitchat, it appears there's a wedding on the horizon and tonight it seems they've come together to discuss the hen night. A pretty girl, tall and athletic, throws a couple of glances Zac's way. He offers her a warm smile in return. Her eyes visibly widen, as though her breath has been stolen away. The girls wander off to a nearby table, but not before Zac receives another interested look. Taking a swig of beer, he relaxes until an aggressive Glaswegian brogue cuts through the music. He peers into the mirror behind the bar and spots Beale pulling up a stool about ten feet to the left of him.

'Hey, sweetheart, give us a double whisky, will yer?' The barmaid eyes him warily and wearily but pours his drink as he taps his credit card on the machine. 'Fucking twenty quid to get into this shithole,' he grumbles. 'It's hardly the Monte Carlo Bay Hotel, is it?'

'Receipt?' the girl asks, refusing to enter the debate.

'Nah... oh, wait, aye, give me the receipt—expenses. It's discrimination, that's what it is. How come the ladies get in for sweet FA and I get stung twenty quid just because I have a big hairy pair of balls and a long swinging dick between my legs? If it was the other way around, the feminists would be outside burning their bras and setting light to their fucking beards by now.' Zac slowly turns to face him. Beale stares back. 'Who the fuck you looking at, boy?'

'No one.'

'Aye, well, keep it that way if you know what's good for you. You pimped up, hairy bag of weasel piss.'

Zac shrugs at the barmaid, who reciprocates by rolling her eyes heavenwards. Both men fall silent for a good five minutes as they nurse their drinks. The girl who was making eyes at Zac returns to the bar and orders another five chardonnays.

'Fast drinking,' Zac says.

'That's because they're half-price before eleven-thirty. May as well get them in whilst they're cheap,' she says with a wide beam and a flutter of the eyelashes. 'Has anyone ever told you that you look a bit like Keanu Reeves?'

'Fuck me drunk!' Beale's voice drifts over.

Zac laughs. 'No, they haven't.'

'Well, you do.'

'Is that a good thing or a bad thing?'

'It's a fucking bad thing—Einstein.' Beale's deadpan accent again.

The girl frowns and gazes along the bar. 'Who's that prick?'

'No idea and I don't wish to find out.'

She refocuses on Zac. 'It's a good thing—Keanu, that is. He's drop dead gorgeous. I haven't seen you in here before?'

'No. First time. I'm in Hull for a couple of nights on work business. I fancied getting out. It can get a tad lonesome stuck in a hotel room.'

'Cry me a fucking river.'

The girl throws Beale a scowl. 'He's obnoxious.'

'Aye. He's probably one of those sad sacks who's alienated everyone in his life, and the only friend he has left is at the bottom of a whisky bottle.'

The girl laughs. 'I love your accent. I know you're Scottish, but where are you from?'

'Edinburgh.'

'Aye, jumped up wee hamburger, tattie boglers,' Beale scoffs.

'What is that guy on?' the girl whispers, completely bamboozled by Beale's derogatory terms for the natives of Edinburgh.

'Ignore the moron. What's your name if you don't mind me asking?'

'Lilly.'

'That's a beautiful name.'

'Someone, anyone, get me a fucking sick bag, please!' Beale splutters.

'And yours?'

He almost says Zac but catches himself in time. 'Ahem, it's Nigel,' he replies, wincing.

Beale snorts derisively. 'Nigel. Fuck me! Aye, you're a Nigel, all right.'

Lilly shakes her head and collects four wine glasses from the counter. 'I'll come back for mine in a moment. Nigel—that's a lovely name.'

'Pig's arse.' Beale again.

Zac watches her as she heads back to the table and frantically whispers to her friends who first gawp at Zac, then at Beale.

'Oi, sweetheart, stick another double in here, will yer?' Beale says, pushing his empty whisky glass towards the barmaid. As she hands him his drink, he stands up from the stool, rearranges his testicles, and pulls his trousers up. 'By the way, darling, which bouncer is called Tiny?'

'He was on the door as you came in,' she replies as Beale taps his card on the machine.

'Aye, but there were two of them on the door. A tall black guy and a short fuck knuckle who looks like a mad professor's biology experiment gone wrong.'

'Tiny's the black guy.'

'Oh, I see. Very droll. I forget... I'm in Yorkshire. The Yorkies are notorious for their dry sense of humour and fucking serial killers. I'm not sure what that says about the place.'

Lilly returns and picks up her wine glass. 'So, Nigel, do you have a girlfriend or wife?' she asks expectantly.

'Yes, I'm a married man.'

Her face drops. 'Oh. Why are all the nice men always taken?' she laments.

Beale leers down the bar. 'Never mind about him, darling, shift your sweet toots down here. There's room for you on my lap. I'm free and single.'

'Why don't you piss off you old, fat, disgusting pig!'

'Old?' Beale is clearly affronted at being labelled old... fat and disgusting he can live with. 'I'm not old. I'm only forty-four.'

'Yeah, and I'm twenty-three. You're old enough to be my dad.'

'If your mother's a skanky-ho like you, then there's a very good chance I could be your dad. But dinnae fash yersel about that. Have you never heard the expression—keep it in the family? We are in Hull after all—it's almost expected.'

Zac stands up. 'Hey pal, don't speak to the lady like that. Show some respect and put a sock in it.'

Beale shrugs and holds his arms out. 'Pardon me for breathing. I only came in here for a quiet drink and all I've copped is abuse.'

Zac resumes his seat as Lilly involuntarily touches him on the shoulder. 'Thanks for that,' she says, gazing at him in admiration.

'No problem.'

'Twenty quid and a mouthful of invective. Some night out this is. I wish I'd stayed home with my vibrating vagina.'

The barmaid catches the attention of Tiny as he comes over to the bar and leans across it. She whispers in his ear. He nods as his eyes swivel onto Beale, then rises to his full imposing, muscular height and saunters over to him.

'Excuse me, sir, but if you keep insulting the other patrons, then I'll have to ask you to leave.'

'Oh aye, you and who's fucking army?' Tiny sticks his chest out and tenses his biceps. Beale chuckles. 'Calm down and put your titties and guns away. I was joshing with you. Actually, it was you I came to see—don't worry, I'm not some repressed Presbyterian father whose daughter you've got up the plum duff, out to exact revenge. I'm here on business. Is there anywhere we can talk in private?'

Tiny eyes him suspiciously. 'You can talk here.'

Beale shakes his head. 'No, we can't. You see that wizened streak of fucking badger piss hitting on the girl with mental and visual impairment,' he says, nodding at Zac and Lilly. 'Well, he's got all the hallmarks of a fucking copper. And I don't want PC fucking McGarry eavesdropping on my business.'

Lilly leans into Zac. 'Are you a copper?'

Zac forces a painful smile. 'No. I'm a tractor salesman.'

'I'd watch him, sweetheart. He couldn't lie straight in bed. They're always the worst. He'll ask you to do things which boggle the mind,' Beale adds for good measure.

Tiny casts his eye over Zac, then back over Beale. 'Follow me,' he says. As Tiny and Beale walk past Zac, Beale bursts into song.

'Here comes the policeman, the big friendly policeman, PC McGarry number 452. Lost dogs, thick fogs, or don't know what to do. Then get a policeman, a big friendly policeman. Hahaha!'

'Thank god he's gone,' Lilly says, emptying her wine glass. 'Imagine being married to that thing? He gives me the creeps.'

'Don't worry, I think his wife will have shipped out a long time ago. Let me get you and your friends a refill.'

'No! Don't talk daft. You'll get charged full price.'

'Not a problem,' he says, pulling out his bogus credit card. 'It will go on expenses.'

'How long are you in town for?' she asks as he places the order.

'Tomorrow night then I'm away back to Scotland.'

The news excites her. 'Are you going to be in here again tomorrow?'

'I can be if you want.'

'Yeah. Yeah, I do.'

———— ◆ ————

Beale is ushered into a semi-lit room containing a desk, filing cabinet and a bookcase. Tiny closes the door, folds his arms and stands in front of him.

'Well?'

Beale surveys the room then pulls out a business card and hands it to him. Tiny takes it and reads. Silence descends for a good ten seconds.

'Sorry, but have you been struck dumb or something?' Beale enquires. 'My apologies. You can't use the phrase—struck dumb—these days. Politically incorrect. What's the term they use now? Non-verbal or some such fucking thing.' More silence as Tiny eyeballs him. 'Okay, I get the picture. You and me are similar. We're both the strong silent types.' More crickets. 'Right, well, let me do all the running here, if I can get a fucking word in edgeways. My name is Talbot McGovern. Heard of me?'

'Should I have?'

'Not necessarily. I'm obviously not as infamous as I thought. Bit of a kick to the ego, but I'll get over it with counselling. You may have heard of my crew—The Caledonian Boys?'

Tiny inspects the business card again. 'Are you some sort of Scottish folk band? Because if you are, then we don't put bands on anymore. They don't pull the punters in.'

Beale rolls his eyes. 'Fuck me! No, we're not a fucking Scottish folk band. We're in a similar business to yours, up in Scotland.'

'And what business would that be?'

Beale pulls the plastic bag from his jacket and dangles the pills in front of him. 'This fucking business. Making people feel good—at a cost—financially and detrimentally to their physical and mental health. But hey, if we didn't hawk this shit around, then someone else would—right?'

'What exactly is it you want...' he reads the card again, 'Talbot McGovern—Procurement Officer for Caledonian Inc?'

'A wee little birdy tells me you are beating the system. As you know, there's a bit of a drought on when it comes to the old sniffing salts thanks to some fucking operation the plods are running. I'm amazed they've been so successful considering most of the coppers I've ever met struggle to open a bag of peanuts and have a lower IQ than the contents. Anyway, until their operation goes tits up or they run out of money, then we are looking for a new supplier.'

Tiny's poker face expression remains the same as more silence ensues.

'Right, well, I can't hang around here all night with you chewing my fucking ear off. Tell your boss I'll be back tomorrow to talk business and sort out a deal conducive to both parties.' He turns and pulls open the door. 'By the way Tiny, if you ever tire of being a bouncer, you'd make a cracking living as a raconteur on the public speaking circuit. You'd have them rolling in the aisles. Right, one for the road then it's time for my beauty sleep.'

He closes the door and heads back to the bar. 'Oi, sweetheart, give me a treble whisky. There's a darling.'

'Oh, god, he's back,' Lilly whispers to Zac.

Beale eyeballs them as he pays for his drink. 'You lovebirds still here? I'd have thought you'd have been back at Nigel's hotel room by now playing hide the sausage. Or have you got the painters and decorators in, love?'

'Get lost, you creep.'

'I intend to,' he says, knocking back the whisky in one hit. 'Last chance, sweetheart. If this elongated hair bear has no lead in his pencil, then I'm available to help a damsel in distress. It's my civic duty. Although, I hope you enjoy being tied up?'

Zac pushes his stool away. 'Listen pal, I've just about had enough of you,' he hisses, towering over Beale.

'Fuck me! You are a tall bastard. What's the air like up there?' He readjusts his pants and makes to leave. As he passes Lilly, he leans in towards her as she automatically recoils. 'I'd give him a wide berth, darling. I could swear blind I bumped into him at the clap clinic earlier today. Sweet dreams.'

26

Zac checks his watch and slugs the last of his beer.

'Well, it's been nice chatting with you, Lilly, but I must be on my way. I said I'd call the wife when I got back to my hotel room to say goodnight.'

'Oh, but it's early yet. Do you have to go?'

'I'm afraid so. I have to be on the road by six visiting local farms.'

'Selling tractors?'

He laughs. 'Aye, trying to.'

She leans in and pecks him on the cheek. 'I'll see you in here tomorrow—yeah?'

'For sure. About ten-thirty. Night, Lilly.'

'Night Nigel.'

Casually walking out of the entrance, he nods respectively to the two bouncers. 'Night lads.'

'Aye, night mate,' they both say.

He buttons his coat against a stiff wind and hangs a right, pulling Beale's tourist map from his coat pocket. He crosses the street as he studies the map and tries to remember Beale's earlier instructions.

'Now, what did the tool say? First left, then left again, down to the end of the street and it should bring me out on his route.' He takes a left onto a road lined with terraced houses on either side. Walking briskly, he takes the first left, noting the street name and reconciling it on the map. Lifting his pace, he breathes a sigh of relief that the night is finally coming to an end. Halfway down the road, he stops. 'I don't believe it,' he curses as he stares at a brick wall in the distance, which demarcates the end of the row of terraces. 'It's a bloody dead end. What did that wanker say—meticulous planning and research. He hasn't walked this out.' Turning abruptly around, he jogs back to where he started, takes another left and heads down the next row of terrace houses. Once again, he comes to a halt as he spots the brick wall at the end of the road.

'Another bloody dead end!'

———◇———

Beale occasionally glances over his shoulder, expecting to see Zac behind him, but the road is deserted. 'Send a boy to do a man's job,' he sighs. He slows his pace as he spots two surly looking youths in their late teens heading his way. As they near, one lad calls out.

'Hey, mate, you haven't got a light, have you?' he asks as he sticks an unlit ciggy in his mouth.

'Aye, sure,' Beale replies as he retrieves his lighter and flicks it alight.

'Cheers.' The lad leans in and cups his hands around the flame to shield it from the biting wind. Beale notices the trembling fingers.

'Are you going through cold turkey, or have you been diagnosed with motor neuron disease, because you're shaking like a shitting dog on the streets of Calcutta?'

As the lad pulls away, puffing on his smoke, the other youth lunges forward and pulls out a knife—or at least the handle of a knife.

'Hand your wallet over, you fat bastard!' he yells.

Beale stares at the blade handle, then at the two lads. 'You know, there's a lot of fat shaming that goes on in this city. I'm not fat. For all you know, I may have a glandular problem.'

'Your only problem is you're a greedy twat,' says the lad who's smoking. 'Now hand the wallet over, otherwise he'll stab you.'

Beale waves his hands around in the air. 'Oh, I'm so scared. Two pock marked monkey spunk drops are threatening me with a knife,' he says in mock fright. 'Listen, Rumple-fucking-Stiltskin, and Rupert the Bear, a word of advice. If you're going to mug someone, then at least press the button on your flick knife to release the blade. Unless you intend cutting me open with the handle, in which case we could be here all fucking night, and I have better things to do.'

The lad glances down, notices his mistake, clicks the button and the blade flicks outwards. 'Wallet now!' he shouts, waving the knife in front of Beale.

'Okay, okay, calm down, Peewee. No need to get agitated. It's me that's being fucking robbed, not you. Now, just to clarify,' he says as he searches his jacket pockets, 'did you want the wallet or did you want the contents of the wallet?'

'Cut him, Bez! He's taking the fucking piss,' says the sidekick with the ciggy.

'Just hand the wallet over and stop pissing about. It's your last chance.'

'Ah, here it is,' Beale says extracting his leather wallet. 'This has sentimental value. My dear old ma bought it for me on my twenty-first. If I gave you my address, do you think you could pop it in the post when you're done with it?'

'Stab him, Bez. He's full of it. Let him know who's boss.'

Beale eyeballs him. 'Oh, you're good you are... standing there like a limp prick at a wedding, barking your orders. Not willing to do the job yourself, though, are you? I know your type; you're all wind and piss and candy floss.'

'Wallet now!' the lad with the blade screams.

'Okay, keep your voice down. You'll wake the old folk. Here's the wallet,' he says as he holds it out in his right hand. The lad lunges for it, but Beale grabs him by the wrist and bends it back in one swift move, ending with an audible crack. The lad screams, drops the knife and falls to his knees, clutching at his wrist. His mate pounces for the blade, but unfortunately for him, it coincides with a violent swing of Beale's leg. His boot catches the lad square in the face, breaking his nose and knocking him out. Beale bends down and picks up the knife.

'I'll take care of this before someone gets hurt,' he says, folding the blade away and dropping the knife into his pocket.

'You've broken my fucking wrist, you bastard,' sobs the lad.

'Oh, stop your snivelling, you wee Jesse. I made sure it was a clean break. Six weeks from now, when the plaster cast comes off, you'll be as good as new. You'll be straight back onto your PlayStation or Sega Gameboys or whatever they're fucking called these days. In the meantime, you'll have to wank with one hand. But look on the bright side—your left forearm will look like Popeye's in a few days' time. Christ, I bet you've never even heard of Popeye,' he adds wistfully. 'That cartoon has been consigned to the history bin of time thanks to the fucking do-gooders and their cancel-culture neo-Nazi manifesto.'

The lad with the broken nose groans and sits up, wondering where the hell he is, who he is and what's happened to his nose. Beale spots the cigarette on the ground and picks it up.

'I'll smoke this for you,' he says. 'I'm doing you a favour. Smoking is bad for your health. Anyway, I cannae hang around here all night blethering with you two test-tube abortions. Why don't you pair of acne ridden, missing links run off home to your cocoa and Rice Krispies.' He draws heavily on the butt of the smoke, then flicks it into the gutter as the two wannabe muggers stagger away. 'Kids nowadays,' he chuckles. 'They don't know they're born.'

———◆———

Zac paces nervously up and down in his hotel room. He glances at the clock again, waiting for the Bat-phone to ring.

'Christ! Where is he? I've been back half an hour. Damn it!'

Heading down the corridor, he breathes a sigh of relief as he smells cigarette smoke. He knocks gently on the door. A few seconds tick by until it's opened. Beale is naked apart from a pair of baggy Y-fronts with dubious stains on them. He pulls the cigarette from his mouth and stares dismissively at Zac.

'Nice of you to turn up.'

'I was waiting for your call,' he says, striding into the room as Beale shuts the door.

'What call?'

'The signal—you were going to ring my room—thrice.'

'Was I?' Beale says as he pours himself a whisky and flops onto the bed and resumes watching a porno film on the television. Zac flicks it off. 'Oi, it was getting to a good part!'

'We're supposed to be having a debrief.' He pulls the tourist map out of his pocket, scrunches it up, and throws it at Beale. 'And so much for your bleeding map! Meticulous research, I've done my homework! You didn't actually walk my route, did you? Otherwise, you'd have noticed the great big fucking walls at the end of every street!'

'Oh, I wondered where you'd got to. I thought you might have headed back to Lilly's place for a clam sandwich.'

'You are the most disgusting man I've ever met… and I work in CID so you can imagine some of the low-life's I've had to deal with.'

'Stop, you're jabbering, man. Help yourself to a beer or whisky.'

'I'll pass—thanks. So, how did it go with you and that Tiny guy?' he says, calming down a little.

'Swell—just swell. Although, he could talk the hind leg off a fucking donkey. Never shuts the fuck up. And by the way, thanks to your cack-handed attempt at covering my back, I nearly got mugged tonight.'

'What?'

'Aye. Two little fuck titties wanted my wallet. Pulled a knife on me.'

Zac takes a seat, concerned. 'Shit! Are you all right?'

'Oh, aye. Thanks for your concern.'

'And what happened to the lads?'

'I dare say they'll be wolfing down the paracetamol as we speak. Which means we're dealing with amateurs.'

'Why? I don't get it.'

'Tiny, or one of his crew, obviously put the wannabe rock stars up to it. I mean, who nicks wallets these days? No one carries cash and I could cancel my cards online before they'd made it to the nearest sweetie shop. Which tells me this so-called drug gang, cartel, whatever the fuck you want to call them, are nothing more than a bunch of amateur chancers. They've spotted an opening in the market and are filling their boots. It's lucky we found them first because if the real drug cartels find out about them, they'll be filling their boots with fucking quick-drying cement.'

'I still don't get it?'

'Sweet roast lamb of god! They wanted the wallet to check my ID—to see if I am Talbot McGovern.'

'That doesn't help us out then, does it? They still don't know who you are who you say you are.'

'Fuck me! That was a poorly constructed sentence. Did you nay pass your English O' level? Anyway, they'll know by tomorrow. That room he took me in, all dark and gloomy, hoping I wouldn't spot the fucking spy cam. They've now got a close up of my rakishly handsome features and a quick internet search for Talbot McGovern and The Caledonian Boys will confirm I'm the real McCoy—or real McGovern.'

Zac brushes his hand through his hair. 'Right, I see. So, what now?'

'We're back there tomorrow. I'll set up a deal. Place an order for twenty kilos to test out the quality. Then it's a matter of finding out how they're getting the coke into the country. Once we've figured that out, a bit more surveillance to make sure we've identified all those involved, and it's goodnight Piccadilly, farewell Leicester Square and kiss my sweaty arse goodbye, Tipperary.'

Zac eyes him suspiciously. 'You've used the pronoun—we—quite a lot.'

'Pronoun? Are you trying to show off because you mangled a sentence before?'

He ignores him. 'After tomorrow night—I'm off this operation. That was the deal. And if I never see you again—it will be too soon. I'm away to my room.'

'It's a good job I've got a thick skin. I've taken a hammering tonight on the insult front. I could end up with an eating disorder. Hey, by the way—you and that Lilly girl?' he grins lasciviously.

Zac shakes his head. 'Nice lass, but I'm married, so put those dirty, grubby thoughts of yours to bed.'

'I'd have been putting her to bed if I'd been in your shoes. Like a rat up a drainpipe,' he cackles. 'Hey, what do you reckon to my performance tonight? I could be on the fucking stage.'

'Aye. Preferably one with a trap door and a noose above it. Night.'

'Oi, put the porno back on!' he shouts out as the door slams shut.

27

Thursday 19th November

Prisha shivers in the crisp morning air as a chill runs down her spine. The darkness of the early November morning lingers, but the promise of a new day is slowly creeping in. A collection of aromas tickles her senses—the earthy dampness of the ground, the sweet scent of heather mixed with a pungent aroma of wild grasses. The occasional distant bleat of sheep and the chirrup from unseen birds drift to her on an unpredictable wind. She and Cartwright clamber back into the car after their third fruitless farm visit. Light rain spatters across the windshield, and grey clouds scud across the sky. She gazes at the barren landscape. If it was daylight, the scene would fill her full of joy and hope—a timeless, rugged beauty. But in this no-man's-land, caught between dark and light, the countryside is full of shadows that creep along behind drystone walls, stalking her.

'Three down, one to go,' Cartwright says as he starts the engine and cranks the heater up.

'And so far, not a dicky bird. No one saw anything or heard anything,' she replies gloomily.

'Hey, cheer up. We've had three cups of tea, a bacon butty and a nice warm by the fire. They're a friendly lot, these Dales farmers, and their wives. There are worse ways to start the day.'

Prisha is not really listening, as she taps at her phone. 'How far can sound travel from a high-powered hunting rifle before it's no longer audible?'

Cartwright pulls out of the farm gate and onto Henside Road. 'Hell, I don't know. A mile or two, I guess. You'd need to ask ballistics or Google.'

'I *was* asking Google.'

'Oh, I thought you were talking to me.'

'You weren't far off the money, Jason. Depending on terrain and weather conditions, the sound would travel between a mile and a mile and a half. The last three farms are roughly two miles from Vertigo Alley.'

'Well then, that's why they heard nowt.'

'Hmm, I suppose. It's odd to think I could have been climbing Malham Cove last Saturday at the same time as they were murdered.'

'And you didn't hear a gunshot?'

'Of course not. Malham Cove is nearly four miles away. All I heard was the screech of an eagle. Okay, next stop Hollybush Farm.'

The car trundles on for another few minutes until they pull off the main road and come to a halt at a farm gate with a homemade sign clumsily attached to the horizontal bars. Daubed in red paint, the scrawl reads—Trespassers Beware!

'Whoever wrote that needs to work on their penmanship,' Cartwright chuckles.

Prisha jumps out to open the gate, but it's padlocked with a heavy chain. She puts one foot in the middle bar and leaps over. Cartwright emerges from the car as his phone rings.

'Hang on a moment, it's the missus. It could be good news,' he says, smiling.

'Take your time. Catch me up in a minute,' Prisha replies as she sets off down the farm track lined with dwarf willows and birch trees.

The track takes a dog's leg to the left and as the trees thin out, she spots a cluster of old barns and the farmhouse not far ahead. She tiptoes past muddy potholes until she's standing in the main courtyard. Her eyes swivel around as she captures the scene. Three old stone barns without doors. One houses a newish looking tractor sporting a pair of forks. Sitting next to it is a brand-new silver Audi A8. The other barns are empty. It's quiet, almost desolate. Not like any farm she's come across before. Something unnerves her about the place as the hairs on the back of her neck stand to attention.

Soft footsteps are followed by a click.

A deafening blast rings out as she instinctively clasps her hands over her ears, closes her eyes and drops to her haunches.

'What the hell do you bloody want?' a gruff, male voice roars.

She looks up and sees the man approaching, shotgun in hand, barrel pointing skywards.

Pulling her warrant card out, she flashes it at the man and yells, 'Police officer! Put down the weapon!'

The man stops in his tracks and lowers the shotgun. 'Oh, sorry. I thought you were a bloody rambler trespassing.'

'I could arrest you for recklessly discharging a firearm!' she shouts as the adrenalin pumps through her veins.

'You were never in any danger. I shot in the air, as a warning, like.'

'Prisha! Prisha!' Cartwright bellows as he comes jogging down the track.

Prisha lifts her hand up. 'It's okay, Jason. I'm fine.' She glowers at the man in front of her. 'What's your name?' she demands, already knowing the answer.

'George Baxter. What's all this about?'

Prisha pulls a plastic wallet out containing photos of the murder victims. 'Have you seen, or do you know, these people?'

Baxter takes the photos and stares at them. 'It's the couple who were murdered, not far from here. I've seen their faces on the local news. But no, I don't know them, and I've never seen them before apart from on the telly.'

Cartwright eventually arrives at Prisha's side, panting hard, red in the face. 'Do you have a valid firearms certificate for that thing?' he scowls, pointing at the shotgun.

'Course I bloody have. You can check.'

'Don't worry, I will.'

Prisha retrieves the photos. 'Have you any other firearms on the property, Mr Baxter?'

'No. Just the shotgun. It's all I need to keep the rabbits and foxes down.'

Prisha's heart rate slowly subsides. 'Have you noticed anyone suspicious around here over the last week?'

'No. It's quiet this time of year. Summer is a nightmare, though. I have walkers trampling over my land, shitting behind walls, snooping around the farm on the pretence they want to buy eggs.'

She ignores his gripes and presses on. 'Can you tell me your whereabouts last Saturday?'

Baxter rubs at the back of his neck, his bulbous red nose glowing. 'Saturday? I woke at midday...'

Prisha interjects. 'Midday, I thought farmers were early risers?'

He looks embarrassed. 'Aye, well, I dare say I had one too many at my local, then a few more when I got home.'

She glances at the Audi. 'Where's your local?'

'Lister Arms, Malham.'

'That's what... three, four miles away?'

'Aye, about that.'

'Drive home, did you?' she asks fixing him with an unflinching gaze.

He stiffens and pulls his neck back. 'No, of course not. That would be against the law. A friend dropped me home.'

'Name?'

'What?'

'The name of this friend?'

'Look, what's your bloody game? Are you investigating a murder or trying to fit me up for drink driving?'

She's unmoved. 'Name?'

'Lewis.'

'Lewis Visser?' she questions, brow creased.

Baxter's a little taken aback and suspicious. 'That's right—Lewis Visser. Know him, do you?'

She doesn't answer as she hands him her card. 'Thanks for your time, Mr Baxter. If you should think of anything, however small, then please call.'

The officers walk back to the car. 'Hellfire! I nearly shat my pants when I heard the shot,' Cartwright says.

'I know. One more cup of tea and I think I'd have embarrassed myself as well. I know that man. He was in the Listers Arms on Saturday afternoon getting blind drunk ranting about hikers. I think we have our first main person of interest, Jason.'

'Really?' he says, less than convinced.

'Time for a warrant for his arrest and a search warrant to investigate a farmer who doesn't farm.'

'What do you mean?'

'No dogs, no animals, no farm machinery, apart from a solitary tractor and a flash car. How much is a new Audi A8 these days?'

'Oh, around the seventy grand mark.'

'Odd car for a farmer. Back at the station, I want you to check the land registry office and determine how big this farm is and where the boundaries are. A perfect hiding spot for a gunman would be behind a drystone.'

'He doesn't look like the sort of bloke who could kill two people in quick succession over a long distance wall.'

'It doesn't matter what he looks like. It's what he's capable of. We know he's violent and hates walkers, and his property is within a couple of miles of the murders. That's enough dots joined to warrant further examination, if only to...'

'... eliminate him from our investigation.'

Prisha smiles. 'Yes. Frank taught me that. Keep ticking off the suspects and persons of interest until you're left with one. Hey, what did your wife want?' she asks as she leapfrogs the gate.

Cartwright beams and lowers his voice. 'Don't tell anyone. It's early days, and she wants to keep it quiet, but she thinks she's pregnant. Home testing kit, so it's not a hundred per cent, but she has an appointment at the quacks next week.'

She holds her arm out to help her colleague down from the gate. 'Congratulations! That's wonderful news!'

28

After wasting the best part of an hour rearranging the tiny office they've been allotted in the station, Prisha is finally happy with the layout.

'Compact and bijou,' she says with a laugh.

'Not enough room to swing a dead cat,' Cartwright says with a chuckle. 'Now for the incident room.'

'No, I'll get a couple of uniform to sort that out. You head over to Forest Beck and catch up with the Roberts brothers. Take a uniform with you. See if PC Claire Darby is available. It will be good experience for her.'

As Cartwright departs, Prisha wanders across to the office of Sergeant Evans. She's noticed his door is continually open, offering him a good vantage point of the station. He obviously likes to keep a close eye on the comings and goings. She taps at the open door and enters as he lifts his head from some papers.

'Inspector. How are you settling in?' he asks coldly.

'Yeah, good.' She's not going to moan about the office. He'd only take some perverse satisfaction from it. 'What can you tell me about George Baxter up at Hollybush Farm?'

He pushes back in his seat and raises a crooked eyebrow. 'George? The farm's been in his family for generations. His wife left him a few years back. He likes a drink and can get handy with his fists, if you know what I mean.'

'Handy with his fists? Rather a benign term for domestic violence,' she states, emphatically.

Evans eyes narrow. 'You don't suspect Baxter of any involvement in the murders, do you?'

'We'll find out soon enough. I'm organising warrants for his arrest and to search the farm.'

Evans lets out a mocking laugh. 'Waste of bloody time. I've read your report from yesterday. It's thought Albert and Maxine were shot from some distance away and in quick succession. First off, I doubt George could hold a gun without it shaking, never mind getting two shots off in quick time. When he's sober, he has the twitches. And when he's drunk, he's really drunk.'

'Take an angry man, mix with alcohol and throw in a firearm and you have a volatile cocktail. How's his farm doing?'

'He's been on his uppers for a while. The banks won't refinance. I wouldn't be surprised if he sold up at some point. That's another thing about drunks—they don't make great farmers.'

'They don't make great anything apart from misery.' She places a list in front of him. 'I've compiled a list of uniformed officers I want on my incident team.'

He studies the note. 'PC Darby? She's still on trainer wheels. She'll be no good to you.'

'And unless she's given chances and responsibility, she'll be on trainer wheels a lot longer than necessary.'

He glares at her. 'Very well. Have it your way.'

DS Cartwright has done well to hide his trepidation in the company of PC Darby. They've made idle chitchat for fifteen minutes, but as the car nears the tiny village of Forest Beck, his concerns jostle to the forefront of his mind again.

Instinctively, he feels the visit to the Brigante clubhouse is a wild goose chase. But he also knows Prisha is right—the task needs to be done, if only to eliminate the Roberts brothers from the investigation. And yet... a sense of foreboding clings to him like a bad smell, and worst of all, he doesn't know why. Even the thought he could be a father doesn't shift the lingering oppression. It could be the mist, which has settled in for the day. It hangs over the desolate landscape like a disease. Or possibly the fact they are in the middle of nowhere, literally. If anything goes wrong, there will be no fearless members of the public to rush to their aid or call for help.

Throwing the young PC a glance, he notices her wide eyes and silent demeanour. He filled her in on the details—who the brothers were, and why the visit, and all was fine. It's when she studied the photos of the brothers, particularly the tattooed face of Steve Roberts, that she went quiet. Maybe it wasn't a good idea to have mentioned the hacked-up body found in a suitcase.

Thinking of Prisha, he wishes she was sitting next to him now. Nothing ever seems to faze her.

'How far to go?' he asks.

PC Darby stares at the GPS. 'Five minutes. There's a right-hand, left-hand bend in the road, like a chicane. Halfway along that we take a right turn onto a gravel road.'

Cartwright slows the car and turns onto the track, which is enveloped by a cavalcade of trees. He peers through the skeletal branches at a recently ploughed field. A murder of crows busily feeds from the soil; one even has the temerity to perch on the outstretched arms of a lopsided scarecrow. Pointing it out to PC Darby elicits a nervous laugh from both of them. The car enters a circular driveway in front of an old stone farmhouse.

'Here we are!' Cartwright says with mock enthusiasm as he stops the engine.

'Sir, I'm scared,' PC Darby says as she unclips the seatbelt. It's not what he wants to hear. But he's an experienced officer with over twenty years under his belt. She's a young kid. It's time for him to man up.

'Nothing wrong with being scared. It gives you an edge. Just don't let it show, otherwise they'll be all over you like a cheap suit. That's how bullies work. They detect fear and prey on it. Remember, these two numbskulls are also scared—permanently. That's why they act tough to cover their own insecurities. Anyway, you've completed your self-defence training, haven't you? Combat and restraint techniques, breakaway tactics, controlling holds, joint locks?'

'Yes. But I'm five-five, with my shoes on. Those two are built like brick shithouses.'

'Don't worry. If anything kicks off, which it won't, I'll take them both down. Underneath this layer of fat is a superheros body. But make sure you have your baton and Taser at the ready in case my right knee locks up.'

She giggles, then takes a deep breath. 'Thanks sir, I feel better now. I was being silly.'

He offers her a warm smile and pats her on the shoulder. 'That's the spirit. Anyway, let's hope these two knuckleheads aren't around. Then we can go for a nice coffee on the way back.'

They exit the car and first knock on the farmhouse door, but receive no answer. The distant sound of reggae music flows through the air.

'That sounds familiar,' Cartwright comments. The screech of an angle grinder occasionally drowns the music out. They walk around the back of the house and spot two large sheds. A cyclone fence and a locked gate surrounds one. Razor wire runs along the top of the fencing. The shed is painted black and is obviously the clubhouse. The club name is painted in giant gothic letters on the side wall—Brigante MCC. Beneath the letters is a boar's head, all professionally done. Cartwright turns his attention to the other shed where he spots the Roberts brothers. Steve is kneeling, holding the angle grinder as he works on the forks of a mean looking motorbike. His brother is behind him spray painting a fuel tank. Cartwright pulls his warrant card out and saunters towards them, fearless, to the untrained eye. The brothers don't notice him and PC Darby until they are virtually in front of them. The angle grinder revolves to a stop, as Steve stands up grimacing and Mike pulls a dust mask from his face and kills the music.

'I'm DS Cartwright and this is PC Darby,' he states confidently, swaying back on his feet.

Steve drops his head and spits on the ground. 'Filth,' he hisses.

Mike moves forwards and touches his brother's arm. 'What do you want?' he says. There is no venom or malice in his tone.

'Just a few routine questions, Mike,' he replies as he pulls two photos from his jacket. 'Do you know this man?'

Mike leans in and studies the image. 'Nah, can't say that I do.'

Cartwright shows the photo to Steve. 'And you?'

Steve gives it a casual glance. 'No. And if I did, I wouldn't tell you.'

'Meaning you could know him?' Cartwright persists.

'He doesn't know him either,' says Mike, almost wearily.

Cartwright shows them the photo of Maxine Wood and receives the same reply.

'That's funny, because their faces have been plastered all over the newspapers, and nightly TV news, and social media sites.'

'I don't read the papers or watch the news. And do I look like the sort of guy who wastes his life on social media looking at dancing cat videos?' Mike says. 'Why are you here asking us about them?'

'Albert Shaw and Maxine Wood were murdered last Saturday, up on Malham Moor. Shot through the head.' There's the merest flicker of something in Steve's eyes as he almost glances at his brother but stops himself.

'That's all very tragic, isn't it, Steve?' Mike says.

'Aye. Tragic,' he sniffs.

'But same question; why are you asking us?'

'We believe Albert was a former member of the Brigante Motorcycle Club. We thought you might know of him.'

The brothers glance at each other, patently confused. 'He wasn't a member. What makes you think that?'

Cartwright points at the design on the clubhouse. 'Albert has that tattooed on his arm.'

The brothers eyeball each other again. Mike inspects the photo again. 'How old was he?'

'Seventy.'

The brothers crack up laughing. 'Fuck me! Maybe he was a member fifty years ago, but we've been running this club for the last twenty years and I've never seen him and never heard his name mentioned,' Mike sniggers.

'Oh, very funny, isn't it?' Cartwright sneers. 'Two elderly people murdered. Where were you two last Saturday morning from 7:30 onwards?'

'We were both here,' weren't we bro?' says Steve.

'We were. Can both vouch for each other.'

Steve turns his attention onto PC Darby. 'It's a weekday love, shouldn't you be in school?' he says with a chuckle.

230

She doesn't flinch. 'What's with the face paint? Is it to intimidate people? Because if it is, it doesn't work. You just look like a twat.'

His face hardens before a wry smile breaks out. 'Fiery. I like that in my women. How about you and me exchange numbers and we could get together sometime?'

'I'd rather gnaw my arm off.'

'Nice comeback. I like it. Anyway, not one of my better ideas. I don't want to be arrested for underage sex.'

'No, and I don't want to catch herpes, so let's drop the idea.'

Mike takes a step forward as he wipes his hands on an old rag. 'I'm sorry we couldn't help you out Sergeant Cartwright, but as you can see, we're busy, so if you don't mind,' he says, holding his arm out pointing toward the farmhouse.

They turn to leave before Cartwright stops and wheels around. 'How many members are in your gang?'

'It's not a gang. It's a club.'

'Sorry... club.'

'That information is restricted,' Mike says.

Cartwright snorts derisively. 'Restricted! Christ, you lot really are chocolate soldiers, aren't you? You actually believe your own hype. Anyway, remember that in our gang we have over sixteen hundred members. And that's just in the North Yorkshire Police alone. Enjoy your day.'

As the officers disappear from view, Mike Roberts taps at his phone.

'What?' a voice answers.

'Just had the pigs around at the clubhouse asking about Albert Shaw and Maxine Wood.'

'Why?'

'It appears he was an ex-member. Had the club colours tattooed on his arm.'

'They're simply tying up loose ends. They don't know anything. Keep your heads down and your mouths shut.'

'Understood.' He ends the call.

PC Darby and Cartwright high-five each other in the car and burst out laughing.

'You handled yourself like an old timer back there,' he says.

'It was all false bravado. I was shitting bricks.'

'Doesn't matter. You didn't show it. They were certainly on their guard. Right, let's find a caff and have a cuppa and a bite to eat. We've earned it.'

29

Sitting in her claustrophobic office, Prisha is studying the drone footage again.

'Hell, I'm becoming obsessed. I'm not sure what I'm even looking for,' she mumbles to herself. Her focus is distracted as the gruff tones of Sergeant Evans echo down the corridor. She quietly opens her door and peeks out.

'For god's sake Edward! When we have the time, I'll send an officer out to see you! But I'm not sure what you want us to do. This week it's the mysterious red lights on the moor. Last week it was a badger digging in your garden, and the week before that you were allegedly attacked by a malevolent goose! I've a good mind to arrest you for wasting police time. Now, if you don't mind, I have more pressing issues! You can see yourself out.'

The old man in a heavy grey overcoat and flat cap shuffles down the corridor muttering to himself. As he leaves the station, Prisha visits Sergeant Evans.

'What was all that about, sarge?' she asks with a grin.

'Edward Harrowby or Edward the Confessor, as he's nicknamed. He's in here every other week with some half-baked complaint. The bane of my life. He should be in a bloody home.'

'What was that he was saying about the lights?'

Evans wipes a sweaty mitt across his balding head. 'Who knows? He reckons he's been seeing red lights in the sky at night for the past month?'

'Aeroplane lights, possibly?'

'I suggested that, but he says they come from the ground into the sky for a few minutes before they disappear.'

'Where does he live?'

'On the outskirts of Arncliffe. Hang on... why are you interested? Shouldn't you be running a murder investigation instead of wasting your time with delusional attention seekers?'

'Just curious.'

Evans relaxes. 'Any developments?'

'Not yet. But I'll be sure to let you know. By the way, I have the warrants in place for George Baxter. My team will go in about four this afternoon, after a briefing at three. I'll need a couple of K-9 units and an explosive detection sniffer dog. I'd appreciate it if you could handle that for me.'

Evans shakes his head in disgust. 'What the hell do you want K9s for?'

'Baxter discharged his shotgun this morning. Admittedly it was a warning shot because he didn't know who I was. However, he's proved his volatile even when sober. The dogs always make people less prone to violence in my experience.'

'In your experience,' he snipes. 'And why are you waiting until 4 pm? Why not go in now?'

'I'm assuming he will head to the pub at about five or six. I want to keep him in custody overnight and interview him tomorrow when he will be struggling with detox.'

Evans eyes her with disdain as she heads down the corridor and out of the entrance. 'Talk about out of her depth. What the hell was Finnegan thinking of, putting her in charge?' he mutters under his breath.

Prisha gazes up and down the street until she spots Edward Harrowby trundling along the high street at a snail's pace. She sprints after him.

'Mr Harrowby! Mr Harrowby!'

The old man is oblivious to her cries as he continues to mumble to himself. 'Bloody police. Don't know their arse from their elbows. Never listen to a word I say.'

Prisha catches up, skips around him, and holds out her warrant card. 'Mr Harrowby, wait. I'm DI Kumar. Can I have a word?'

He comes to a stuttering halt and observes her warily. 'What about?'

'I overheard your conversation with Sergeant Evans about the lights.'

'Conversation? You don't have a conversation with that man. He only does lectures.'

'Where are you heading?'

'The terminal to catch a bus back to Arncliffe.'

'I tell you what, I'm headed that way myself. Why don't I give you a lift and you can tell me about the lights?'

He considers the proposition for a moment before begrudgingly accepting. 'Aye, I suppose.'

As she parks up in the driveway, Prisha isn't looking forward to entering the quaint stone cottage. During the car ride, she formed the distinct impression Edward Harrowby has been a widower for quite some time. In the past, she's known quite a few younger men who lived alone, and their places were always disgusting. With Edward's advanced years, she's expecting something much worse. Although, she notes the small gardens are well maintained. Edward puts his key in the lock and pushes open the door.

'Go through to the lounge room, love and make yerself at home. I'll stick the kettle on and make us a brew.'

She winces at the thought but follows him inside. Pleasantly shocked, she moves from the kitchen and into the lounge room. It definitely stood still in the 1970s and the place is a little tired, maybe even threadbare, but it's meticulously clean and tidy. The view from the window is magnificent, and she instantly takes a liking to the place. It's snug and cosy, with a wood burner radiating heat from an old fireplace. Navigating the room, she stops at a bookcase and peruses a few books for a couple of minutes then picks up a photograph of Edward and a woman she assumes was, or is, his wife. As she hears Edward approach, she places it back down.

'Here we go, lass. Take a seat,' he says as he places a tray containing a teapot, a pair of cups, a jug of milk and a plate containing a slice of fruit cake.

'No milk for me,' she says as he does the honours. 'How long have you lived here, Edward?'

'Since I was eighteen.'

'Wow! And how old are you now?'

'Ninety-four.'

A little stunned by his age, she thinks of all the things he's lived through. 'And is that your wife?' she says, pointing at the photograph.

'Aye. That's Deidre,' he says sadly. 'Passed away over twenty years ago. I still miss her every waking minute. You'd think the pain would pass after all this time—but it don't.'

'Have you children?'

'No,' he says passing her the tea. 'We were never blessed. God's way I guess.' They make small talk for a few minutes as Prisha devours the moist slice of cake and sips her drink. Edward slumps back in his chair and gazes at her.

'So then, lass. What can I do for you?'

'You were going to tell me about the lights, remember?'

'Was I? Oh, aye. That's right.'

'When did you first notice them?'

'About a month back, maybe longer.'

'And where were they?'

'Follow me.' He leads her into the kitchen and stands at the window, which captures another glorious view over the

Dales. 'Out there,' he says pointing at thousands of hectares of emptiness.

She has a lightbulb moment. 'Could the lights be from RAF Fylingdales, possibly?'

'Nay, nay, nay lass!' he cries, apparently appalled at the suggestion. 'You're not from around here, are you?'

'No,' she replies sheepishly.

'Out there is heading west towards Settle, over Malham Moor. Fylingdales is on the east, eighty mile that way,' he says pointing indiscriminately.

Suitably chastised at her novice error, she continues. 'Can you describe what you saw?'

'Red lights. Four of the buggers coming up from the ground.'

'What time of night?'

'Late. About one in the morning?'

'That is late.'

'Aye well, I don't sleep much these days. I can get by on four or five hours a night. I stay up until about one or two, listening to the radio or reading.'

'And how long are the lights on for?'

'Not long. Ten minutes, max.'

'Could they be coming from Settle or a nearby town?'

'That's what I asked Sergeant Evans. I thought there might have been one of those laser shows or Christmas lights or summat. But he said there wasn't anything like that in town.'

'Roughly how far away would you say the lights were?'

'I'm not sure. Hard to tell. Could be a mile or twenty mile.'

'Are they static or do they move?'

'Nay, they don't move, lass. Just straight up in the air.'

'Is there anything else you can tell me about them?'

He leads the way back into the lounge room. 'No. That's about it. What are you going to do about it?'

Prisha finishes her tea. 'I'm not sure there's much we can do, Edward. We don't know what they are or even where they are and as far as I'm aware, there's no law being broken.'

'Oh, I see,' he replies. Concluding she's wasted her time, she edges towards the door and decides against leaving her card in case he constantly calls her mobile.

'Thanks for the tea.'

'Hang on, don't you want to know about the red strip lights I saw as well?'

'Red strip lights?'

'Aye, flashing ones.'

She has a soft spot for Edward, but it's becoming apparent that maybe his mind is addled. Escape is imminent as she pulls open the front door. 'And how many times have you seen the flashing lights?'

'Just the once. They were on the ground. It was foggy as hell, but you couldn't miss what they were. Red strip lights.'

'Hmm... I see. It really is a puzzle, isn't it Edward?' she replies, humouring him as she crosses the threshold. She scampers briskly down the garden path as he shuffles after her.

'Aye it is, queer. On, off, on, off for a good ten minutes then they were gone.'

Slipping into the car, she offers one last platitude. 'I'm sure it's nothing to worry about, Edward. Now you take care,' she adds, firing the engine.

He leans against the top of the door and stares down at her. 'Aye, on and off for a good ten minutes.'

'Goodbye, Mr Harrowby.' The car reverses at speed down the narrow driveway. 'Evans was right. A bloody time waster. Focus Prisha, bloody focus!'

30

The officer opens the jaws of the bolt cutter and places them around the chain. Squeezing the handles together, there's a moment's resistance from the steel before it pings and padlock and chain fall to the ground. He swings the gate open.

Prisha speaks into her radio. 'This is DI Kumar. All units proceed to the farmhouse with caution. Move in and secure the premises and detain George Baxter!'

Two K9 units, two patrol cars, and Prisha and Cartwright in their Ford Focus follow one riot transit van. The vehicles speed down the gravel track, sirens blazing and screech to a halt in the courtyard. Shouting, the rumble of boots, and barking dogs disrupt the serene setting. Two burly officers burst through the door of the farmhouse, followed by two snarling Alsatians and their handlers.

'This is the police! Present yourself!'

A moment later, George Baxter is dragged from the house, handcuffed and sporting an expression of bewilderment, fear, and alarm.

'What the bloody hell is all this about?' he yells.

Prisha marches up to him. 'George Baxter, I am arresting you in connection with the murder of Albert Shaw and Maxine Wood. You do not have to say anything. But it may harm your defence if you do not mention when questioned something which you later rely on in court. Anything you do say may be given in evidence. You'll be taken to Settle Police Station and handed over to the custody sergeant who will explain your rights. Take him away!'

'You're not setting me up for bloody murder!' Baxter screams. 'I've nowt to do with it. I'll bloody sue the lot of you!'

As Baxter is led to a patrol car, the search team gets underway.

'Inside or outside?' Cartwright asks.

'I'll take inside, you search the barns,' she says as Cartwright heads off followed by four uniforms.

Inside the house there's the smell of cooking. Prisha enters the kitchen and stares at a pan of stew bubbling away on the stovetop. She turns the gas off and pops a lid on the pan.

'Looks nice. Shame it will go to waste,' she mutters as she pulls on a pair of latex gloves. Within ten minutes, there's a yelp from a dog followed by Cartwright's booming voice.

'Inspector Kumar!'

Prisha scurries down the stairs and sprints across the yard into the barn, housing the car and tractor. 'What is it?'

Cartwright points into the gloom. 'Rifle bag in the corner,' he says as the handler puts the sniffer dog back on its lead. The barn is constantly lit up by the flash of a camera as the police photographer takes a series of shots.

'Are you done?' Prisha asks as she ventures into the murky corner of the barn.

'Just about, ma'am,' the photographer replies.

'Don't go anywhere. Get some shots as I unzip the bag.' She stares at the gun scabbard made from khaki canvas leaning against the old stones. Picking it up, she pulls at the zip, extracts the rifle and examines it. Stamped onto the barrel is the manufacturer's name—Tikka. There's a smooth groove on the buttstock, where the serial number used to be. She slips the rifle back into the scabbard as the camera flashes and clicks, then hands it to Cartwright. 'Okay, bag and label it. We need to get it to forensics as soon as.' She marches out of the barn shouting. 'Keep searching! We need bullets, empty cartridges, shooting rest, gun scope—anything to do with firearms.' Back inside the farmhouse, she issues more orders. 'Shoes, boots, trainers, I want them all bagged, along with the contents of his laundry basket. Search the rubbish bins inside and out. We're looking for rubber gloves, tissues which may have blood on them.'

As the search continues, Prisha grabs her laptop and walks around the back of the farm and stares at the panorama of fields divided up into random shapes which stretch on for as far as the eye can see. Opening the laptop, she clicks on the link to the drone footage PC Jarvis captured the day before. She scrolls the video forward until an aerial shot of Hollybush Farm comes into view. The camera hovers above the farmhouse, barn, and courtyards before moving at a slow pace west over the fields. As the footage plays, she occasionally looks out across the fields to take her bearings. The camera stops over the peculiar rectangular shapes that dot one particular paddock. As the drone descends, the markings become less distinguishable. From high above, they are as clear as day, but ten feet off the ground, they are almost invisible.

Pushing open a farm gate, she follows a drystone wall for three hundred yards as it snakes across the land. Checking the drone footage again, she stares at the slight ridge peppered with a scar of white rock running along the top. She looks up and spots the same ridge, but in real-time.

'X marks the spot,' she says to herself as she slowly stalks the ground, head down, eyes scanning for any sign of the peculiar imprints. After fifteen minutes, she closes the lid on her laptop and sighs. 'Waste of time. What are you doing, Prisha?' she chastises. 'What the hell has this got to do with a murder investigation?' As she sets off back toward the farmhouse, something catches her eye on the other side of a drystone wall. Peering over the stones, her curiosity is piqued. Placing the laptop on the ground, she clambers the wall and drops to the other side. She squats and picks up a fragment of pale-yellow timber about the length of a pencil. She pulls an evidence bag from her pocket and drops the sliver of wood into it. Studying the area, she notices quite a few other timber fragments clustered together. The ground around them is covered with a fine white dust.

'I wonder what it is?' she murmurs, pulling another plastic bag from her coat. Using two fingers, she carefully scrapes together a small clump of soil and bags it. 'Fertiliser, possibly?' She takes a series of photos, then heads back to the search team.

———◆———

Two hours into the search, Prisha is becoming dispirited and heads out of the house into the courtyard. She spots Cartwright emerging from the barn.

'Jason, how's it going?'

'Good, how about you?'

'No, I meant the search. Anything else of note turned up?'

'No, not really.'

'Which one is it—no, or not really?'

'Erm... no.'

'You scoured the car and tractor?'

'Yes. I went over it myself. Nothing.'

She puffs out her cheeks and spins around, taking in the courtyard. 'Okay, let's call it a day. Get all the items off to the lab and expedite the rifle and footwear. There may be traces of blood on the soles.'

'Will do. I've got to take my hat off to you,' he says with a wry chuckle.

'You're not wearing a hat.'

'Funny, funny. No, I mean it.'

'Why?'

'Because I think we have our man.'

Prisha raises her eyebrows, a tad incredulous. 'I don't.'

'What?' he says, clearly surprised. 'This morning you said we had our first main suspect, and I was sceptical. Now, after finding a hunting rifle in his barn you don't think it's him. There's no keeping up with you.'

'Don't even try. I can't keep up with myself. Some days my mind is like a bloody roulette wheel, constantly spinning, waiting for the ball to drop.'

'Why the doubt?'

'We've found no other shooting paraphernalia to go with the rifle. No bullets, no scope, no rifle rest.'

'It's a big farm. He could have hidden them anywhere.'

'He goes to the trouble of disposing of the bullets and scope, but leaves the rifle conveniently leaning up against the side of the barn. Ballistics will tell us if the bullets found at the crime scene came from that rifle or not, and if they did, then it wasn't George Baxter who fired them.'

'You think he had no involvement in the murders?'

'I'm not saying that. He's a dodgy character, that's for sure, and it's possible he's an accessory, although I even doubt that. But he's not our killer.'

'You think the rifle was planted there?'

'Yes, and in a hurry. Right, round the team up and let's head back to the station.'

31

Zac is sitting on the high armchair in Beale's room as he waits for the unhinged buffoon to emerge from the shower. He spots a pile of papers on the desk and takes up a seat behind it. There's a raft of papers about the activities of The Caledonian Boys which make for fascinating, if disconcerting, reading. There are photographs of all the main team, including Talbot McGovern and his brother, the leader—Hamilton McGovern.

He pauses and cocks his head to one side. The shower has stopped running. He skims through the rest of the photos of the Caledonian gang. None of them are bonny looking buggers, although Hamilton scrubs up quite well. He's taut, lean, and wears snazzy suits—but still—that mug could put anyone off their breakfast. Shuffling the photos, he picks one up of Talbot McGovern coming out of what looks like a massage parlour. He's oblivious to the camera shots taken. Zac is amazed at the uncanny resemblance between McGovern and Beale.

'I wonder if they're actually related?'

The door to the bathroom opens, followed by a billow of steam and the unattractive flabby body of Beale with a towel wrapped around his waist.

'Sorry about the wait. I was hither and thither between the twixt and the twain.'

'What are you talking about?'

'I couldn't make my mind up.'

'About?'

'Whether to help myself to a hand-shandy or not. I erred on the side of self-restraint, having noticed a knocking shop down the road earlier today masquerading as a massage parlour.'

'Christ,' Zac murmurs, shaking his head.

'Simple choice really; an all over body massage by an illegal Latvian immigrant, finished off with a glorious rub and tug, or a quick five-finger shuffle in the bathroom. I mean, come on—it's a no-brainer—right?'

'I wouldn't know,' Zac replies wearily as Beale squirts deodorant under his armpits, which resemble an Amazonian rainforest, then sprays half the can over his ridiculously hairy chest. The man looks like a gorilla on testosterone implants.

Zac checks the time. 'It's nearly nine-thirty now. I thought I'd head to Bojangles a little earlier tonight. It will appear more random.' Beale drops his towel and lets his crown jewels swing freely in the wind. 'For the love of god!' Zac exclaims. 'There's no need for that. It's like a blind cobbler's thumb! Put some bloody underwear on, damn it!'

'Calm down, hairy Maclary from Donaldson's dairy. It's not a come on, so stop drooling.' He picks up the towel and sticks it between his butt cheeks and flosses. Discarding the towel, he sprays another dose of deodorant over his genitals, then across and up his butt crack. 'It can get a little whiffy up there in the brown zone. Just because they're working as illegal sex workers doesn't mean you shouldn't give them the same consideration as legal sex workers,' he says.

'You're all heart. Right, I'm out of here. I was going to grab a shish kebab before I went to the club, but I've lost my appetite for some bizarre reason. Anything you'd like to go over before I depart—you know, tactics, scenarios, what could go wrong, escape routes?'

'Nah! Waste of fucking time. It's in the bag—trust me. It's game, set, and hairy snatch. I'm all over these lemon-sucking, pasty-faced pussycats like scabies. I'll see you in there later, unless I have a coronary during ejaculation.'

'Aye, that would be a happy ending for so many, many people. Remember—my role in this pantomime ends tonight,' Zac calls out as he leaves the room, slamming the door behind him.

'That's what you think—big boy—that's what you think,' Beale chuckles as he pops a pill and swills it down with a hefty slug of whisky. Standing in front of the mirror, he splashes aftershave on his face. 'Okay, big boy, tonight is your night! And tomorrow, I'm homeward bound away from this rat-infested, sinkhole.'

Against his best efforts, Zac is falling for Lilly. Guilt fights it out with intense attraction and joy. His marriage has been rocky for twelve months thanks to his gambling addiction, which left his family perilously close to financial ruin. And although he hasn't made a bet in many months, there is still something standing between him and his wife. And now she's working night shift at the hospital for the next three months, they barely see each other. Lilly is young, fresh, and fun. It's easy to be all those things when you don't have kids, responsibilities, and a gambling husband, he thinks to himself.

As he pays for the drinks, he checks his watch. Beale is due in another fifteen minutes. Maybe another ten, twenty minutes for him to set up a deal, then he'll depart, which means Zac will have to leave, as well. A painful stab of longing sits in his guts. He passes Lilly her wine, but she immediately places it back on the bar.

'Come on!' she yells, grabbing his hand. 'I love this song. Let's dance.'

The opening bars of Tainted Love blast out across the sparsely populated club. Despite yanking at his hand, Zac remains rooted to the spot.

'Oh, no. I can't dance. You go. I'll stay here.'

'Don't be daft. There's no one on the dancefloor. I'd look like Nobby-no-mates. Come on, it will be fun.'

'No, it won't,' he says, feeling his will slip away.

'Please,' she begs, pulling a puppy dog look.

'Oh, bollocks. Okay, one dance and that's it.'

'Yeah!' she screams, leading him towards the flashing lights.

Initially embarrassed at his lack of prowess in the dancing department, as the song progresses, his inhibitions slowly evaporate. Lilly, on the other hand, is quite the performer. Perfect timing, handclaps, and high leg kicks accompanied by a gratuitous knicker flash entices several other patrons onto the floor. As the song finishes, they fall giggling into each other's arms, as Lilly plants a peck on his cheek.

'Okay, enough dancing,' he says as a buzz of adrenalin swamps his body. He's momentarily taken aback as he spots Beale at the bar, roaring with laughter.

'Oh god,' Lilly groans. 'It's that bloody creep again. What's he doing here?'

They resume their seats at the bar and grab their drinks. Beale's laughter eventually subsides as he wipes tears away from his eyes. He turns to Zac, whisky in hand.

'What the fuck was that, big fella?' he says, still recovering from his hysterics.

'What?'

'The whole dancefloor thing? I almost reached for my phone to call the paramedics. I thought you were having a medical emergency. You looked like a frog trying to take the wheel nuts off a moving car.'

'Just letting my hair down,' Zac replies curtly.

'You were letting the fucking human race down, pal. Although, on the flip side, your little piece of sweetmeat can certainly shake her tush. Nice G string by the way, love,' he says with a leer. 'Ever thought about going commando?'

'Oh, piss off,' Lilly spits. 'You are the most repulsive man I've ever met.'

'Come on, sweetheart, all this passive aggressive nonsense isn't fooling anybody. It's simply a protection mechanism to mask your true feelings. I've seen the way you've been slowly undressing me with your eyes. Come on, admit it.'

'I'm going to powder my nose,' she says to Zac.

'Aye, okay.'

'Think about me while you're taking a slash!' Beale calls out. She turns and gives him the finger.

'Can you turn it down a bit?' Zac whispers. 'You're going too far.'

'What are you talking about? I've barely fucking started, yet.' He knocks his whisky back and orders another as he spots Tiny in the mirror, heading his way. 'Here he comes, chattering Charlie. Looks like it's on,' he murmurs. Zac stands up, collects the drinks and heads off to a table in a dark corner of the club.

———◆———

Tiny knocks once on the door, then opens it, and holds his arm out, indicating for Beale to enter. Beale takes a deep breath and ambles into the room as Tiny closes the door behind him. He stares at the two men sitting behind the desk, thankful Tiny didn't enter the room. Two against one are not good odds should something go down. Three against one are impossible odds. He studies the men staring at him. Mid-thirties, muscular, one with short cropped hair, the other with a shaved bald head, tattoos up his neck and over his face.

Beale juts his thumb over his shoulder. 'I'm glad Tiny didn't join us. Once he starts with his amusing anecdotes, you can't shut the fucker up. Some people were born to hog the limelight. I had tinnitus after meeting him last night,' he says with a laugh which receives nothing but impassive looks. 'Okay, I see you two are about as verbose as your bouncer mate. Is this a Hull thing or an English thing?' Silence. He pulls a chair up and flops down into it. 'It's going to be a little difficult holding a business meeting between us if I'm the only one who's going to fucking talk.' Still no response. Beale blows air through his lips. 'Maybe it's my accent. Should I try sign language, or maybe semaphore signals?' He sticks his hand in his pocket and retrieves the flick knife he took from his would-be muggers the previous night, then tosses it onto the desk. 'You can give it back to the two little balls of pimple puss who wanted my wallet. Very amateur. Made me think twice about even showing up tonight.' He throws his wallet onto the desk. 'All you had to do was ask.'

The short haired man picks it up, and half pulls out a credit card, studies it, then slips it back inside and pushes the wallet across the desk towards Beale. 'Talbot McGovern,' he says.

'Now there's a fucking coincidence, because that's my name too,' Beale says.

'You're a funny man,' the tattooed guy says with a scowl.

'Thanks. You've gotta have a laugh, haven't you? Without laughter, what have you got—a tsunami of fucking tears and misery.'

'I hate the Jocks,' he says, curling his top lip up.

'I don't much care for them myself, if truth be told. But what I hate more is fucking wannabe caramel gangsters who've watched too many Martin Scorsese films and think they can muscle in on some action when they should really stick to nicking little girls' bikes. Now, you have twenty seconds to start talking otherwise the next time you'll see me I'll be with my crew, and we'll torch this fucking place, and you two donkey turds will be part of the next fucking bypass they build around some godforsaken one-horse fucking town.'

The seconds tick by. Beale pushes his chair back, the legs squealing against the hard floor. He picks up his wallet, drops it into his coat pocket and turns toward the door.

'Wait!' says the short haired guy. 'Sit down.'

'Pretty please?' Beale replies with a genial smile as he resumes his seat. 'Okay. I can see you're not one for manners. Now, what are your names?'

'No names,' says the tattoo guy.

Beale stares heavenwards. 'Please god, help me out here. These two wank muppets are testing my patience.' His gaze returns to the men. 'You know my name and who I represent. I think it only fair I know your names.'

The short haired man speaks. 'I'm Razor, and this is Wolf.'

'Fuck me! What were your parents thinking of? Don't tell me—your father worked for Gillette and your mother was half werewolf, half beetroot? Okay, Razor, and Wolf, let's get down to business as I have more enjoyable things to attend to, like cauterising my fucking haemorrhoids. I know you're importing shit loads of cocaine into the country. Fuck knows how, as nearly every other importer has had their means of supply shut down because of Operation Dragnet run by our intrepid fuckwit friends in blue. I dare say it will be short term; maybe three months, six months, possibly a year, but nevertheless, it's causing a lot of headaches. And I don't like headaches ever since my old da died of a brain haemorrhage. So, here's my proposal: once a month I want a delivery of cocaine—we'll start off with twenty kilos, and if it's good gear and not cut with any shit, we'll up it to fifty kilos a month.'

The two men look at each other. 'We import fifty kilos twice a month. That would mean you want half of our supply,' Wolf says.

'Fuck, you're good with numbers. Is that a problem?'

'We have agreements with other gangs,' Razor adds.

'Fuck the other gangs. If they give you any shit, my crew will deal with it.'

'That's not how we operate. An agreement is an agreement.'

Beale sighs heavily. 'I see, men of honour. You're not going to last too long in this game with that attitude. Okay, here's another idea—simply import more.'

'It may be possible,' Razor says, thoughtfully. 'Don't you want to know the price?'

'Do I look like I was born on the back of a bus? I know the price. For bulk wholesale purchase it's between twenty-five and thirty-five grand a kilo. We'll pay you thirty-five K for the first drop, then after that, thirty K. And that's being generous. In cash, of course,' he adds with a chortle.

'No cash,' Razor says.

Beale nearly falls off his chair. 'No cash?'

'We want paying in Ripple.'

'What's that, a new type of chocolate bar? You must have one hell of a sweet tooth.'

'Ripple is a fungible cryptocurrency.'

Beale waggles his little pinky in his ear. 'Sorry, Razor, either my hearing's going or you're fluent in fucking gobbledygook.'

'You've heard of Bitcoin?'

'I've heard the term bandied about and some fucking egghead once tried to explain it to me, but after about two minutes I'd lost the will to live.'

'Ripple is similar to Bitcoin. When a payment is made, it's instant. It is impossible to trace, from either end.'

'Hmm... I'm warming to this idea. So how long does it take to set up something like that?'

'Thirty minutes, max. All you need to do is create an account on a cryptocurrency exchange, deposit funds, then purchase Ripple.'

Beale rubs his chin thoughtfully. 'Aye, that's above my pay grade. I have trouble booting up my fucking phone some days. But my older brother, he's into all that shit. Insider trading, stocks, and shares and bulls and bears. He's a bit of a geeky boffin type, although you wouldn't think so if you saw him. He looks more like a fucking confused plumber. Right, gentlemen... I take it we have a deal,' he says holding out his hand. Razor and Wolf shake it, cautiously. 'Now, I assume you deliver the product to a location of my choosing?'

'No. You come to us. We don't come to you,' Wolf says.

'I see. Okay, fair enough. Let's arrange our first exchange for next week. The natives in Scotland are getting restless without their white powder.'

The brothers exchange looks. 'Next week?' Razor says.

'Aye. Problem?'

'No. Short notice, but I'm sure we can arrange it.'

'Right then. You best give me a contact number and the rendezvous point.'

'No. All communication is via Wickr.'

Beale has heard of the app but plays dumb. 'Here we go again. What the fuck is that?'

'It's a messaging app. It offers end-to-end encryption, self-destructing messages, encrypted file transfers, and secure group chat options. The messages are completely untraceable and deleted after a pre-set time chosen by the user.'

'Fuck me blind. I'm getting too old for this game. I suppose I'll have to download it to my phone?'

'Obviously.'

'And how do I get in touch with you?'

'You don't. We get in touch with you via SMS. We'll send you a QR code. Scan it then add the contact to your Wickr account.'

'I think you boys have watched too many James Bond movies. This is all getting very technical. I can feel the onset of a migraine. Let me just make a mental note before I forget. Ripple for payment; Wickr account for communication; fucking QR code to get your contact for Wickr. Right, all set. So, what day next week? The earlier, the better.'

'Wednesday.'

Beale stands up and heads towards the door. 'I need a double whisky after all that. And at the pickup point, tell your boss to be there—the real boss, because I know for a fact you two bozos haven't got the combined brain cells to put a caper like this together. If I'm doing business, I want to meet the organ grinder, not the two fucking monkeys. Oh, and one last thing; I hope this isn't some elaborate undercover, police entrapment, sting. Because if it is, I *will* hunt you both down and kill you and every member of your fucking family—slowly. I like to be upfront with people. Sweet dreams.'

32

Zac watches on as Beale makes his way to the bar, orders and pays for a large whisky, necks it down in one, then head towards the front doors.

He stands up and checks his watch. 'I'm sorry, Lilly, but I really should get back. I've another early start tomorrow. I have to be in Somerset by eight.'

Her disappointment is obvious as she rises. 'Oh no! Really? You have to go? It's only eleven thirty.'

'Really, yes, I do.' There's a stilted impasse as they both gaze at each other. From the corner of his eye, he sees two men appear from the room Beale was in. He turns slowly towards them.

Shit!

His heartbeat quickens at an alarming rate. The two men stop for a moment and slowly scan the room. Zac grabs Lilly and plants a passionate kiss on her lips. There's a moment of resistance until she relaxes and reciprocates enthusiastically. Zac opens one eye and squints at the men. Their gaze passes him by, and they head towards the entrance. When they are safely out of sight, he breaks away from the embrace.

'I'm really sorry about that, but I saw a couple of dodgy guys who I used to know, and I'd rather not speak to them again.'

'That's why you kissed me?'

'Aye,' he says, checking over his shoulder to make sure the Roberts brothers haven't suddenly returned.

'Bastard!' The slap across his face takes him by surprise and stings like hell. Lilly storms away, heading towards the exit.

Zac runs after her and grabs her by the arm. 'Lilly, wait! It came out wrong. I did kiss you for that reason, but it doesn't mean I didn't enjoy it,' he pleads.

Her vicious pout softens. 'You mean that?'

'Yes.'

'Okay. Then kiss me again.'

'What?'

'You heard.'

Guilt and unbridled lust go head to head once again. There can only be one winner as he takes her in his arms, and they indulge in a tender and sensual kiss. Eventually, he pulls away.

'I really must go.'

'Will I see you again?'

'Probably not. But it was nice to experience passion like that. It's been a long time.'

'I thought you said you were married. Oh... I see. You and your wife are...'

'Things between us are tricky at the moment. I tell you what, give me your number and I'll call you in a couple of days—for a friendly chat.'

'Do you have a pen?' He hands her a pen, and she scribbles her number on the back of his hand. 'Promise you'll call?'

'I promise.'

———◦———

Much to Zac's disgust, Beale has stripped down to his baggy Y-fronts as he leisurely packs his suitcase.

'I wanna be away at first light. This place is no good for my soul,' he says griping about England again. 'All in all, it's been quite a successful undercover op. Although, you were superfluous to requirements. About as much use as titties on a bull.'

'Excuse me. I was watching your back.'

'Watching my back? Fuck me, you were more interested in chatting up the local tarts and making a complete twat of yourself on the dancefloor. Oh, that was funny,' he says, chuckling away to himself.

'Thanks to me, you know who you're dealing with. Mike and Steve Roberts from the Brigante Motorcycle Club. I investigated their operations a few years ago. I've saved you a lot of time.'

'AKA Razor and Wolf. What a pair of clowns. Aye, I'll give you a wee credit for that one. But there's at least one Mr Big behind those two nuff nuffs. We need to nail that fucker, as well as Tweedle Dee and Tweedle Dumber.' He pauses and eyes Zac suspiciously. 'Have you heard of a thing called Ripple?'

'Yeah. It's a form of cryptocurrency.'

'Prick. That's what they want paying in.'

'So what? It's easy enough to arrange. I'm sure DCI Keegan and his team will be able to set something up.'

'I guess. Now we play the waiting game.'

'There is no—we. I'm officially done. I don't want to see you ever again.'

'I have feelings, you know. And I don't think you are done. By the way, what's that number on your hand?'

Zac pulls his shirt sleeve down. 'It's nothing.'

'Well, it must be something. Oh, I see,' he says with a leery grin. 'Lilly. I can't say I blame you. If you had any sense, you'd be rooting her rigid right now instead of eyeballing my meat and two veg. I know you'll be fighting with guilty emotions, but believe me, the first time you cheat on your wife is the hardest. It gets a lot easier after that.'

'You really are a piece of work, aren't you?' Zac says heading towards the door. 'Hey, I don't suppose you asked them how they're getting the drugs into the country?'

'What—and make them suspicious? No, they're either bribing someone who's working on Operation Dragnet to turn a blind eye or they're flying it into a remote landing strip. Right, if you don't mind, I'd like to watch a bit of porno, if you catch my drift. And I'd rather be alone,' he says clicking his suitcase shut, then pouring a generous whisky.

'Unreal,' Zac mutters as he closes the door behind him.

33

Friday 20th November

DI Kumar and DS Cartwright are sitting opposite George Baxter and his solicitor in the interview room. She presses the record button on the digital recorder and reads out the standard police caution. Baxter folds his arms, eyes swivelling between inspector and sergeant.

'George, before we get into the nitty gritty of our investigation and the evidence we've accumulated, a simple question which could save everyone a lot of time; did you kill Albert Shaw and Maxine Wood?'

'No,' comes his gruff reply.

'Okay, we'll begin then,' she says as she flicks open a folder on the table. 'You don't like walkers, hikers, ramblers, do you?'

'No. Don't mean I go around killing them, though.'

'You said a similar thing to me yesterday morning, a few seconds after you fired a shotgun above my head.'

'It wasn't above your head. I shot it in the air to give you a start, that's all.'

'You said last Saturday morning you slept late, waking about midday... is that correct?'

'Aye.'

'Sleeping off a hangover?'

'I suppose you could call it that.'

'You like a drink or two, don't you, George?'

'No law against it. Not yet anyway. What I do in my own time is up to me.'

'Unless you break the law. Then it's not up to you. Moving on. Have you any witnesses to verify you slept until midday?'

'No. Who has bloody witnesses to when they're asleep?'

'Wives, children, family members, friends?' she says slowly, methodically trying to get under his skin.

He involuntarily twists at the neck and tightens his arms. 'None of the above.'

'I see. DS Cartwright, would you show George exhibit-A, please?'

Cartwright pulls on a pair of latex gloves and retrieves the rifle from a box on the table behind them. He holds it up for all to see.

'Oh, don't you bloody dare,' Baxter snarls.

Cartwright clears his throat. 'For the recording, I am holding a Tikka T3x UPR Ultimate Precision Rifle. It was found in George Baxter's barn during our search, yesterday. It has recently returned from the forensic lab. The bullets that killed Albert Shaw and Maxine Wood were fired from this rifle.' He carefully places it back in the metal box.

'Bollocks!' George snarls, suddenly unfolding his arms. 'You bloody planted it there! You found it somewhere else and you're trying to fit me up with murder because you can't find the real murderer!'

Prisha ignores his intense outburst and calmly continues as she flicks a page of her notes over.

'You see, George, once the gun goes to the ballistic experts, they fire a round from the gun, then compare the markings on the test bullet against the markings on the bullets recovered from the crime scene under a microscope. It's like a fingerprint... the markings are unique.'

'Bullshit!' he snaps, becoming more agitated.

'No. It's not bullshit. It's forensic science, which when explained in layman's terms to a jury, is very convincing. To recap; you have a motive—you hate hikers tramping over your land. Your alibi is unverifiable, and we found the murder weapon in your barn. Not looking good, is it, George?'

'No comment.'

'That's enough evidence already for the CPS to be rubbing their hands in glee. A jury would take about ten minutes to return their guilty verdict.'

'No comment.'

'And there's your bank account,' she adds. 'Over to you, DS Cartwright.'

Cartwright opens his folder. 'I only went back five years, but I see you've been doing it pretty tough, George. Your average annual income from two hundred and fifty acres has been around the twenty-thousand-pounds mark per year. You don't do much hands on farming anymore, you rent your land out on a yearly basis to two local farmers. Livestock is mainly sheep, a few cattle. Your land is on high ground, so the grass is not the best. You had debts to the bank, tried to refinance for the fourth time and was declined. Like I said, doing it tough. Then, lo-and-behold, about two months ago, suddenly you pay off all your debts and buy a new car from an Audi dealership in Leeds. I must admit, you got a good deal. Standard drive away price is normally seventy-five Gs. You got a five grand discount. No hire purchase, no lease, no bank loan. And I've got to say, your bank balance is still looking very healthy. I wish mine looked like yours.' Cartwright's mocking tone presses a few buttons.

'I thought this was a bloody murder investigation?' Baxter snarls. 'Now you're snooping around in my affairs. Well, do your worst. Everything's legit!'

Prisha takes up the gauntlet. 'We're CID, George. We don't really care about your income. It's simply another indicator. Of course, our colleagues in the Fraud Squad and the Inland Revenue would be very interested in your sudden accumulation of wealth.'

'It was inherited. An old aunt died and left me everything.'

'Of course she did. Name of this aunt?'

'None of your bloody business.'

Prisha closes her folder, adjusts her jacket, and relaxes back into her chair. 'Here's the rub, George. Something's bugging me. I've been watching your hands and they're shaking. I don't think you're easily intimidated. You can handle yourself and give as good as you get. The reason you're shaking is because it's over thirty-six hours since you last had a drink. You're an alcoholic, George. Not that I'm judging. But I don't think you are capable of murder with a high-precision long-range rifle. You're either drunk or recovering from being drunk. Not great attributes for a marksman. So, my question is—who are you covering for?'

'You're going nowhere with this, are you?' he sneers.

'That's what you think. As I pointed out, the case against you is extremely strong. Think about the jury when they're presented with the evidence—motive, alibi, murder weapon. This is DI Kumar suspending the interview for lunch,' she says as she presses the stop button on the recording. She smiles at Baxter. 'Whichever way you look at it, George—it's not good! Murder or serious fraud? If you could help us out, then maybe those fraud charges could be mitigated—a slap on the wrist?'

'Piss off.'

———❖———

Prisha relaxes on a park bench and munches on a sandwich, idly watching some young children as they play on the swings. Their carefree and joyous manner bring a welcome relief to her fatigued mind. She's feeling the pressure of expectation. Cartwright and some from uniform view her as some sort of Superwoman. Then there are the others, like Sergeant Evans, who see her as an imposter, and are waiting for her to fail. Truth is, she's neither Superwoman nor an imposter. Finishing her lunch, she brushes the crumbs away and takes a swig of water. She taps at her phone.

'Prisha, what can I do for you?' Frank asks.

'Are you busy?'

'No. I'm in my office staring out at the trawlers while trying to eat my way through a pasta salad. I told Meera, pasta is supposed to be eaten hot. It doesn't belong in a bloody salad. Go on, fire away.'

She smiles at the imagery. 'I've completed round one with Baxter, and I wanted your advice.'

'I'm all ears.'

'On paper, at least, we have all the essentials; motive, murder weapon, and no alibi.'

'But you don't think it's him?'

'No. It's all too obvious. If we'd found the rifle stashed away under the floorboards in a back bedroom, then it would have been more convincing. Plus, he's not capable of firing an accurate shot from a long distance, or any distance for that matter. I'm not sure what my next step is, Frank.'

'Have you checked the firearm certification records?'

'Yes. Baxter's registered for his shotgun and that's all.'

'What about the manufacturer of the rifle?'

'They're manufactured and sold by a company in Finland who only supply to one dealer in England. Cartwright spoke with the dealership, but without the serial number, they said it would be hard to trace. Although, the finish on the gunstock is quite distinctive. It's made from glass fibre and has a desert sand finish, a sort of mottled white colour. We've sent them a photo, and they said they'd have a look at their records.'

'Any DNA on the rifle?'

'Yes, but it's not Baxter's and there's no match on the database. I've hit a brick wall, Frank.'

'Don't get dispirited. It's early days. You know how long murder cases can drag on for sometimes. Your options are to release him under investigation with or without bail, or charge Baxter with possession of an unregistered firearm, then release him on bail. If a blood match or DNA from Albert or Maxine turns up on his clothing or shoes, then it's a game changer, but at the moment, I tend to agree with your initial premise that Baxter is not our killer. We can always charge him at a later date for the firearm offence. The thing at the moment is not to get distracted from your primary focus.'

'Hmm... charging him could muddy the waters down the line.'

'How do you mean?'

'When we catch the real killer, I can see their defence counsel bringing it up in court that we charged Baxter with possession of the murder weapon. They'd have a field day with that information. It's the sort of thing which brings doubt into a juror's mind.'

'Good point. Your decision is simple, then. Release him under investigation. Would you consider him a flight risk?'

'No. The only place he'll be fleeing to is the pub. Thanks, Frank. I feel a lot better just speaking to someone about it.'

'No problem. Put Baxter to one side and focus on other potential suspects. I take it you'll be working the weekend?'

'No. Me and Cartwright are heading back to Whitby this afternoon.'

'Oh, I see. I usually...'

'Yes, I know what you usually do, Frank. But I believe in giving people a rest, a chance to recharge. If the murders had just been committed, then the team would work the weekend. But nearly a week has passed, and everyone has been putting in long hours. They need a break.'

'Okay. Different strokes for different folks. And is Cartwright still performing?'

'Can't fault him. He's really knuckled down. I think all he needed was a little TLC.'

'That's good to hear. Okay, got to dash as Superintendent Banks wants to see me.'

'Bye, Frank.'

Prisha waggles a pencil up and down against her teeth as Cartwright taps away at a keyboard. She checks her watch.

'Jason, why don't you head off back to Whitby now?'

He looks up from the screen. 'It's only two. I thought we were heading back together?'

'I've got some reports to update. I'll take one of the pool cars. You haven't had a chance to check out Craig Shaw's alibi yet, have you?'

'Sorry, no. I've been meaning to, but it's a four hour round trip from Settle to Pickering and I haven't had time.'

'I understand. It's not a bollocking. You can do it on your way back to Whitby.'

'Yeah, I will,' he says, shutting the lid on his laptop.

'Hey, how'd you go with the online dating agencies? Did Maxine Wood show up on any of them?'

'No. Me and PC Darby spent about four hours on it. I rang Julie Wood and asked a few more questions. She said there'd be no way in a million years her mother would have signed up to an online dating app. Wasn't her scene at all. And definitely no other men in her life.'

Prisha follows him out into the corridor. 'I'll see you back here Monday morning. Good luck with the darts tournament, by the way.'

'Thanks. And cheers for this week. I feel like a copper again, thanks to you,' he says softly.

'You feel like a copper again thanks to yourself, you mean? You've done some excellent work. Keep it up.'

'I intend to. Make sure you get some rest. You look tired.'

'It's not rest I need. It's exercise and healthy food I'm craving. I intend to go for a long run tomorrow, down to Robin Hoods Bay and back. Blow the cobwebs out of my hair.'

'Rather you than me. I'll catch you later.'

'Yeah, bye.' She gazes at him as he hurries into the car park. As she turns to head back to her office, she nearly bumps into George Baxter, who has just finished with the custody sergeant.

He smirks at her. 'That was a right waste of everyone's time, wasn't it?'

'Simply doing my job, Mr Baxter.'

'Aye, well, learn how to do it better. Arresting innocent men when there's a murderer on the loose. You don't know what you're doing, if truth be told,' he adds belligerently as he heads towards the entrance.

'I wouldn't be so cocky if I were you, George. I have released you without charge, but you are still under investigation. I'd say your troubles are only just beginning.'

Sneering back over his shoulder, he says, 'I suppose I'll have to make my own way home.'

'I can arrange for a patrol car to drop you off if you like. I'll ask the officer to drive as slowly as possible through the town.'

'Don't bother. I'll get a cab,' he snarls as the door swings shut behind him.

The squeaky boots of Sergeant Evans telegraph his presence as he sidles up to her shoulder. They both watch Baxter pass the side window and disappear.

'Motive—tick. Murder weapon—tick. No alibi—tick. And you let him go without a charge,' he whispers, a sly grin on his face. 'I hope for your sake he doesn't kill again, otherwise I wouldn't want to be in your shoes.'

34

Frank rubs wearily at his eyes as his mind drifts back to the day when his and Meera's life changed irrevocably. He manages to circumnavigate the memory on most occasions by keeping busy. But sometimes, when his guard is down, the thoughts creep into his brain like malevolent nymphs and unleash a Pandora's Box of guilt.

'Stop it, Frank! This is another reason why I don't want to retire—too much time to think.'

Thankfully, there's a knock on the door followed by the appearance of Superintendent Banks.

'Anne. You wanted to see me?'

She sports her usual frown and solemn disposition, like a low hanging greyish cloud that threatens rain. 'Yes. I haven't long, just a quick heads up,' she says, glancing at her wristwatch. 'I have a meeting with the chief super at three to discuss last month's KPIs.'

'Sounds like fun.'

He receives a pout and a glare, which replaces her usual spoken rebuke. 'It's about Cartwright. There's no point letting these things fester. I've made my decision and I'm going to tell him next week. Can you let him know I want to see him at 4 pm sharp, next Friday?'

Frank's heavy frame creaks in the chair. 'Tell him what?' he asks, already knowing the answer to the question.

'I'm moving him back to uniform. He'll be more use to them than he is to us. And he's now got the experience of CID under his belt. It will add another string to his bow. I've discussed it with head office. I'll complete the paperwork next week.'

'Anne, don't you think you're being a little hasty? I've been in regular contact with Prisha about this double murder, and by her own account Cartwright's turned over a new leaf.'

'You bewilder me sometimes, Frank. How many more chances are you willing to give him? It's Cartwright we're talking about. It's one step forward and two steps back with him. It always has been. And you have been one of his biggest critics over the years. No, my decision is made, and I won't be going back on it. It's good to take the broom out every now and then and sweep the floor. I'm sure he'll prosper back in uniform, and it means we can bring in some fresh blood. Regeneration, Frank, regeneration!'

'We only brought Prisha in three months back.'

'Talking of which, the other day you were complaining about the chain of command. Well, I have two candidates in mind to replace Cartwright. They're a couple of bright up-and-coming PCs from York who are looking for a transfer. They've both passed their detective's test with flying colours. So that will give you a detective constable to add to your two detective sergeants.'

'And wouldn't the obvious solution be to leave Prisha as inspector, then we have a royal flush?' Anne grimaces. 'It's the highest hand in poker—jack, queen, king, ace.'

'Oh, I see. No, as I explained before, Prisha is new on the block, and I want to assess her performance before I make my decision. It's easier to promote than demote someone, as proved by Cartwright's case.'

Frank stands and edges towards her. 'Please, Anne—reconsider? I know I've whinged about Cartwright in the past, and maybe some of his failings are a reflection on me, but let's give him one more chance. I'm begging you, Anne, please.'

'No. He's had more lives than a cat.' She spins around and heads towards the door. 'A week on Friday, Frank, then he's gone. And keep it to yourself!' she shouts as the door slams shut behind her.

He flops into his chair and stares out at the river. 'That is one hard-nosed bitch!'

35

Saturday 21st November

It's a cold and blustery morning, with a few speckles of rain. Prisha jogs past the old Whitby Lighthouse high on the coastal path as a fine spray from the sea falls on her bare arms. The wind whips around as the frigid air stabs at her heaving lungs. Pushing the pain aside, she lifts her pace until she feels she's almost flying, free and unshackled from the burdens weighing her down. As she nears the abbey, she bears left past the Malting Pot Brewery. The chuckle and mew of seagulls, and the crash of distant waves bring her comfort.

By the time she's showered, dressed, and devoured a healthy breakfast of porridge and fruit, it's nearing ten o'clock. Heading to the station with her laptop slung over her shoulder, her clarity of thinking returns as she trawls over the previous week's events. She still doesn't believe Baxter is the killer, so who planted the rifle in his barn, and why Baxter's barn? Was it random or is someone trying to fit him up? And where has he obtained a glut of money from? Cartwright said the deposits were all cash payments. It contradicts Baxter's version that he inherited it from a deceased aunt—not that she believed that for one moment. His financial rebound has only muddied the waters even further.

It's an unwelcome distraction, unless there's a link between the murders and the money. But what?

She grabs a coffee on her way and skips up the station steps and into the CID room. She's surprised to see Zac sitting at his desk, looking tired and a little worried.

'Hi stranger. What brings you in on a Saturday? I thought your boys played football on a weekend?'

He forces a smile. 'Hi Prisha. The lads have a bye this weekend. Thought I'd catch up with some paperwork so I don't have to face it on Monday.'

'Fair enough. I'm glad you're here. I wanted to pick your brains about two scuzz-buckets who briefly entered my world last week.'

'Who would they be?'

'Mike "Razor" Roberts and his brother Steve "Wolf" Roberts.'

He pulls his head back in surprise. 'Now that *is* a coincidence.'

'Why?'

'This undercover thing I've been working on. Well, those two reprobates are involved.'

She pulls up a chair. 'I'm intrigued. Tell me more.'

'I'm not supposed to. It's all hush-hush at the moment.'

'Come on, kiss and tell. There's only you and me here. I won't say anything... cross my heart and hope to die.'

Zac peers sheepishly around the room. 'Okay, but not a word, right? This week has been a nightmare.'

'I must admit, you look stressed, which is most unlike you. Hit me with it, big boy.'

'Remember last week when those two guys came into Frank's office accompanied by the super?'

'Yes.'

'Well...'

———◆———

Thirty minutes pass while both officers relive their past week. Prisha occasionally has to hold back the laughter as Zac relates his experience with DS Beale, whereas he has to suspend disbelief when he hears about Cartwright's miraculous resurrection.

'So you don't think the Roberts would have had anything to do with the murders?' she says as they wrap up.

'I can't see it. That's not their style. If for any reason Albert Shaw was mixed up in the drug importation and he was causing the brothers problems, they'd give him a good hiding. Maybe break a leg or something. But not cold blooded murder of two elderly people.'

'What about the body in the suitcase? If they were involved, it proves they're capable of murder.'

'Yeah, but my gut instinct was that the suitcase was a random find and nothing to do with them. It just so happened to be not too far away from their marijuana farm, and because they're bad boys, they were implicated.'

'Hmm... well, we know there was only one person who pulled the trigger because the bullets were fired from the same rifle within a few seconds of each other.'

'And that's another thing. During our investigation, we discovered nothing to do with firearms.'

'So as strange as it seems that they've turned up in your undercover op and my murder investigation, it's purely chance. Two different lines of enquiry briefly intersecting.'

'I'd say so, yes.' He checks his wristwatch and closes the lid on his laptop. 'Right, I'm done here,' he says as he stands and throws his overcoat on.

'How do you think they're getting the cocaine into the country?' Prisha questions.

He pulls at the zipper on his coat, then packs his laptop into its case. 'We live on an island, which means there's only two ways—by air or sea.'

'What about the Chunnel?'

'That's classified as sea. Right, I guess I'll see you when I see you.'

Prisha rubs at her head and grimaces. 'Yeah, catch you later.'

He gazes down at her. 'Headache?'

'Yes. I think I'm dehydrated.'

'There's paracetamol in my top drawer. Help yourself,' he says as he heads towards the door.

'I think I will. Thanks.' She refills her water bottle from the cooler and heads back to Zac's desk and pulls open the drawer. Picking up the packet of pills, she pops two out and swallows them down with three large gulps of water, then tosses the pills back into the drawer. She hesitates and picks the box up again. 'Price

Slashers Discount Chemist Warehouse,' she murmurs, reading the labelling. 'Lewis Visser... you dark horse.'

36

Sunday 22nd November

Prisha struggles up the staircase with her suitcase and fumbles the door open to her room. She immediately opens the window and breathes in the fresh air and takes in the scene over Settle. It's mid-afternoon, and the town is relatively quiet as persistent mizzle falls from overcast skies.

'Does it never stop raining in Yorkshire?' she whispers. After taking a quick shower and donning her running gear, she unpacks her suitcase and scans her phone for any missed calls or messages. There are none. The room is silent, and she experiences a twinge of loneliness.

'I never thought I'd hear myself say this, but I wish Cartwright was here.' A thought springs to mind, one that has visited a few times over the last week. She had been expecting, or at least hoping, Lewis Visser may have called her. She's barely had time to think about him, but on the rare occasions when she did, she experienced a warm tingling in the pit of her stomach.

'Damn it! What's the worst he can say—no? Nothing ventured, nothing gained.' Taking a deep breath, she taps at his number and waits. 'Please don't go to voice mail,' she mumbles. 'I always get tongue tied and end up sounding like a right dipstick.'

He answers. 'Ah, Prisha, I was just thinking about you,' he says.

Smooth talking bastard. 'Oh, really. What sort of thoughts?' *No, no, no... that sounds weird.*

'I was looking at my calendar to see when I was next available for a climb and wondered if you'd like to buddy up. Unfortunately, I'm pretty busy for the foreseeable future and the weather is so unpredictable at this time of year.'

'I'd love to do another climb with you. Let me know when you're free and call me.'

'I will. So, what can I do for you?'

'What?'

'Your call?'

'Oh, yes. I'm back in Settle and I was wondering if you were available for dinner tonight? That's if you're around, of course. My shout, as you bought the meal last week.'

There's a pause. 'I'd love to, but unfortunately tonight I have other commitments, which is a shame as I am in the holiday house at Malham.'

'Okay. How about tomorrow night?'

'I'm afraid not. Monday and Tuesday I'm away on business.'

'Wednesday?' *Fuck! I'm sounding desperate now.*

'This sounds awful, but I'm tied up with something on Wednesday night as well.'

Well, that told you, girl. Idiot! 'I see. Busy, busy,' she laughs nervously. 'Maybe another time.'

'Definitely. I'd be delighted. Sorry, Prisha.'

'No need to apologise. Have a pleasant evening.'

'You too.'

She hangs up and slumps onto the bed, feeling foolish and slightly humiliated.

'What was all that about? Did he just give me the cold shoulder? He's fifteen years older than me. He should thank his lucky stars I even called him. Maybe I'm overreacting? He's a busy man. That's all it is... I'm sure... I think?'

37

Predictably, George Baxter made up for lost time after missing out on a night's drinking. He got smashed on Friday and Saturday night at his local in Malham, telling anyone who would listen about his wrongful arrest and how the young female inspector is incompetent. Loud, boorish and an angry drunk, it didn't take long before people gave him a wide berth.

It's 5:30 pm on Sunday evening and he's itching for a drink but first he has work to attend to—and it's not farming work. As darkness sweeps across the stark landscape of the dales, he fires up the tractor and navigates into the field behind his farmhouse. Parking up, he waits impatiently, leaving the engine running for the heater to keep the chill away. Taking a little nip of brandy from a hip flask, he stares up at the sky and checks his watch again—5:45 pm.

Jumping from the cab, he strides with purpose to the drystone wall. From behind the wall, a small solar panel is mounted atop a metal pole. He crouches down and flicks a switch. A second later, four red lights in the corners of the field burst into life.

The lights are faint until he nudges a lever on the switch and the intensity of the beams grows brighter. Heading back to the tractor, the familiar low-pitched, steady hum of the plane in the distance travels to him. Back in the cab, he turns on the full beam of the tractor and re-checks his watch. 5:50 pm.

'Let's hope the bloody parachute deploys properly this time,' he mumbles to himself. He cranes his neck and gazes up towards the east and spots the red flashing taillight of the single engine Cessna. He switches the tractor off, pulls down the window, and listens. The engine noise steadily grows louder, then takes on a different tone as the plane rapidly descends. A last glance at his watch—5:55 pm.

'Bang on time,' he confirms. The distinct outline of a plane nears the field about a thousand feet off the ground.

'And there she blows,' he says with a chuckle as the billowing chute suddenly fills with air and makes the attached wooden crate below it jerk violently upwards. 'Come on you bastard, hit the target,' he curses under his breath as he restarts the engine. The chute and illegal cargo land with a heavy thump fifty feet in front of him. The tractor lurches forward and rumbles towards the crate. Baxter makes light work of removing the chute and stashing it in the cab, then carefully lowers the forks until they slide effortlessly under the crate and lift it from the ground. He spins the tractor around and heads back to the farmhouse.

The black transit van is already waiting for him in the barn as he returns. The brothers are standing at the back of the van and as the tractor enters the courtyard, they yank open the rear doors. Baxter slows the tractor, lowers the forks and carefully deposits the crate inside the cargo hold. The van rocks from side to side with a creak and a groan. Baxter kills the engine as one brother approaches the cab and jumps onto the footrail. He passes a bulging backpack through the window.

'How come another drop so soon?' Baxter asks as he snatches the bag and drops it in the footwell.

'New customers and major players, by the sounds of it. This thing is only going to get bigger,' he says, sporting a rare grin.

'I'm going to have to find somewhere else to store my money,' Baxter says.

'Why?'

'The police have been snooping around in my bank accounts. They want to know where the sudden influx of money came from.'

'For fuck's sake! You were told at the start to set up a cryptocurrency account, but you insisted on cash.'

'I don't understand all that shit! I'm a farmer, we deal in cash, always have done.'

'The police are your problem, pal! But if you mention anything about this operation or any names, then you're a dead man! Understand?' he yells, making Baxter flinch.

'Calm down. I'll take care of it. I'm not a grass. Every thing's cool, all right?'

The brother glares at him, leaps from the tractor and climbs into the transit. A squeal of tyres, and the van takes off from the courtyard and speeds up the gravel path.

———◇———

'Yes, I understand. With the aid of binoculars, I can see his car in the pub car park right now. He's been in there over two hours. I called in last night for a quick pint and he was there spraying his mouth off. He can't hold his beer or his tongue. Yes, I agree, he's become a liability. I think it's time you and your brother bought a few acres and earn yourselves some extra money. It's safer with the three of us. You know the route he takes home? Yes, Tarn Road. A lot of sharp bends on that road. Could be treacherous for a habitual drink-driver. I'll text you when he leaves. No mistakes. Another four months and we can all retire extremely wealthy men.'

———◇———

As Baxter emerges from the pub, he burps, then chuckles to himself. The persistent drizzle which set in when he arrived three hours ago has now turned in to heavy, driving rain. He scurries to his car, head down as though it will protect him from the weather. The car beeps twice and he climbs into the driver's seat and starts the engine. The wipers spring into life as music blares from the speakers. He steers the vehicle out of the car park, turns left and sedately drives another two hundred yards before he hangs another left onto Tarn Road. Gently squeezing the foot pedal, the car accelerates as the wipers automatically increase their tempo.

There's a loud rumble as the wheels hit a cattle grid, but the car hugs the road with ease.

Baxter sings along to the song—Rain Drops Keep Falling On My Head. He occasionally interrupts his singing to laugh loudly, pleased with himself. Alcohol has fuelled not only his recklessness but also his sense of invincibility. The car increases in speed as it whizzes around tight bends, the high-beam marking out the narrow lane, ambushed on either side by the ubiquitous drystone walling. After a few minutes, he's almost blinded as a solitary light appears in his rear-view mirror.

'Turn your high-beam off you dickhead!'

The motorbike tails him for a good mile until Baxter reaches a straight piece of road.

'Okay, big boy! You wanna race? I'll give you a fucking race.' He floors the accelerator as the engine screams in annoyance and the car leaves the motorbike in its wake.

'Hahaha! Wanker!' he bellows. Spotting a corner rapidly approaching, he hits the brakes and the engine thumps down through the gears. He has this. It's a safe car, and he's a skilful driver, especially when he's had a few. Halfway around the sharp bend, he spots a large, darkened object rolling towards him. Swinging the car violently to the right and hitting the brake pedal hard, the car slews across the road, crashing through a wall. It rolls twice before coming to rest in a field on its roof, thirty feet from the road.

It took less than three seconds.

Music continues to play as the engine dies. The tractor quickly reverses, using the breach in the stone wall, and heads back the way it came as the motorcyclist pulls up at the crash scene and dismounts. He pulls a hammer and a twelve-inch screwdriver from a pannier, then twists a piece of rag around the tip. Walking over to the car, he bends down and peers inside. Blood drips from Baxter's head and nose as he emits a dazed groan. The rider moves to the back of the car, places the screwdriver tip against the side, and with one hefty thwack punctures the fuel tank. The pungent aroma of petrol quickly fills the air as he removes the cloth from the screwdriver and holds it under the trickle of fuel. Taking a few steps back for safety, he pulls out a lighter, ignites the rag, and tosses it to the ground. He rushes behind the stone wall as the fuel ignites into a thunderous fireball. Crouching low until the last pieces of debris have safely plummeted back to earth, he swings one leg over his motorbike and revs the engine. With a powerful roar, the machine thunders into the night, its headlights spearing through the darkness. Baxter's piercing screams continue to echo in the frosty air for a few seconds before they fade into silence. The music ends. The only sound now, the crackle and hiss of burning plastic, metal, and human flesh and the pit-a-pat of heavy rain hitting stone.

38

Monday 23rd November

Prisha struggles to find a car parking space outside the police station and instead parks under a sign which reads—Police Notice—No Parking. She strolls into the reception and exchanges pleasantries with the desk sergeant, who greets her with a welcoming smile. Pushing open her office door, she stops dead in her tracks and does a double take.

'Morning, Prisha,' Cartwright says, sounding happy and looking well groomed.

'Jason! It's seven-thirty. What are you doing here?'

'Arrived at seven.'

Prisha removes her coat and hangs it up on the back of the door as she detects a pleasant scent of Jason's aftershave, mingled with freshly brewed coffee.

'That would mean you left Whitby at five?'

'Up at four. A quick shower and shave. A bowl of porridge and brew then into the car,' he explains, beaming widely. 'There's a coffee on your desk. It should still be warm. I only got it five minutes ago from a nice little cafe on the high street. Right, are you ready to go or do you want a bit of time to get into it?'

She grins. 'No, I'm raring to go. What have you got?' she says as she takes a seat behind her desk.

'More results from the lab. I did a printout. They're on your desk.' She picks up the sheets and studies them. 'No DNA or blood traces from the victims were found on any of Baxter's clothes or footwear.'

'Hmm... so I see,' she says, disappointed but not surprised.

'But the interesting bit is on page two. That soil sample you scraped together.'

She reads out the breakdown from the lab. 'Clay, silt, sand, gravel, phosphorous, potassium, nitrogen. In other words—soil, duh!' she says, raising her eyebrows.

'Carry on reading.'

'Benzoylecgonine, methylecgonine, and cinnamoylcocaine and cocaine hydrochloride!'

'Aye. What the hell is all that about?' Cartwright says, puzzled.

'Not sure. Cocaine?' She falls silent as her mind becomes a cloudy cauldron of snippets of information and past conversations. Taking a sip from her cup, she stands and peers out of the window.

'Prisha!' Cartwright asks, a little concerned. 'Prisha, are you all right?'

Spinning around, her face is full of excitement. 'I think I have it.'

'The murderer?'

Wincing, she says, 'No, not the murderer.'

'What then?'

'I caught up with Zac on Saturday, at the station. Last week he was working undercover on a big drugs case. Some new players are bypassing this big operation they have running at the moment to stop drugs entering the country by sea.'

'And?'

'The lights.'

'What bloody lights?' Cartwright quizzes becoming increasingly confused.

'The lights Edward Harrowby kept seeing on the moor.'

'Okay, you're freaking me out now. Who the hell is Edward Harrowby? Have we been living in a parallel dimension?'

Prisha ignores him and snatches at the lab report again. 'There's got to be more. I collected a fragment of wood.' Her finger moves quickly down and across the page. 'Here we are; cellulose, lignin, hemicellulose, and extractives, or in layman's term—pine timber.'

'So what? Not an unusual find on a farm.'

'A packing case or a crate,' she murmurs absentmindedly. 'It's all coming together. That's where he's been getting his sudden influx of money from the conniving, devious, toad.'

'Baxter?'

'Yes. The lights Edward Harrowby saw came on for about ten minutes. Four red beams pointing upwards. I bet the drugs are being parachuted in by plane. One of them must have had a heavy landing and split open, hence the coke and fragments of wood in the field.'

'Are you saying Baxter is a dealer?'

'No, no. He's the first receiver, I think. A remote farm is perfect for a drugs drop by air. George doesn't do farming anymore, but that's why he's still got a tractor. To collect the drugs from the field. Guess who else is involved in this drug ring?'

'Lord Lucan?' Cartwright replies, realising any attempt to join the dots would be futile.

'Your friends, Mike and Steve Roberts from the Brigante Motorcycle Club. Zac spotted them at a nightclub in Hull as part of the undercover op.'

'You're shitting me?'

'It's true. I bet they're the dealers, not street dealers, but I reckon they sell wholesale to the big gangs. They have quite a reputation, so no one is going to muscle in on their business. Well, I never,' she says, taking her seat, feeling quite pleased with herself. 'Quite a sophisticated operation.'

'Hell. To look at them all, you wouldn't think they'd have the brains to come up with something like that.'

Prisha's self-satisfied smile mutates into a severe frown. 'No, you wouldn't. Zac said they thought there was at least one other person involved in the operation. Someone with brains, contacts, nous.'

'That's all very interesting, but it doesn't help us catch our killer, does it?'

'No, it doesn't.'

A loud knock on the door and Sergeant Evans marches in, red around the jowls and sporting a scowl. He bypasses any early morning pleasantries.

'I take it you haven't heard the news yet, inspector,' he bellows, hands behind his back, rocking back and forth on his heels.

'What news?' Cartwright asks.

'Last night, around 10 pm there was a single vehicle fatality on Tarn Road a few miles out of Malham.'

'Oh, that's always tragic,' Cartwright sympathises, missing the implication. It doesn't pass Prisha by as she feels a knot in her stomach tighten.

'Any guesses who the deceased was?' Evans continues, revelling in his cat-and-mouse game and expecting no reply.

'George Baxter,' Prisha murmurs, her mind once again spinning.

Evans narrows his eyes. 'Aye, it's not one hundred per cent confirmed yet, as there's not much left of him. But we recovered the vehicle identification number and a partial number plate, and it matches his Audi A8. We sent a couple of officers over to his farm earlier and there's no sign of him. He was last seen leaving the Lister Arms around ten last night—five sheets to the wind.'

Prisha shoots Cartwright a look, telepathically asking for an interpretation.

'Pissed,' he explains.

'I'll let you know when we get a positive identification on him.' He half turns to leave, then stops. 'If he was the murderer, he won't be going to trial now, will he? Maybe it would have been wise to charge him and keep him on remand,' he states with condescension. The door is slammed shut harder than necessary as he departs.

'What an arsehole,' Cartwright says.

'Worse than that, he's a bloody hypocrite. When I first bandied Baxter's name around, he scoffed at the idea he could be involved in the murder. Said I was wasting time. Then when we found the murder weapon at Baxter's barn, he suddenly sees him as Yorkshire's new serial killer.'

'Some coppers are like that. They get obsessed with the shiny, new, bright object until another shiny, new, bright object happens along. You don't think we ruled Baxter out too quickly, do you?'

'We didn't rule him out. He was still under investigation, but I'm damn sure he didn't kill Albert and Maxine.'

'Here's a thought, Prisha. What if Albert and Maxine saw the parachute with the drugs attached? Baxter clocks them and panics. How could he be certain they wouldn't report it to the police? Or what about the Roberts brothers. They'd be damn better shots than Baxter.'

Prisha isn't convinced but considers the suggestion. 'Hmm... Charlene Marsden said the entry points of the bullets indicated they were looking up at the sky. It is possible Albert and Maxine saw the parachute. But we've narrowed down the time of their death to between 9:30 and 1 pm. Who would do a drugs drop by parachute during the day? Too risky.'

'You were in Malham on Saturday. Have you forgotten what the weather was like?'

'No. It turned to shit.'

'Maybe they knew they wouldn't be able to make a drop that night because of the weather and brought it forward. A little risky but with mist and rain around in mid-November, there'd be fewer walkers about.'

'Okay, let's analyse the scenario. Albert and Maxine spot the parachute. Baxter or the Roberts brothers see them, panic and take them out. Think of the risk factor for them. Two walkers go missing. After a few days, the place will be swarming with police, rescue volunteers, the public, sniffer dogs, drones. And just for good measure, someone is stupid enough to leave the murder weapon in Baxter's barn. Come on, really? Why wittingly invite all that attention to the area? Now let's look at another scenario. If Albert and Maxine spotted the drop, so what? After finishing their walk and returning to Settle by bus, which is about another two hours, they may, or may not have reported their sighting to the police, and what would their response have been? Maybe send an officer up there to have a nosey around. They wouldn't even know what they were looking for and by the time they arrived, the drugs would be somewhere else, probably at the Brigante Clubhouse. Which scenario sounds more plausible?'

Cartwright ponders. 'Aye, you're right. Why bring attention to yourself? It doesn't add up.'

'Exactly,' Prisha says slipping into her coat.

'Okay, boss, what's the go?'

'Get at least six uniforms together and head to Baxter's farm. Take someone who knows the area well to identify the boundaries. I want you to walk every wall of his land and find those lights. A car battery or solar panel must power them.'

'Wilko. Where are you going?'

'I'm going to pay another visit to Mr Harrowby.'

'Aren't you going to tell Zac what you know?'

'What I think I know. Yes, I'll call him from the car. If you find the lights, then it confirms our suspicions. By the way, I forgot to ask. You called in at Pickering on your way home on Friday to check on Craig Shaw's alibi. How'd you go?'

'The landlord confirmed Craig entered about one-thirty on Saturday. Had a couple of pints then left. Maybe there for about forty minutes.'

'And didn't Craig say he was at his mother's on Saturday morning about nine, to make her breakfast?' she says hurriedly, fastening the buttons on her coat.

'That's right,' he says with a frown. 'She seemed a bit confused.'

'Understandable, considering.'

'She thought it was Sunday that Craig made her breakfast.'

'Really?'

'Yes. Then she backtracked and said maybe it was Saturday.'

'Hmm...' she says.

'I know your—hmm. What are you thinking?'

'Considering her condition, and the fact he only lives five minutes away, wouldn't you think he'd have made her breakfast on both mornings while Albert was away?'

Cartwright shrugs. 'Maybe he did, and she's forgotten or got muddled up. Or possibly on Sunday he wasn't around.'

'Yeah. I guess. When you get a free moment, work out the timings based on our estimated time of murder and Craig's alibi.'

'Will do. By the way, you haven't asked how my team went in the darts comp on Saturday night?'

Prisha widens her eyes, appalled at her faux pas knowing how much it means to him. 'So sorry, Jason. I clean forgot all about it. Well, how did you go?' His downcast face telegraphs the answer. 'Oh, Jason, I'm so sorry for you. Never mind, there's always next year,' she says softly, like a mother comforting a child.

He jumps from his seat and pumps the air. 'We only bloody went and won! We're into the regionals now.'

She walks over and gives him a big hug, even though her interest in darts is less than zero. 'I'm so pleased for you. When's the next game?'

'Match.'

'Sorry, match.'

'Next Saturday in Scarborough. It's gonna be a tough one but I'm feeling confident. Two more wins and we're into the nationals.'

She has no idea what that means and isn't going to ask. 'Great. Tell me which pub it's at and I'll come along and support you.'

His face drops. 'Oh no,' he says gravely. 'I don't even let my missus come and watch. Sorry to sound sexist, but wives, girlfriends, or female acquaintances are a no-no. They're a jinx. The team would tar and feather me if you showed up.'

She laughs as she heads to the door. 'Yes, that is sexist, but I'll turn a blind eye this once. To be honest, I'd rather read a good book.'

39

Entering the narrow driveway of Edward Harrowby's idyllic cottage, she finishes her call with Zac, parks up, then raps the doorknocker three times. As she waits, she marvels at the unspoilt beauty of the countryside.

I could live here. The house would need a complete renovation, but the location is stunning. A four-hour round-trip commute to Whitby every day wouldn't work. I'd have to get a transfer to York or Northallerton. Still over an hour each way, though.

She knocks on the door again, this time louder as grumbling emanates from inside.

'Hold your 'osses! What's the bloody rush?' The front door swings open. 'Nah then, lass, what does thee want?' Edward asks scrambling his spectacles onto his head.

Prisha holds her warrant card out. 'It's me Edward, Inspector Kumar. We spoke last week about the lights.'

He gazes at the badge, oblivious to her explanation. 'Is this about those little buggers I saw legging gravel at passing cars t'other day?'

'No, Edward. It's about the lights—the red lights you saw on Malham Moor. You remember? I was here last week.'

Squinting at her, he suddenly recalls the event. 'Oh, aye. That's reet. Come in, lass, you should have said.' She rolls her eyes and enters the kitchen. 'I'm making a cuppa. Do you want one?'

'No, thank you.'

'Suit thy sen.'

'Last week, as I was leaving, you mentioned something about strip lights flashing on and off.'

'That's reet. On, off, on, off, on, off.'

She takes a deep breath as he fills the kettle. 'And you saw them only once?'

'Aye.'

'Do you remember what day you saw them?'

'I do,' he says, as though accepting his wedding vows.

'Well?' she persists.

'Well, what?'

Agitated, she rubs at her neck. 'What day did you see the flashing lights?'

'The ones that went on, off, on, off or t'other ones which went straight up?'

She's quickly losing the will to live. 'The ones which went on, off, on, off.' *Christ, he's got me at it now.*

'What about them?'

She resists the urge to scream and stab him with a sharp object. 'The-day-you-saw-them,' she spits the words out slowly... enunciating clearly.

'The on, off, on, off, lights?'

'YES! The bloody on, off, on, off, lights!' she yells.

'Nay, lass. No need to shout. I'm not deaf tha knows.'

She drops her head into her hands and nearly weeps. 'Please, Edward, just tell me the day?' she implores.

'Week last Saturday. The same day as those two murders. Have yer found the bastard who did it yet?'

'No. Not yet.'

'They should be hung, drawn and quartered when you find them. Killing old folk out for a peaceful walk. The world's going to hell in a handbasket.'

She's contemplating cutting her losses, having got the answer she came for. But she'd really like to confirm a time of day but runs the risk of being up on a murder charge herself.

She pulls her chest back and fills her lungs. 'You're certain it was a week last Saturday... the fourteenth?'

'Aye. Dead set.'

She assumes that's a confirmation. 'Last question, Edward; do you recall the time of day?'

'About nine-thirty in the morning coz the news on the radio had just finished.'

Sweet merciful lord, I thank you! She turns to leave, having survived the ordeal. 'Thank you for your time, Edward. You've been very helpful.'

'Saw them again last night.'

She stops. 'The lights?'

'Aye,' he says as the kettle clicks off and he busies himself with pouring the boiling water into an ancient teapot.

Dare I ask which type of lights? I could end up here for the rest of my life. 'Which type of lights were they?'

'The usual lights. The ones that go straight up. Came on about ten minutes before six.'

'At night?'

He stares at her as though she's stupid. 'I just bloody said that, didn't I? You need to clean yer lugholes out, lass. Sure you can't stay for a brew?'

'Maybe next time, Edward,' she says as she makes a quick exit. 'Thanks again.'

She scurries towards her car as he stands on the threshold. 'And what yer gonna do about those young 'uns legging gravel at cars? They need their arses tanned.'

<hr />

Back at the station, as she awaits the return of Cartwright, she makes another call to Zac then rings Frank to give him an update.

'I agree, it is unlikely, but don't rule out the Roberts brothers all together,' Frank says. 'They're running a sophisticated drug importation business which is making them very rich, very quickly. If they felt their operation was compromised, who knows what they're capable of? People have died for far less.'

'I'll keep that in mind. Our only other suspect at the moment is the son, Craig Shaw.'

'When you spoke with Mary, did she indicate whether Craig and Albert had a fractious relationship?'

'Well, no, but I didn't ask. It was a missing persons investigation at that point, initially categorised as—absent.'

'Okay. You will need to interview her again, but tread lightly. And remember, our killer may not have even walked onto the stage yet, so keep all your options open.'

———◆———

Munching on a tuna sandwich, she scans her emails and notices a message from the gun dealership in London. Attached is an Excel file, which she quickly prints out and studies. There are thirty-five names on it who purchased a rifle which matches the make, model, material, and colour of the murder weapon. She traces her finger down the column of names, but none jump out. Next, she checks the addresses which cover a fair breadth of the country. Near the bottom of the list, she pauses. An address of interest—a post office box in Pickering, but unfortunately the name tallies with a Mr Brown.

Damn it! Who the hell is Mr Brown?

A clatter of voices and laughter break her attention as the search team arrives back at the station. A moment later, Cartwright walks in grinning like the proverbial Cheshire Cat and carrying a plastic bag.

'I take it by the smile on your dial you had a win?' she says.

'Aye, a big win,' he says donning a pair of latex gloves then carefully lifting an object from the bag. He places it on her desk. 'Don't touch it.'

'It looks like something from a car's suspension.'

'It's a high-powered laser light. One of the lads in uniform is a part-time DJ. He reckons these things are pretty powerful. You can buy four of them for less than a grand. They were mounted on fixings attached to the walls in the field immediately behind Baxter's farmhouse. Powered by a solar panel. We've left the other three in situ and taken photos. The police photographer will load the images onto the system straight away he's had his lunch.'

'You'll need to return this and reattach it,' she says.

'Yeah, I know. And...' he says pulling out his phone. 'I got a few snaps of my own. A big plastic tarp and rolled up inside—a bank of red LED lights. Covers about four-square metres,' he explains, passing her his mobile.

'Ah, it's the on, off, on, off, lights,' she murmurs, scrolling the images.

Cartwright stares at her, puzzled. 'The on, off, lights?'

She waves her hand at him. 'Never mind. Why two different lighting systems?'

'According to the lad in uniform, he reckons lasers are great at night but weak during daylight—something to do with diffusion. But coloured flashing LED or halogen lights can be clearly seen during the day. Think of your car brake or indicator lights.'

'I see. So they've got night time and day time drops covered.'

'Yep.'

'Hey, we received some info back from the gun dealership,' she states as Cartwright pulls a pork pie from the small bar fridge in the corner and takes a seat. 'A rifle was sold to a Mr Brown of Pickering eighteen months ago.'

'Address?'

'PO box. After lunch, I want you to call Craig Shaw and ask him to come into the Pickering Police Station tomorrow—voluntarily. Tell him we need to clear up some details. Before that, go to the post office and obtain the address of the owner of the PO box. You'll need a warrant.'

'Yeah, I know. I have been doing this job a while,' he says, clearly annoyed.

'Sorry. That's unforgivable. You know what's happening to me—I'm turning into Frank. Oh, my god, I've become a micromanager without realising it.'

Cartwright chuckles. 'Don't worry about it, Prisha. I inadvertently do it to senior constables in uniform. There's no malice intended.'

'Yes, but we're both sergeants on the same level.'

'No, we're not. You're an inspector now.'

'Acting inspector until the end of the month, then I'm back down to sergeant.'

'Bullshit!'

'It's true.'

'Superintendent Banks?'

'Yep. She doesn't want to make the position permanent as she thinks it will be interpreted as a token gesture.'

'That's crap. You've worked on two high-profile cases in the last three months and been fore and centre of them. Without your skills, they may never have been solved.'

'Thanks for the compliments, but it was more about Frank than me.'

'I disagree. Frank's good, but you're right up there with him. How do you feel about going back to sergeant?'

'Angry at first, but now it's made me more determined than ever. How does the song go—I get knocked down...'

'... and I get up again. Aye, classic tune. Back to the murders. Is Craig Shaw now in your sights?'

She waggles her cheeks from side to side. 'He wasn't, but after what you said about Mary not being sure which day he called to make breakfast, he's on the radar. Although, we have the mysterious Mr Brown from Pickering, who's entered the game. If you obtain his address from the post office tomorrow, and track him down, then he needs to produce his rifle.'

'If he can show me his rifle then he's off the hook.'

'Exactly. And if he can't, then he's suspect number one and we bring him in for questioning.'

'Why do you want me to interview Craig at the station instead of at his home?'

'A police interview room is more intimidating. I want you to witness his body language. Although, just because someone acts nervous, or jittery, is not an admission of guilt—despite what the old hands say. We know a lot more about anxiety and depression these days.'

'I've interviewed guys who went down for cold blooded murder, and they were as cool as cucumbers, and some were quite likeable. Killers come in all shapes and sizes.'

'Very true. We need to spend the rest of the day tying up the loose ends around here, because tomorrow, we're going to be in Pickering for most of the day. While you chase up Mr Brown and Craig Shaw, I'm going to visit Mary Shaw again, which is not going to be pleasant.'

'We'll lose four bloody hours in the car.'

'Can't be helped.' She collects her lunch rubbish and drops it in the bin. As she pulls open the door, she glances over her shoulder, first at Cartwright, then at the laser light on her desk. 'Jason?'

'Yes,' he says devouring the last of his pork pie.

'Why did you bring the laser light back to the station?'

'Thought you'd like to see it.'

'But we have photos.'

He shrugs. 'I guess.'

'Hmm... get it back to where it was as soon as. We don't want anyone noticing it missing, otherwise they'll be suspicious.'

'Oi! What does the hmm... mean?' he shouts after her as the door closes.

40

Tuesday 24th November

The wiper blades squeak and shudder across the windshield, leaving a streak of watery trails in their wake. A ray of sunshine occasionally pierces drab clouds overhead, illuminating fallow fields and spindly thickets on the undulating hills.

Feeling groggy from a restless night, Cartwright wipes sleep from his eyes, and takes a slurp of his sugary coffee. Prisha flicks the indicator and accelerates onto the main road that leads to Pickering. The car radio is tuned to a local station, a mixture of news and talkback callers airing their grievances. Being in a rural area, most complaints are about council bylaws, roadworks, and the price of stock feed.

Something niggles at Prisha. If Craig Shaw, and the mystery man—Mr Brown—are eliminated from their investigation today, she's back to square one, with no other suspect apart from the unlikely Roberts brothers and the deceased George Baxter. Has she missed something, or could Frank be right? Maybe the killer hasn't even entered the frame yet?

They drive on in relative silence for a good hour and stop off in Harrogate to refuel the car and grab a coffee and a cheese toasty. The food appears to revive Cartwright, who relives his victorious darts match in graphic detail to Prisha. She feigns interest, but her mind wanders back to the investigation. As Cartwright's detailed account of his team's triumph finally ends, she jumps in before he can retell it again.

'Did you do any work on the timeline regarding Craig Shaw's alibi?' she asks.

'What? Oh, aye,' he replies, retrieving his notebook from his jacket pocket.

'Hit me with it,' she says, turning the radio off.

'Okay. I've been going over the notes again. Albert and Maxine left the guest house at 7:30 am. It's a two hour walk to Vertigo Alley where they were found, making it 9:30 am. Maxine asked Mrs Winterbottom, the owner of the guest house, what time the tea rooms opened in Malham, she said, 9:30, to which Maxine replied, good, we should be there before eleven. The walk from Settle to Malham via the cove takes three hours and fifteen minutes. Add another fifteen minutes for a rest stop and the timeline is bang on with what Maxine indicated their intentions were. Let's say our killer is Craig Shaw. If he shot them at 9:30, returned to Settle, which takes two hours, making it 11:30, then drove from Settle to Pickering, which is another two hours, the earliest he could have got back is one-thirty.'

'The time he went to the pub.'

'Yes.'

'So theoretically, it is possible?'

'Yes, but bloody tight. If Albert and Maxine took a detour for anything longer than say, fifteen minutes, then there's no way Craig Shaw could have got back to the pub by one-thirty.'

'You're assuming he parked in Settle, followed them, then returned. What if he parked near to the murder spot and waited for them? That would give him ample time to get back to Pickering.'

'Then why not show his face sooner back in Pickering? And how would he know where Albert and Maxine were heading to? Even Mary didn't know.'

'Hmm... you're right. And what's his motive? Angry that his father is cheating on his mother? That sort of thing can lead to a big family fall out, but a double murder is unlikely.'

'Aye, it is a bit of a stretch.'

'What about his vehicle, the Land Rover? Have you checked the ANPR records?'

'Yes. It's registered in Mary's name. He probably gets cheaper insurance. Older lady driver and all that. There's no record of it on any of the main roads on the day of the murder.'

'What about the days before? Remember that Albert and Maxine arrived in Settle on the Friday.'

'Yep, checked that. Even went back as far as Wednesday, and zippo. But there are plenty of back roads you can take from Pickering to Settle without being pinged by a camera. But it obviously takes longer.'

'Meaning it's even less likely he could have arrived back at the pub by one-thirty.'

'Correct.'

'It's all very flaky. What time did you ask him to come to Pickering Police Station?'

'One.'

'What did he say?'

'Asked why we couldn't talk over the phone. I told him I had some mugshots I wanted him to look at.'

'The Roberts brothers?'

'Yes, a ruse to allay his suspicions.'

'Good work, Cartwright. Frank will be proud of you. Good old-fashioned methodical police work. I'm intrigued to find out about this Mr Brown. He's looking more like a potential candidate.'

'Yeah, what are the odds of an exact copy of the murder weapon being purchased by someone from a tiny village where Albert and Maxine lived? Very fishy.'

———◦———

The car pulls up a hundred yards from Mary Shaw's address.

Prisha grabs her bag from the backseat. 'I shouldn't be longer than thirty minutes. I'll meet you at that caff we visited last week. Say about, midday?'

'Sounds good.'

'I'm looking forward to this like a hole in the head,' she adds as she steps out of the car, and Cartwright slips across into the driver's seat with some difficulty. 'Wish me luck.'

The elderly postmistress is less than enthusiastic with Cartwright's request.

'We take the privacy of our customers very seriously sergeant,' she says, peering over her glasses at him.

'I'm sure you do Mrs...'

She's not forthcoming with her name. 'It's a matter of trust and confidentiality,' she adds in a hushed whisper as a customer enters.

'My investigation is also very serious, Mrs...'

'It's a small town and gossip spreads like wildfire.'

'I can assure you; I will be discreet. The gentleman in question won't even be aware of how I obtained his address. And I have the appropriate warrant, as issued by a magistrate, to obtain the address of the man in question,' he adds more firmly.

'May I ask what your investigation is concerning in relation to Mr Brown?'

'I'm sorry. That's confidential. We wouldn't want to start the gossip mill, would we?'

She pouts, gives him a good once over with her beady, mistrustful eyes, and heads into a backroom. 'Give me a moment.' She returns and holds out her clenched fist. 'Here. I've jotted it down,' she whispers as she drops the slip of paper into Cartwright's hand.

He smiles. 'Thank you, Mrs...'

'Good day sergeant.'

He saunters outside into the mizzle and pulls his collar up. 'It's never easy,' he mutters to himself as he reads the address. For a split-second, he experiences a sense of déjà vu, but it immediately vanishes.

Parking outside the small semi-detached house he suddenly feels quite nervous.

If this guy is the killer, then his reaction could be unpredictable when I ask to see his rifle. What's he going to do? Shoot me? As if!

His positive reaffirmation doesn't quell his unease. He ambles up to the front door, fills his lungs with air, then presses the bell, warrant card at the ready. He sees a shape behind the frosted glass. The click of a latch and the door opens.

'Oh, it's you,' says the man.

Cartwright's mind turns to mush as the strict laws of reality melt away.

41

Prisha takes her time as she strolls to the rendezvous with Cartwright. Her meeting with Mary Shaw was painful for all concerned. Thankfully, Mary's sister was by her side to offer her comfort and reassurance.

She explained that her impromptu visit was a courtesy call to see how she was coping and to give her an update on the investigation, and also some good news—if you could call it that; the coroner's inquest was complete and Albert's body would be released back to the family, meaning they could now organise the funeral. As good news went, it wasn't up there with winning the lottery. The sordid issue of what Albert was doing with Maxine Wood was never raised. Her name only came up once when Mary referred to her as—*that* other woman. Prisha tiptoed around the thorny issue of her son's alibi, explaining it was standard police procedure to ascertain the whereabouts of all close family members, solely to eliminate them from the investigation. It was a half-lie, or maybe a half truth. If Prisha was hoping for some ground-breaking revelation, she was sorely disappointed. Mary couldn't be sure what day Craig arrived to make breakfast, vacillating between

Saturday and Sunday, before finally saying she thought maybe he visited her on both days.

Checking her phone, she notes there's no message from Cartwright, meaning his mission probably proved negative, as well. If Mr Brown couldn't produce his rifle, then Cartwright would have been onto her straight away to let her know he was heading to the station with Mr Brown under arrest. Her worst fears were materialising rapidly. No further headway with Craig Shaw and a possible dead end with Mr Brown.

Walking into the café, she spots Cartwright sitting in a corner. Oddly enough, all he has in front of him is a cup of tea. She waves to him, but he doesn't see her, obviously caught up in his own thoughts. Ordering a Cornish pasty and a cup of tomato soup, she heads to the table.

She takes a seat and bites into the pasty. 'You first,' she says, mumbling her words. 'I'm starving.' Cartwright stares back, white faced, eyes on stalks but says nothing. 'What's wrong with you? And why aren't you eating? Are you unwell?'

'I can hear Frank's booming voice right now,' he drawls, lost in a daze.

Prisha grimaces and places her food down on the plate. 'What are you talking about?'

'He'll be red in the face, jowls wobbling, yelling. Shoddy, sloppy police work, Cartwright! You're a disgrace to the uniform. What were you thinking? You weren't bloody thinking, were you?'

Prisha reaches out and touches the back of his hand. 'Jason, take your time. Deep breath. What's happened?'

'Mr Brown,' he stammers, then stops.

'Yes, what about Mr Brown?'

'Mr Brown is...'

She's losing patience fast. 'Mr Brown is?' she prompts

'Mr Brown is... Craig Shaw.'

42

It takes a moment for the enormity of his words to sink in before her mind goes into overdrive, whereas Cartwright's mind seems to have given up the ghost completely. Prisha sees a massive breakthrough. Cartwright sees only ignominy.

'Did you ask to see the rifle?'

'No. I was flummoxed. I said I was in the area to see some other witnesses and was passing and called by to say I'd put the meeting at the station back by half an hour.'

'Why did you say that?'

'I froze. I lost it. From day one, I assumed his last name was Shaw. I never checked. Then when I got his details at the rugby ground after the search was called off—the address was the same as Mr Brown—but I missed it.'

'So what? How many addresses are we supposed to keep in our head? Anyway, you only got the address thirty minutes ago.'

'There's more. Again, at the rugby ground, I briefly questioned him about his work.'

'He said he was a handyman.'

'Yes, but something else he said that I didn't jot down.'

'What?'

'He said he received a small pension.'

'He's ex-services?'

'I assume so. Now that I think about it, he looks the type.'

'Fuck!'

'Exactly. How many stuff ups is that? Three at least... and counting. Frank will do his nut.'

Prisha is understandably livid with him about not mentioning the pension. As for the last name, well, she was as guilty as Cartwright in assuming his name was Shaw. Obviously, Mary was previously married before she met Albert.

'Right, listen to me, Jason, and listen good. First up—pull yourself together. This is a good thing. We could be a few hours away from arresting our killer. We have a motive—money. When Mary passes away, which won't be long, then the house and their joint savings would have gone to Albert. And when he goes, who's he going to leave everything to? His own daughter in Australia or his stepson? Next: opportunity. We've established it's possible to have been at the murder scene on Malham Moor at nine-thirty and still get back to Pickering by one-thirty. And one thing we didn't consider about the timeline—we based it all on a steady walking pace. Craig Shaw is a fit-looking man. If he jogged back, he could have knocked thirty to forty minutes off the time, which means he could have taken the back roads. We know there was only one shooter as the bullets came from the same gun. Which means a top marksman made those shots. I'll bet you Craig Shaw... sorry Craig Brown was in the Army, the infantry or maybe even the special forces with those shooting skills. We also have unidentified DNA on the rifle to fall back on, and if Craig can't produce his rifle, then where is it? Motive, opportunity, and ability.'

'But when Frank finds out about the pension, I'm for the high jump. It was last Wednesday when Craig told me about it. That's a whole a week wasted,' he laments.

'And how will Frank find out if a pension was mentioned? I won't tell him.'

He appears surprised. 'You won't?'

'No, and neither will you. If he asks you straight up about it, then yes, you're going to have to front up. But what are the chances of that?'

'What if Craig brings it up when we interview him?'

'Do you think Frank's going to listen to hours of interview tapes? That's our job, not a DCIs.'

'Maybe, but the CPS will.'

'If they do, and they spot it, then so what? You fucked up, as we all do occasionally. We're humans, not bloody machines. It's not a hanging offence. All Frank and the CPS are bothered about is collecting enough solid evidence to get a conviction.'

He breathes a sigh of relief as the colour returns to his cheeks. 'Okay, I feel better, I think.'

'I need you with me Jason, we've a shitload of work to get through this afternoon and I can't manage it without you. Are you back onboard?'

A whisper of a smile passes over his lips. 'Yeah, sorry. I really dropped my shit for a moment.'

'Good. At one-thirty you're going to arrest Craig Brown. Once the custody sergeant has finished with him, put him in the holding cells and get his DNA swab off to forensics ASAP and tell them it's bloody urgent. We'll interview him first thing tomorrow, which gives us a bit of breathing space to line our ducks up in a row. Now get your lunch because you're fading away in front of me,' she adds with a grin.

He stands up. 'What's the Cornish like?'

'Bloody delish.'

'I might try a couple. I am feeling peckish. Thanks, Prisha. I won't forget this.'

43

The phone rings on Cartwright's desk.

'Cartwright,' he says confidently, belying his inner turmoil.

'I've a Craig Brown in reception. He says he's got a one-thirty with you,' the desk sergeant says.

'I'll be right out.' He adjusts his tie, brushes his jacket down, and strides out into reception. Craig is sitting on a chair, wearing a dark green parka, hands thrust deep into his pockets. He rises as Cartwright approaches.

'You said this should take a few minutes, yeah?' he asks.

'Slight change of plan,' Cartwright replies.

'Go on?' he says, a little suspiciously.

'Craig Brown, I am arresting you on suspicion of the murder of Albert Shaw and Maxine Wood. You do not have to say anything. But it may harm your defence...'

44

Zac is not in the best of moods. He was hoping he'd never see DS Beale again and now here the man is, in the Whitby CID room, sitting in Zac's chair with his feet resting on *his* desk. Zac places the cup of tea down in front of him and pulls up a chair.

'How was your weekend?' Beale asks as he takes a sip of the brew and grimaces. 'I hope it was better than your tea making abilities. This tastes like essence of turd mixed with hot water.'

He ignores the barb. 'Weekend? Good, I think. Long time ago now.'

'Two fucking days ago, that's all.'

He's not used to small talk with Beale, and it slightly unsettles him. 'How was your weekend?'

'Nice of you to ask. Fucking shite, if truth be told. I spent Saturday morning in the office as some geeky, spotty faced fucking muppet gave me a crash course on the intricacies of cryptocurrency on a Zoom conference call. Not only that, but I was nursing the mother and father of all fucking hangovers after my ma's seventieth birthday bash the evening before. Christ, I drank some piss that night. When I woke up the next day, I was pleasantly surprised to find myself still alive, until I rolled out of bed. Then I wished I'd fucking choked to death on my own vomit during the night. I've only just come good today.'

'How did you go with the cryptocurrency stuff... up to speed?'

'You take a punt. I barely had a pulse and was suffering from triple vision as the little weasel turd banged on and on and fucking on. Four hours he was at it. The snivelling, wee, pustule. He was barely out of nappies. At one point I could swear his nanny came in to breast feed him—although I put that down to my blurred vision. It looked like one tit sucking on another tit from where I was sitting.'

'It's safe to say you're none the wiser then?'

'Correct. It doesn't matter though. They sent the walking, talking, limp-pricked computer chip over to set up my phone with everything I need. Just one app, apparently. The account is all set up. They've transferred forty grand into it. All I've got to do tomorrow night is pull my phone out and hover my finger over the Transfer Now button once I've seen the cocaine. Then the cavalry arrives, led by none other than your good self.'

'Yeah, thanks for roping me into the sting operation. It's appreciated.'

'No worries, fur ball. Share the kudos, that's my motto. You may even get a promotion to inspector if this little shit show goes according to plan. Of course, if it goes tits up, you could end up dead, or worse.'

'What's worse than death?'

He scoffs. 'Loads of things. You could be a Rangers fan, or have an inverted penis, or be trapped in a lift with a ghost—or god forbid—all three.'

'A ghost?'

'Aye, a fucking ghost. I don't trust the wispy, see-through little bastards.'

Zac knows Beale is socially delinquent, but he's now considering the fact he could be mentally unstable. 'No, they cannae be trusted,' he murmurs, humouring him.

Beale looks around impatiently. 'Where the fuck are DCI Finnegan and Keegan? It's past two now.'

'They went to lunch together.'

'Oh, how fucking sweet. Do you think they're old lovers?'

'Something tells me not.'

'You never know. Stranger things happen at sea. By the way, thanks for the intel on the bonehead brothers and the drop point in the dales. Funny that fucking farmer should die in a car crash, though. What's his name?'

'George Baxter.'

'Aye, that's the one. Do you think it's sus?'

'Not sure. Collision investigation are still preparing their report.'

'Sounds dodgy to me. Anyway, one less scrote in the world has got to be a good thing.' He takes another sip of tea. 'Fuck, that's disgusting. Of course, I'm blaming you, but it's probably the shitty English water.' He leans back in his chair and smirks.

'So, big man, how are you going with that little piece of skirt from Hull? What's her name, Tilly?'

Zac nervously looks around the office. The only other person in the room is an older woman civvy performing data entry. Luckily, she's out of earshot.

'Her name's Lilly, and I'd be grateful if you never mentioned her again,' he hisses in a strained whisper.

Beale holds his hands up in apology. 'Okay, point taken. What happens on tour stays on tour. I'll never mention her again. Cross my heart and hope to die.'

'Thank you.'

'So, have you banged her little tush yet or what?' he says, grinning.

The door is thrust open and in walks DCI Finnegan and DCI Keegan, laughing and joking and in excellent humour unlike a certain other police detective in the room.

'Thank god,' Zac moans.

Beale leans in towards Zac and whispers. 'Look at them. Like two young lovers. Which one do you reckon's the pillow biter? I'll put my money on Keegan. Can't imagine Frank taking one up the rusty bullet hole. Not his style.'

With the other three seated in Frank's office, DCI Hedley Keegan runs through the operation with the aid of the whiteboard.

'We've dubbed tomorrow night's sting, Operation Greenhorn,' he says, writing the name on the board in perfect block letters.

'Fuck me,' Beale murmurs under his breath.

Frank chuckles, 'Nice name, Hedley. This new gang is inexperienced and, luckily for us, naïve.'

'Indeed,' replies Keegan. 'However, it doesn't mean they're not dangerous and we mustn't underestimate them. Thanks to the intel from DS Stoker, we've pinpointed where and how they are getting their supply of cocaine.'

'I can't take credit for that, sir. The intel came from DI Kumar working on a murder case in the dales.'

Keegan smiles at Frank. 'You have a good team around you, Frank.'

'Aye. I'm proud of them all.'

'Sheesh,' Beale mutters under his breath.

Keegan continues. 'Twice a month, a Cessna 172 Skyhawk has been taking off from a private airstrip outside Rotterdam. It flies up the east coast as far as Scarborough before banking left. As it approaches Malham Moor, it rapidly descends from eight thousand feet to a thousand feet, and once it nears the markers on the ground, red laser lights, or flashing LED lights, it jettisons its cargo. From there, the now deceased landowner, George Baxter, collected the cargo. We're uncertain what happens to it after that, but we're guessing the Roberts brothers pick it up, then drive it to places unknown. We know they must have a tablet press and an encapsulation machine to turn the powder into tablets and capsules. It's quite a clever marketing ploy. If you want a longer lasting hit from the cocaine, you simply swallow a tablet. If you're after an instant high, you pull the capsule apart and snort the contents.'

Beale stifles a yawn. 'Aye, whoever thought of that should be on Mastermind.'

'And as noted at our first meeting, the tablets are stamped with a boar's head, which is the emblem of the Brigante Motorcycle Club, of which Mike and Steve Roberts are president and vice president.'

'Aye, that idea will be the fuck knuckle twins. They may as well have stamped their fucking address on there as well.'

'Ahem, yes, continuing. The brothers contacted DS Beale this morning via an encrypted messaging app, namely Wickr.'

'Do you mind if I take it from here, sir?' Beale asks, becoming increasingly bored with DCI Keegan's long-winded manner. 'After all, it is me who will walk into the lion's den.'

'No, of course not. The floor is yours.'

Beale shoots a glance south. 'I'm not sure I want the floor by the state of it. When was the last time this thing was steam cleaned? But anyway, the message specified a day, a time, and two coordinates. I could understand the day and time bit; tomorrow, Wednesday night, at eight-thirty—I'm gifted like that. As for the coordinates, they may as well have been speaking double fucking Dutch. But we got some snotty nosed, habitual masturbator onto it and they pinpointed the location as a layby off the A65 close to a place called Hellifield, which is a fifteen-minute drive from the Brigante Clubhouse, and a twenty-five-minute drive from George Baxter's place on Malham Moor.

'I studied the map around that area for at least five minutes and it's just one big open space of fuck-all. My theory is, I'll meet one brother at the layby. They'll either put me in their vehicle and drive me to the exchange point, or one of them will blindfold me and drive my car there. Oh, one other possibility—they've found out I'm an undercover copper, and not the Scottish gangster, Talbot McGovern, and they put a bullet through my head, then dice me into dog food and I spend the rest of eternity in a second-hand suitcase under a fir tree. Not my idea of fun. It would be worse than speaking with the ex-missus... hang on, maybe not? Putting both those gruesome possibilities aside for a moment, they're going to frisk me for sure and turn off the GPS tracking on my phone. They may be as dumb as dogshit, but no one's that dumb. So that means no weapon, no wire, no tracking. My car will have a tracking device fitted, but if they put me in their vehicle—then the game changes. Which worries me. And I'm not the worrying type. Unless, I'm further than ten feet from a toilet after eating a Phaal curry on top of twelve pints of Guinness.'

Frank raises his hand. 'If I may interject. Zac has spent the morning working on this. Zac, if you'd care to elaborate?'

'I've put together a specialist, elite team.'

'Okay, ding, ding! Time out. That word concerns me for a start,' Beale interrupts.

'What word?'

'Elite. That usually means you've scraped together a bunch of dropkicks who are after a bit of overtime because their mortgage payments have recently gone up.'

'Can I finish?'

'Pardon me for breathing. Pray continue—not that it's your fucking neck on the line.'

'I have recruited two experienced officers from the Drug Enforcement Unit; six officers from the Armed Response Unit, and two K9 units. There's also myself to coordinate, and Frank, DCI Keegan, and six officers from uniform.'

'Okay, for starters, you can cancel the uniforms and dogs. We want a successful arrest, not a fucking bloodbath. And reduce the gung-ho, Arnie Schwarzenegger wannabes from the armed response unit down to two good men—or women—or what's the fucking new thing now? Transgender fucking no-names... they, them, it... I don't fucking know. This is supposed to be a clandestine rendezvous, in the middle of fuck-alls-ville, on a dark, stormy night. I don't want it turning into the beach landing from the opening scenes of Private fucking Ryan!'

Zac shakes his head wearily and glances at Frank. 'Boss?'

Frank glances at DCI Keegan, who merely shrugs.

Beale is not as reticent. 'It's my cods on the chopping block—I call the shots. I shouldnae even be here in this... this... fuck, I cannae find the words to describe the place.'

'England?' Zac suggests.

'Aye, fucking England! I've asked to meet with the big man behind this op. That means at most there'll be Wallace and fucking Grommet there, and maybe one other. We don't need the entire cast of Westside Story to take those fuckers out. Have you lot not heard the phrase—less is more? What I want to know is how you're going to track my whereabouts if I'm in *their* vehicle, and how am I to give you the signal to storm the place once I've eyeballed the cocaine and Mr Big?'

Zac tosses a ballpoint pen and a pair of spectacles onto the desk. 'Try them on,' he suggests.

'The ballpoint pen?'

'Ha, ha—not. The pen and glasses have a micro voice transmitter, and GPS tracking fitted. Can you spot where they are?'

Beale studiously investigates the objects, which is hard to do as he's left his own spectacles in his car. 'No, I can't. But if five naked dancing girls walked through the door right now I could mistake them for Jehovah's Witnesses.'

Keegan speaks up. 'State-of-the-art. Flown in from America overnight. The latest and greatest technology.'

'From America, you say?'

'Yes.'

'I hope the technology isn't based on the Windows operating system, otherwise I'll waste twenty minutes waiting for the things to boot up before they freeze and crash. Then I'll receive an email asking me to fill out a satisfaction survey and can I leave a fucking review.'

Frank and Zac slowly swivel their eyes onto DCI Keegan. He gets the message.

'DS Beale... Danny, we seem to have wandered off-piste. Can we recalibrate?'

'What?' he says, trying the spectacles on. 'Hell, what strength are these lenses?'

'DS Beale!' Keegan shouts, losing patience.

'Oh, aye. Sorry. Where were we?'

'We'd just finished deciding the make-up of the back-up team. If we can proceed to your intended plan once you are at the exchange location, and a code word for the back-up team to storm the building, if it is indeed a building.'

'Once I've checked out the coke and made sure it's kosher, my code word will be— excuse me while I blow my nose.' The other three wait for the inevitable nose blowing ritual, which is not forthcoming. Beale eyeballs them suspiciously. 'What the fuck are you all gawping at?'

'We're waiting for you to blow your nose,' Zac replies.

'No! That *is* the fucking code word.'

'What? Excuse me while I blow my nose?'

'Correct! Right, are we done here? As this could be my last night on planet Earth, I'd like to let my hair down.'

Zac is concerned. 'I don't think we are done. We've barely started. We need to play out some worst-case scenarios, risk mitigation, consider the what-ifs.'

Beale scoffs and stands up. 'Don't overthink it, sunshine. Paralysis by analysis. Sometimes you must live by your guile, and cunning. I'm away. Oh, by the by, does Whitby have any titty bars?'

Zac and Frank watch from the office window as Beale and Keegan head off across the CID room and disappear out the door.

'I'm not happy about this at all, Frank. Not happy.'

'Exactly which part of the op concerns you?'

'Just one part—Beale. The man's unpredictable, unprofessional, and unhinged.'

'He's a maverick. I'll admit that much.'

'Yes, and police work is about teamwork, not lone rangers.'

'True, but give him his dues—he volunteered for this job, he didn't have to do it.'

'Aye, and I wager his super couldn't sign the release forms quick enough.'

'Stick to your original plan for the back-up team, Zac. Beale won't know until it's too late. He's an oddball, and a deviant, but so are the criminals we're chasing. And this may sound mercenary, but I'd rather it be him in the firing line than one of my own officers.'

45

Wednesday 25th November

Cartwright stares at the clock on the station wall as the second hand plods its way around the digits with a noticeable lack of urgency. Pulling a handkerchief from his pocket, he dabs at his forehead, then takes another drink of water.

Prisha bustles into the office, bristling with energy and excitement. 'Got the bastard!' she declares.

'Forensics?'

'Yes. Just came in. It's Craig's DNA on the rifle. He obviously gave it a good clean, but they found a tiny amount in the crevice where the cheek piece meets the stock. I think we had enough evidence already to get a conviction, but this is the final nail in his coffin. Right, five minutes and we're in there. All prepped and ready to go?' she says as she glugs down the rest of her coffee.

'Erm... yeah,' he replies, pulling at his tie.

She detects his nervousness. 'What's the matter? You've done this a hundred times before.'

'Not a hundred, and never a double murder. In fact, I haven't interviewed a murder suspect for at least five years. Frank hands it over to Zac these days for high-profile cases. I get the shoplifters and street dealers. Are you sure you don't want to take the lead?'

'You're the arresting officer. You should lead. I have faith in you. We spent two hours on the drive over here, going over all the details for about the fourth time. You'll nail it. If you forget anything, I'll jump in. You calmly present the evidence and at the end give him a moment to digest it all. Then I'll go in hard with the emotive angle. Emotion is a very underrated tactic in these situations.' She leans forward and tightens the knot in his tie. 'There you go. Now you look the part.'

He forces a smile. 'You're right. Come on, let's do it,' he says as his confidence returns.

———◦———

With the digital recorder on, and cautions, risk assessment, and formalities over, Cartwright opens his folder. He places a photo of the Tikka Ultra Precision Rifle in front of Craig and his solicitor.

'Do you recognise this rifle, Craig?'

He casually glances down. 'Yeah, I had one like that, same model.'

'Had, as in past-tense?'

'Yes.'

'You don't have it anymore?'

'No.'

'That would explain why we couldn't find it when we searched your house and vehicle yesterday. What happened to the rifle?'

'About five months ago I went on a deer shoot up in Scotland with a few old buddies and the forestock developed a fracture,' he says, tapping his finger on the photo at the forestock. 'It was

334

knackered. It was no use to me anymore, so I took a hacksaw to it and cut it into bits, so it didn't fall into the wrong hands. Then I took it to the local tip with some other rubbish.'

'Five months ago, you say?'

'Yeah, early July.'

'And you don't have any other rifles?'

'No. They're not cheap. I'm saving up for one.'

'Our ballistics and forensics experts determined the bullets that killed Albert and Maxine were fired from this rifle.'

'I've read the rumours on social media. Everyone's an amateur detective these days.'

'It's estimated the shots were fired from quite some distance, anywhere between four hundred to eight hundred yards away. That's some shooting, wouldn't you say?'

'It's up there.'

'As a marksman in the infantry, you'd appreciate the skill and accuracy of the shooter, if not the targets?'

He leans back and folds his arms. 'I see where you're going with this,' he says with a smile.

'You joined the army at sixteen, is that correct?'

'Yes.'

'It's a very young age. Couldn't wait to leave home?'

'No. Just wanted to get on with my life once I left school.'

'We spoke with your mother's sister, your Aunty Karen, yesterday. She said you left because you were constantly at loggerheads with Albert, and you couldn't wait to leave.'

'Aunty Karen is old and her memory's not what it was. Me and Albert weren't best buddies, but we had a mutual respect for each other and always got along. I was a little shit for a few years when I was in my teens. I see that now. That's probably what Aunty Karen was referring to.'

'When I interviewed you at the rugby ground last Wednesday, you gave me the details of your movements from the previous Saturday—the day Albert and Maxine were murdered.'

'Yes.'

'You said you woke about eight, then visited your mother about nine. Made her breakfast and returned home about ten. You continued with renovations to your house and worked until approximately one-thirty then visited your local. You had a couple of pints over a period of around forty minutes before returning home again. Is that correct?'

'Yes.'

'There's nothing you want to change?'

'No. That's the truth.'

'Except your mother can't verify whether it was Saturday or Sunday when you visited her.'

'Hardly surprising, considering what she's going through. She's confused.'

'Yes. Totally understandable. Inspector Kumar, would you show Craig, exhibit-A, please?'

'Certainly.' Prisha rises and walks to a table containing a metal box. She pulls on a pair of latex gloves, takes out the rifle wrapped in plastic and holds it up in front of Craig.

Cartwright continues. 'For the tape, DI Kumar is holding a Tikka T3x Ultimate Precision Rifle. Craig, is this the same make and model of rifle you once owned before you disposed of it?'

'Yes.'

'What about the material, the finish, the colour?'

'Yes. Identical.'

'Identical?'

'Yes.'

'But it can't be yours, can it? Because your identical rifle went to landfill last July.'

'That's correct. They're a popular rifle.'

'Not that popular. There are only thirty-five in the whole of the UK. So, the rifle DI Kumar is holding is not yours?'

'Correct.'

'Can you explain why forensics detected your DNA in the crevice of the cheek piece?'

He sits upright, unfolds his arms and drops his hands under the table. 'What? No, there must be a mistake.'

'Extremely unlikely, unless you have an identical twin?'

He pulls a thoughtful expression. 'Wait. Now I think about it, before I bought the Tikka, I tried one out on the Rhyader rifle range in Wales to test its capabilities.'

'When?'

'I can't put an exact date on it now, but within the last year.'

'And obviously before July, when you destroyed your gun?'

'Yes, obviously.'

'Inspector Kumar, can you show Craig, exhibit-B. For the recording, this is digital footage taken from CCTV.'

'Of course.' Prisha hits the play button. The computer monitor in the corner of the room crackles into life as the grainy video plays.

'As you can see from the date stamp, it is Saturday the 14th of November, at precisely 7:38 am. Coming into view now are Albert and Maxine. They set off from the guest house a few minutes earlier and walked up Duke Street, which eventually leads to the start of the trail to Malham via Malham Cove. It's clearly recognisable as Albert and Maxine, and the clothing clearly matches what the deceased were wearing when their bodies were found. If you would fast forward, please, Inspector Kumar.'

'Certainly.' Prisha points the remote control and the footage speeds forwards until she hits the play button.

Cartwright continues. 'As signified by the date and time stamp on the bottom left-hand corner, it is now 7:51 am, just over thirteen minutes later. There's a figure entering the frame now. The man is five-ten, about twelve stone, fit, well-built, wearing a dark green parka with a black bobble hat pulled down low over his forehead. Remind you of anyone, Craig?'

'I hear your insinuation, Sergeant Cartwright, and I'll readily admit it looks a bit like me. But the footage is very grainy, and there's a million guys of my age of similar height and weight. And those parkas are from the Army and Navy stores—second-hand. Fifty quid a pop. They're good value and they're everywhere.'

'You're saying it's not you in the video?'

'It's not me. How could it be? I was still in bed in Pickering at the time.'

'Can you rewind the footage a few seconds, DI Kumar?'

'Of course.'

Prisha replays the footage.

'Craig, the camera shot is from the left. Have you noticed what's hanging from the man's right shoulder?'

He squints. 'Hard to tell, but it looks like a rifle or possibly a fishing rod.'

'It's a rifle scabbard. Inspector Kumar, can you show Craig, exhibit-C?'

Prisha takes the scabbard from the metal trunk and places it on the table.

Craig shrugs. 'It's a rifle carrycase—a scabbard. It's a popular brand. Some of my mates have them.'

'When we searched your house yesterday, we found no rifle and no carrycase. You've explained the whereabouts of the gun. What about the scabbard?'

'The handle broke, and the stitching was coming away from the seams, so I got rid of it.'

'When?'

'Probably about the same time I got rid of the rifle, although I can't be certain.'

'You don't seem to have a lot of luck with the rifles you buy?'

'It's like anything—sometimes you get a beauty which will last you a lifetime. Other times you end up with a lemon.'

'DI Kumar, can you open up the scabbard?'

Prisha pulls at the folds of the canvas bag and points at a few white dots inside.

'So?' Craig says.

'We sent the scabbard back to forensics yesterday and asked for a re-examination of the interior part of the scabbard. They came back with the results overnight.'

'Bully for you.'

'You've been renovating your house. Repainting all the rooms?'

'Yes, amongst other things.'

'The dots inside the scabbard are paint drops. It's a Dulux brand. To be specific, a vinyl matt emulsion ceiling paint. The same type you've been using on your ceilings. We took a sample from the paint tin in your back bedroom.'

He snorts. 'Give me a break. That scabbard doesn't even belong to me. And I'm not the only person in the country painting their house right now with bloody Dulux paint.'

'The thing with paints, Craig, although they're mass produced, paint particles are unique. Chemical analysis is used to measure the physical characteristics of the paint particles, such as their shape, size, and composition. By comparing samples from your house and the scabbard, forensic investigators determined they are the same paint. The paint spots on the inside of the scabbard matches the paint in your bedroom.'

'I don't believe it. You're making it up, or if you're not, then they're wrong. That scabbard is not mine.'

Cartwright pulls another photo from his folder and slides it across the table. 'For the recording, I'm showing Craig a photograph of a dark green Land Rover Defender. The photo was taken by DI Kumar a week last Monday on the driveway of Mary Shaw's house. The vehicle registration number is S110 TAK. Is this your vehicle, Craig?'

He pushes the photo back to Cartwright dismissively. 'Yes.'

'It's registered in your mother's name?'

'It makes the insurance cheaper.'

'You must be doing it tough if you need the car to be registered in your mother's name to save what... seventy, eighty quid?'

He shrugs. 'It all counts.'

'For the record, I'm showing Craig a photo of a Land Rover Defender parked in Booths Supermarket car park in Settle. The date and time stamp, record it as Saturday 14th November at 7:35 am.' He slips another photograph across the table.

'There are hundreds of Land Rovers knocking about all over the dales. Looking at that photo, the number plate is unrecognisable.'

'You're right, it is very blurry. But this enhanced photo of the same vehicle clearly shows the number plate as S110 TAK,' Cartwright says, placing another image carefully down on the table. Even the solicitor raises his eyebrows. Silence ensues for a few minutes as Craig falls into a glassy-eyed stupor.

As the clock ticks, one mind desperately tries to find a believable answer—but comes up with nothing.

Prisha eventually intervenes. 'It's not looking good, is it, Craig? The evidence keeps on piling up. How do you explain your vehicle being in Settle on that day and at that time when by your account you were at home in bed?'

'I, erm, that's right, I forgot. A buddy of mine borrowed the Rover on Friday for the weekend.'

'Oh, come off it, Craig. Is that the best you've got? You're playing us for fools. I'll tell you what I think happened. Knowing your mother hasn't long left, you realised all her money and assets would go to Albert. The house, the savings, the shares they jointly own. And when Albert passes away, who's going to get the inheritance? You, the stepson, or his daughter in Australia, his own flesh, and blood. You murdered Albert and Maxine out of greed, pure nasty greed for your own benefit, without ever thinking once about the pain and anguish your mother would have to endure in her final few months. What sort of loving son would do that?'

He taps at the table with his fingers, agitated, but fails to respond.

Prisha gives him a few seconds to ruminate, then continues. 'I spoke with your old army commander earlier—Lieutenant Colonel Jones. He said you were an impeccable soldier, one of the best. A good man. True, honest, did your duty without grumbling. Got the job done. The finest marksmen he's come across. Because that is what you were in Afghanistan, wasn't it Craig... a marksman, a sniper? But since you left the army, you haven't had much work. You managed to get a mortgage, buy a house, but your army pension is not enough to cover all the bills, is it? In fact, you're in arrears with your payments. According to the bank, you're one more missed payment away from repossession. Times are tough for many people. I feel your pain, Craig. Is that why you killed Albert, to sort out your debts?'

His fingers tap at the tabletop with an increasing tempo as his knee involuntarily flits up and down. But still no response.

'I feel sorry for your mother the most. Hell, what an end to her life. There's no Hollywood happy ever after for her, is there? No slipping peacefully away in her sleep, or on a bench in the garden admiring the daffodils. Just cancer, drugs, a murdered husband who's been cheating on her. And now a son who killed her husband simply to pay off his debts. Your army commander was wrong about you. You're not a good man. You're a bad man, Craig. A bad man.'

He explodes. 'Don't you dare talk to me about fucking good and bad, about pain and anguish,' he snarls, slapping his hands on the table and lurching forwards. 'I've done my time—twenty years in the army, three tours of duty in Afghanistan. You sit there, judging others, with your photographs and CCTV and fucking forensics. I've seen the horrors of war! Things you couldn't possibly imagine. Women, children, babies, shot, butchered, cut into pieces. Entire families wiped out because the daughter dared to attend school. You think you have it tough dealing with rapists, murderers, drug dealers—you've no fucking idea—that's a doddle. Imagine every person you meet could have ten kilos of high-explosives strapped to them, ready to hit the detonator button, willing to die and take you with them. Imagine holding your best mate in your arms with his fucking legs ten feet away after a roadside bomb has gone off. I came out of it physically unscarred. Not a mark on me. But what about up here?' he yells, jabbing a finger violently at his temple. 'No one can see inside here. What about my nervous system, my mental health, my mind? I bet you sleep easy on a night—don't you? Well, I don't. That horror show visits me every fucking night. That's why I can't hold down a job. That's what Albert never understood. He thought I was a shirker because I couldn't get regular work. I went to see him a month ago to ask for a short-term loan, just to tide me over Christmas and New Year when things are quiet. Said I'd pay him back by April. I have a bit of work lined up. The greedy, miserly bastard wouldn't lend me a penny. Said there was plenty of work around for those who wanted it. As I was leaving, he said that once my mother passed away, he intended to rip up their joint will and write a new one and I wouldn't be getting a single bean. My god, he said it with such contempt, like I was shit on his shoe.'

'And that's when you decided to kill him?'

'No. I was angry as hell, but I never thought about killing him until a few nights later. I was coming home from the pub. I walked past Maxine Wood's house. I didn't even know who she was, or that she lived there. I spotted Albert come out of a side door, then kiss Maxine on the lips, a full-on kiss. I realised he'd been cheating on my mother. The dirty old fucker couldn't even wait a few more months until she'd gone. That's when my anger boiled over. I'd teach him and her a lesson and solve my money problems at the same time.' He grips his face and sobs uncontrollably into his hands, his shoulders heaving with the intensity.

'Craig, did you kill Albert Shaw and Maxine Wood?' she asks gently.

'Yes, yes, yes! I killed them!' he weeps.

———⋯◇⋯———

Cartwright places two cups of coffee on the desk and closes the office door, then stares at Prisha.

'I should feel on top of the world,' he says, in reflection. 'But I don't.'

'No, me neither,' she sighs, gazing at a blank wall. 'Oh, what a tangled web we weave, when first we practise to deceive.'

Cartwright screws his nose up. 'Didn't realise you were a poet.'

'I'm not. Marmion—Sir Walter Scott,' she murmurs softly. 'It's the anti-climax I hate. You're on a massive buzz as all the evidence falls into place. Then when you get a confession like that, it jabs a pin in your balloon. Why couldn't he have been a cold-hearted killer whose only motive was greed? I actually feel sorry for him, and Mary, and Albert and Maxine. It's all a stinking mess.'

'And it could have been so easily avoided if Albert had simply found some charity in his heart.'

'Yes. A little understanding and empathy can go a long way.'

46

The sleek black Jaguar XF pulls into the layby and idles as the rain pitter-patters on the windscreen. DS Beale turns the headlights down and waits. It was his idea, the Jaguar. He'd scoffed when he was offered an unmarked Vauxhall Astra.

'What self-respecting crime boss would drive around in an Astra?' he bellowed. 'I need something to reflect my status.' The Jaguar was hastily hired, with strict instructions not to damage it.

Now he waits, gently singing the Skye Boat Song to himself as he drops salted peanuts into his mouth.

> *'Speed, bonnie boat, like a bird on the wing, onward the sailors cry; carry the lad that's born to be King, over the sea to Skye.'*

———◇———

Zac is behind the wheel of an unmarked Vauxhall Astra less than a mile away, on a vantage point high on a hill. Frank is in the passenger seat, and DCI Keegan is in the rear. Behind them is a small convoy made up of the rapid response team; a black transit van containing a driver and five officers from the Armed Response Unit; another unmarked vehicle with two drug squad officers; and lastly, two K9 dog vans.

The disagreeable, out of tune singing of Beale's rendition of the Skye Boat Song filters into all the vehicles via the radio.

> *"Sing me a song of a lad*
> *that is gone, say could that*
> *lad be, I?"*

'Christ almighty,' Zac mutters. 'He's massacring that tune. Is there nothing we can charge him with, Frank?'

'Disturbing the peace is the only thing that springs to mind.'

'What about GBH or crimes against humanity?'

Frank pulls out a pair of night vision binoculars from the glove box and exits the car. Standing on the side of the road, he zooms in on Beale's Jaguar in the distance.

'No sign of the suspects,' Frank mutters.

'Still another five minutes until the rendezvous time,' DCI Keegan calls from the back seat as he sticks his head out of the window.

Laughs and giggles emanate from the black riot van before a chorus of voices joins in with Beale's uncoordinated dirge. Frank half smiles and shakes his head. He ambles over to the van and bangs on the side panel.

'Very funny! Keep it silent in there. We're supposed to be undercover.' High-pitched whining erupts from the two dog vans as Frank now focuses his attention on them. 'Can you keep those bloody mutts quiet?' he hisses in their direction.

One officer pops his head out of the window. 'Sorry, Frank. It's the discordant nature of the singing. The dogs think someone's in pain or in need of help.'

'They'd be right on both counts,' Zac's disembodied voice calls out.

'What a pantomime,' Frank says as he climbs back into the passenger seat.

"Loud the winds howl, loud the waves roar, thunderclouds rend the air; baffled, our foes stand by the shore, follow they will not dare."

'How many verses has this song got?' DCI Keegan asks, in obvious discomfort.

Zac turns the radio down. 'Depends. There are many versions. I think one of them has about twenty verses.'

'Sweet merciful crap!' Frank exclaims. 'Let's hope he's throttling the abridged version. This is torture. No man can endure this for long.'

———◇———

DS Beale puts his all into the final chorus, blissfully unaware of the detrimental effect it's having on his colleagues a mile away. Proud of his efforts, he pulls out his cigarettes and sparks up a smoke, not even bothering to wind a window down. He checks his watch, then takes a nip of scotch from his hip flask.

'Ah, that's the ticket,' he murmurs as he launches into The Bonnie Banks of Loch Lomond.

> *"By yon bonnie banks and*
> *by yon bonnie braes, where*
> *the sun shines bright on*
> *Loch Lomond."*

In the distant, rainy hills of the Yorkshire Dales, a collective groan is followed by the gnashing of teeth and threats of self-harm.

*"Oh, ye'll tak' the high road
and I'll tak' the low road,
and I'll be in Scotland
afore ye!"*

Thankfully, for all concerned, his grating caterwauling abruptly halts as he spots a headlight in the rear-view mirror.

'Hello, hello, what have we here then? Looks like the game's afoot, boys.'

The throaty roar of a motorbike prowls up behind him and comes to a halt. The rider dismounts and surveys the scene, cautiously, suspiciously. He walks to the window and taps at it with a gloved knuckle. Beale hits a button, and the window rolls down, releasing a billow of cigarette smoke.

'Which one of the Krankies are you, then?' he asks, staring at the helmet.

'Phone,' the rider states, voice muffled by his helmet and visor.

'Aye, I'm doing fine, thanks. Nice of you to fucking ask. Manners cost nothing,' he says as he fumbles in his pocket and retrieves his mobile and flashes it at the rider.

'Turn it off and hand it to me,' he demands.

'How far to the exchange point?' Beale says as his phone screen goes into the shutdown sequence.

'Not far.'

'Six inches? A mile? A light-year?'

'Not far.'

'Fuck the dog,' he sighs. 'Okay, Peter Personality, let's get on with it. Your scintillating charisma is making me feel inadequate,' he says, passing him the phone.

The rider straddles his bike and spins around. Beale drops the Jaguar into drive and swings to the left, then spins hard to the right to do a U-turn. There's a thump and clunk and the tinkling sound of glass.

'What the fuck was that?' he curses as he puts the car into reverse to see what he's hit. As the car speeds backwards, whining violently, a scraping sound comes from the front and back passenger doors. As the left-hand headlight is now smashed and non-operational, he manoeuvres the car until he picks up the object in the solitary headlight. 'What dumb-arsed, tit-monkey put that there!' he groans, staring at an ancient, stone waymarker which reads, 175 Miles—Glasgow 230 Miles—London.

The rider revs the engine of the motorbike, showing his impatience, then speeds off. Beale pulls out onto the road and floors the Jag to catch up.

'I said they were amateurs. He didn't even frisk me. What a numpty,' Beale says, speaking to his unseen listeners. 'By the way, a slight accident. Nothing that won't buff out. Can one of you inform the lads from Highway Patrol that if they see a black Jag with a near side headlight missing, not to pull it over, because that will be me.'

As the convoy moves off, Frank shakes his head. 'That's a good start,' he says. He speaks into the police radio. 'Okay team, we're moving. I'll lead the way. try to space yourselves out. Let's not make it obvious we're all together. Dog units to the rear—and another reminder—keep the bloody muzzles on those dogs unless we actually need them. I've got history with those two vicious bastards.' He studies his phone as a red dot slowly moves along the screen, the signal transmitted from Beale's vehicle. 'They're taking the back way, heading northeast along Hellifield Road towards Airton.'

Silence descends amongst the occupants of the convoy as the tension ramps up.

'We should be thankful for small mercies,' Frank states.

'Go on?' Zac says as the rain intensifies.

'At least the prick has stopped singing.'

Zac and DCI Keegan chuckle as the suspense is briefly dispersed.

47

Even Beale, who is normally overbearing, garrulous, and bombastic, is feeling the pinch as he trails the motorbike. His one headlight illuminates a road sign.

'Entering a town called Kirby Malham,' he says, his state-of-the-art spectacles in his breast pocket relaying the information to the convoy. 'Leaving Kirby Malham,' he adds a few seconds later. 'Slap my hairy arse. I've heard of one-horse towns, but that takes the fucking biscuit. I think even the horse has given up on this feudal sinkhole.'

A few minutes pass before he notices the brake light of the motorbike sparkle through the rain.

'What's knucklehead doing?' he murmurs as he glances around the countryside, seeing no sign of life, not even a solitary light. The bike turns tight into an empty field as Beale cautiously follows behind.

'Shit in my shandy,' he groans.

The rider dismounts, swings a gate shut and locks it.

'We've entered a field on the right-hand side and the brain's trust has shut and padlocked the gate. I hope one of you elite fuckers has brought a pair of bolt cutters with you.'

The bike carefully descends the field, traversing the wet, slippery grass, occasionally the back wheel slewing to the left and right. Beale follows the tyre marks of the bike as best he can with one light. The bike skids again, this time sending a wall of mud onto the windscreen of the Jag.

'Fucking wonderful,' Beale hisses as he presses a button to release a squirt of water onto the glass. The mud turns into a slurry as the rider stops and signals something to Beale, but he can't make out what the semaphore is supposed to mean.

'What are you trying to tell me, you numpty!' he says. The Jag hits something hard and comes to an ungainly halt as Beale is jettisoned forward, the seatbelt pulling hard into his shoulder and ample gut. 'Oh, I see. You were indicating there's a big fucking rock in the way. You need to work on your sign language, pal.'

He continually presses the button to rinse the screen until finally there's a narrow patch of glass he can barely see out of. The car reverses before moving forward, bypassing the impediment. The rider alights and performs the same procedure with the second gate—waving Beale through, then locking it shut.

Beale re-evaluates his hastily conceived plan, wishing now he'd actually spent more than two minutes contemplating worst-case-scenarios.

'Houston, we may have a problem,' he whispers. 'The field is a quagmire full of rocks, not to mention two locked gates. I can see a farmhouse ahead. I suggest you find another route to the location. And Zac, maybe next time, put a bit more thought into your contingency plans. I'll have to buy some time until I *think* you've arrived. That's if you can even hear me, of which I've no fucking idea. Yet another cock-up on someone's part.'

'I knew it!' Zac yells. 'I bloody knew it! Don't overthink it. Paralysis by analysis. Sometimes you have to live by your guile, and cunning. What a dipstick!'

'Calm down, Zac,' Frank advises as he studies the map on his phone. He presses his police radio. 'Okay everyone, pull over for a moment while we figure something out.'

DCI Keegan leans forward, holding his phone out. 'Take a look, Frank. Beale is here, nearing a farmhouse,' he says, pointing at the screen. 'But the access road to that house is slightly past Kirkby Malham, about four minutes back the other way.'

Frank eyeballs the route. 'Aye, you're right.' He hits the radio again. 'Okay everyone, we need to turn around. Stay in position until the lead vehicle has passed, then follow along. I'll let you know when to kill your headlights.'

Beale gets out of the car and examines the extensive damage, as the rider kills his engine and removes his helmet.

'Oh, it's you—Inky McStinky,' he says to Steve Roberts, who grins at the state of Beale's Jag. 'You think it's funny? Take pleasure from other's misfortune, do you?'

'A good panel beater will put that right in no time,' he says with a chuckle as he hops into the passenger seat. 'Get in.'

'Where to now?' Beale asks getting behind the wheel.

'Across the courtyard and hang a left by the barn. Watch out for protruding objects.'

'Very fucking amusing.' The car navigates down the side of the barn and into a wide driveway.

'Stop here.'

'Nice new red shed,' Beale says as a clanking noise breaks the silence. Mike Roberts appears and leans his back against the edge of the door and pushes it open. Beale drives forward into the brightly lit interior as the door clanks shut behind him. He takes a quick look in the side mirror, as Mike walks towards the car.

They haven't locked the shed door. These two are as dumb as dogshit.

Both men step from the car, as Beale takes in his surroundings, which don't fill him full of cheer. He squints at both men under the harsh fluorescent lighting.

'Okay, where is he?' he asks.

'Who?' Mike replies.

Beale saunters up to him. 'Don't play fucking games, sunshine. Your boss, the head-honcho, the man from fucking Delmonte—where is he?'

'It's just the two of us.'

Beale guffaws for a moment until his laughter lines are replaced by a mean sneer. He leans against a bench in the middle of the shed, takes a shot of whisky from the hip flask, sparks up a ciggy, then blows smoke into the air.

'Let me tell you about my day. I had a shocking night's sleep as the missus was up all night chucking her arse up. I told her to keep off the oysters as I thought they smelled a bit off. Did she fucking listen? Of course not. She's a woman and what the fuck do I know? I then pick up my brand-new Jag from the dealership.' He stares at it disdainfully. 'It now looks like it's taken part in a re-enactment of the Battle of the fucking Bulge. I've been driving for over four hours. I'm tired, hungry and my haemorrhoids are giving me merry hell. On top of all that, I'm going to have to find somewhere local to stay for the night as I can't drive back to Glasgow in that fucking thing, with one light out,' he says, poking a leg at the Jag, 'which makes me nervous. Because it means I'll have to transfer twenty kilos of coke from boot to hotel room and back again in the morning. And, I didn't bring my overnight bag, so I can't even brush my fucking teeth. I'm not one to complain but, I will say this, I haven't been this pissed off since 2014 when we lost the vote.'

'What vote?'

Beale's eyes narrow to slits as he tugs on his smoke. 'The Scottish referendum vote,' he snarls.

'Too bad about that,' Mike says, grinning.

Beale gives a shake of the head. 'Anyway, my point is this: either the main man shows his face right now or I'm out of here and the next time you two bozos see me is when you're strapped to a fucking bed with a clothes iron on your chest and I plug the power cord in—get it?' he says, in a low growl. There's a click from the back of the shed and the sound of footsteps as Beale peers into the gloam.

'At last!' Beale exclaims as a man walks towards him. 'Here's papa.' He assesses the slender frame that approaches, sporting a warm smile. Slender he may be, but his skin is taut, full of vim and vigour, and he moves with a languid, agile gait as if he has all the time in the world. Exuding calm and confidence, he holds his hand out to Beale.

'My sincerest apologies, Mr McGovern, or may I call you Talbot?' says the man as the brothers part to make way for him.

Beale gives him the stinky eye for a moment, before relaxing and shaking his hand, which is firm but not vice like.

Medium height, slim, lithe, slight accent—maybe South African, German, Dutch? Relaxed, disarming, handsome, likeable—I've met one or two of these fuckers over the years, and they're always dangerous—very dangerous. Far scarier than the two throwbacks standing behind him. Tread carefully, Danny, tread carefully.

'Aye, Talbot's fine. I prefer first name terms in my business relationships.'

They release hands as both men continue to evaluate each other. 'I'm sorry for all the clandestine, covert tomfoolery, but when we take on a new client, we are always cautious.'

'Apology accepted. And I know where you're coming from... erm.... I didn't catch your name?'

'Lewis.'

'Lewis, I take it the boys told you of my organisation's requirements should your product be up to scratch?'

'Indeed. We have twenty kilos for you tonight. If it proves satisfactory to your clients, then you require fifty kilos once a month. Correct?'

'Correct. And we're agreed on the price?'

'For the moment. Cocaine is a commodity like any other and it can fluctuate wildly, depending on supply and demand. Supply is weak at the moment and demand is high. There'll be no surprises from our end. We will always inform you if the price has changed before you purchase the next shipment.'

'Fair enough. I'm cool with that. And the game we're in, the increased cost gets passed onto the consumer, anyway.'

'Indeed. As for the damage to your car, let me know what the cost is, and I will deduct it from your next payment.'

'Thanks for the offer. But no need. It's pin money. Right, let the dog see the rabbit.'

Lewis shoots a glance at the brothers. 'He wants to sample the wares,' Mike explains.

'Ah! Of course.' He nods at Steve, who bends down and pulls a bulging suitcase from under the bench and drops it onto the counter.

Beale pulls at the two zippers.

'Wait!' Lewis shouts, pulling a pistol from his jacket pocket. He places the barrel against Beale's forehead.

48

The convoy inches over the narrow farm track, the only sound the ever-present rain and the occasional muted crunch of gravel under the tyres.

'That doesn't sound good,' whispers Zac.

'No. They were getting on like a house on fire. Why did he shout, wait? There was anger and urgency in his voice,' Frank says.

'Maybe they knew all along he was undercover.' Keegan suggests.

Frank ponders for a moment. 'If that was the case, why not put a bullet through his head at the layby? But something has spooked this Lewis character. Pull over, and kill the lights,' he whispers to Zac as they see the farmhouse in the distance. He picks his radio up. 'Armed response; on foot from here, then take up your positions.'

Beale's deep baritone crackles through the car's sound system. 'Lewis, take the gun away from my head.'

'Shit! They've pulled a gun on him!' Zac says with alarm as the three of them leap from the car.

———◆———

Beale is perplexed by the developments. 'What the fuck is this? You wanna be careful with that thing, Lewis? It could go off. Problem?'

'Your fingers,' he states cryptically, staring at Beale's hands.

'What about them?' Beale asks, puzzled.

'I've done my research—Mr Talbot McGovern. On the fingers of your left and right hand you have the words—Love and Hate tattooed.'

Beale glances at the back of his hands which are bereft of any ink. He thinks back to two nights ago when he fell asleep in the bath.

Fuck!

He chuckles. 'They were falsies. They were real once, but the wife hated them, so I had them removed by laser. Incessant nagging can wear a man down after a while. I get the falsies put on every now and again to piss her off. It's the way to keep a marriage alive—a bit of tension. The tatts only last a few days before they wash off.'

The Roberts brothers exchange glances as Lewis lowers the gun and slips it back inside his jacket pocket.

'Continue,' he says.

Beale relaxes and pulls at the zippers on the case and flips back the outer shell. He quickly counts the contents. 'Forty bags. I'm assuming five hundred grams in each. I can see you're an honest man, Lewis, but I will weigh them with high-precision digital scales once I'm back in the Motherland. Anyone got a razor on them?'

Lewis pulls out a small scabbard containing a scalpel. 'Here,' he says, handing it to Beale.

He inserts a small cut into the plastic and a flurry of powder spills onto the bench top. Quickly and expertly, he chops at the powder before fashioning it into a six-inch line. Pulling a twenty-pound note from his wallet, he rolls it into a cylinder, sticks one end in his right nostril and hoovers up half the line before repeating the process with his other nostril. His bulbous nose takes on a grotesque quality as he scrunches his face up, then violently shakes his head.

'Fuck! That is good shit,' he says as his heart rate takes off in a northerly direction.

'I randomly test all my supplies, Talbot. And that is the finest Columbian. Its purity level is consistently between ninety and ninety-five per cent.'

Beale is experiencing a sudden rush of euphoria and energy. He zips the suitcase up and presses a button on his fob key and the boot of the Jag clicks open.

'Would one of you boys be kind enough to put the suitcase in the boot while I sort out payment?' he says, addressing the brothers. 'Oh, and hatchet face, I need my fucking phone.'

Steve passes him the phone then picks the case up and heads towards the car as Beale stares at his mobile as it boots up.

Okay, Danny, it's nearly death or glory time. Priority number one—take out Lewis as he has the gun. I need him to be in front of me. Then a quick headbutt should do the trick. But watch out, he looks like one of those sneaky little fuckers who is an expert in martial arts. Remember what happened last time you came up against one of them... you copped a right belting. Out of action for six weeks.

'Ah, here we go,' he says, as he slips his spectacles onto his head. 'I may need your assistance, Lewis. I'm not good with technology. It's my brother, Hamilton, who's the egghead. I've been known to get into difficulties with a toaster.'

Lewis moves around from the other side of the bench. 'Of course, let me take a look.'

Beale holds his palm up and wiggles his nose. 'Wait. That coke has set my sinuses off. Excuse me while I blow my nose.'

A second later, the shed is thrown into darkness, as the doors rattle their annoyance. A dull popping echoes out as all hell breaks loose with shouting and screaming, accompanied by a hissing sound.

'Armed police! On the ground, now drop any weapons!'

———◆———

Beale lifts his head from the bucket of water. His bloodshot eyes and swollen facial features do nothing to improve his appearance.

'Who's fucking bright idea was the tear gas?' he says, coughing and wheezing as he peers through narrow slits, as Lewis and the Roberts brothers are escorted to waiting patrol cars.

'Armed response,' Zac chuckles. 'It's best to leave these things to the experts. I thought it went amazingly well.'

'And what's so funny?' he gasps.

'Nothing... Mr Pumpkinhead.'

Frank and Keegan saunter over in good spirits.

'Excellent result,' Keegan declares. 'We've blocked the breach in the damn wall, recovered twenty kilos of cocaine and have three men under arrest. All in all, I'd say it was a good night's work. What do you say, Frank?'

'Aye. A very satisfying outcome, Hedley.' His eyes wander to the inside of the shed. 'Apart from the state of the Jag,' he says, shaking his head. 'We'll be lucky to get a few quid from the wreckers yard for that thing.'

Beale would like to tell them all his thoughts, but he's having enough trouble breathing.

'Okay, let's wrap this up,' Frank declares. 'By the way, DS Beale, next time you traverse the invisible border between Scotland and England, any chance you can leave your singing voice behind?'

Beale tries to reply with an expletive laden comeback but his stinging eyes and rasping lungs prevent anything more than an arthritic wheeze.

49

Thursday 26th November

Prisha passes Cartwright in the corridor of the station.

'This is the last box,' she says.

'Good. I'll give the office a last once over to make sure we've haven't missed anything.'

Turning her back to the swing door, she sticks her bum out and pushes it open, spinning around. She bends over and drops the box into the back of the hatchback. The guttural throb of a diesel engine from a nearby rubbish truck drowns out the squeaky sound of Sergeant Evans' shoes.

'Leaving us already, inspector.'

His voice gives her a start as she lifts her head sharply, catching it on the door. 'Christ!' she says, rubbing at her head.

'Sorry. Didn't mean to make you jump.'

She slams the door shut and stares at him. 'Yes, all done,' she says, replying to his original question.

He leans in, too close. 'Of course,' he says in a whisper, sporting a leer, 'if you'd had the foresight to have checked out Craig Brown's former occupation as a priority, this case would have been wrapped up a week ago.'

'If only hindsight were foresight, sergeant, then every crime would be solved within a few hours of being reported. We had a lot of other leads to check out.'

'Like red lights on the moors?'

'That information led to the arrest of a small drug cartel last night in a successful operation which will shut down the importation of over a hundred kilos of cocaine a month into North Yorkshire. I'd call that a win, wouldn't you?'

He snorts derisively. 'It's like catching rats. As fast as you catch them, another one moves into the empty nest.'

'So what's the answer? Throw our arms up in the air and do nothing?'

'Just saying.'

Cartwright bustles out of the station, appearing rather pleased with life. 'I can't believe it,' he says, staring at the sky. 'The sun is out.'

Evans eyes him with disdain. 'Have a safe journey back to Whitby.' He turns on his heels and squeaks into the station.

'That man is an insufferable prig,' she says, angrily.

'Don't let him needle you, Prisha. He's been left behind by the world and it's made him bitter,' Cartwright says as he hops into the driver's seat.

Prisha climbs in and fastens her seatbelt. 'You're right. I won't let him spoil our day. We've solved a double murder, and Zac and Frank have nicked a trio of drug smugglers. Unfortunately, there goes my climbing partner.'

'Lewis Visser?'

'Yes. I should have twigged when I realised he owned a string of chemist discount shops. Being a pharmacist would come in very handy when cutting cocaine with filler and manufacturing pills and tablets. The sneaky sod. I certainly know how to pick them. No wonder he was so bloody busy this week. And I thought he was giving me the cold shoulder.'

'Don't worry. Plenty more fish in the sea. You'll find Mr Right one day.'

'Hmm... I'm not so sure.'

50

The officers share idle chatter and a few jokes as they take the scenic route back to Whitby, crossing high over the North Yorkshire Moors. The temperature is cold outside, but the sky is aqua blue, daubed with occasional wispy clouds, the verdant rolling hills a stunning backdrop.

As the conversation turns to Cartwright's hopes and dreams as a father, Prisha studies him. He's animated, alive with a sense of optimism and hope for the future. A far-cry from the dispirited and slovenly man—in all his ways—when he first accompanied Prisha to Pickering at the start of the missing persons case ten days ago. She smiles, only half listening as he reels off a list of baby names he and his wife have been considering.

'She really likes Petra if it's a girl. I told her, no bloody way. Petra's a dog's name.'

Prisha laughs. 'Petra was the daughter of Zeus. The name means rock, in Greek. It's associated with strength, a strong will, and independence. I like it.'

He half turns to her. 'You do?'

'Yes. Petra Cartwright. It's a powerful, noble name.'

'Petra Cartwright,' he repeats quietly. 'Petra Cartwright.'

'I'm embarrassed to ask you this, but I don't even know your wife's name.'

'Amanda. If you ever meet her, for god's sake, don't call her Mandy whatever you do.'

She giggles. 'I'll bear that in mind.'

As the car rounds a corner and clears the crest of a hill, Cartwright excitedly declares, 'And there she is—the North Sea. We should be back at the station by three-thirty.'

'Oh, I had a chat with Frank earlier. He's offered to take us all out for a slap-up meal tonight—on expenses.'

'All?'

'Yeah. Me, you, Zac, obviously Frank, and partners are invited along too—not that I have one. I'm taking a rostered day off tomorrow, so I can let my hair down and have a few drinks. You up for it?'

'Am I ever!'

'He also asked if you'd checked your calendar lately.'

'No, not for a while. Why?'

'Apparently the super wants to see you at 4 pm.'

Panic spreads across his face. 'The super! Why does she want to see me?'

'Not sure. Frank didn't say.'

'Oh, that's not good.'

'Calm down, Jason. I'm sure it's nothing untoward.'

'I've been in CID eight years, and I've been in her office three times.'

'And?'

'Always to receive a bollocking and a dressing down.'

Prisha laughs. 'You're overreacting. She might want to give you a slap on the back and a few words of encouragement for a job well done.'

'As if.'

'It's possible. I've been telling Frank what an asset you've been on this investigation.'

'Really?'

'Yes, really. He's probably passed it on to the super.'

He relaxes and grins. 'A pat on the back from Superintendent Banks. That will be a feather in my cap. Wait until I tell Amanda. She'll fall off her perch.' He pauses as his frown reappears. 'Eh, she's not coming on this shindig tonight, is she?'

'What do you think?'

'No, not her scene.' He takes one hand off the wheel and fumbles in his jacket pocket. 'Here, take this. I was going to wrap it up and give it to you, but now is a good a time as any.'

Prisha takes the small medallion and stares at it. 'What is it?'

'It's the first darts medal I won in a major competition when I was twenty-one. After that final I felt on top of the world—like I could achieve anything, be anyone. Things didn't quite turn out like that for me. But that's life.'

Prisha is touched. 'Why are you giving this to me? It must be precious to you.'

'Because I have that same feeling now, on top of the world. And it's all down to you... well, you and the baby.'

'But...'

'Don't say another word. You can do what you want with it. Stick it in a dusty drawer, throw it in the bin or even toss it into the sea. It's worth nowt. But, as you say, it means a lot to me and I wanted to give you something meaningful and valuable as a token of my thanks.'

As they near Whitby, Cartwright peers into his wing mirror.

'What the hell is this bloody dickhead doing?' he says with some alarm.

'What?' Prisha asks, peering over her shoulder.

'A bloody car weaving in and out of the traffic. Keeps overtaking into oncoming traffic then darts back inside. He's going to kill someone.'

Prisha spots the vehicle about four cars behind as it nips back into the left-hand lane, followed by the blare of a horn.

'I hate that. It's a bugbear of mine—reckless driving,' she states.

'It will be a boy-racer or some jumped up, shiny-shit, middle manager late for a meeting. Hang on, here the dickhead comes again.'

Prisha again spins around to witness a metallic blue Subaru WRX move out to the right-hand lane and speed past the vehicles in front of it, as oncoming traffic veers onto the hard shoulder.

'Christ, they're flooring it,' she remarks as she reaches for her police radio. The speeding car pulls in front of the Ford Focus, causing Cartwright to hit the brakes hard. The back of the Subaru is encrusted in mud.

'Sierra Oscar 52, this is DI Kumar. A blue Subaru WRX is driving erratically, heading east along the A171 approximately four miles out of Whitby. Only a partial number plate is visible; first two letters are alpha foxtrot and the last two numbers are six seven. Request Highway Patrol assistance, immediately. It looks like two male occupants but can't be sure.'

The vehicle swerves out onto the oncoming traffic and takes off again as headlights are flashed and a cacophony of horns blares out.

'What a knobhead!' Cartwright yells. The car is out of sight within a few seconds as the road veers to the left.

'They're going to end up killing someone driving like that.'

'Never a dull moment, is there?'

They drive on for a few minutes as the traffic in front slows down, nearing a roundabout.

'There they are,' Prisha says, pointing out of the window at the Subaru parked up next to a petrol pump.

Cartwright taps the indicator. 'I suppose we should do the honours before they take off again,' he says as he drives onto the forecourt and parks up behind the Subaru. Prisha pulls at the handle of the door.

'I'll do it,' Cartwright says. 'You radio control and get a patrol car here. They can make the arrest and handle the bloody paperwork. I think me and you deserve a rest.'

'You should know there's no rest with this job,' she jokes as Cartwright retrieves his warrant card and strides towards the

Subaru. Prisha picks up the radio and immediately drops it, startled as a thunderous blast deafens her.

She raises her head and stares out of the windscreen as Jason falls backwards onto the concrete, arms spreadeagled. A split-second takes an aeon to pass as her mind refuses to accept what she's witnessed. Her heart rate hits dangerous levels as she screams.

'Nooooo!'

Time stops. People cower. The roar of an engine, the violent shriek of wheels. A blue flash takes off. Pushes open the door. Staggers the twelve feet to his body. Drops to her knees.

'No, no, no, no,' she wails, willing the nightmare to end. Places her hands together, palms down on his chest. Pushes. Recoils in horror as they sink into a hole and are flooded with warm, sticky blood. An attendant nervously exits the shop, trying to understand what he's witnessed.

She pulls her coat off, screaming, 'Ring for a fucking ambulance, now!'

He turns on his heels and darts back inside. She bunches her coat up and presses it hard into the wound, realising it's a futile endeavour. Cartwright blinks, staring at the sky.

'Jason, Jason, hang in there. There's help on its way,' she pleads. His eyes flicker shut.

'No, no, don't you fucking dare!' she screams. She prises his mouth open and closes her lips around his and blows air into his lungs. A distant siren drifts on a lazy breeze.

51

Superintendent Banks marches into the empty CID room and scowls. The blinds to Frank's office are closed. She strides towards his door on the warpath.

'Frank! Frank!' She bursts into the office and notices Prisha and Zac facing him. He's standing behind his desk, fists on the surface, propping himself up. 'Where the hell is Cartwright, Frank? I said four sharp, and it's already ten past. I'm not putting this off any longer.'

'I tried calling, ma'am,' he replies in a grave, hushed tone.

'My phone is on silent. I've just returned from a medical appointment. You haven't answered my...' The demeanour of the three officers in the room breaks through her angry annoyance. Prisha turns to face her. Mascara is streaked down her cheeks, her hands stained with blood, white blouse splattered with crimson patches. Superintendent Banks clasps her hand to her mouth.

'It was a car driving erratically, ma'am. We spotted it in the petrol station on the outskirts of Whitby and pulled in to detain the occupants until patrol arrived. It happened so quickly. I heard the gunshot and saw him fall. I tried to, to...' The sobs take over.

Anne shifts her stunned gaze onto Frank. 'Where is... is he still...'

'He's been airlifted to Scarborough Hospital. I've been on the phone with them. He's in the trauma centre.'

'What are his chances?'

Frank's barrel chest expands as he tries to contain his emotions. 'Slim to none. Lost a lot of blood. They shot him from point blank range. We have not apprehended the suspects yet, ma'am. Details of the car have been widely circulated. We don't know if there is a connection yet, but there was an armed robbery on a jeweller's shop in Middlesbrough earlier in the day.'

Anne shakes her head. 'I'll need to lodge the incident with the Independent Office for Police Conduct straight away.' She focuses on Prisha. 'I know this is raw and painful for you, Prisha, but we will need to interview you as soon as possible, while all the details are still fresh in your mind.'

Prisha nods and sniffs. 'Yes, yes, I understand,' she says, regaining some composure. 'He was on such a high after his work on the murder investigation, his darts match, and the news about him becoming a father. Like a new man. He was buzzing.'

'Christ,' Frank whispers.

'A father?' Zac slumps into a chair and drops his head into his hands.

'What about his wife?' Anne asks.

'Amanda,' Prisha murmurs.

'She's on her way to the hospital now accompanied by a PC and a FLO,' Frank says.

'Right, I better inform the chain of command,' she adds, turning to leave.

'What... what did you want to see him about, ma'am?' Prisha stammers.

'Pardon?'

'When you came in, you said—I'm not putting this off any longer. What did you mean?'

Her eyes dart to Frank, who hangs his head in shame. 'It was... ahem, it was nothing important. A mix up on his expenses,' she says as Prisha's bewildered gaze tunnels into her.

'Oh. He thought you were going to give him a dressing down, but I said you were probably going to congratulate him on his recent work,' Prisha half laughs half cries.

'Yes, yes, I was going to commend him on his recent turnaround once we'd sorted out the expenses. Right, all we can do now is hope and pray.'

'And catch the bastards who did it,' Zac growls from his seat.

52

Friday 27th November

Dressed in running shoes, a pair of shorts, and a flimsy top, the icy wind slices into her flesh like a switchblade. She sprints up the 199 Steps and past the omniscient abbey. Although numb, her fingers and toes throb. Throat, dry as desiccated cardboard. Sucks salty air into her stinging lungs. She's not impervious to the weather and the torture it maliciously inflicts upon her. She welcomes the pain, the agony. It's her penance.

It was she who opened the car door first. It was she who should have casually sauntered over to the vehicle. It was she who should have taken a bullet to the chest from point blank range.

Her feverish mind works overtime.

One small thing. Just one insignificant action changed the course of so many lives. Maybe seeing a female, plain-clothes officer brandishing her warrant card could have changed events. No, it wouldn't. Who do you think these guys are—chivalrous gentlemen who couldn't possibly shoot a woman? To them, a copper is a copper, and all coppers are scum regardless of age, colour or gender.

Sprinting down the track, with the enraged sea to her left, lactic acid burns in her legs. She's barely slept, hasn't eaten for eighteen hours and is dehydrated. She wants to fly, to hit the zone where the endorphins kick in and transport her to Nirvana, but energy in equals energy out. Coughing and spluttering, she collapses onto the soggy ground before she's even reached the old lighthouse. The rain arrives in a sudden incensed outburst from above, harsh, stinging, as though Zeus himself is stabbing icicles into her. She pulls the medallion from her pocket and rolls her thumb over it as the tears finally breach the invisible wall she has built around her emotions.

For twenty minutes she sobs until there's nothing left but a few pathetic whimpers. She stands precariously close to the cliff edge, with the howling wind whistling a ghostly requiem.

'Heads or tails.' She flips the medal in the air, catches it in her palm and stares at the disc. 'Everything's chance,' she murmurs.

With all the power she can muster, and accompanied by a scream that could wake the dead, she launches the medallion high into the bruised sky. It rises, momentarily floats, then plummets into the frothing, waves below.

'Life or death. It's up to you now, Jason... you and chance.'

She turns on her heels... and keeps running.

Thank you for reading. If you'd like to jump headfirst into the next instalment of the DCI Finnegan series, follow this link to book4, Whitby Toll.

Let's Keep In Touch

Thank you for reading. If you enjoyed the book and have time, a rating or review would be greatly appreciated.

Whitby Toll, **Book 4 in the DCI Finnegan series, is available now.**
And it get's really interesting, as it continues on from the climactic finale of Vertigo Alley. Tempers are frayed, emotions are running high, and sometimes... good coppers can cross the line.

If you would like to be notified of new releases, back-stories, and future writing projects, then sign up to mu monthly newsletter. Here's the link;

Sign up to Ely North Newsletter. Alternatively, on the **Contact** page below, is a QR code for you to scan.

I thank you for giving me your time, a very precious and finite commodity. It is appreciated. All the best... and keep on reading!

Ely North – May 2023

Also By Ely North

DCI Finnegan Yorkshire Crime Thrillers
  Book 1: **Black Nab** – Text M For Murder
Book 2: **Jawbone Walk** – Text V For Vengeance
Book 3: **Vertigo Alley** – Text K For Killer
Book 4: **Whitby Toll** – The Bell Rings... But For Whom?
Book 5: **House Arrest** – Escape Can Be A Deadly Road
Book 6: **Gothic Fog** – The Strawman Cometh
Book 7: **Happy Camp** – Discipline, Godliness, Fun!
DCI Finnegan Series Boxset: **Books 1 – 3**
DCI Finnegan Series Boxset: **Books 4 – 6**
  Prequel – **Aquaphobia** – The Body in the River (Free ebook
for newsletter subscribers)

*Note: All books are available from Amazon in ebook, paperback, and in **Kindle Unlimited** (excluding Aquaphobia). Paperbacks are distributed widely via online retailers (Apple, B&N, Kobo, Amazon etc). **Boxset print editions are one book compiled from three books. They do not come in a box. *** Pre-orders only apply to ebooks.

Contact

ely@elynorthcrimefiction.com

Follow me on Facebook for the latest
https://facebook.com/elynorthcrimefictionUK

Sign up to my newsletter for all the latest news,
releases, and discounts.

Printed in Great Britain
by Amazon